CIRCLE
WILLIAM

━━━━━━━━━A NOVEL

BILL HARLOW

SCRIBNER

SCRIBNER
1230 Avenue of the Americas
New York, NY 10020

Designed by Brooke Zimmer
Set in Janson
Manufactured in the United States of America

1 3 5 7 9 10 8 6 4 2

Library of Congress Cataloging-in-Publication Data

Harlow, Bill
Circle William: a novel/Bill Harlow
p.   cm.
I. Title.
PS3558.A624257C57   1999   98–27775
813'.54—dc21   CIP

ISBN 0-684-85039-7

*For My Mom and Dad, Both Navy Vets
and
for Family, Friends and Shipmates*

ACKNOWLEDGMENTS

I am indebted to the men and women of the United States Navy who serve with courage, skill and good humor. They are the inspiration for *Circle William*. Special thanks go to a small group of friends who generously provided technical expertise, guidance, and support. Many did so while asking not to be publicly identified. That group included three former commanding officers of Arleigh Burke class destroyers; a former carrier air wing commander, a submariner, several Navy SEALs, a handful of former intelligence officers, and a well-known journalist. Thanks go to RADM Bill Schmidt, USN, who lent his name to one of the principal characters in this book. My sister, Peggy, like me, a retired naval officer, provided excellent advice and counsel on making the manuscript readable. I am grateful to Sloan Harris, my agent at ICM, for his careful guidance, and to Scott Moyers, who acquired the book for Scribner, enthusiastically supported *Circle William*, and skillfully served as the book's editor throughout much of the production process. And finally, I would like to thank Rene Harlow for her excellent editorial help, insight, and professional encouragement.

CIRCLE WILLIAM

Circle William: The designation for access and ventilation fittings on board the ship which are only closed when the ship expects chemical, biological, or radioactive attack. These vents and fans throughout the ship are designated with a black W contained within a circle. When an attack may be imminent, the Captain will direct the crew to immediately close vents and immobilize fans marked with the Circle William to prevent the spread of toxins, fire, and smoke.

—USS WINSTON CHURCHILL (DDG-81)
Damage Control Manual

1

The captain prepared to jump overboard.

The destroyer USS *Winston Churchill* drifted slowly south on the warm Mediterranean Sea. Her captain, Commander Bill Schmidt, had ordered the engines stopped an hour earlier and announced a swim call, a very rare occurrence on most ships, but a regular event on *Churchill*. During swim call, a ship would drift lazily and routine work would come to a halt. It was an impromptu beach party, minus the beach.

As Schmidt turned to head back to the fantail, he saw his second-in-command, *Churchill*'s Executive Officer, coming onto the bridge. Lieutenant Commander Thomas Oliver Ellsworth III looked preoccupied and slightly nervous, as usual. "XO, I'm going to go back aft and jump in. Everything taken care of for the swim call?"

Schmidt saw his XO grimace for a moment. "Yes sir, we've got the shafts locked, a boat in the water, cargo nets up on the sides, and a rifleman standing by in case of sharks. I've also got the Master at Arms bringing up some blankets for the steel beach . . ." He looked balefully at his commanding officer.

Bill Schmidt was, in every respect, a typical naval officer. He was of average height, and average weight. He bore no unusual scars under his mop of sandy hair. Schmidt had an easy smile which often bordered on a smirk, and rock-solid self-confidence, which sometimes got him in trouble.

"What about the DJ, Tom? Did you set up the big speaker system?"

The XO shuddered slightly. "Sir, do you really want to get into the music today? We can't just drift all afternoon if we're going to make Toulon on time tomorrow morning."

"We can if we go *real* fast, XO. Get the DJ up. And throw out a couple of cases of that nonalcoholic beer and the sodas we picked up in Rota."

Another darn picnic, thought the XO. Ellsworth was the kind of officer who never swore, even to himself.

What a dipshit, thought Schmidt. "Relax, XO. It'll be fine," said the *Churchill*'s captain as he walked away, shaking his head. He said those precise words to his XO at least a dozen times each day. Schmidt was beginning to doubt if Ellsworth, the son of a retired three-star Admiral and a card-carrying member of America's informal naval aristocracy, had the makings of a destroyer captain. Or at least the kind of destroyer captain Bill Schmidt wanted to sail with. During his career, Schmidt had run across dozens of similar flag officer progeny. With rare exception, the navy juniors displayed an expectation of privilege and promotion. Their attitude, he thought, would have been more appropriate for the Royal Navy at the end of the nineteenth century than the U.S. Navy at the beginning of the twenty-first.

Schmidt's trip aft was interrupted by the blare of the ship's announcing system, known as the "1 MC." "Commanding Officer, please dial one-zero-zero-two."

Schmidt's call to the bridge was answered by Ensign Marshall Madison, a newly commissioned and very inexperienced Junior Officer of the Deck. "Captain, there's an unidentified submarine on the surface heading straight toward us at over twenty knots. We've tried calling her on bridge-to-bridge but she doesn't answer." Unless they were emitting some sort of electronic signals, the identity of approaching submarines at sea was nearly impossible to discern.

"Unidentified? What's her CPA?"

"CPA?" There was a long pause. Schmidt guessed that Madison was trying to figure out why his commanding officer wanted to know the name of the submarine's accountant.

"Marshall, please put the Officer of the Deck on the phone." Schmidt heard the crisp voice of Lieutenant Debbie Smith, *Churchill's* Antisubmarine Warfare Officer and one of his best bridge watch standers. "Officer of the Deck, sir."

"What is the CPA, Debbie?" Schmidt quickly asked again.

"The submarine's closest point of approach is . . . let me recheck on the radar . . . CBDR."

Constant Bearing Decreasing Range. Collision course. Christ, thought Schmidt, here I am with both shafts locked, about half the crew in the water, an XO trying to set up a disco on the fantail and a submarine bearing down on me.

Perfect.

At six feet tall, Debbie Smith was a full two inches taller than her commanding officer. She moved about the bridge briskly, with an athleticism that had served her well in her days as a volleyball player in college.

"Looks like the submarine is picking up speed, sir. CPA is dead on the bow. I'm trying to get the crew back aboard."

"Break out some flares, and have the signalmen flash her continuously. We need to know a nationality. I'm on my way up."

When Schmidt stepped into the pilot house, the Boatswain's Mate gave the traditional call, "Captain's on the bridge." Schmidt got a quick update from the OOD and walked straight to the radio.

"Surfaced submarine, this is United States naval destroyer *Winston Churchill*, channel sixteen, over."

Silence. The submarine's sail was clearly visible cutting through the water, perhaps four miles away. There was a big wake behind them. Man, they are clipping, thought Schmidt, and coming right for me.

"Submarine, submarine, dead ahead on my bow, this is U.S.

naval destroyer *Winston Churchill*, channel sixteen. Request you alter course immediately. I am dead in the water and cannot maneuver. Request you alter course."

Nothing. Schmidt tried channels sixteen, thirteen, and twelve. The sub was closing fast. Inside of three miles. The more alert members of *Churchill*'s crew were starting to climb the cargo nets to get up the side of the destroyer. Eric Clapton's "Layla" was blasting out of the fantail speakers.

Ellsworth, who had been standing and fidgeting next to the captain throughout the radio calls, began imagining how a collision with a submarine would end his career. I can't believe I'm steaming around the Med with this idiot cowboy CO, he thought. If my dad knew how many swim calls we've had in the last month, he'd roll over in his crypt at the Naval Academy cemetery.

Schmidt was getting slightly nervous. Who is this bozo? he wondered. The Russians hadn't been deploying to the Med much in recent years. The Syrians and the Israelis didn't venture this far east. Maybe the Libyans had finally figured out how to operate those Kilo-class subs they bought from the Soviets a decade ago.

Schmidt turned to the quartermaster. "Sound six blasts on the ship's whistle."

The few crew members who heard the horn blasts over the music began scrambling on board in earnest. The Master at Arms, Chief Petty Officer John Browner, tried to get the attention of the rest of the crew with a whistle he always carried around his neck like a badge of office. Unfortunately, he was largely drowned out by Peter Gabriel's "Sledgehammer."

Back on the bridge, a crackle on the radio . . . static . . . a burst of white noise, then "*Churchill*, this is American submarine. Is your Charlie Oscar available?"

No shit I'm available, thought Schmidt as he grabbed the radio. In the phonetic alphabet Charlie Oscar, the letters C and O indicated commanding officer. U.S. submarines rarely identified themselves on open circuits, even when everyone knew who they were. Secrecy carried to idiotic lengths, thought Schmidt. But he had to play the sub's game.

"Submarine on my bow, this is *Churchill*, Charlie Oscar. I am conducting hydrographic investigation in this area and have my shafts locked and divers in the water. Request you maintain at least a two-mile clearance from me, over."

The bridge team exchanged glances and smiles. Several didn't know exactly what "hydrographic investigation" was, but they knew *Churchill* wasn't doing it.

Static. A buzzing sound. The submarine slowed perceptibly, her range about four thousand yards. Her bow slowly swept away from *Churchill* and pointed west. Someone on the submarine's sail was waving his ball cap.

"*Churchill,* this is American submarine Charlie Oscar. Bill, this is Chet Hollomaker, and trust me, I don't need a periscope to see you're doing swim call. Hydrographic investigation. Right. You haven't changed since Annapolis."

At the sound of his Naval Academy classmate's voice, Bill Schmidt grinned. He'd heard that Hollomaker had recently taken command of the Los Angeles-class submarine *Hartford.* He looked around the bridge. Everyone was now smiling except Ellsworth.

Hollomaker and Schmidt had been in the same company when they were midshipmen at the Naval Academy. As a result, they'd spent a lot of time together during those trying four years. They had become friends, as close friends as two young men with completely different interests and personalities could be.

Hollomaker could have been pegged as a future submariner from his first day as a plebe. A physics major, he spent most of his very limited free time in his room poring over textbooks. *The Lucky Bag,* the academy's yearbook, listed the chess club, computer club, and the cross-country team as his only extracurricular activities. Schmidt, on the other hand, was rarely seen with his nose in a textbook. A liberal arts major at Annapolis, he told classmates that he saw studying as a sign of weakness. The arts and sciences are based on common sense, he said, and if you have a knack for them, you shouldn't need to study. *The Lucky Bag* listed a dozen organizations of which he was a member, including, in his senior year, the "Irish Cultural Society." Despite the fact that he had no Irish blood, Schmidt thought joining the group was a good idea, if for no other reason than to enjoy their parties.

Hydrographic investigation, thought the XO. The man has no shame.

"Hart . . . err American submarine, this is *Churchill*, roger, Chet. Slow down a little, will you? You looked like Victory at Sea powering down on me like that, and you scared the hell out of my crew, over."

"*Churchill*, this is American submarine, they don't look too scared to me. I can hear the music from here. Just thought we'd do a slow flyby and motor on. We're headed to Marseilles for some French Navy Day thing. Have a safe day, classmate. I think we're in an exercise together in the eastern Med in July, over."

"American submarine, this is *Churchill*. Roger, Chet, looking forward to it. You can come down my port side at a couple of thousand yards if you want. We'll be in Toulon while you're in Marseilles—maybe we could meet in Saint-Raphaël at the Excelsior Hotel. Send me a P4. Either way, we'll see you off Syria in a couple of months, over." Schmidt made the Excelsior his unofficial headquarters whenever his destroyer was in the Riviera port, and he hoped he could see Hollomaker. The P4 was Navy shorthand for a "Personal For" message, sometimes used as an informal communication between commanding officers.

"*Churchill*, this is American submarine. Roger, Bill, I'll see how the schedules look. We'll see you around the pond. American submarine standing by channel sixteen, out."

"*Churchill* standing by channel sixteen, out."

Schmidt ruminated as he walked back to the fantail for his slightly delayed swim. He could never serve on a submarine, he thought, although the extra sub pay would be nice. The seventy-day deterrent patrols of the ballistic missile submarines would have driven the sociable Schmidt to distraction. He wouldn't have been able to handle the isolation. Bill needed to be able to get away from his work from time to time and blow off steam. That wasn't possible as a bubble head. And he couldn't have endured life aboard a fast-attack submarine like the *Hartford* either. Although they get into port more often than the ballistic missile boats, when they are underway, those onboard see the same one hundred shipmates in very close proximity for days on end. The gregarious Schmidt needed more variety in his life.

He knew that the careful checklists and constant vigilance of submarine duty were beyond him.

Flying wasn't his thing either. The naval aviators Bill knew spent countless hours doing maintenance, preparation, and paperwork for every hour they spent in the air. It was a good thing he loved destroyers.

Destroyers are for stable extroverts, Schmidt thought. His classmates with excessive amounts of hubris chose aviation. You have to think you are invincible to try to land a jet aboard an aircraft carrier. The brainy introverts in his class tended to end up in submarines. They didn't mind the isolation and enjoyed memorizing countless tech manuals and checklists. But destroyer drivers were team players. They enjoyed taking their swift and agile ships on all manner of missions. They sprinted ahead of and around aircraft carriers, protecting the behemoths from harm. They hunted submarines and scanned the skies to keep unwanted and unknown aircraft away from the capital ships. They made solo visits to obscure ports to project U.S. power and interest. Destroyers gave Schmidt the freedom and opportunities he craved.

Not a brilliant student at Annapolis, Schmidt had survived by his gift for gab, a keen eye for "the gouge," information one needed to slide by, and above all the ability to come through in the clutch. There was a wildness about him that intrigued women and either appealed to or angered men, depending on their own level of self-confidence.

The fact that Schmidt had achieved command of *Churchill* just seventeen years out of Annapolis was a surprise to many of his classmates. Some considered it a miracle. Still single, captain of one of the best-equipped, most powerful destroyers in the world at age thirty-eight, and headed for a swim in the Med. Not bad, he thought, for a guy whose highest aspirations at Annapolis were making the lacrosse team and drinking a lot of Heineken.

As he crossed the after missile deck, Schmidt glanced at the sixty-four vertical launch cells, each containing a Tomahawk land-attack missile, a Standard antiair missile, or a rocket-propelled torpedo. He reflected about the strike power of the ship's cruise missiles that could fly over a thousand miles, the two heavily armed helicopters, the big five-inch gun up forward, the huge phased array radar and all the electronics known to man. All the best toys. Inwardly, he sighed. Still, a ship is a ship, but the crew is the heart, he thought. Bill Schmidt wasn't big on formally articulating his command philosophy, but that was basically it. And it worked pretty well for him. This was only the second deployment for the *Churchill* since she was commissioned in 1999. She was still state-of-the-art.

A crowd of *Churchill* crew members still concerned about the mystery submarine gathered around their captain as he emerged on to the fantail. "Nothing to worry about, folks. Just an old classmate of mine from Boat School playing 'Chicken of the Sea.' "

Schmidt looked around at the relieved smiling faces of his crew and momentarily felt the weight of his responsibility for keeping them safe. Over three hundred people on board who think I'm their daddy. Schmidt felt the need to break the mood. Although it was a late April morning, the Mediterranean sun had produced a steamy day that felt like midsummer. "Hey, let's get wet," Schmidt shouted. He kicked off his black uniform shoes and jumped feet first off the fantail ten feet into the sea, fully clothed in his khakis. On the way down, he flashed his customary V for Victory symbol, in honor of his ship's namesake.

The crew cheered, laughed, and did a ragged wave on the fantail in approval. As they did when their CO did something unusually crazy, many of them turned to each other, shrugged, and said "Schmidt happens."

The comment echoed over the sea as Schmidt's brown hair bobbed above the surface. He started an easy crawl around the hull of the slowly drifting ship. I wonder what my big brother is doing today, thought Schmidt. He could be making half a million a year at IBM, and instead he's a government worker, flacking for the President. Well, to each his own. I'll bet Jim doesn't get to go for a swim in the middle of his work day, Bill thought. Ah, this is the life.

• • •

A FEW HOURS later and four thousand miles to the west, the crew of the M/V *Valetta* held a swim call of their own. Theirs was a very different event. In the cold, predawn darkness, two divers slipped over the side of the Maltese-owned, Panamanian-registered freighter moored at the Dundalk Marine Terminal in Baltimore, Maryland.

All was quiet except for the call of a couple of seagulls and the gentle lapping of the tide against the piers.

The aged vessel had arrived a day earlier with a cargo of Maltese textiles. M/V *Valetta* was scheduled to depart the following day after unloading the fabric and taking aboard a shipment of U.S.-made consumer goods destined for Europe.

At 3:00 A.M., even the busiest ports in America can be fairly quiet. The *Valetta*'s Master had requested and been assigned berth three; one of the least desirable locations. Only four of the thirteen berths at Dundalk lacked the big cranes necessary to unload so many of the modern container ships, and this was one. The master chose the location in part because it was farthest away from the shed on berth 11 which housed the U.S. Customs, Food and Drug Administration, and Agriculture Department inspectors. *Valetta*'s unloading would have to be accomplished with her own shipboard-based crane.

Customs officials had been onboard *Valetta* shortly after she pulled into Baltimore. After a cursory tour of the ship, inspection of the vessel's documents, and a visit to the Master's cabin for a chat and a shot of brandy to ward off the chill, the inspectors declared everything in order.

Now, in the early morning fog, the port area was bathed in the eerie yellow glow of halogen lamps. With her starboard side moored to the pier, the superstructure of the *Valetta* blocked much of the light. The port side, facing the water, was cast in shadows.

Unable to use searchlights, the divers relied on their sense of feel as they dove beneath the vessel. Valetta's twenty-foot draft left about fourteen more feet of water between the keel and the harbor's muddy bottom. Moving quickly ten feet below the waterline and about a third of the way forward from the ship's stern, they found what they were looking for. Where the sides of the ship started dramatically curving inward toward the keel, a ten-by-ten-foot long compartment had been attached to the hull. Known as a "blister," the addition was invisible from the surface, even on a bright day in clear water.

The blister had a dramatic effect on the navigation of the ship. The increased drag added twenty-four hours to the normal nineteen days that it took *Valetta* to sail from the Maltese port of Marsaxlokk to the East Coast of the United States. But speed was not what mattered here.

The divers carefully removed four bolts which allowed the blister cover to drop away, exposing eight chrome canisters, each three feet long, secured to the ship's hull. After attaching flotation devices to the containers, the divers released them from their holding racks and silently guided them to the surface.

Waiting crewmen stood around the deck of the *Valetta* while their colleagues worked beneath them. As the hidden cargo broke the surface, the crewmen used a boat hook to corral the canisters and one by one gently lifted them aboard the vessel. On board *Valetta*, the chrome containers were inspected and gingerly dried off. Then they were slipped inside coverings which made them appear similar to the bolts of fine Maltese textiles which *Valetta* was importing.

When the sun rose, the crew of the *Valetta* set about unloading the textiles, taking special care with one truck, which they said would be taking samples of the material to potential future buyers.

The Dundalk Terminal was a beehive of activity once again, but few people paid much attention to the rusty old European freighter or the trucks alongside her. As the driver of the delivery truck passed through the terminal exit lanes he provided his paperwork to the waiting clerk. After executing a few swift key strokes on his computer, the clerk found everything in order and waved the truck through with a sweep of his arm and a thumbs-up gesture.

Within minutes the driver had driven the two-and-a-half miles to Interstate 95, the Main Street of the U.S. East Coast, from which he could go virtually anywhere.

2

It all became clear when he saw the six-foot-tall rabbit walking along Constitution Avenue. Until that moment, Jim Schmidt hadn't understood why the early morning traffic near the White House was worse that usual. The man in the bunny suit reminded him that today was the annual Easter egg roll on the White House lawn.

Schmidt steered his aging Volvo past the barricades on E Street and wended his way toward the West Executive Avenue entrance just south of the presidential mansion. Traffic had been perpetually screwed up ever since Pennsylvania Avenue had been blocked off due to concerns about terrorists.

Across the nearby open space called the Ellipse and down every street in sight, parents led hundreds of sleepy children toward the White House gate that wouldn't open to them for several more hours. Some folks will do anything to get their kid a free wooden egg and a picture with Willard Scott, Schmidt thought. His car edged forward, stopping and starting, as he waited his turn to clear security and enter the heavily guarded eighteen-acre compound. What a zoo, he thought. That rabbit will feel right at home.

His car lurched forward to the position where the guards were inspecting security passes and using mirrors to check under cars for bombs. Officer Clarence Jackson of the Uniformed Division of the Secret Service recognized Schmidt. After all, the President's press secretary was on TV nearly every night. "Good morning, Mr. Schmidt. Pop your trunk for me, would ya?" Jackson took out his flashlight and quickly inspected the Volvo's trunk, looking for stow-aways. "Have a good day, sir," Jackson said as he gave his partner a thumbs up, signaling the okay to open the iron gates leading toward the West Wing.

Until the middle of the FDR administration, West Executive Avenue was a public thoroughfare. Citizens routinely drove along it, just a few dozen yards away from the oval office. World War II brought tighter security, and threats of terrorism caused the layers of protection to be greatly expanded in recent years.

Have a good day. Not much of a chance of that, thought Schmidt. As he pulled into his prime parking space near the west basement entrance, his mind went back again to his gaffe of the day before, a mistake that would demand much more of his attention today than would the Easter egg festivities on the south lawn.

Who would have guessed that those microphones were still on—and that they were so sensitive? The day before, at a Rose Garden ceremony, Secretary of State Blair D. Harden III had made a speech in which he blathered on about the importance of his efforts to secure a new pact to amend a flawed old treaty banning chemical weapons. Schmidt always had trouble stomaching Harden's immense ego. On this occasion, during one flight of oratory, the Secretary referred to a recent parcel of policies as "the Harden Doctrine." Even in Washington, home of the world's largest egos, this was amazingly self-serving.

When the Rose Garden event ended, Schmidt, who had been standing off to the side of the familiar blue presidential lectern, turned away from the audience and muttered, "What a windbag." Quietly, he thought, but apparently not quietly enough. An open C-SPAN microphone had carried the spokesman's verdict over cable systems across the country.

It was late that night before Schmidt learned that his private assessment had been broadcast across America. An avid C-SPAN watcher had tipped off the *Washington Post*, and the newspaper glee-fully reported this rare bit of capital candor in the "In the Loop" column of this morning's edition.

As Schmidt got out of his car, he dreaded the ordeal that awaited him. He knew that no White House staffer would be able to resist reminding him of his slip of the lip. He imagined that each one would make some lame joke at his expense, deepening his embarrassment. Worse, he would have to face the White House press corps. For the most part, the press liked Schmidt for his easy humor, his unflappability, and his record of honesty. They especially liked the fact that Schmidt was a true insider on the President's team. He knew the President's mind on any given issue. But per-sonal feelings aside, Schmidt knew that the press wouldn't cut him any slack over the Harden jibe. Even though most probably agreed with him, it was just too juicy to pass up.

The worst part of the day, Schmidt knew, would be the obliga-tory phone call to the Secretary of State. He would have to grovel, beg forgiveness, and humbly ask understanding from the sort of man who gave out autographed pictures of himself as Christmas presents.

Schmidt walked under the canopied entrance to the West Wing basement. He passed through the outer lobby and through a wooden doorway that cleverly masked a sophisticated metal detec-tor. The hallway was decorated with antique furniture. It doubled as a waiting room for people trying to see officials who occupied the tiny ground floor offices. The same officials could command large airy offices across the street at the Old Executive Office Building. There they might have windows, balconies, and even working fire-places. But those offices were eschewed for the opportunity to work in windowless, closet-size offices which had the cachet of a West Wing address.

Schmidt came upon another Uniformed Division officer sitting at a desk at the entrance to the West Wing. The desk hid sensitive monitors for unlikely threats, such as radiation and poison gas. The officer glanced at the pass that was hanging from a chain around Schmidt's neck and his stone face broke into a smile. It was only then that Schmidt looked down and noticed that the officer had a copy of the daily White House news summary, a compilation of newspaper clippings. Even upside down, it wasn't hard to read the headline of the lead story: "What a Windbag!"

Instead of immediately going up to his office, Schmidt turned right, went down a few steps, and entered the White House mess. There he thought he could grab a cup of coffee, a danish, and a moment to reflect on how he was going to get out of his predicament. Jim usually skipped breakfast, but he would fortify himself on days when he felt particularly overwhelmed by his challenges. This might be a three danish day, he mused.

On difficult days, Schmidt found the dark wood paneling of the mess somehow calming. He noticed, not for the first time, the nautical decorations about the place. At the entrance stood a model of the "Lone Sailor" statue, a miniature version of one displayed at the Navy Memorial a few blocks away down Pennsylvania Avenue. On one wall, behind glass, was the dinner gong from "Old Ironsides," USS *Constitution*. These items were reminders that the mess was operated by the U.S. Navy. And they reminded Schmidt of his little brother, Bill.

At times like this, he really envied Bill. Commanding Officer of his own boat. Make that "ship." Bill hated it when Jim called it a boat. At sea, Bill was in charge of all he surveyed. He didn't have to kowtow to thousands of reporters, 535 members of Congress, hundreds of contributors, scores of presidential advisors and staffers. That was the life. Jim wondered how Bill was doing and hoped that Bill would not learn of Jim's "windbag" comments at sea. Bill would never let him hear the end of that one, especially because the comment sounded like something Bill would say.

Jim looked up from his table to see the President's National Security Advisor, Wally Burnette, approaching his table. Here it comes, he thought. The first person of the day to bust my balls over the Harden screw up.

Burnette, a retired Army general, walked briskly up to Schmidt. He paused for a moment, leaned down, and put his arm around the younger man. "Jim, your words have given wings to the thoughts of many. You are a great American." With that, Burnette stood erect, saluted, did an about face, and headed off. Schmidt smiled and for the first time thought that the reaction to his comments would not be too bad. That thought wasn't to last long. Schmidt left the mess and walked the short distance to the stairs. The walls were adorned with massive candid color photographs of the President. How odd it must be for the boss, he thought, to walk down here and every two feet see another view of his own smiling face. On the other hand, if you don't like that sort of thing, you probably shouldn't get into elective politics.

Schmidt went up the steps near the Cabinet Room and made a hard left turn toward his own office. As he approached the door he came face-to-face with his worst nightmare: Alice Kenworthy, dean of the White House press corps, sitting on the credenza near his doorway. Like a troll near a bridge, no one would be able to get past without her permission. Alice had been covering the White House since the Nixon administration. Her thick southern drawl had been made raspy by decades of chain smoking. Dictates in recent years that banned smoking in the White House had done nothing to improve her already cranky nature. White House spokesmen over the past several administrations had learned to be wary of Alice on rainy days when her mood grew more foul with every cigarette she puffed in the White House driveway.

Alice spotted the spokesman approaching and whipped out her notebook and handheld tape recorder. "Do you plan to insult any more cabinet officers today?" she asked.

"No, but I am thinking about working on a few heads of state," Schmidt blurted, instantly regretting it.

Kenworthy didn't pause as she launched another round. "Is it true that the Secretary of State has called the President demanding that you be fired?"

She's fishing; it is too early for Harden to have gotten a call through, he thought. "Nah, I hear he wants to offer me a job. Say Alice, is Ambassador to Iran a good post?"

She gave a brief chuckle of admiration at Schmidt's bravado. The unwritten rules and her own sense of propriety would keep Kenworthy from reporting the spokesman's attempt at humor.

Sensing that she wasn't going to get him to say anything of substance on the record, she stepped aside. Schmidt entered his office
and quickly shut the door.

By White House standards it was a spacious office, with windows looking out on the north driveway and a bank of four TVs.
Since it was spring, Schmidt was unable to use his favorite perk, the
fireplace. Jim did feel a little guilty every time he called for one of
the men from the National Park Service, the only ones actually
authorized to light the fires.

Jim hung his jacket on an antique wooden cigar-store Indian
that he had purchased years ago and plopped down in the chair
behind his desk. He felt tired and old. The press secretary's job was
a tough one, and Jim's friends thought he had aged about ten years
in the three years he had held it. His sandy brown hair was beginning to show signs of gray. Still in his early forties, Jim looked like a
thicker version of his brother Bill. There was one other difference.
There was something about Bill's face which always made him look
happy, even when he wasn't. Jim's countenance took the opposite
turn. People were constantly telling him to cheer up even when he
was feeling just fine. Schmidt's secretary, Natalie, disrupted his day-
dreaming when she scurried in with a copy of the news summary,
the day's second cup of coffee, and a typed list of fifteen news organizations. Each had already called seeking confirmation and comment on his review of yesterday's speech by the Secretary of State.

Might as well get it over with, Jim thought. He asked Natalie to
place a call to Secretary Harden for him. What made this more
galling was that Harden was known to be a major self-promoter and
one of Washington's premier leakers. Jim knew that minutes after
his call begging forgiveness, Harden would phone one of his friends
in the press and "on deep background" describe the call in the most
self-serving fashion.

"The secretary's assistant, Margaret, is on the line," Natalie
said.

In the most cheerful voice he could muster, Jim said, "Good
morning, Margaret."

"Morning, Mr. Schmidt," was the icy reply.

Uh, oh, this isn't good. She always calls me Jim. He was placed on hold for several minutes. Margaret was extraordinarily devoted to her boss. She bore an uncanny physical resemblance to the secretary's wife, "Miss Jane." Margaret wore the same type of clothes and styled her hair in the same fashion as Mrs. Harden. Long-time State Department employees often said there was nothing she wouldn't do for her boss.

"This is Secretary Harden," the old windbag finally intoned.

"Sir, there is little I can say other than to offer my most sincere and abject apology," Jim groveled.

"Young Man, Your Wanton Attempts to Ridicule My Statecraft Have Done Grievous Harm to the Cause of World Peace." Whenever Harden spoke it sounded as if his words were capitalized. Any doubt in Jim's mind about the accuracy of his assessment of Harden yesterday were immediately erased. The phone call went downhill from there.

Upon hanging up, Jim gazed out his window and saw scores of White House staffers streaming by with children in tow. One of the privileges of working on the compound was the ability to place your children, your relatives, or your neighbor's kids at the head of the line for the Easter Egg Roll. Those folks all look like they are having a great time, Jim thought. Sure wish I was.

There was one more challenge to surmount: the press briefing. If he could get through today's briefing without being brutalized too badly, perhaps the "windbag" storm would blow over. With luck, it might be a one-day story. Maybe I'll get lucky, Jim thought, and somebody else in government will screw up even more colorfully than I did.

Looking out at the kids streaming across the north lawn, an idea struck him. Due to the vagaries of the President's schedule, Jim's daily press briefing was usually held any time between 10:00 A.M. and 2:00 P.M. What if he held his briefing at 9:00 A.M.? Many of the press corps would probably be with their kids and Peter Cottontail on the south lawn, too preoccupied to pester Schmidt about his self-inflicted wounds.

Schmidt's staff did a good job of quickly gathering the information he needed for the daily briefing. Answers to questions about the latest unemployment figures, the status of the Administration's crime bill, and reports of a coup in Burundi were assembled. There were about twenty people on Schmidt's staff. Most were young, just a few years out of college, and yet most had worked on political campaigns since they were teens. They were more experienced and more cynical than most Americans of their age. Jim knew that many of his staffers were sons or daughters of major donors to the President's party. There were more BMWs and Mercedes at the outer reaches of the White House parking area, the Ellipse, than could be found inside the gates where Jim's ancient Volvo rusted.

He was hoping to dodge a bullet at the briefing, but in the end, Jim knew, there was only one topic of intense interest on this day.

At precisely 9:00 A.M., Jim walked into the tiny White House press briefing room. Visitors were always amazed by how small it was compared to the way it looked on television. Less than fifty theater-style chairs were available in the room Nixon built above an old indoor swimming pool where FDR paddled and, it is said, JFK canoodled. Prior to the construction of the press room, reporters were allowed to simply hang around the entrance of the West Wing lobby. There they could buttonhole officials en route to meetings. Nixon wanted his visitors to be able to come and go without running the gauntlet of reporters, and so the current facility was built.

The first row of the briefing room was reserved for AP, UPI, Reuters, and the three main broadcast networks. CNN and the *Washington Post* were among those blessed with seats in the second row. The luckiest news magazines, out-of-town newspapers, and organizations of lesser clout were assigned seats farther back.

Most of the 1500 credentialed members of the press did not show up on any given day, thank God. And most of those who did had no assigned seat. They had to stand along the side or back of the room, or jump into an empty seat left temporarily vacant by a late arrival.

But today, many of the seats were empty and others were filled with youngsters whose moms and dads were part of the press corps. Clearly the kids were anxious to get outside where there were free toys and food rather than sit in a small crowded room listening to

Schmidt's lengthy opening statement about the Consumer Price Index. Children were running up and down the narrow aisles, tripping over TV cables and the jungle of ladders left about by the still photographers.

Jim decided to brief the press on the President's travel plans for the next several months. He read a half-dozen personnel announcements, including some critical appointments to the American Battle Monuments Commission. Finally, he ran out of filler and opened the floor to questions.

By tradition, Alice Kenworthy got the first question. "Do you think you undermined U.S. diplomatic efforts yesterday when you called the Secretary of State a 'windbag'? What were you thinking of?"

Pausing for a moment, Jim saw his opportunity. "What was I thinking of? Well actually, my comments were misunderstood. I was thinking of my upcoming summer vacation. My wife wants to go to the beach but I want to take the kids camping. And I must have mumbled 'I want a *Winnebago.*' "

The press erupted in laughter at the attempt to construct some plausible deniability. Then Jim nodded to one of his assistants, who opened the double doors on the side of the briefing room leading to the Rose Garden and the noise outside. In marched Willard Scott and the six-foot-tall Easter bunny. "Hey boys and girls, who wants to help me and my rabbit friend find some Easter eggs!" Scott shouted. As the noise level in the room grew even louder, the press corps kids began to shriek. Under the cover of the confusion, Jim said he heard someone say "Thank you," the official signal that the press have had enough. He declared the briefing over and retreated to his office.

3

The bow of the *Winston Churchill* swung sharply to port. On the bridge, Bill Schmidt cursed softly to himself. He had clearly let Glen Johnson, the conning officer, a young Ensign making his first approach on a pier, go too far. Toulon harbor, in the center of the Riviera, was a major French naval base. Schmidt knew that many of the French officers, including the port Admiral, would be watching the American ship's landing.

"Midship your rudder, Mister Johnson," Schmidt said to his conning officer. The French pilot standing next to him, a short man in a slightly dirty white uniform, turned and breathed garlic at the *Churchill*'s commanding officer. Navy ships routinely used civilian pilots, as did merchant vessels, to assist them in entering and leaving ports. The pilots were specialists, familiar with the tides, currents, and hazards to navigation peculiar to a particular harbor. "Ah would lock to bring zee tug in now, Captain," said the pilot.

"No thanks," said Schmidt, intently staring at the pier, then at the ship's bow. "I think we've got this one wired."

"Wired?" The Frenchman was confused. First the crazy Ameri-

CIRCLE WILLIAM • 33

can had insisted on letting the young Ensign drive the ship: then he refused to take his advice; now he refused tug services. *Merde!* He was a Rambo, this one.

"Captain, I think we'd better get the tug in under the bow," said Ellsworth, nervously twisting his hands. As usual, visions of *JAG Manual* accident investigations danced in his head, most featuring questions like, "Where was the ship's Executive Officer when the bow was crushed against the pier?" Ellsworth's father had always told him to avoid Judge Advocate General Corps lawyers, a notion Ellsworth had more fully accepted after watching the movie *A Few Good Men*. He had admired the Jack Nicholson character, even if he was a Marine.

"Relax, XO. Just keep the pilot off my back. Mister Johnson, put your starboard engine back two-thirds, port ahead one-third. And speak up to the Helmsman."

The Ensign complied, his voice cracking slightly. "Umm, I think the stern is coming in too quick, sir."

"Relax, Glen. XO, call the foc'sle and the fantail and have the line handlers stand by to shoot lines over. We'll just hold her steady here for a minute and then pull her in with the lines. All engines stop, Glen."

"All stop!" the conning officer shouted, his voice cracking.

"All engines are stopped, sir!" the Lee Helmsman replied.

Meanwhile, the mistral wind was kicking up from the west, pushing the ship sharply off the pier. The mistral, it was said, could blow the ears off a donkey, even in late spring. The ship was maneuvering in a narrow slip with the French aircraft carrier *Clemenceau* just off the starboard side.

"Captain, we're drifting down on the French carrier!" Ellsworth was screeching slightly with nervousness. The bridge crew were glancing at one another expectantly.

The Boatswain Mate, Petty Officer Second Class Jorge Maderias, turned to whisper to the Helm Safety Officer, Lieutenant Abraham Shakespeare Hahn. "Okay, sir, here's the deal: the XO's going crazy, everyone's ignoring the pilot, we got no tugs, a big huge wind, foreign flagship right next to us with some Admiral watching, and a conning officer who doesn't know jackshit, let alone port from starboard. A typical *Winston Churchill* landing."

Lieutenant Hahn, a former enlisted man who had served on a previous ship with Schmidt, was widely acknowledged in the crew to have the best tattoos on board. He chuckled softly, having watched Schmidt pull out of a dozen shiphandling situations tougher than this one without breaking a sweat. "Watch this."

Schmidt seemed to lean in closer to the conning officer, his hand resting lightly on the small of the young officer's back. His eyes began a constant rotation from the bow of the ship to the pier to the stern. He quietly coached the Ensign, giving orders to manipulate the engines and the rudders, alternating each, thereby holding the ship essentially parallel to the pier. The wind howled across the deck, pushing the ship toward the French carrier.

The French pilot moved slightly forward, started to say something, then abruptly stopped. He licked his lips. Then he just watched, realizing he was in the presence of something beyond technical competence, beyond professional skill; he was watching the exercise of a gift.

Schmidt was seldom serious, but when he quietly turned to his XO, his voice carried extraordinary authority and meaning. "Lines over now, XO."

Twin pops, fore and aft, from the line-throwing guns. Strong, light lines went first. Heavier six-inch hawsers were then quickly pulled over by the French linehandlers. Working the engines and rudders, and mentioning most orders to the Ensign as "suggestions," Schmidt held the ship parallel to the pier despite the thirty knots of wind blowing hard across the destroyer's decks. Fore and aft, the deck crews quickly ran the ship's lines to the capstans and began winching the *Churchill* inexorably toward the pier.

Schmidt relaxed and his hand dropped from the Ensign's back. "Nice job, Glen. XO, give Mister Johnson a hand adjusting the lines."

Behind him, Hahn and Maderias exchanged glances. Hahn repeated Maderias's words, "A typical *Winston Churchill* landing." The XO bustled toward the conning officer. Ellsworth said, "Great job, great job. Just like I was telling you guys in the wardroom last week, you don't need tugs if you know what you're doing. Okay, okay, let's get lines one and six over . . ."

Schmidt rolled his eyes. The only thing worse than Ellsworth's limited leadership skills were his shiphandling efforts. Schmidt wondered at times what he was doing carrying Ellsworth along. But he believed in working with the officers sent to the ship by the Bureau of Naval Personnel, and he figured Ellsworth couldn't do that much damage anyway. He doesn't have enough nerve to get us in any serious trouble, Schmidt thought.

As the ship settled in alongside the pier, the Captain walked slowly down the two decks to his in-port cabin. He sat for a minute and reflected on their arrival in Toulon harbor. Schmidt knew he shouldn't have stayed so long with the swim call. They had needed a real high speed run—almost twenty-seven knots—to make it into Toulon on time. He wondered if the Sixth Fleet operations officer would be able to decipher their movement reports and identify the excessive fuel burn. Navy ships weren't supposed to cruise at more than fifteen knots to conserve fuel. Oh well. What are you gonna do? Got to make port on time.

The entrance to Toulon harbor had been simple enough, and the beautiful natural bay opened easily once they had cleared the short channel and cleared the fishing village of Mandrian to the west. He had been lulled into a false sense of confidence by the relative quiet of the harbor, the ease of the channel, and the obvious professionalism of the French pilot who had swung easily on board as they lined up on the pier. Then the damn mistral wind had kicked up, and Schmidt knew he hadn't been paying enough attention. If you want the Ensigns to learn to drive, you've got to let them make some mistakes. But he'd let Glen Johnson, a young officer who would soon be leaving for nuclear propulsion training, go a little too far with a port rudder near the pier, and the wind started to push them sharply off the pier and toward the *Clemenceau*. Only by stepping in and taking over had he been able to avert a real problem. Of course, he could have used tugs, but Schmidt hated tugs. They destroyed the paint, took away the interesting aspects of shiphandling seamanship, and made the captain look like he couldn't handle the vessel.

Schmidt's shiphandling thoughts were disturbed by the officious entrance of his Exec. "Captain, I've got the ship tied up. I'll be in the wardroom taking the port brief. Do you want some coffee or something sent in?"

"No thanks, Tom. Just have Attila the Hahn stop by, will you."

What does the captain want with that gnarly LDO? Ellsworth had a dislike for former enlisted officers that was perfectly clear to the wardroom. He felt they were somewhat bothersome with their attention to the technical aspects of the ship, such as how the radars worked and so forth. Ellsworth knew radars and sonars and other sensors were important, but felt it was up to the troops to keep them running. His job, as he saw it, was to be selected to command a ship some day. And this CO isn't being much help, he thought to himself, as he looked at Bill Schmidt.

Schmidt was thinking that Ellsworth was becoming a real no-load around the ship—someone who wouldn't get the job done, but spent a lot of time acting like he did. Well, maybe he'll shape up after some liberty in the Med, he thought. This is a man who could stand some serious loosening up. A tattoo wouldn't hurt.

A few minutes later, Attila the Hahn walked into the CO's cabin. "Cap'n, were you lookin' for me?" Hahn had a thick New York accent and a face that looked like it had withstood a thousand quarterdeck watches in the rain. His rumpled khaki uniform was spotted with grease. It was clear that Attila's mind had wandered a bit this morning since there were several patches of beard on his otherwise clean-shaven face.

"Attila, yeah, I was thinking this might be a good port for us to do that CO, LDO, and Warrant Officer dinner we talked about. You know any good spots in Toulon?" Schmidt prized his collection of four former enlisted officers, two Limited Duty Officers who were Lieutenants and two Chief Warrant Officers. Not only could they fix anything on the ship with a screwdriver and a hard look, but Schmidt felt their experience lent a certain seasoning to the younger junior officers. They also know all the good bars, thought Schmidt, looking affectionately at Hahn.

The Lieutenant, a burly forty-year-old, was an expert gut crawler, a sailor who knew where to go in the nightlife district, the "gut" in Navy Mediterranean parlance. As the senior former enlisted officer in the wardroom, he had invited their CO out for a liberty run with the four Mustangs.

"Do I know any good spots in Toulon? I love it when you ask me these trick questions, Cap'n. Yes Sir, I think I can find something interesting to do here. How about we meet you on the quarterdeck around eighteen hundred, sir. We'll show you the sights . . ."

"Okay, Attila. Give me a call when you're all down there and we'll roll. And go by the foc'sle and check the forward lines for me, will you?"

"You got it, Cap'n."

4

Libya is like a really bad novel, thought Commander Chet Hollo-maker, commanding officer of the U.S. nuclear attack submarine *Hartford*. Having spent sixteen years bouncing around the U.S. Navy submarine force, and fully half of that time submerged, he had read a lot of bad novels. At times, it felt like he was living in one himself, mostly when he tried to explain to his wife, Donna, why he needed to spend yet another tour assigned to sea duty. She said she understood. They had a nice home near Groton, Connecticut, and she and the kids had a lot of activities to keep them busy while Dad was deployed. But the separation was increasingly hard on Hollo-maker's wife. It seemed that the car always broke down, the dish-washer gave up the ghost, and the snow piled up the highest when Chet was away.

Hollomaker spun the periscope around the horizon quickly, surveying the calm Mediterranean waters off the coast of Moammar Gadhafi's workers' paradise. Through the haze, he could make out a place called Janzur Village, a Mediterranean beach haven for the wealthy few. It was a weird landscape of large satellite dishes and small white-washed bungalows. Eavesdropping crewmen heard Eric

Clapton playing on the radio sandwiched between broadcasts of Gadhafi's manic sermons.

Bill Schmidt would fit right in here, thought Hollomaker. Too bad we got diverted and missed the chance to hook up on the Riviera. The thin submariner said aloud, "XO, let's close in a little further. And let the guys in the tank know they can start anytime."

The mission was pretty basic for *Hartford*. Linger within monitoring distance of the Libyan coast and collect signals intelligence. Chet Hollomaker had performed similar missions off the coasts of every rogue state on the planet—North Korea, Syria, Cuba, Iran, Iraq—and now Libya. They would intercept and record communications from within the country and send the recordings back to the U.S. for analysis.

Chet thought of the briefings they had attended in Naples about this mission. As he entered his thirty-second year in power, Gadhafi's Great September Revolution was in serious trouble. Store shelves were empty, civil servants and military officers went unpaid, and years of United Nations sanctions had resulted in a country that was completely isolated from the rest of the world. The plumbing didn't work, the streets were the only things more crooked than the political leadership, and Gadhafi himself, as he entered his fifty-ninth year, was balding and tired.

State-sponsored terrorism was a timeless problem. Although the techniques of terrorists had evolved in recent years and other countries had received more notoriety of late, the one constant over the past three decades was that Libya never stopped spawning terror around the globe.

Gadhafi constantly needs to reinvent himself, Hollomaker's briefers had stressed. One minute he wore the outfit of a western brain surgeon, complete with white coat and stethoscope; the next he appeared clothed in a Bedouin tribesman's ceremonial robes. The intelligence briefer said that we didn't know why Gadhafi did this. Some thought he was trying to inspire the common folk and create a myth about a leader who could do anything. Others thought that Gadhafi had a messianic streak and himself believed that he could accomplish anything, even challenges that had eluded the most brilliant minds on the planet. No matter what he wore, he was showered by rose petals on his tours of the city in his BMW convertible. A perfect symbol of today's Libya, according to the briefers: recently a camel was sacrificed in honor of Gadhafi as he opened the most modern hospital complex on the African continent.

Hollomaker turned his head from the periscope and rubbed his eyes. He knew that his submarine was not lingering off Libya just to keep track of Gadhafi's clownish activities. The noise from Libya was becoming increasingly shrill and ominous.

Chet's mind returned to his briefing. Growing dissent from fundamentalists had caused Gadhafi to try to ingratiate himself among the hard-liners. He had recently shown great interest in the Palestinian problem and had publicly vowed to help them establish a homeland. Gadhafi ratcheted up his rhetoric each time he spoke. And each time, Israel responded with a salvo in the press, questioning Gadhafi's motivation, his qualifications to render an opinion, and at times his sanity. Middle East experts at the State Department were troubled by the crudely dismissive tone of the Israeli comments, and they asked the intelligence community to increase its coverage of Libya in an effort to spot any Libyan response.

Hollomaker was snapped out of his memories of the briefing by his Executive Officer's voice.

"Captain, the intell guys say we need to close the beach about another mile. I checked the charts. It looks okay . . ."

"Let me take a look. Just hold it here until I talk to the navigator." Hollomaker eased his way around the navigation table and glanced down at the annotated charts of the Libyan coast. He could see the site southeast of Tripoli where the chemical weapons plant had been completed in 1998. Tarhouna, it was called. While he couldn't be sure of it, his strong suspicion was that the sudden diversion of the *Hartford* toward the coast of Libya was also linked to events in Tarhouna. Ever since it had opened, the administration had wanted more and more information about the plant. Makes sense, he thought. Just hope we haven't waited too long. Should have knocked the goddamn place out back in 1995.

Hollomaker knew that the Libyans had been producing higher and higher yield chemical weapons over the past few years. Swiss,

German, and Austrian engineers. Thai workers. Why the U.S. hadn't bombed the place years before was an international mystery. Probably got something to do with lobbyists, Hollomaker thought. Too bad we didn't figure a way to get the Libyans to use Thai engineers and Swiss workers. The tunnels wouldn't have connected and the labor costs would have closed the place down.

"Captain, the intercept team is rolling tape on the signals collection. We'll get word from the tank about outcomes later on tonight. You might want to get some downtime. I can stay up here," said the Exec.

"Okay, Tom. I'll crash for an hour. Call me if we get too close to the beach. And keep the scope down."

The Janzur Village radio station was playing Traffic's "The Low Spark of High-heeled Boys." Chet Hollomaker shook his head. Too weird. That's one of Bill Schmidt's favorite songs.

As he walked aft toward his stateroom, Hollomaker listened carefully to the sounds his boat was emanating. There were hardly any. Despite the fact that the 360-foot-long metal tube was crammed with sophisticated machines, it was constructed in a way that dampened virtually all mechanical noise that could reveal the sub's position.

Down in the tank, the intell team collected, and collected, and collected. Within hours, their data streams would be headed toward Washington. I hope the guys in the Puzzle Palace like Steve Winwood, thought Hollomaker as he fell asleep.

5

Irv Gartenhaus could not get the word *kvetching* out of his mind. Kids, car, crabgrass, his life was a royal pain, and he had been doing a lot of kvetching lately.

Chronic complaining, whining, griping artfully and endlessly against the system—kvetching was one of those great Yiddish words that needed ten words in English to do it justice. Irv knew the word came from even further back in the complicated family of central European languages, from High Middle German, he guessed: *quetschen*, meaning to squeeze.

Gartenhaus knew languages. Lots of them. In his job as an analyst and linguist for the National Security Agency, he had heard kvetching in over twenty languages over the years. Last night, he had listened to a tape from Libya, someone talking on and on. And this guy has a real kvetch against the system, Irv thought. He was looking forward to hearing more today.

He drove his wheezing Yugo along the Washington beltway, heading toward the sprawling Fort Meade, Maryland, complex where the NSA existed more or less in an orbit of its own. The site had more satellite dishes and antenna farms per square inch than anyplace else on earth.

It was an agency that didn't quite fit, not part of the Washington scene and not quite a military command. It represented one of the largest and perhaps least-known parts of the intelligence community.

Irv and the NSA were both born in 1952. That year, President Truman directed the establishment of a central organization of codemakers and codebreakers to handle signals intelligence for the U.S. government. In later years, the agency added the mission of protecting national security information systems. Over the years, NSA became one of the largest employers of mathematicians and linguists in the world.

Irv found his way to intelligence the way most people find jobs, through an ad in the newspaper. As a graduate student at NYU he was beginning to think his father was right, he should have majored in accounting rather than Middle Eastern languages. How in the world was he going to earn a living? Irv had no patience for teaching. His opinion of the UN was too low to consider a job there as a translator. It was then that he saw the employment advertisement saying that the Marine Corps was looking for a few good linguists. It wasn't until his third interview that he learned that his prospective employer was really the NSA.

The amount of raw data pouring into the NSA at Fort Meade was astounding. The product of countless spy satellites, microwave intercepts, and electronic and old-fashioned wiretaps were funneled into the huge facility night and day. Those who worked at NSA suffered mixed emotions. They had the satisfaction that came from ferreting out some of the world's great secrets, and the frustration of realizing that hardly anyone would know what they had done. They were unable to share with their neighbors, friends, or even families exactly what they did.

Still, things were better than they were a few years ago. Now, NSA even had its own public World Wide Web page. Near the grounds of Fort Meade, a museum of cryptology gave civilians a brief glimpse of the magic that is performed inside the headquarters. Yes, for people who worked there, it was frustrating that their friends and neighbors didn't understand what they did. But the biggest frustration for NSA analysts like Irv Gartenhaus was that even *they* weren't always entirely sure about what they produced. Individual analysts would know only snippets of information. It was almost always the case that only after the massive Cray computers synthesized the output of hundreds of analysts, working on data culled from thousands of sources, would a big picture emerge. That picture would normally be visible to only a handful of the most senior people.

Gartenhaus entered his cubicle following yet another tough commute. Like most of his coworkers, Irv's workaday environment consisted of modular furniture which the manufacturer described as "earth tone" but which was a color that did not exist in nature. The space was minimally personalized. Three "Dilbert" cartoons were posted on the wall with push pins. Irv's grime-encrusted coffee mug emblazoned with a circling buzzard and the phrase "Don't Let the Turkeys Get You Down" rested nearby.

Why the hell do I live in Frederick and drive sixty miles a day? Thank God the Center's computers do the heavy lifting, Gartenhaus grumbled to himself.

After settling in with a cup of coffee, Irv adjusted his hearing aid. NSA employees received their health care from the onsite Army medical clinic, but the new hearing aid they gave him didn't quite fit correctly. Typical Army product, Irv thought. And he'd missed three days at work attending the hearing aid school the Army required before actually providing him with the device.

Two Ph.D.s in linguistics, and they want me to go to hearing aid school for three days. Perfect, thought Irv. And if I want miracle ear, I've got to pay for it myself. You'd think they'd want a linguist to be able to hear okay.

Irv had the output from some of the most powerful computers in the world in front of him, computers that decoded and unscrambled encrypted messages and sifted through literally millions of written and oral communications in search of specific words and phrases that would signal the need for human attention. Only useful if my hearing aid works right, Irv muttered to himself.

It was the communications selected by the computers that Gartenhaus was tasked to review. Using his understanding of the nuances of Arabic, Irv would look for warnings and indicators that would be of interest to the leadership of the intelligence community. Gartenhaus preferred listening to intercepts of communications from Israel's neighbors. People there tended to speak colorfully and openly. Working on Libyan material was tedious. No one in Libya seemed to speak their mind. Everyone seemed afraid of offending the man who had ruled the country since 1969, Colonel Moammar Gadhafi. Thirty years and still a colonel. You'd think he'd get a promotion by now, Irv mused.

Today Gartenhaus was listening to telephone conversations that had recently been intercepted by an American submarine lingering off the coast. The fifth call he listened to this afternoon was from the same soft-spoken professional man he'd listened to the night before. It wasn't clear where he worked, but it was clear that he was most unhappy. Boy, this guy is really kvetching, Gartenhaus thought. And if I didn't know better, I'd swear he's been at the cooking sherry.

As the call went on, it became clear that the kvetcher, whose name apparently was Mustafa, was very unhappy with his Exhalted Leader. This might be promising. I might get some insights about what the middle class really think about their Leader for Life, Irv thought.

What he heard next startled the jaded NSA employee. "I can't believe he is going to do it. A planeload of our 'special product,' on the Zionists. Right on the Knesset."

This statement also shocked the person on the other end of the line, apparently Mustafa's brother, Ibrahim, but for different reasons. "Shut up! No one may speak of it. Tarhouna must remain unsaid."

Gartenhaus leaned forward. Tarhouna, he knew, was the site of Gadhafi's chemical weapons production plant. He strained to hear more, but the brothers quickly ended their call.

Gartenhaus typed a brief summary of the conversation into his computer and with a push of a button sent it to his superiors with a "flash override" priority attached. Calm down, he told himself. This guy could be just a delusional drunk . . . or Gadhafi could be planting the story to play with us. Yeah. It must be something like that.

Irv's bosses read his summary and then listened to the intercept themselves. As usual, they were divided on its meaning. The leading school of thought was that even Gadhafi wasn't crazy enough to use CW on Israel. Surely he knew that would provoke a massive response he could not hope to survive. And yet Gadhafi had demonstrated an ability to get involved in other terrorist acts and to proclaim his innocence. The La Belle Disco bombing in Germany, the downing of the Pan Am 103 over Lockerbie, Scotland, the funding of the IRA and Hizballah—his track record was not pretty. Perhaps he was mad enough to believe that he could pull this off, deny responsibility, and forever change the equilibrium in the Middle East. And Gadhafi was not getting any younger. Perhaps he wanted to make some grand gesture, to leave his mark on history.

Such an act would be crazy. Gadhafi had already been burned by earlier U.S. reactions to far less provocation. But he had been known to make apparently illogical decisions in the past few years. Maybe he was about to make the biggest one yet.

This was not the type of intercept that could be dismissed by applying logic or by making an assumption. More information to confirm the threat or disprove it was essential.

The tapes that Irv had been listening to represented only a small portion of the "take" from the American submarine. He had been given only those tapes deemed most suspicious by the Cray 4. Now Irv and his colleagues were directed to go back and review every conversation captured during the submarine's two-week mission.

The computers worked overtime trying to single out other communications that would shed light on the call. New key words were entered into the hot list profile, tops among them "Mustafa."

I never knew there were so many Mustafas in Libya, Irv groaned as he was handed a large stack of tapes. Eventually voice prints would eliminate almost all of them. But for the time being, every Arabist was given a pile of tapes, a list of key words and a headset, and told to get to work.

Gartenhaus grew weary of listening to endless, pointless conversations from mounds of Mustafas. Then, five hours into his task, he heard it. That same voice. The kvetching was unmistakable. He looked at the time/date stamp on the tape container. This conversation was intercepted just two days after the first. "I don't feel badly about the Jews," Mustafa slurred. "But that is just the beginning . . ."

"I've asked you not to talk like this!" his obviously agitated brother, Ibrahim, interrupted.

Ignoring his frightened brother, Mustafa continued: "Tel Aviv is just a warning. The next target would be America."

"Don't be ridiculous," Ibrahim blurted. "After a strike on Israel, even a masterful planner like Brother Gadhafi couldn't get the material onto American soil."

"Ah, but that is the genius of the plan, my brother." A short silence. "You see, the material is already there."

6

Bong, bong. Bong, bong. The ship's bell sounded over the 1MC public address system, ringing clearly throughout Toulon harbor and the French naval base. It was followed by the traditional announcement of the captain's chosen moment for leaving the ship: *"Winston Churchill,* departing." Bill Schmidt flashed his V for Victory sign to the four sailors on the quarterdeck, who smiled and responded in kind to their CO. Schmidt, who tended to dress somewhat eccentrically, had only one constant in his wardrobe: he always wore cowboy boots on liberty in foreign ports. Always let 'em know where you're coming from, he figured.

"Anything you need us to check on, Cap'n?" asked Lieutenant Commander Brad Moseman, the day's Command Duty Officer and the Combat Systems Officer aboard *Churchill.*

Schmidt looked appreciatively at Moseman. He was an exceptional officer, an Annapolis graduate who had played on the hockey team at school and wrote computer programs in his spare time, several of which had earned him royalties from software design firms. Schmidt—who on a good day could get his computer turned on, and even occasionally used the word processing program—looked on Moseman as the new breed of naval officer: motivated, smart, computer literate, career oriented. At a comparable age, Schmidt had spent most of his duty days on the ship figuring out which bars had free munchies on which nights. He'd thought of it as his version of strategic planning. He knew that Moseman, on the other hand, would be working on a software patch for the ship's computerized reporting system, after which he would probably hit the ship's gym and lift weights for an hour.

"Check the lines again around ten, Brad, and tell the XO I'll probably stay on the beach somewhere tonight. I'll call with my number when I get settled in." He paused. "Maybe." Moseman grinned. A confirmed bachelor, Schmidt was occasionally elusive in ports overseas, much to the affected distraction of XO Ellsworth. The crew loved it.

Schmidt walked down the steeply angled brow. He saw the rental car on the pier, with the large bulk of Attila the Hahn in the driver's seat. In the backseat three more big Mustangs, officers who'd come up through the enlisted ranks, were squeezed in. All had spent ten or more years as enlisted men before attaining their officer's commissions. Four different aftershave lotions fought a losing battle with the waterfront's aroma of fuel, old wood, and sea air.

"Okay, boss, hop in. We'll show you Toulon from the Mustang perspective." Toulon was a navy town. It had been since the Romans used it as a base for their Mediterranean fleet. The harbor was described as the finest natural basin in Europe. That and its favorable weather made it a popular port for sailors going back hundreds of years. Napoleon Bonaparte became a hero to his countrymen by driving the British out of Toulon in 1794. More recently the Germans captured the port during World War II and the city suffered massive damage from subsequent Allied bombing. Now extensively rebuilt, the city, sitting thirty miles east of Marseilles, managed to maintain its old-world charm. But the Captain's companions did not have sightseeing in mind.

Schmidt looked the group over. They all grinned at him. He sighed, knowing what was ahead. "All right, Attila. You know the deal. I get to pick the dinner place first. Got to eat a good meal in France. Then it's over to you guys for the rest of the agenda. No tattoos and no beers over two bucks, right? Everything else goes, unless I have a seizure or something."

Attila chuckled. It was 7:00 P.M.

About seven hours later, Schmidt thought, *well*, at least I don't have a tattoo. Or more accurately, I can't remember getting one. He thought vaguely that he'd need to carefully do a full body search in the shower the next morning to double-check the tattoo thing. Maybe I can find some nice French girl to help, he thought wistfully. The luxury of a long hot shower would be nice after the limitations of the ship, with its constant need to conserve fresh water.

Schmidt and Hahn were walking down the hill from the Hotel Tour Blanche where they had dropped off the other three officers, no longer mobile, at Schmidt's room.

As the two survivors walked down the hill toward Toulon, Schmidt mentally reconstructed the evening's gut crawl thus far. On the way to dinner, Schmidt had checked in at the hotel. He always stayed at the Hotel Tour Blanche in Toulon, which was reasonably priced and situated on the side of Mount Feron, rising above the city. It offered a spectacular view of the harbor—a vantage point from which he could keep an eye on the *Churchill*—as well as a great dining room and an excellent bar. He'd had the hotel recommended to him by Sophia Largent-Lemieux, the president of the French Riviera's American Navy League. An American expatriate lawyer who had lived on the Riviera for decades, she'd never steered him wrong over the six cruises he'd made in the Med, and Hotel Tour Blanche was one of her best calls.

At his insistence, they had started with dinner up at the hotel. They had dined on zucchini stuffed with oysters, lobster salad, roast lamb with aubergine and parmesan, and too much wine. "Christ, Cap'n, did you ever see so much cheese in your life?" said one of his LDOs when the after-dinner cheese basket was presented.

Schmidt smiled. "Yeah, Mike, and all the waiters are foreigners."

After several glasses of armangnac, Schmidt, Hahn, and the entourage headed down the steep slope of Mount Feron and into the gut of Toulon.

In the gut of any seaport you will find cheap beer, bad bars, and easy virtue. Schmidt's companions knew this very well. But they began to speculate about where the term actually came from. "Well, I imagine that it is a short version of the word *gutter*, as in the gutter along a street," Schmidt said. And, inhibitions having been loosened by the first few rounds of drinks for the evening, he demonstrated his liberal arts education by quoting a line from Oscar Wilde about people and society at large: "We are all in the gutter. It is just that some of us are looking at the stars."

Schmidt immediately regretted the statement. I don't believe I just quoted Oscar Wilde to a bunch of Mustangs, he thought. To repair any damage to his reputation, Schmidt offered a variant to Oscar Wilde's line. "And gentlemen, when you are drinking hard near a gutter, always fall with your name tag down. Keeps you out of trouble in the long run."

The Royal Navy had used the term *gut* for centuries. There were frequent eighteenth-century references to British sailor antics in "the gut of Gibraltar." In the American Navy it was initially an Atlantic Fleet term applied to the worst parts of the worst port in the Mediterranean—Naples. The term had spread throughout the fleet and thus throughout the world. Subic Bay, Pattya Beach, Athens, Sydney, Toulon all had "guts." Bill Schmidt figured he knew guts like Ronald Reagan knew tax cuts, and he had personally crawled most of them at one time or another.

This particular night's gut crawl was much like any other. Only the language, street signs, and brands of beer were different than in other places. The initial stop was at Madeline's on the Rue Des Trombades, a simple place with a tiled floor and wooden beams, six tables and a microscopic bar. But Attila had known the owner from previous cruises, and the beer was half priced.

After laying a nice foundation of cheap French beer, they had headed west through the heart of the old city and switched to Martinique rum. Schmidt thought he remembered bars named "Pizza New York New York," "Les Bikers Chicks," and "Legion Etrangere," which he was told meant Foreign Legion by a cab driver who also warned them not to go in. He seemed to recall a large group of very hard-faced men drinking bottle after bottle of screw-top brandy and staring at them. Not the warmest French guys I've ever seen, he thought. Got to be either drug dealers or Legionnaires.

Wonder if they like Jerry Lewis? He decided not to ask. Eventually, they had moved on, after Attila explained in very loud English that they were stagehands for a rock band from Seattle. The Legionnaires—if that's what they were—hadn't seemed impressed, but they had let them move back out to the Avenue de la Republic unmolested.

So now, at 2:00 A.M., it was just Schmidt and Hahn left standing. Each was determined not to be the first one to recommend calling it a night. Conducting a proper gut-crawl was important to Hahn. He had a reputation to uphold. Old-time Navy men, and Hahn saw himself as one, thought that carousing correctly was a significant part of their job. They even likened it to sailing their ships. They called it "steaming."

Attila, who gave new meaning to the term *bottomless pit*, announced he was hungry, so the two men were on the lookout for a small restaurant that Sophia had recommended, called the Dauphin, on the Rue Jean-Jaures, somewhere near the large park on the outskirts of the French naval station. As they turned the corner, Schmidt heard the words every U.S. Navy destroyer captain dreaded most in a foreign port: "Captain, come on over and have a drink with us!" uttered in a loud, drunk, and highly excited tone of voice.

Well, I hope this one doesn't make the papers, Schmidt thought. Before him were about a dozen sailors from the good ship *Winston Churchill*, sitting in a park in the heart of Toulon, France, surrounded by a number of opened and unopened bottles of cheap French wine, roasted chicken, and loaves of French bread. A perfect picnic, if your idea of a perfect picnic included sitting in the flower beds of the municipal park of a foreign city with drunk American sailors at about 2:00 A.M.

"Captain! Captain! Want some chicken?" An entire rotisserie chicken was being waved unsteadily in his direction by a sailor with red wine stains on the front of his white jumper. Schmidt recognized Boatswain Mate Second Class Jorge Maderias, *Churchill*'s master helmsman.

"Maderias, for Christ's sake, what are you doing in your uniform? And no, goddamn it, I don't want any chicken."

"Captain! The French sailors said we'd do better with the women if we wore our whites. And they showed us where to buy this really cheap wine. And they gave us a cork screw thing. But the women don't like the uniforms and act like they don't speak English so we thought we'd have a picnic . . ."

Attila the Hahn surveyed the crowd, most of whom were sobering up fast, and several of whom were starting to drift away. "Get up." He didn't say it very loudly. He didn't have to. A big man, his voice penetrated the haze of alcohol, chicken, and crusty French bread. The sailors stood, shuffling their feet nervously.

Schmidt smiled. Okay, Attila can deal with this. Then he looked at the ground where his crew had been picnicking. They had been sitting on a large French flag.

Jesus Christ! He froze. We've got to clear. Throughout his career in the Navy, especially at Annapolis, he'd learned to know instinctively how to find open water. He knew that surviving an incident involving a dozen drunken American sailors using a French flag for a tablecloth required a very dramatic sprint for open water and a great deal of luck.

"Attila, get these guys out of here. Now." Schmidt started to move toward the French tricolor. It was enormous. He wasn't sure if he should ask his men where they had gotten it, then realized he had to. Hahn saw it at the same moment.

Just as Hahn started to open his mouth, Schmidt was startled to hear in the distance the distinctive Klaxon of an approaching French police car. All they needed was Inspector Clouseau, Schmidt thought. For a second he thought Hahn was doing one of his famous imitations. Hahn could make sounds that no human being should be allowed to emit. But the thought was the product of wine and wishful thinking.

As if from nowhere, three French police cruisers, blue lights swirling, pulled up to the curb about fifteen yards away. *Merde*, Schmidt thought, this is going to be ugly.

7

The exceptional nature of the two intercepted phone calls meant that they received extraordinary handling. Normally, the transcripts of significant intercepts would be simultaneously routed via electronic means to regional analysts at both the CIA and the Defense Intelligence Agency. Not in this case.

General Lew Firman, head of the National Security Agency, picked up the hand set on his Defense Red Switch secure telephone and hit the speed dial button for Cleveland Forbes Stevens, the Secretary of Defense. The line was answered by the secretary's Senior Military Assistant or MA, Rear Admiral Al Myers. Firman asked for an immediate meeting with Secretary Stevens. The tone of his voice convinced Myers of the necessity of finding time on the boss' calendar.

Getting in to see SECDEF on short notice would not be easy. The day was supposed to be committed to hosting his counterpart, the Minister of Defense from Luxembourg. These ceremonial meetings took up much of Stevens's time, especially now that NATO had expanded from sixteen nations to twenty-seven. The founding NATO member nations such as Luxembourg required special stroking, ever since countries like Latvia and Estonia had gained equal status.

Told he could have thirty minutes of the secretary's time later that afternoon, General Firman called and invited the only other outsider he wanted in the room, the Director of Central Intelligence. Firman told her nothing, other than the fact that he urgently needed her to meet him in the Secretary of Defense's office at 3:00 P.M. Raw intelligence, information of the kind contained in the intercepted phone calls, would not normally be immediately disseminated to the leadership. Analysts would normally pore over the intercepts, trying to glean the real meaning of the calls and would struggle to put the information into some sort of context. Normally, only after this was accomplished would a written "spot" report be issued to alert senior officials about a potentially significant discovery.

Firman's driver made the trip from Fort Meade to the Pentagon in record time. Unfortunately he could not drive up to the usual entryway; access was blocked because of the arrival ceremony for the Luxembourger taking place outside the River Entrance. In the distance, Firman could see the honor guards from the Army, Navy, Air Force, Marines, and Coast Guard as well as the Army's Old Guard Fife and Drum Corps. The ceremonial troops honoring this guy probably outnumber the total Armed Forces of Luxembourg, he thought.

A career intelligence officer, Firman had spent more time in the Pentagon than anywhere else in his thirty years in the Air Force. He had a love/hate relationship with the place. The bureaucracy, backbiting, and budget drills were maddening. But the sense of being involved in big things made working there worthwhile. Now that he was up at Fort Meade as the head of NSA, however, he had the best of all worlds. He could visit the Pentagon when his presence was really needed, but spent most of his time at his own headquarters where, for one of the few times in his career, he was totally in command.

Firman's sedan rolled up to the Pentagon's Mall entrance. It was somewhat farther from there to Stevens's suite, but not an unmanageable walk. From this doorway, the most direct route would have called for Firman to turn left after passing through the security checkpoint and walk about 500 feet to the escalator that would take him to the corridor near the secretary's third floor office. Unfortunately, this route would also have taken him directly through the Correspondents Corridor, the area where the Pentagon press corps worked. Although Firman was among the lesser-known generals, he decided that today of all days he did not want inquiring minds asking why he was in the building. A more circuitous route was called for.

So he walked briskly straight ahead, down the MacArthur Corridor. Ever since the Bicentennial, the Pentagon had taken to dressing up some of its 17.5 miles of hallways and giving them names. As the last display case honoring the old soldier faded away, Firman came upon the alcove known as the Hall of Heroes, recognizing the 3,427 recipients of the Medal of Honor.

He turned left and ran into a wall of tourists. About seventy-five well-fed sightseers, most in Bermuda shorts and slogan bedecked T-shirts, clogged the wide hallway. "Excuse me, excuse me please. Pardon me." Firman finally got the attention of a large woman who was impeding his progress. When she saw stars on his shoulders she was momentarily stunned. "You someone important?" she asked. Without waiting for a response she turned her Instamatic camera on the General and opened fire. At least a dozen of her fellow tourists joined in the barrage, including several armed with camcorders.

So much for maintaining a low profile, Firman thought.

True to the expectations of someone in her post, Director Fiona Nelson of the CIA made a much more subtle entry into the Pentagon. Her driver used a little known garage entrance, allowing her to access the building via the secretary's private elevator.

Nelson was a woman in her mid-forties with a magnolia and mint julip accent which gave some people the impression that she was a gentle thing. She was not. Agency insiders knew her to be a demanding boss who presided over endless meetings with an iron hand. Even the most ambitious and self-confident agency staffers would go out of their way to avoid briefing her. Nelson often shredded analyst and operator alike in her meetings. Her ass-chewings of staff members were so complete that the recipients were often left in a state of shock, able to mumble only "Yes, sir" to each of her directives. Fiona Nelson knew what she wanted and usually got it.

Firman arrived at the Secretary's suite off the Eisenhower Corridor just in time for his 3:00 P.M. meeting. He was escorted past the ceremonial outer office to the inner outer office. Here he was greeted by the Secretary's personal assistant, Kitty Gorton. Gorton was someone with no interest in policy but who was fiercely loyal to her boss. Firman knew the importance of stroking people like her. In Pentagon parlance she was a "moat dragon." Unless you kept her happy, you would never escape alive.

"Kitty, I am terribly sorry for disrupting your schedule. I really appreciate your accommodating me." Wise officials knew that she viewed the secretary's schedule as her own.

Before she had a chance to respond, the secretary returned to his office, fresh from the arrival ceremony. He had Director Nelson in tow and waved Firman to come along.

They were joined only by Admiral Myers, the senior MA. Secretary Stevens invited the visitors to take seats across from a doleful painting of one of his predecessors. James Forrestal, the first Secretary of Defense, had not responded well to the burdens of life and this office. He left both over fifty years previously when he committed suicide by jumping off of the top floor of the Bethesda Naval Hospital.

Meetings were rarely held in the Secretary of Defense's office without a previously agreed agenda. Staff officers prepared background briefings, option papers, and talking points for the most mundane and the most complex of gatherings alike. But Firman had convinced the Secretary's MA that whatever was on his mind was so sensitive that it could not be addressed in advance, even over the secure telephone.

Firman was quite used to giving briefings to senior officials. He quickly outlined the facts of the current Libyan situation, taking care not to present the details in a way that would cause his listeners to come to a premature conclusion on the accuracy of the possible plot report.

When he finished, the others sat for a moment in stunned silence. Secretary Stevens spoke first, asking what level of confidence NSA placed on the intercepts. "There is no doubt that the conversations took place. A Navy submarine intercepted them quite recently. And I have had the translations triple-checked." Firman sighed and continued. "What I cannot tell you is whether our friend Mustafa is crazy or drunk, or whether this is some sort of set up. I am afraid that the DCI and her people will need to sort that out."

Stevens turned and looked at Director Nelson. "We know that Gadhafi has been behavin' even more erratically than usual," she said. "His pattern has been t' cause trouble with the West, get spanked, and then lay low for a while. Each time he eventually resurfaces and his conduct gets bolder and bolder. But somethin' like this? I have a hard time believin' that even Gadhafi is that crazy."

"Well, a couple things are clear to me," Stevens said. "We need to confirm—or God willing, deny—the accuracy of Mustafa's plot. And we need to do it now." Turning to his military assistant, Stevens said: "Al, any thoughts?"

"Two, sir. One, if word of this threat gets out, there will be panic. And two, I think you need to notify the President—right now."

8

From the pier, Sue O'Dell looked almost straight up a ladder rising to the main deck of the Navy command ship *La Salle*. The heavy gray ship loomed over the wide pier, the three-star flag of the Mediterranean's Sixth Fleet Commander flying atop her mast. Sue wished she had followed the advice of the Sixth Fleet's Public Affairs Officer and worn slacks and low-heeled shoes. Instead, she had on what was for her a fairly conservative outfit: a somewhat tight khaki business suit, with a skirt that hit her about mid-thigh, dark blue silk blouse, and medium heels. Damn. I'm going to be showing a little leg going up this thing, she thought, looking up the steep accommodation ladder to the flag offices up far above. Oh well, she thought, it won't be the first time.

A veteran of three years of the foreign service of the *Washington Post*, Sue had moved to the Style section of the paper the previous winter. She had become tired of the endless seriousness of the European Community—NATO, the Partnership for Peace, the European Parliament—it all seemed so *boring*. Table after table with those little crossed flags, miniature bottles of mineral water, and tiny bowls of candy, which no one ever touched. Toward the end of her third year, she had started to fantasize about going up to the table in the middle of some delegate's speech and grabbing a bottle of Evian water and a Belgian flag.

Ever since graduating from the University of Virginia ten years earlier, Sue had been looking for something well paid, fast paced, and interesting. Journalism seemed logical, and she had initially thought something serious would suit her best. But about three hours into covering her fifteenth meeting of the European Economic Union, she realized it wasn't fast and it wasn't fun.

After a year of badgering her editor back in D.C., Sue was moved to the Style team. Given her background on the international beat, she had been a logical choice to remain overseas and fill a new position working on international style pieces for the *Post*. She tried to vary the locations of what she sent home, moving smoothly from the Toledo Film Festival to the Berlin zoo; from a story describing Peter Mayle's new novel about hotel management on the Riviera to the hip-hop dress code of the emerging Moscow Mafia. Maybe it wasn't as important as covering the endless shuffles of the British Parliament, she realized, but at least it wasn't dull.

When she heard about a series of Navy embarrassments—the so-called "liberty incidents"—along the French and Italian Riviera throughout the winter and spring, she thought it would make a good piece. Readers back home were always fascinated with Ugly American stories, and what could be more ugly than crazy American sailors running amok along the Riviera? The next step was to request an interview with the commander of all afloat U.S. naval forces in the Mediterranean. She had thought he was headquartered in Naples, but discovered the Sixth Fleet Commander was actually embarked on a ship—the *La Salle*—homeported in the small town of Gaeta, just up the Tyrrhenian coast.

This Navy angle might be good for the Style section, she thought. At least it got me down to Naples. Sue loved Naples, and had spent three nights there before driving up for her interview with the Admiral commanding the Sixth Fleet. An old boyfriend from college, now a trade negotiator for an international consortium of deep seabed mining companies, had joined her briefly. During the three-day stay in old Napoli, they had hit what she considered the three best pizza restaurants in the world: Santucci's on the Mermaid Square, just off Margilina Harbor, Fangoli's near Dante Square, and Mattricia's up near the National Museum. After a three-day pizza binge, Sue had dropped her old boyfriend at the Naples airport, rented a black Fiat Spyder, put the top down, and drove the hour or so up the coast to Gaeta. She'd parked on the pier, right under an officious No PARKING sign. Hey, she thought, that doesn't apply to the press.

And now she was walking up the long ladder behind the slightly nervous commander who was the Sixth Fleet Public Affairs Officer. "Admiral Barnswell is looking forward to this interview, Sue," he said.

"I'm glad," she said, adjusting her Oakley sunglasses. "Can I get a full hour?"

"He's very busy right now," said the PAO. "We have a major multinational exercise coming up, you know."

Sue looked at him thoughtfully through the lenses of her shades. "Exercise? I would have thought he'd be a lot more concerned about the Navy's image in the South of France. It's not every day that a bunch of drunk sailors use the French flag for a table-cloth."

Oh boy, he thought. This is going to be a real treat. What a bitch.

"Actually, we spend a lot more time thinking about real problems of national security," said the commander. "Like tracking Russian submarines. They're back operating all over the Med. And Syria has missile boats all over the eastern parts of the Med, too. And Libya. Plus the challenges of integrating operations with our Allies."

Sue didn't say anything else. She wished the Public Affairs Officer would just disappear. PAOs are useful in setting up interviews, she thought, but they can be a real pain when they try to "spin" you. And when they monitor interviews with senior officials, their sole purpose seems to be to wrestle the official to the ground if he or she is about to say anything newsworthy.

The two of them cleared the ship's quarterdeck, where a group of young sailors sitting on the deck chipping paint tried to pretend they weren't attempting to look up Sue's skirt. She smiled at them, and they immediately returned their attention to removing paint from the steel decks just beyond the immediate area of the ship's ceremonial quarterdeck. Practically slave labor, she thought. Only the Navy would think of removing paint with a hammer.

Vice Admiral Johnson Barnswell was old Navy in the best sense of the expression. A Rhodes scholar after Annapolis, where he had been the captain of the squash team and Brigade Commander of his class. A naval aviator and combat veteran from the Gulf War, he was well known among his classmates, and the entire Navy, for his ready smile, a tolerant attitude, and a desire to keep the Sixth Fleet combat ready. Sue wanted to interview him about a series of liberty incidents along the French coast; and he wanted to talk about how the Navy was dealing with real world problems of international security: not a good combination.

"Good morning, Admiral." She tossed her short blonde hair to one side and smiled winningly.

"How are you, Sue? Thanks for coming all the way up to Gaeta."

They smiled insincerely at each other.

Oh boy, thought the PAO, they're really gonna hate each other. Knowing the dynamics of both sides as he did, he shuddered internally.

Everyone settled into the leather chairs in the Admiral's expansive cabin. The *La Salle* had been completely overhauled in the U.S. in the early 1990s, and was well appointed to carry the three-star officer and his staff. Iced tea, fresh lemon slices, and a plate of warm chocolate cookies were on the low table between them. The Public Affairs Officer took a discrete seat across the room. Sue pulled out a tape recorder. The commander, a veteran of several other *Washington Post* interviews, pulled out a slightly larger tape recorder. They smiled at each other thinly.

As the interview unfolded, it became increasingly clear that Sue wanted to focus only on the crazy liberty incidents. She had been following the exploits of the *Winston Churchill*, and knew there was a good story. The Admiral was equally determined to merely recount how "a few isolated incidents" should not be used to judge the Navy's presence in the Mediterranean; and how the Navy was really focused on the serious security problems of the region. The interview was going nowhere fast, and the Public Affairs Officer was wondering how to separate the two gracefully.

Suddenly the Admiral's telephone on the other side of the room rang once then clicked loudly to indicate it had been automatically answered. The speaker function was on.

The Admiral was up and moving toward his desk, but it was a long way away. The Public Affairs Officer, who was slightly closer, also lunged at the desk and managed to knock the Admiral off balance and onto a navy blue couch.

"Admiral, we've got a problem," said the metallic voice of the Sixth Fleet Chief of Staff over the speaker phone. "Those idiots on the *Churchill* apparently kidnapped a British model in Cannes and wouldn't let her go unless she agreed to a date with their captain. About a half dozen are in a French jail and the Chief of Naval Operations is on the outside line and—" Admiral Barnswell managed to hit the speaker button and shut it off. The PAO was gaping in terror at Sue's tape recorder.

"Thank you, Miss O'Dell. We've certainly enjoyed having you aboard. Please feel free to take a few cookies with you for the road."

9

It was a habit that went back to his college days at Syracuse. Whenever Jim Schmidt felt he was under the gun, he would lift his spirits by listening to oldies. It was hard to take yourself too seriously while humming along to "Who Put the Bomp (in the Bomp, Bomp, Bomp)."

Jim shared a passion for these old songs with his younger brother, Bill. They shared a lot growing up. The Schmidt family lived on a rural road outside the small city of Binghamton, on the Susquehanna River near the Pennsylvania border. There weren't many neighbors nearby, and those there did not have children close to Jim and Bill's ages. So the two brothers learned to rely on each other for friendship. They made up games that required only two people to play.

Their father held a series of jobs. The best of which, from their points of view as the boys were growing up in the sixties and seventies, was manager of a Howard Johnson's restaurant on the interstate highway leading out of town. Each week their father brought home a new flavor of ice cream for them to sample.

Because their home was isolated from town, it was hard for the boys to visit their classmates after school. And because it was nestled between two hills, the Schmidt household's TV was often fuzzy at best. As a result, the boys spent a lot of time listening to the radio.

As he grew older, radio became more than a pastime to Jim. While attending journalism school he worked as a disc jockey at WSYR, a radio station in Syracuse. Jim left that job with an appreciation for music and a stack of bootlegged tapes that he still played.

As a DJ, Jim prided himself on running a tight board. He could seamlessly blend the music, chatter, and commercials without a gap. He would talk over the musical lead-in to a song—giving the weather, or wry observations—and end a split second before the vocals kicked in. Now, some two decades later, he kept in practice by occasionally announcing the impending start of his briefings over the Press Room public address system with musical accompaniment.

So this day he intoned over the PA, "Ladies and gentlemen of the press, the briefing is about to begin," at the precise moment he turned up the volume on his tape deck as The Animals sang: "I'm just a soul whose intentions are good/Oh Lord, please don't let me be misunderstood."

Jim knew that some of the White House senior staff who had caught his DJ act in the past thought it was beneath the dignity of the White House. That's what's wrong with this outfit, he thought. No sense of humor. I need to keep the press loose if I have a chance to get them to forget the "Windbag" fiasco.

The timing of the day's briefing had an unintended and useful side effect. By drawing the reporters and photographers into the briefing room it prevented any of them from seeing the three limos drive through the West Executive Avenue gate and up to the West Basement entrance.

The cars assigned to the Secretary of Defense and Director of the CIA were large armored affairs, while the Director of NSA's vehicle was considerably more modest. All three were relatively unremarkable on purpose. If a reporter had seen the three officials arrive together, he or she might easily have wondered what the occasion was. The tourists passing the White House gate probably took no special notice. Tourists were unaware of what Schmidt called the "Antennae Law of Inverse Importance," a principle that held that the importance of an individual in a Washington limousine was inversely proportional to the number of antennas on the car. The head of the Bureau of Mines, for example, had no less than eight antennas on his car, while the President's car had but one.

While the press were tied up sparring with Schmidt, Secretary Stevens, Director Nelson, and General Firman were able to sweep into the lower West Wing entrance unnoticed. They were taken up the narrow back stairs and ushered immediately into the National Security Advisor's spacious office.

Wally Burnette's office looked out onto the White House driveway, where members of the press regularly ambushed visitors to the executive mansion. Since the press had free run of the driveway, Burnette was forced to keep his curtains drawn, lest meetings like this become public knowledge.

The three visitors gave Burnette an abbreviated version of their concerns. Burnette, who had been through innumerable crises, gave no visible sign of shock or alarm. He nodded and said, "Well, I can see why the three of you were so insistent about getting in to see the big guy. I told him that you were coming over on some mysterious mission. I will be able to get you into the Oval in about thirty minutes."

"Obviously," Secretary Stevens said, "this potentially is a matter of extraordinary sensitivity. Especially if the report is true. Is there anyone else the President will want to join him for this briefing? The Secretary of State, for instance?"

"Oh, Jesus," the DCI drawled. "Ah thought you wanted to keep this quiet." There was not a lot of admiration for Secretary Harden among his colleagues in the cabinet.

"No, I think we can stumble along, at least for the moment, without the sage wisdom and counsel of that old wind . . . I mean wise man," Burnette replied. "The one person he will want in there is Jim Schmidt."

"The press guy?" blurted General Firman, making his first comment of the meeting.

"The President relies on him completely. One way or another, this thing is eventually going to hit the press. And Jim has told the President not to expect his spokesman to be able to explain this Administration's crash landings unless he is allowed to be on board for the takeoffs."

"Of course it's the President's call," Firman said, "but in my experience the press is often *the cause* of a lot of crash landings."

"Well, Lew, you need to keep in mind that Schmidt isn't the press," Burnette replied. "He's just the lucky guy who gets to deal with them on a daily basis. Besides, if you are worried about Jim feeding the press to make himself look good, you'll appreciate Schmidt's Cockroach Law of Bureaucracy. He thinks the key to survival is keeping a low profile."

At that moment Schmidt would have loved to have been able to achieve a low profile. The briefing had just ended, but before he could retreat to his office he was called upon to break up a cat fight. Helga Heinemann, perhaps the most unusual member of the White House press corps, had leapt over the briefing room seats and was in the process of trying to muss the lacquered hair of network correspondent Claire Barnes.

Heinemann was the sole employee of the Heinemann News Service, an organization bequeathed to her by her late husband, Benny. HNS had long since lost its last client, which freed Helga from the annoyance of actually having to report about anything. But Benny invested wisely and left his wife with enough funds to travel with the White House press corps and live the life of a correspondent. Now, well into her seventies, Helga had become more than a little eccentric and had pretty much taken to living in her cubicle beneath the briefing room.

Helga and Claire never hit it off. A pack rat, Helga kept her cubicle stacked to the ceiling with old newspapers, magazine articles, plastic shopping bags, and the remnants of quite a few meals. Helga always seemed to wear the same blue dress, although she said that she had several of the same design.

As a network correspondent, Claire rated slightly more luxurious accommodations. She toiled in a tiny five-foot-by-ten-foot booth a floor above Helga. Most of the counter space in her booth was taken up with makeup, hair spray, mirrors, and a stack of copies of a three-year-old edition of the issue of *People* that had rated Claire one of the twenty-five most fascinating women in the world.

Bystanders said that the argument had erupted because Claire had objected to Helga installing a toaster oven in the downstairs cubicle. The aroma of baking macaroni and cheese had driven the constantly dieting Claire to distraction. Claire suspected that those few extra pounds she had put on of late were the reason she was not chosen as one of *People*'s "most fascinating women" in either of the past two years.

So Claire filed a formal complaint to the White House Correspondents Association, saying that cooking in the workplace presented a fire hazard, particularly in a confined, paper-strewn area like Helga's cubicle. The association ordered Helga to cease her culinary efforts. The receipt of the association's written decision, delivered just before the briefing, caused Helga to attack Claire's most prized possession, her hair. Fortunately, Jim and other briefing room occupants were able to separate the two before serious damage was done.

When the combatants were banished to their corners, Schmidt headed back toward his office. Before he could reach it, Natalie approached with the message that he was wanted in the Oval Office. A day rarely passed that Jim wasn't summoned to the Oval Office without advance notice, yet he never got over his wonderment at being invited into the inner sanctum and his fear that he was being called in over something dumb he might have been quoted as saying. Jim remembered being called into the Oval Office after one of his first briefings at the start of the Administration. It seemed that the Speaker of the House had objected when Jim told reporters that the newly elected President planned to take the "high road" in dealing with Congress because he didn't think he would encounter much traffic.

Jim was surprised to see the National Security Advisor, Secretary of Defense, Director of Central Intelligence, and a general he didn't know all standing outside the Oval Office. Light was streaming in through the windows that looked out on the Rose Garden. "What's up? Are you going to give me a purple heart for the fight I just broke up in the Briefing Room?"

"No, but I look forward to hearing about it," Burnette replied.

"Were there any injuries?" Stevens asked hopefully.

"Just some pride. Say, you aren't all still pissed off about that 'windbag' crack, are you?"

"No," Secretary Stevens replied. "Actually, the rest of the cabinet has put you in for the Presidential Medal of Freedom."

The general mirth was interrupted by the President's personal assistant, Graham Hall. "Gentlemen, and Director Nelson, President Walsh will see you now."

10

The evening had started calmly enough. As the sun set over the Bay of Cannes, *Winston Churchill's* centerline anchor splashed into the perfect blue water. The ship was positioned a few hundred yards from the Vieux Port, the old harbor. From the bridge, the watch-standers could see headlights moving slowly up and down the famous harborside boulevard Rue De La Croisette, a long strip of glittery hotels framed by palm trees and fronted with small chic cafes.

On the bridge of *Churchill*, Bill Schmidt commended his Officer of the Deck, Ensign Marcello Baptista, on a smooth approach to the anchorage. Looked a lot better than when Glen Johnson almost hit the French carrier in Toulon, he thought to himself. We might make a ship driver out of this one. Then he stretched, yawned, and turned to his XO.

"I'm going to crash for an hour, XO. Just make sure the anchor is set and post a good watch here in the pilot house . . . you never know when the mistral wind is going to blow up. You can go ahead and do the port brief for the crew and let them go on liberty as soon as it's done."

Ellsworth paused and pursed his thin lips. Here comes something really stupid, thought Schmidt.

"Captain, I was thinking of holding the crew on board tonight to clean up the ship. We may have some press interest tomorrow with the film festival starting, and I want the ship to look good. I think Sixth Fleet may be coming to town for part of it. When my dad was here as Sixth Fleet, he *always* came to Cannes for the festival."

On the bridge, the ten or so enlisted men and women within earshot all rolled their eyes. This was classic Ellsworth, overworking the crew to be able to make a better impression on some visiting VIP. Fortunately for the crew, Schmidt disliked such posturing almost as much as the crew did.

"Forget it, Tom. The ship is in pretty good shape as it is. And this crew didn't join the Navy to come to Cannes and chip paint. Get 'em on the beach. Usual rules . . . buddy system, situational awareness, a good shore patrol. And get the Ensigns out to the hotel to set up the Admin. I'll go ashore around twenty-one hundred or so." In most liberty ports the members of the wardroom would chip in and rent a hotel suite called an Admin, which would serve as the officers' unofficial headquarters and hospitality suite for the duration of the visit.

Ellsworth started to reply, then thought better of it. He confined himself to berating the ship's Quartermaster about sloppy navigational plotting of the anchorage as Schmidt left the bridge. The Boatswain's Mate of the Watch called out "The Captain's off the bridge," and the Quartermaster of the Watch dutifully noted the event in the ship's log. Schmidt climbed down the two decks to his cabin. His bridge crew looked after him affectionately.

An hour later, the liberty brief complete, a group of *Winston Churchill* sailors were gathering on the port quarterdeck to await a ride in the liberty boats to the shore. "Hey, I heard the goddamn XO wanted to keep everyone on board to have a field day," announced Jorge Maderias to a group of fellow Boatswain Mates.

They nodded their heads. A "field day" in Navy terminology meant an intensive cleaning session.

"That jerk doesn't give a shit about the crew," agreed a quartermaster.

"But the Cap'n wouldn't let him do us like that," added one of the ship's cooks, a Second Class Petty Officer named Arlen Thomas. "The captain is always looking out."

"He's the best," said Maderias.

"Yeah. We're lucky."

"What could we do for Cap'n Schmidt?"

"I don't know. Maybe we could buy him drinks ashore or something . . ."

"Nah, he's always got drinks. And whenever we try to buy him more, he looks nervous. What he needs is a date. He hasn't had a date all cruise, and he's not a married guy or nothing."

"Yeah, a date. But where are we gonna find him a date?"

"I'm thinking we might set him up with some kind of model or movie star or something from the film festival. Why not? You know he could handle it. We just got to get the ball rolling."

Amidst general agreement, the liberty boat's departure was announced by three short strokes on the ship's bell. The sailors saluted the in-port Officer of the Deck, Ensign Marshall Madison, who was proudly manning his post. After receiving the ceremonial permission to go ashore, the sailors ran down the accommodation ladder to the gently rocking boat below.

After a short boat ride ashore, the group of six sailors walked along the Rue De La Croisette. They gaped at the huge and beautiful hotels along the boulevard: the Martinez, the Ritz-Carlton, the Noga-Hilton, each with its trademark striped umbrellas and cafes populated with Pastis- and Pernod-sipping tourists. Endless lines of Maseratis, Rollses, Mercedes, and Porsches swept down the boulevard. The crew especially enjoyed the convertibles, most transporting glamorous-looking women in for the festival. The women glanced at the shabbily dressed Americans and slowly turned away.

The night was young, the women were beautiful, and the sailors were on the lookout for a perfect date for their beloved CO. It was a bad combination.

Ever since the liberty incident in Toulon, the Sixth Fleet Commander had kept a special eye on the travels of the good ship *Winston Churchill*. They had effectively been kept at sea for a month of penance. They had missed the final several days of their scheduled visit to Toulon, and were likewise kept underway through a proposed visit to Schmidt's favorite Riviera city, Saint-Raphael. The only reason they'd been scheduled back into Cannes was a long-standing commitment to the influential Navy League of the Riviera, which had badgered the Sixth Fleet commander for a visit by one of the newer *Arleigh Burke* destroyers. Sophia Largent-Lemieux, the president of the Navy League's Riveria Chapter, had personally asked for Bill Schmidt's ship, having taken a liking to him on one of his previous cruises.

In a sharply worded personal message, sent directly to Schmidt, with information copies to his battle group commander and destroyer squadron commander, Vice Admiral Barnswell had enjoined Schmidt to "get his crew under control, or prepare for an unscheduled change of command." Barnswell, being an aviator, wasn't known for his subtle approach, and Schmidt knew this was serious. Given the situation, the Captain would have been very nervous if he'd known what was going through the minds of his sailors at that moment.

They had rented a bright yellow Suzuki Samurai, taken the top off and thrown it away, and loaded a cooler in the backseat. It contained a case of cheap French Côte du Provence rosé wine in liter plastic bottles, purchased for eighty francs at the Bon Marché supermarket. This was deemed expensive until Thomas had pointed out it worked out to less than $2 a bottle. Ice cold, the wine went down easy, and the six sailors quickly worked their way through eight of the twelve bottles. They were discussing whether to replenish their wine supplies or begin the quest for their captain's date. Unfortunately for Schmidt and the *Winston Churchill* the "Dating Game" advocates won the argument, and the plans to find their captain a date began to get serious. They had even identified a possible candidate, an English model named Kate Iverson.

They stared at her across the Croisette as they sat in the Suzuki Samurai, parked near the Hotel de Ville and the harbor park. She was walking around the esplanade George Pompidou, just outside of the Palais Des Festivals Des Congres, the harbor side theater that was home to the Cannes Film Festival.

"Wow. What a babe. She looks just like that actress with the thing near her lip, what's her name . . ."

"She's a model. Her name is Cindy Crawford. And this babe is better looking. Like by far."

"Okay, okay, who is going to go explain this to her?"

Jorge took another slug of the Côte du Provence. He tucked in his red T-shirt, which said DON'T MESS WITH TEXAS in Old English lettering and showed a bull with a lusty look on its face chasing a cow through a glow-in-the-dark meadow. "I guess that would be up to me, as I'm the senior Boatswain Mate here."

Weaving across traffic, he came up behind the British model and decided to use a subtle approach. She was, after all, about six inches taller than he was.

"Excuse me, but would you like to meet the captain of my ship? I'm an American sailor, and my captain is very rich and is the captain of our American destroyer."

Kate Iverson stared at Jorge as if he was a Syrian paratrooper who just landed in the middle of a bar mitzvah. He sensed it wasn't going well. Across the Croisette, his shipmates began to yell encouragement. One of them threw a bottle into the middle of the street.

"Pardon? Your captain is from what ship? A cruise ship?"

"We're from a destroyer. An American destroyer. The *Winston Churchill*. It's named after a British guy," he added helpfully. "That's it out there." He pointed to the sleek gray vessel anchored in the harbor.

Iverson glanced over Jorge's head at her publicist, Reggie Devons, who was starting to interpose himself between Jorge and Kate. The model thoughtfully looked at Jorge. He smiled hopefully. She turned and conferred with Reggie.

"It's all right, Reggie. I'd like to meet their captain. Maybe we could do some publicity shots on the ship, like Cher did on that American battleship. And I've another idea." Reggie stared at her in disbelief.

Jorge spoke again. "You could come for a ride with us. In our car. We have a convertible. And we could take you to the ship to meet him. Not in the car to the ship, we'd have to take a boat out. But we could go anytime. And it's not like Tailhook or anything."

Jorge felt this might soothe any concerns she might have. He tried to look sincere.

Kate Iverson paused and smiled at him. "Just a moment, let me talk to my fellow here." She turned again to Reggie, out of earshot of Jorge. "Reggie, this is perfect. It'll be a great story, just on the night of the festival. I'll go off with the sailors, and you call the police and tell them I was abducted. We'll sort it out later, but it'll be a great stunt! Think of the pictures." She turned and laughed gaily. "Don't wait up, darling. I'm off with the American Navy!"

As she jumped into the Suzuki and drove into the warm French night with a car full of cheering sailors, Reggie turned and walked a hundred yards up the Croisette to a pair of dark French Gendarmes who were lounging near their black Citroen. Each had the serious, slightly cynical look of French police officers. They wore the insignia of the French antiterrorist police branch.

Reggie took a deep breath and said in his best Oxford French, "Look here, *monsieur, nous avons un grande problem*. A very *grande* problem . . . *c'est tres serieux.*"

At that moment, the captain of the *Churchill* was stepping out of his ship's small boat and coming ashore in the Vieux Port at the Fleet Landing. His supply officer, Lieutenant Melissa Jones and his Combat System's Officer, Brad Moseman, had ridden in with him. Schmidt liked to go on liberty with various members of his wardroom. It gave him a chance to get to know them better. Besides, it was lonely at the top. And regulations and common sense forbade him from getting too close to any one person on his crew.

"Well, what's the first stop? I hope you aren't going to get another tattoo, Melissa," Schmidt kidded.

"Not tonight, Captain. How about a leisurely walk around the harbor until we find a good place to have a Pastis somewhere. I just want to forget about all the problems in Toulon."

Schmidt smiled ruefully and looked down at his cowboy boots. "Hey, can't be perfect. The kids joined the Navy to have some fun. We've just got to keep it cool here in Cannes."

Both Jones and Moseman, who spent a great deal of time protecting their CO from his forgiving nature and wild streak, looked at each other behind his back. "Okay, Cap'n. Sounds good."

They turned to the east and began walking toward the enormous Palais De Congres.

"Hey, isn't that Maderias driving that yellow Suzuki?" said Brad. Schmidt and Jones looked up and both grinned as the car slid by down the Croisette.

"Yeah. I can't believe it. There's some good-looking woman in the front seat and some of our other guys in the back. They're probably on their way to some party. I can't get over Maderias. He always ends up lucky." All three laughed.

They turned the corner. Coming up the Croisette, police sirens blaring, were three French police Citroens. The drivers looked extremely serious. They were forcing car after car off to the side as they fought their way through the crowded evening traffic, intent on something up ahead. Behind them was a large antiriot vehicle with a turret and fire hose at the top. French SWAT officers jogged along behind, dressed in head-to-foot black, gas masks dangling at their waists. Pedestrians were staring in disbelief.

"Wow, that looks serious," said Jones. "I wonder if it's some kind of terrorist thing. They said in the port briefing that something crazy always happens when the festival is in town." All three stared as the French riot force turned the corner.

"Well, hopefully it'll keep any little problems our sailors get involved in off the front page," said Moseman.

"Yeah," Schmidt said, shaking his head. "Whoever those guys are after is going to be sorry he ever set foot in Cannes."

11

All his life, Bill Schmidt had disliked authority. His older brother always asked him why the hell he was in the military if he didn't like being told what to do. Jim Schmidt told Bill that he found it strange that his little brother had gladly joined an organization in which 400,000 people got up every morning and essentially put on the same outfit to go to work yet was himself a true nonconformist who bridled at the thought of a policeman asking for a driver's license.

Recognizing his shortcoming, Bill was thinking seriously about sending his Executive Officer to the Cannes Municipal Jail. "Nobody can kiss butt better than that guy" were the precise words that came to Schmidt's mind when he thought about Lieutenant Commander Thomas Oliver Ellsworth III. The problem was that the XO—whom the crew referred to by a wide variety of insulting names, the most printable of which was "Tommy Triple Sticks" for his family numerals—was also liable to do something incredibly stupid if he felt threatened himself.

And the situation was delicate. Schmidt had to figure out how to get the French Police Special Unit 703, an elite antiterrorism group, to release six of his crew members. Schmidt figured the initial flurry of press interest was over, although the British model/actress, Kate Iverson, continued to give interviews about her alleged "kidnapping" by the American Navy. She described her experience as "Euro-Tailhook," and the label was sticking.

Also sitting on his desk was the phone number of someone named Sue O'Dell, a reporter for the *Washington Post* who wanted an interview. Below it were a stack of Navy messages, each stamped "Personal For" across the top, indicating that they were for his eyes only. Schmidt noted that every level in his chain of command, from his immediate Destroyer Squadron Commodore, a Navy Captain, right up through the four-star Admiral who was the commander of the Atlantic Fleet, had decided to weigh in and express disapproval concerning the latest liberty incident. He was ordered to get his crew aboard, persuade the French authorities to release the "Cannes Six" from the local jail, and get to sea. He also had messages from the Sixth Fleet Public Affairs Officer, his brother Jim back in Washington, and Sophia Largent-Lemieux.

He knew only his brother and Sophia Largent-Lemieux would be sympathetic, and figured brother Jim was busy, so he picked up the ship's cell phone and called Sophia's house in downtown Cannes. "Sophia, this is Bill Schmidt. We're still at anchor here in the Bay of Cannes, but I guess you heard about my six sailors getting into a spot of trouble."

"Darling, it would be hard to miss. Two days on the front page of all the papers, that awful British girl calling them Euro-Tailhookers, and the protesters down at the Fleet Landing. It must be terrible for you and the crew."

"I've been in trouble over liberty incidents before, but this one looks bad, Sophia. I've got a stack of P4s here that are so hot they're smoking, and I've got to figure out how to get my guys out of jail."

"The Cannes Six? The papers are howling for justice as only a French newspaper can, calling for La Belle France to mete out an appropriate punishment to the American bandits, especially that short one, Madonna or something . . ."

"Maderias. My boatswain mate. Yeah, he's a real danger to society. Jesus, Sophia, we need some help here. Do you know the mayor?"

"Michele Mouirret? Quite well, of course. Hmmm. He's in trouble himself at the moment, something about a five million Franc gratuity he accepted for allowing the installation of a new casino on top of the Noga-Hilton Hotel. He probably isn't too interested in taking on more political problems with releasing the Cannes Six to your jurisdiction. Not without some serious advantage to himself."

"Can't you tell him about all the money the Navy ships bring into Cannes and the Riviera? *Churchill* isn't that big, but when the carriers come into port . . ." Schmidt felt as if he was clutching for a life ring that was floating just beyond his reach.

"Oh William, he knows that . . . but it won't make him intervene with the police. I think perhaps the best I can do is try and convince him that by helping liberate the 'Cannes Six' he will strike a public blow against the British expatriates in town. All the French hate the British community here, especially since Peter Mayle's books about Provence enticed all the tourists from Cannes into the rural parts of the region every summer. It has hurt the local economy."

"Sophia, I hope you can pull something off, or we're really in trouble."

"I'll try, William. And while I'm working on the mayor, your best bet is to go down to the police station with a case of that Jack Daniel's bourbon you are always handing out." Sophia knew that Bill kept several cases stowed away on board *Churchill* to provide to dignitaries and VIPs wherever the ship called. The last time he'd needed to pull it out, Schmidt was trying to get officials in Palma de Majorca not to press charges against several crew members who had pushed a grand piano into a hotel swimming pool.

"My bourbon. Oh well. Whatever it takes, I guess."

"And William? Be charming."

As Schmidt hung up the phone, the ship's Executive Officer bustled officiously into the Captain's cabin.

"Captain, there is a young woman on the quarterdeck to see you. She hired a private boat to run her out. Her name is Sue O'Dell. She says she's called a dozen times and urgently needs to speak with you."

"Christ. She's the reporter from the *Washington Post*, XO. Okay. I can handle this. Send her up."

Ellsworth looked doubtful. He knew the regulations cold, and was sure ship COs were not supposed to give off-the-cuff interviews without contacting the Navy's local public affairs representative, in this case the Sixth Fleet's PAO.

"I don't know, sir. Shouldn't we contact the Fleet PAO?"

Schmidt reflected on the yet-to-be returned phone message from Admiral Barnswell's Public Affairs Officer. No, I can handle this, he thought. Confidence was never Schmidt's problem.

"Don't worry about it, XO. Here's the plan. You go down to the municipal jail. Take a dozen bottles of Jack Daniel's and Attila the Hahn. Sophia Largent-Lemieux is going to work it through the mayor's office. When you talk to the police, play up the British angle . . . you know, they tricked our sailors, you know the story. And be smooth, XO. You can do this."

Ellsworth straightened visibly.

"Well, I must say my father often told me how to deal with for-eigners, particularly the French. His service here in the Sixth Fleet is still quite well remembered. I suspect that will help our cause a great deal."

Only if he doesn't remind them that his father was famous for calling the French Navy "the frog leg fleet" behind their backs, thought Schmidt. He was about as popular in the Med as a prostate checkup. "Great, XO. I know you can handle it. And send up that reporterette. I can deal with her."

Sue O'Dell swept into the Captain's cabin. She was wearing stone-washed blue jeans and a black cotton sweater with a single strand of pearls. She looked terrific. Schmidt was sitting comfort-ably at his desk and looked appreciatively at her figure as she entered. He rose and greeted her smoothly.

"Good afternoon. I'm Bill Schmidt." Schmidt flashed a warm smile. How bad could this be? he thought. She sure doesn't look like the barracudas that Jim keeps telling me about. They shook hands and he guided her toward the small pair of facing couches in the corner of the small cabin. The steward, now known in the polit-ically correct Navy as a "Mess Specialist," entered and set up coffee and a platter of freshly baked brownies.

Sue O'Dell was primed for this interview. She had spent the past week all along the Mediterranean coast, interviewing shop owners, merchants, police officers, embassy personnel, and anyone else who would talk to her about the adventures of the destroyer *Churchill*. After a good deal of thought about how to conduct the interview, she had decided to try and make friends with the CO. He looks pleasant enough, she thought. Gosh, I was expecting someone older. Actually, he's kind of cute . . . but a little too clean cut. He's probably not too bright. After all, why would he be doing this for a living?

"Captain, thanks for agreeing to see me. As you know, I am a correspondent with the *Washington Post*." Sue found that she got more respect when she referred to herself as a "correspondent" rather than as a "reporter."

"I'm very interested in your reactions about your cruise. I know you've been in the Med for three months, so you're about halfway through your deployment. Tell me how you think it's been going overall." She smiled encouragingly.

She seems pretty reasonable, Schmidt thought to himself. This may go okay.

"Sue, please call me Bill." When he had first taken command, Bill got a kick out of being called "Captain." It still sounded pretty good to his ears, except when it came from a good-looking young woman. Okay, better keep your mind on the job at hand, he thought.

"Well, Sue, I think *Churchill* has done a good job with our key missions of peacetime engagement, active deterrence, and preventive defense. I believe . . ."

Schmidt began quoting from the public affairs course he had been given before deploying. The Navy public affairs officers had stressed focusing on the ship's mission, not on liberty calls. He thought he sounded pretty good.

But on the opposite couch, Sue O'Dell's eyes were glazing over. After several minutes, she realized this wasn't working. So much for the "get to know him" approach. I'll just go for the throat, she thought to herself.

She smiled and gently interrupted. "Captain, may I be frank?" She touched his arm gently. Bill smiled back and momentarily felt that he had really connected with Sue.

"Of course. Go right ahead."

"You sound a little like one of those slick little pamphlets the Department of Defense hands out about Strategy 2010 or whatever. I'm here to talk about the *Churchill* and specifically your crew's record for causing, what do you call them?—'liberty incidents?'— wherever they go." She warmly smiled again, eyes twinkling. Bill told himself that she was just doing her job, but that secretly she was genuinely impressed with his pitch. Or was it that she was impressed with *him?*

Sue glanced at her notes. "Let me start with Rota, Spain . . . *Churchill's* first liberty port, I believe. Is it true that four of your crew members set up a 'Free Condom Clinic' outside a Spanish bar, and across from a convent school, while wearing their uniforms? Do you have a comment on that incident?"

Schmidt felt the interview taking a turn for the worse.

Sue referred to some notes and continued. "And I'm also interested in reports that a dozen *Churchill* crew members used a French flag as a picnic blanket in Toulon last month. What about that incident? Also the reports that in Corfu, Greece, there was an all-day ship's barbecue held at Heraklio Beach at which your crew members hired a prostitute to dress like a shoe shine boy and walk through the crowd offering—let me get this straight—shoe shines and . . . umm . . . various sexual services . . ."

Schmidt sat up straight and interrupted. "She wasn't dressed like a shoe shine boy. And it wasn't a ship's *official* function, and the rumors about various . . . er, services was started by one of our sister ships."

Sue referred to her notes again, flipping pages rapidly through a small spiral-bound notebook. "And I'm also very interested in a story that on the door to the Chinese embassy in Rome, two *Churchill* sailors hung a sign saying, NOTICE: NO MORE WHORE-HOUSE! IN FUTURE, WE TRY TO BE LAUNDRY HOUSE." She looked up and smiled sweetly at Schmidt.

As he rambled through a series of long explanations of *Churchill* adventures—saying that the crew was a bit rambunctious but good hearted—Schmidt noticed that Sue had a tape recorder out and running. He hadn't seen her start it. *I hope this is going okay,* he thought. Sue was also nodding encouragingly and writing furiously. Whenever he made a particularly colorful point, Sue would look down at her tape recorder and jot down the number on the machine's digital counter. I wonder if I should have gotten the Fleet PAO involved in this, he thought. Naw. Those guys are about as useful as a dashboard indicator light telling you the air bag just deployed. I'm doing good here. She's buying this big time.

An outsider reading a transcript of the interview would have rated it an unmitigated disaster for Schmidt. But there was something about the way that she carried herself, something about the way she gently asked the questions and smiled at his answers that gave him an entirely different sense.

The interview lasted two hours. Schmidt walked away feeling he had given a good, honest picture of all the excellent things *Churchill* had accomplished during her Mediterranean cruise so far. He also felt certain he had provided solid explanations for the most egregious incidents, putting a good spin on every event. He knew he was doing well because she kept smiling and quite often would reach out to touch him and laugh. As she got up to leave, Sue glanced at Schmidt's photos and mementos displayed about the cabin. One bulkhead, standard throughout the fleet, was known as the "I love me" wall. In addition to his elaborately framed commission were pictures of Schmidt assuming command of the ship, plaques from his past duty stations and other memorabilia. One particular picture caught her eye. "How did you meet the President?" she asked, pointing at a photo of Bill shaking hands with the commander in chief.

"I was the one-millionth person in line for the White House tour," he replied.

"No, really," she said. As she looked closer, she noticed a third person in the picture, the President's spokesman.

"Well, actually, my big brother Jim is the President's press secretary. The last time I was in Washington, I visited him at work and he brought me in for show and tell." Sue gave an enormous smile. Bill figured she must really like his sense of humor.

Schmidt walked Sue to the quarterdeck, pointing out various damage control features of the ship as they went along. Sue tried hard to appear interested, even though military hardware held no fascination for her. He is really proud of this boat, she thought. That's actually kind of sweet. He doesn't know how folks back in Washington are going to react when they read about his oversexed sailors overrunning Europe. Poor thing. He's cute but clueless, she thought.

At the quarterdeck, Sue turned and said, "Captain Schmidt. Bill. I've enjoyed talking with you. I appreciate your candor, and I want you to know I plan on a very interesting story about the *Churchill*. I hope when you read it, you will think that I have been accurate and fair."

Schmidt smiled with relief. "Sue, I've really enjoyed talking to you. We're looking forward to the story. I guess we could use some good publicity for the Navy right now. The *Churchill* has hit some rough patches, but when you hear all the facts, I think it puts things into perspective. Thanks for coming out. Come visit us again!"

Good publicity! Sue thought. Was this guy in the same interview I was? God, I'm going to hate doing this to him. He's so naive.

Lieutenant Commander Brad Moseman stood with his captain watching Sue climb down the accommodation ladder into the waiting boat that would take her to the pier in Cannes. They both waved at the reporter as the boat shoved off. "How did it go, sir?"

"Pretty good, Brad. She started off a little hostile, but I warmed her right up. I never would of thought I could like a *Washington Post* reporter, especially after all I've heard from my brother. But she's a great listener. I could talk to her for hours. I think we're going to get some good PR out of this."

Moseman looked doubtful. As Sue's hired speedboat roared off to the pier, Schmidt pointed a pair of binoculars toward the Cannes Fleet Landing. He saw his sedan pulling up along the quay, driven by Attila the Hahn, with *Churchill*'s XO seated beside him. Behind it was some kind of French police van. Even at that distance, he could see it was full of his sailors.

"Brad, we finally get a break!" he said. "Looks like the Cannes Six are liberated." I finally found something the XO is actually good at—if they ever make international butt-kissing an Olympic sport, he's going to make the front of the Wheaties box for sure. "Let's start the Sea and Anchor Detail checklist and get the hell out of Dodge."

An hour later, *Churchill* lifted her centerline anchor to the water's edge. Bill Schmidt allowed Lieutenant Debbie Smith to take charge and gently twist the ship in the Bay of Cannes. Within minutes of weighing anchor, the destroyer was standing smoothly into the Mediterranean Sea.

Sitting in his starboard bridge wing chair, Schmidt saw the lights of Cannes disappear into the evening haze. The bridge was bathed in a soft red glow from the ship's gauges. From his elevated perch, Schmidt looked down on the bridge watch team.

Good thing I talked to that reporter personally. I think she really came around, he thought to himself. I suppose you never know about these things, but I walked away from that session feeling really good. Brother Jim would be really proud of the way I handled the press.

12

Every weekday morning, shortly after 5:30 A.M., Jim Schmidt would venture outside his Mount Vernon home and search the bushes for his copy of the *Washington Post*. On days when he could find the paper, he would bring it into his kitchen and read the front section to see if it was safe for him to go to work.

Jim would quickly scan the A section, first looking for headlines that contained the words *White House* or *the President*. Next he would go back and read the other major stories with an eye toward stories that would raise in the reader's mind the question: What is the administration doing about this? Those stories, he knew, would generally drive his day.

Finally, if time permitted, he would quickly flip through the rest of the paper. He had developed an amazing knack for spotting obscure stories in which his own name was mentioned.

It required no special skill to spot the story which led the *Post's* Style section today.

The *Washington Post*
Page D-1
'Schmidt Happens'
Navy Ship on Raucous Trip
by Sue O'Dell

CANNES, FRANCE—"What can you do with a drunken sailor?" is more than an old sea chanty to Bill Schmidt. It is a daily challenge. Commander Schmidt, the captain of the U.S. Navy destroyer *Winston Churchill*, and his crew—currently pillaging their way through the Mediterranean—might consider a slightly more modern tune as their theme song: "Born to Be Wild."

Traditions die hard in the Navy. In recent years, the service has tried mightily to live down the image of the Tailhook Convention debacle. But the reputation of hard drinking, womanizing, and general carousing was well earned. The crew of the *Winston Churchill* seems hell-bent on keeping it alive.

The European deployment of the Norfolk-based ship is scheduled to last six months. Since the admirals who run the fleet demand that at least a little of that time be spent at sea, the men—and women—of the *Churchill* appeared determined to make the most of their time ashore.

Most destroyers keep their records in ships' logs. *Churchill* just uses a police blotter. Even old hands in some of the roughest liberty ports in Europe say that this ship has set new highs in hijinks.

Commander Schmidt, a boyish 38, says that his ship's mission is "forward presence, peacetime engagement, active deterrence, and preventive defense." His crewmen seem to have taken that to heart. They have demonstrated some of the most forward behavior by visitors to Europe since the Vandals and the Huns.

Consider a few examples. While visiting heavily Catholic

Spain, public-spirited *Churchill* crewmen conveniently set up a "free condom clinic" outside a convent school.

In France, a group of *Churchill* sailors honored our Gallic allies by adopting their national ensign for use as a blanket for a 2:00 A.M. picnic.

At a ship's barbecue in Greece, fun-loving crewmembers dressed a local prostitute in a shoe shine boy's outfit and sent her around offering topless boot-blacking and a few other services, apparently subsidized by the ship's "morale" fund.

Not to be outdone by their male colleagues, several women crew members, who reportedly had been overserved at a local drinking establishment, took it upon themselves to rearrange the letters on a marquee outside a hotel in Gibraltar. The original message to a wedding party of "Good Luck, Lucy and Geoff" was reconfigured to offer an entirely different evaluation of the bride's marital skills.

Most recently, while in this beautiful Riviera port, several crewmen thought it their civic duty to offer a visiting British model a tour of the ship named after her countryman and a date with their captain. The fact that she apparently did not want a tour or date did not dissuade them. The sailors bundled her off with the French antiterrorist police in hot pursuit.

The perpetrators, known as the "Cannes Six," languished in the municipal jail until officials could explain away the Euro-Tailhook incident as an "unfortunate misunderstanding."

Their captain, with a winning smile and a gleam in his eye, says all these incidents were just misunderstandings. The crew—to a man (or woman)—he says are "as fine a group of sailors as you'd ever want."

Schmidt apparently learned to put the best possible spin on a bad situation at the knee of his big brother, White House spokesman Jim Schmidt.

Well, how is it that bad things keep happening to this good crew? Perhaps the answer lies in a saying that the crew has for the regular occasions when their skipper runs into life's shoal waters. They like to say: "Schmidt happens."

The story jumped to page D-3 and continued with outraged reactions of local officials from the towns that the *Churchill* had visited and comments from Navy officials trying to put the ship's deployment in the best light. A handful of defense critics, ranging from the Center for Defense Information, the Federation of American Scientists, and the National Organization for Women all chimed in with reactions of their own. None were positive. Billy, Jim thought, what kind of trouble have you gotten yourself into?

13

The Lincoln Town Car idled in the predawn hours outside the McLean, Virginia, residence of Secretary of the Navy Frederic C. Fiske. Fiske's neighbors—lawyers, lobbyists, and diplomats—were still sound asleep. Most of the nearby two-story brick houses sported three-car garages. In the driveway of each home lay a plastic bag containing a folded copy of the *Washington Post*. The secretary's driver, Lance Corporal Bennie James, stood in a modified parade rest position next to the vehicle, ready to open the door and accept custody of his boss' overstuffed briefcase. James was dressed in civilian coat and tie and did his best to look like a professional driver. But his whitewall haircut gave away his true profession.

Until a few years ago, the secretary's driver was a civilian. That individual, who was never called a chauffeur, drove the secretary to early morning power breakfasts and late-night soirees on Capitol Hill. Unfortunately, the secretary had to order that the gentleman be reassigned when an audit revealed that with all the overtime the driver was logging he was drawing a larger salary than the man riding around in the backseat. The solution was simple for someone who controlled three-quarters of a million uniformed sailors and

Marines. An enlisted man could be assigned the driving duties, and wouldn't draw overtime unless he worked more than twenty-four hours in a single day.

The secretary's personal aide, a Navy lieutenant, rode shotgun in the front right seat. Observers might assume that he was there for security reasons, but his real mission was to provide the third person needed to allow the car to take advantage of Washington's car-pool lanes.

Corporal James had already been to the Pentagon that morning to pick up the overnight classified dispatches for the secretary. The military called it "message traffic." The State Department called them "cables." A civilian might call them telegrams. Whatever you called them, Fiske found them a bore.

Secretary Fiske folded his large frame into the back of the Town Car and grabbed the stack of messages that had been left for him in the left rear seat. He pushed the messages aside, not knowing or perhaps not caring that his executive assistant had arrived in the office two hours earlier solely to highlight the more pertinent parts of the messages for him. Fiske had long since learned that on the rare occasions that there was something significant in the messages, a staff member would summarize it for him in his first five minutes in the office. "What do you think about that collision at sea?" the staff would ask. "Tell me what *you* think about it," Fiske would say. He would quickly get the *Reader's Digest* version of what was contained in his messages without having to labor through them.

Most days as soon as he got in the car, the secretary could safely set aside his messages and reach for the item which would almost invariably set his agenda for the rest of the day, "the Early Bird."

"The Bird" was a twenty-four-page dossier of the top defense-related stories clipped and reprinted from newspapers around the world. The Defense Department's top brass read it religiously. For the Pentagon press corps it was the yeast in their daily bread.

Fiske adjusted the goose neck lamp in the back of the sedan so he could better read the Bird. He was a bit uncomfortable in the Lincoln, not because it lacked amenities but because Fiske had made his fortune selling Cadillacs. Donating several million dollars to his party and serving three years in the naval reserve in the late

'6os while trying to avoid the draft were the credentials that earned Fiske his current job.

The editors of the Early Bird didn't often lead their publication with a feature story, but they didn't often have a feature story like the one that skewered the *Winston Churchill*. The secretary read through the article, blood pressure rising with the recounting of each liberty incident. Fiske wondered how he could explain to the White House the actions of this rogue captain and undisciplined crew. He also wondered why he hadn't heard about these incidents before. Maybe I *should* be reading that damn message traffic, he thought.

Lance Corporal James barely had a chance to bring the Town Car to a stop at the Pentagon's Mall entrance when Fiske bounded from the vehicle and went charging up the building's steps. Pausing at the guard desk only briefly to ensure that his framed photo there was hanging straight, Fiske charged ahead to the one-way escalator (up in the mornings . . . down in the afternoons) and ascended to his fourth-floor office.

Bursting through the doorway at 7:49 A.M., Fiske immediately told his Executive Assistant, a Navy Captain, to summon the Chief of Naval Operations to the secretary's office to explain the offensive behavior of his sailors in the Mediterranean. The Captain looked at his watch and smiled. It was not that he enjoyed seeing the four-star CNO get called on the carpet. But the order did mean that the Captain had won the office pool, guessing that it would take forty-five seconds from the time the secretary's car rolled up before he would go to General Quarters. The CNO had guessed it would take a minute thirty.

Admiral Bushrod Custis did not become CNO by being unaware of how to manipulate Service Secretaries. He glided down the narrow private passageway that separated his office from that of the Secretary and charged into Fiske's office without knocking. "Mr. Secretary, I know what you are thinking and you are absolutely right!" the Admiral thundered. They didn't call him "Burning Bush" for nothing.

Fiske was pleased that the Admiral knew what he thought, because he wasn't too sure.

"The U.S. European Command, with all those Army and Air Force weenies running it, they probably set our guys up!" Custis continued.

Fiske nodded his head slowly in an effort to conceal that not only had he not thought of this possibility before, he couldn't make heads or tails of it now.

"Yessir, those Army guys are always running amok with their tanks in Germany. Why, they have a huge slush fund just to bail them out when they run over the Burgermeister's cow for sport." Custis was just getting up a head of steam. "I'll bet they fed this *Washington Post* gal the story on our guys. They are always trying to make it look like our forward presence is a thing of the past."

The tactic worked. Fiske began thinking of the *Winston Churchill* crewmen as victims. Custis kept up a running commentary about past misdeeds by Army and to a lesser extent Air Force troops in Europe. If half the stories were true, those GIs would have put Genghis Khan to shame.

After delivering a broadside to the *Churchill's* accusers, Custis moved on to do some damage control concerning the reputation of the ship's captain. "Mr. Secretary, I don't know this Commander Schmidt personally, but folks who do tell me that he has a fine sea-man's eye and a knack for ship handling." Custis, himself a Surface Warfare Officer rather than an aviator or submariner, had credibility on that account. "Sure, he might be a bit unconventional but you've got to have an independent streak if you are going to take a fast ship"—he paused—*"In Harm's Way."* Custis knew that the sec-retary loved that phrase, even if he thought of it as the title of a John Wayne movie, not a John Paul Jones quote.

As the top civilian and uniformed leaders of the Navy Depart-ment, Fiske and Custis had a pretty good relationship. The secre-tary knew that the CNO had forgotten more about the Navy than he would ever know. And the Admiral was certain that Fiske knew more about politics than he would ever want to know.

Service Secretaries and their Uniformed Chiefs did not always share this comfortable relationship. Every once in a while a Presi-dent would appoint a Service Secretary who knew enough, or thought he did, to want to tinker with strategy and tactics. It would take the brass months, sometimes years, to teach their upstart bosses that the concept of civilian leadership of the military did not extend to actually obliging those in uniform to actually follow the Secretary's direction.

While the Army and Air Force had nothing to do with planting the *Churchill* story, their press officers in the Pentagon did their best to keep it growing. All day long they would seek opportunities to chat up the Pentagon press corps and in their most genial conversational tones check to make sure that the reporter had not somehow missed the O'Dell article. This was done not with malice but with a sense of sport.

At Foggy Bottom, the leadership was not amused. At his 9:30 senior staff meeting, Secretary of State Harden, in his usual uppercase declaration, directed his spokesman to use the State Department's daily press briefing to express "Shock, Dismay, and Outrage at the Cavalier Treatment Afforded Our Gallant Allies."

To ensure that the message got through, later in the day Harden invited in Albert Janoska, his favorite *New York Times* correspondent, for a "deep background" chat on world affairs. The *Times*man did not disappoint and quickly asked for a reaction to the O'Dell story. Harden hinted darkly that the incidents might upset the delicate understanding he had achieved with the French on the new chemical weapons treaty.

In his finest statesmanlike tones, Harden said that it made no difference to him that the commander of the *Winston Churchill* was the younger brother of the President's spokesman. "And Al, even on the deepest of background, I will not discuss the rumors that are floating around town that this young Schmidt chap had a less-than-sterling record and obtained his captaincy through political influence. I Simply Will Not Discuss It."

14

Jim Schmidt sat behind the curved desk in the Press Secretary's office, listening to his oldies tapes. Sam Cooke's "Wonderful World" played softly in the background. His little brother's world was probably not so wonderful at the moment, he thought.

He looked at his In box piled high with government reports he would have to defend from the briefing room podium but would never have time to read. Thank God for executive summaries, he thought. Next to his In box was a second basket dedicated solely to documents requiring his signature. There were a half-dozen forms requesting reimbursement for expenses incurred during Jim's recent travels with the President. Also awaiting signature were a score of thank-you notes that Natalie had drafted for people who helped facilitate press coverage on the trips, and about half as many notes of apology to people who had been offended by the White House advance team.

Traveling for the White House staff was a mixed blessing. On the plus side, it usually resulted in a bump up in the President's poll numbers, which in turn resulted in an improvement of the President's mood. This was a highly desirable outcome for those who worked closest to the man. On the down side, the trips chewed up a lot of time. And there was the tyranny of deadlines and the In box. Whenever Jim was away from the White House, it seemed that people would sneak into his office and leave behind complex, controversial reports and proposals which he was "invited" to comment on. The deadline for response was invariably the day after he returned to the White House. If the policy initiative later went badly, the proponent could always say "the Press Secretary was fully informed of the project. Since he made no objections, it must be assumed that he was supportive."

Try as he might to focus on the paperwork, his mind kept drifting back to the fix his brother Bill was in thanks to the *Washington Post.*

His overall sense—or perhaps it was a hope—was that "Schmidt happens" would be a one-day story. And he took comfort in the fact that Bill's connection to the White House wasn't mentioned until deep into the article. Most folks will probably quit reading before they get that far into the story, he thought.

In any case, Jim couldn't give the story much attention because of the mound of routine work he had before him and the very unroutine threat of chemical weapons. He turned his attention back to his music, trying to relax before the meeting in the Situation Room. As he did so, he asked himself, not for the first time, how the hell he ended up there.

After college, Jim briefly held a job at a small radio station in Cheyenne, Wyoming, spinning records, giving farm reports, and doing the news. In his newshound role he covered and later befriended the city's youthful mayor, Sean Walsh. When Mayor Walsh ran for and won Wyoming's sole seat in Congress, he surprised Jim by asking him to come along to Washington to serve as the congressman's press secretary. Over time, the congressman turned into a senator. Ten years later he found himself in the Oval Office. With each promotion Jim was asked to come along and help formulate and articulate his boss' views.

The President had made his reputation largely through leadership in domestic issues. As a result, Jim had developed a certain expertise in discussing farm price supports, welfare reform, and even urban housing issues—despite the fact that Wyoming was blessedly free of urban woe, or even urban areas.

If there was a weakness in the President's background, and thus in Jim's, it was a noticeable lack of experience in foreign affairs and national security issues. It was because of this weakness that the President appointed Blair Harden to be his Secretary of State. The President quickly learned that this was a terrible selection, but having picked Harden, he felt he was stuck with him. Given his own weak record on the diplomatic front, he felt he could ill afford to sack the fat-headed windbag.

After two years in the White House, both the President and his spokesman had grown somewhat more comfortable with foreign policy. Jim looked around his office at the photos of himself with the Russian President, the Pope, and Fidel Castro, the latter taken during a historic White House rapprochement. Quite an on-the-job training program.

Still, Jim was apprehensive about his own lack of depth in national security issues. Other than having a brother in the Navy, Jim's only experience with the military was his three-year stint in the Army Reserves when he was trying to earn money for college. A relic of those days also hung in Jim's office. It was a plaque from his Army Reserve Public Affairs unit. The plaque showed a tank encircled by laurel. Diagonally across the face of the tank was a red quill pen. Beneath the image was the Latin phrase *Non pugnabimus, nec cogi possumus*. Jim had an idle fantasy about inviting John McLaughlin to his office to see if the former Jesuit priest could correctly translate the motto: "We won't fight, and you can't make us."

Jim's reverie was broken by his secretary, Natalie. It was time for his next meeting.

It is a wonderful world, Jim thought. A kid who don't know much about national security gets to be part of a Crisis Working Group and pretend he's Norman Schwartzkopf. God, I hope somebody at this meeting knows what he's doing.

Jim kept reminding himself that as unprepared as he was to deal with issues involving international terrorism and chemical warfare, he was better equipped than most members of Congress and the vast majority of executive branch officials. With his three years in the Reserves and a brother who was a career military officer, Jim had some familiarity with the importance of the armed forces. At least I don't treat defense as a not-very-necessary evil like some of these guys do, he thought.

Elsewhere in the White House, the routine business of governing went on. It was photo-op day and a steady stream of people with special interests were lined up in the West Wing lobby and the Roosevelt Room waiting to be ushered into the Oval Office for a three-minute picture session with the most powerful man on earth.

There were two routes Jim could take to get to the Situation Room. When the mood struck he would take the path via the West Wing lobby because of the never-ending wonders that might be found there.

In one corner of the lobby, sitting in front of a huge antique clock, was a group of Native Americans in their ancestral garb. One of them held a stuffed fish. On a settee across the room was a young woman with a sash across her chest which identified her as Miss Psoriasis. Her handler was drilling her on two lines she was supposed to ad lib to the President when the photographers covered her visit. In the far corner was a retired senator, now a lobbyist, who was using the telephone to call some of his clients. "I'm over at the White House seeing the President. Had a minute before our meeting and thought I would touch base with you . . . "

Just outside the West Entrance door, Jim looked out on a U.S. Marine in full dress uniform. The Marine, too young to have seen service in the Gulf War, would someday be able to tell his grandchildren how he served his country. He was a doorman at the most prestigious address in the world.

The absurdity of the scene greatly amused Jim.

Leaving this three ring circus, he crossed the waiting room, went through a door, and walked down a staircase to the basement level. He squeezed past staffers hustling up the very narrow staircase and strode the short distance along the corridor to the Situation Room entrance across from the White House mess. He prayed that he could correctly remember the three-digit code for the cipher lock which controlled access to the area. If not, he could always pick up the wall phone and ask the duty officer for admittance, but that would mark him as someone who was not one of the regulars.

His memory didn't fail him and he heard a welcome click. As he entered, Jim reflected on the fact that the Sit Room was not very aptly named. It was actually a series of rooms with offices, a command center, a secure teleconferencing facility, and a small conference room. The floor of the facility was raised, and Jim wondered how many miles of computer cables ran beneath it.

Jim stuck his head in the portion of the facility which served as a communications center. There, a half-dozen young men and women detailed to the White House from the CIA, Defense Department, NSA, and State Department kept watch on the world for the President.

"How's the planet holding up?" Jim asked with a smile. He always made a point of saying hello to the team because he knew that they stood their twelve-hour watches largely unappreciated by the rest of the senior staff.

"Under control, Mr. Schmidt. At least that's what I hear on CNN," the senior watch officer replied.

Most of the White House staff were on a first-name basis with one another. Jim noticed that the Sit Room crew were among the few who treated him with some deference. Sometimes he liked being called "Mr. Schmidt," but mostly it just made him feel old.

"Mr. Schmidt is my father. Call me Jim."

After bantering a bit more with the watch team, Jim entered the comfortably appointed conference room, the design of which was intended to defeat even the most sophisticated attempts at electronic eavesdropping. Decorated in leather and earth tones, the windowless room was pleasant but not plush.

The back of the chair at the head of the table was slightly higher than the others. It was meant for the President, but at this meeting it was occupied by National Security Advisor Wally Burnette, whom the President had put in charge of this ad hoc crisis working group. Along the sides of the table were the Secretary of Defense, the Director of the CIA, the head of the National Security Agency; and the Chairman of the Joint Chiefs of Staff, General Leroy Sundin. Normally for significant matters of national security a "principals meeting" would be called. The Secretary of State and, when necessary, the Attorney General and Secretary of Treasury or Energy might be included. Jim noted that there were two people present who would not normally be invited, the head of NSA and himself.

Still, not a very big group. And this is probably the first meeting I have attended at the White House that didn't include an official notetaker, Jim thought.

He took his place at the end of the table and waited for Burnette to begin. The retired general quickly reviewed what was known about the situation. "The President wants me to stress the critical importance of keeping this threat secret. If Gadhafi is toying with us, we don't want him to think that we have taken the bait. If he is seriously planning some action, we don't want to show our hand until we know more." Burnette turned to the Director of the Central Intelligence Agency.

Jim had heard the horror stories attributed to her staff that had been swirling around about Director Nelson, but he had seen only the southern belle side of her personality. They had had only a few official dealings. On two occasions, Nelson had called Jim seeking his help in trying to dissuade a major news organization from publishing some story which she felt would cause great harm to U.S. interests. "Jimma," she would say. "If they run that story, someone who has been verra hepful ta us might dah." Schmidt tried to lend the weight of his office to Director Nelson's plea. In one case he was successful, in the other he was not. As far as Jim knew, no one died as a result. The DCI was warmly grateful for Jim's attempts. It was odd, Jim thought, to have the Director of Central Intelligence flirt with you. But not at all unpleasant. She was what was called in some parts of the country a handsome woman. In her day, Jim imagined, she must have been quite striking. "Fiona, tell us what the agency is doing," Burnette asked.

"We are turning evrah national technical means onta the problem," she said. "We have energized all of ouah HUMINT resources in the region and, without telling them why, we have turned ta the Brits, French, Italians, and other allies and have them trolling for data as well."

"Director Nelson, unless things have changed very recently, I believe that our—our human assets on the ground, the ah, HUMINT . . . are quite thin, are they not?" Secretary Stevens asked.

"Well, Cleve, there ah a couple places on earth that are moah closed ta us. But I have ta admit that I am not entie-ly sanguine about ouah chances of gettin' the plant superintendent of Tarhouna to walk in and spill his guts ta us."

"Let's back up a step here," Burnette said. "Fiona, do your analysts have any idea about whether Gadhafi might pull a stunt like this, and if so, why?"

This same question had been troubling Jim, but as the person present with the least amount of foreign policy experience, he had been reluctant to ask it.

"The agency's psychiatrists ah quite worried about Gadhafi's stability," Director Nelson offered. "It is they-ah analysis that he is beginnin' to see his own mortality. The UN sanctions against Libya have hurt and he feels unappreciated by his Arab brothers. They-ah is a real likelihood that he may do something' dramatic which, in his mind, would enhance his standin' in the Arab community and make his mark upon his-tory."

"With that kind of mindset, we can't count on him to act rationally," Burnette added.

"This may seem like a dumb question," Jim Schmidt spoke up for the first time in the meeting. "But I am not real clear on what Gadhafi could hope to achieve by this whole thing."

"No, that's a verra good question," Director Nelson replied.

I hope she isn't just humoring me, Jim thought.

"Ouah best guess is that Gadhafi wants to make his place in history and undermine his domestic opposition. We know that he is increasin'ly undah attack from the fundamentalists. A group whose name translates inta somethin' like 'Fightin' Islamic Group in Libya' in particulah has been causin' him fits. Ouah estimate is that his plan is to attack Israel and demand that the West Bank be turned intah a sovereign Palestinian state. He would demonstrate his seriousness by the attack on the Knesset and would then try to splinta Israel's support by threatenin' an attack on the U.S. unless we back his scheme."

"Clearly, if he thinks that kind of plan would work he has a screw loose," Burnette replied. "And we need to pull out all the stops in locating the CW stash in the United States, if there is one. Okay, let's talk options." He turned to the Chairman of the Joint Chiefs. "General Sundin, do we have the capability of taking out Tarhouna in a preemptive strike?"

"Can we hit it? You bet. Can we knock it out entirely? Hard to say. Gadhafi has buried that sucker in a mountain. We could drop a lot of ordnance on it and only rearrange the sand. Unless you are going to authorize me to use nukes. Then I could pretty much guarantee a successful mission."

Depends how you define "success," Jim thought.

Jim found it impossible not to like General Sundin, known by his friends in the Pentagon as "the Big Swede." Everything about the man was big, especially his ears. Whenever the administration needed someone to go on television and carry a strong message, Sundin was willing. A bomber pilot by trade, he was not known for being subtle. Jim enjoyed the way the General always waved around a cigar—unlit, as a concession to modern sensitivities.

Sundin made few other concessions. In an era of so-called "political" admirals and generals, he was a throwback to the old-style warrior. He would punctuate his points by pounding the table, gesturing with his big black cigar, and blasting his opponents into silence with his hundred-megaton personality.

"You know, a mission like this is why we designed the damn B-61 warhead a few years back," Sundin shouted.

I thought that was a vitamin, Jim mused.

"The B-61 is long, thin, and relatively light-weight. It's like dropping a dart from ten thousand feet." General Sundin was warming to the topic. "What this baby does is bury itself in the ground . . . maybe fifty feet deep. Then it sets off a mini nuclear explosion that'll bust just about any bunker. And the collateral damage would probably be quite light."

"The collateral damage around Tarhouna might be light, but I am afraid that the fallout around the world from our using a nuclear weapon would be quite severe," Wally Burnette injected.

"And a preemptive strike might be hard to explain to the international community," Director Nelson seconded. "'Course, that is not really mah portfolio." At that moment, Jim acutely felt the absence of any representative of the State Department.

Apparently sensing this concern, Burnette spoke up. "The President was very explicit about the makeup of this little group. He wanted to keep it limited to as few people as possible. And he wants to ensure that whatever action we recommend be driven by concern for the safety of our citizens first and then of our allies."

With that, Schmidt made his second contribution to the meeting. "Gadhafi's credibility around the world is pretty weak. If we have to conduct a conventional preemptive strike, I think we can convince reasonable people that we were taking a prudent action of self-defense. But nuclear . . . that would be an awful hard sell."

"Whether we can take out Tarhouna, and whether we can convince the world that the action was necessary, seems to me to be a moot point," Secretary Stevens injected. "Even if we destroy Tarhouna, Gadhafi may have chemical weapons stashed in New York, or St. Louis, or San Francisco. His agents could detonate those weapons as soon as the smoke cleared in Libya. What's more, Gadhafi could claim that he was just retaliating for an unprovoked attack upon him."

"Other options?" Burnette asked.

Director Nelson took a deep breath and offered one. "We could contact Gadhafi clandestinely and tell him that we ah on to him and that if a single whiff of gas should evah appear in Israel or the United States we will create a majah roofing problem for his family tent," she said.

General Firman, the head of NSA, reacted first. "The one thing we have going for us now is that we have some idea of what he is planning and he doesn't know it. I'd sure hate to tip him off. He's liable to clamp down on communications and change his plan, and then we'd have no hint as to when, where, or how he will hit us."

"Lew may be right," Burnette said. "Gadhafi is so unpredictable we cannot assume that he would react rationally to the news that we are on to him. That news alone might be enough for him to order the stash in the U.S. to be used. Leroy, I understand you had your people put together a little tutorial on chemical agents. Do you want to give a brief rundown now so everyone here has an idea of what we might be up against?"

The General snapped open a leather-bound folder with gold metal corners. "Sure thing, Wally." The Chairman cleared his throat. "We suspect that the Libyans would most likely employ a nerve agent like sarin or VX. Characteristically, these types of agents are extremely toxic and have a very rapid effect. The agent might be a gas, aerosol, or liquid. Generally, it enters the body through inhalation or through the skin, although poisoning can also occur through the consumption of liquids or food contaminated with the agent." Looking around the room, Sundin could tell that he had everyone's attention.

"The route for entering the body is important because it has an impact on how quickly the agent starts to work. Usually, it works fastest when it is absorbed through the respiratory system. That's because the lungs have lots of blood vessels and the agent can rapidly enter them and get out to target organs."

Jim noticed that no one was breathing very deeply.

General Sundin pressed ahead. "The respiratory system is most important. If a person is exposed to a high concentration of nerve agent, death may occur within a couple minutes. Poisoning takes a little longer when the agent enters through the skin. The first symptoms might not show up for twenty or thirty minutes . . . but after that things go pretty rapidly."

Director Nelson broke in. "Remind us, if you will. What ah the symptoms?"

General Sundin flipped ahead several pages in his brief. "If you are exposed to a low dose, you might have increased production of saliva, a running nose, and a feeling of pressure in the chest area. The pupil of the eye becomes contracted, which impairs night vision. There also could be headaches, slurred speech, hallucinations, and nausea."

"And that's foah the low dose?" Director Nelson asked.

"Right. Higher doses bring more, ah, dramatic results. Difficulty in breathing, coughing, and the like. Then comes discomfort in the gastrointestinal tract. Cramps, vomiting, involuntary discharge of, well, every sort of bodily fluid." Sundin looked up from his notes. "It gets kind of messy, Madame Director."

"How about cutting to the chase, Leroy?" Burnette asked.

"Glad to. Then come the convulsions, paralysis, and death. It's kind of a death by suffocation. Not very pleasant, really." Sundin closed his leather folder to punctuate the remark.

There was silence in the room for half a minute.

"I don't think we are in a position to make any useful recommendations to the President right now," Burnette finally said. "We are in desperate need of some additional information. Fiona, Lew, Cleve . . . you need to pull out all the stops to find out when the attack on Israel might occur and where the stash in the U.S. is located. General Sundin, you need to work on a plan to take out the Tarhouna facility with certainty. And you need to be able to do that with conventional weapons."

Burnette looked up at the ceiling and sighed. "My mission," he said, "is to figure out how to get the Federal Emergency Management Agency to increase their chemical weapons disaster drills without getting anyone concerned."

15

Bill Schmidt sipped appreciatively at the mug of coffee Petty Officer Maderias had just handed him. The *Churchill*'s captain was leaning back in his starboard bridge wing chair, his feet up on the railing in front of him. The coffee was hot and dark.

"Captain, me and the other guys just want you to know we are really happy to be out of the French jail. And we're sorry, too. We just wanted to introduce you to that British girl, and . . ."

"Boats, let's face it, you guys just got carried away. And it was bad. But it's over now. We talked about it at mast." Schmidt had held nonjudicial disciplinary hearings on the Cannes Six upon their return to the ship and assigned each of them thirty days restriction. "Looks like your restriction will be served out at sea anyway with this new special operation in progress. We're *all* kind of on restriction, as far as I can see anyway."

"Roger that, sir. We didn't mean no harm. And we're sorry."

"I know, Boats." Maderias started to walk away.

"Hey Boats, one other thing. I never heard the whole story about how the jail thing worked out from your viewpoint. How did the XO get you guys out of the lockup?" Schmidt had heard Lieutenant Commander Ellsworth's version of events, which included a long and detailed negotiation supposedly carried out in French and including closely reasoned legal arguments which had overwhelmed the French.

"It was simple, sir. Lieutenant Hahn started waving around the case of bourbon you sent and opened up a couple of bottles. He was drinking with the cops when they released us. I saw the XO in the corner trying to talk French with some officer, but the French guy just kept answering in English. XO looked pretty pissed off that the French guy wouldn't talk French and kept talking louder and louder."

Lucky he didn't mention his father, Schmidt thought.

"I think maybe the XO was gonna get himself in trouble," Maderias continued, "until Lieutenant Hahn grabbed him and we all blew out of there. In the van on the way back, Mister Hahn was telling the XO that just 'cause you talk louder in bad French doesn't mean they understand it any better, and then the XO really got pissed off. Anyway, it wasn't that big a deal by the time the XO and Mister Hahn got there 'cause I think the mayor's office had said to let us go anyway."

Schmidt took another sip of his coffee. "Thanks, Boats. It's good to have you back around here. Nobody can make coffee like you."

Maderias flashed a smile at his captain. "I used that Cuban dark roast you like, sir."

Schmidt turned his attention to the horizon. The central Mediterranean was churning a bit, giving *Churchill* a very lazy roll as she powered south at twelve knots. He could see a few squall lines ahead in the purple twilight. A stiff breeze raked the deck.

His orders were pretty clear. First and foremost, gather the Cannes Six back aboard. *Check.* Then get underway from Cannes. *Done.* Third—and most interesting—head south and await further direction. This was really an odd set of orders. Schmidt also noted a lack of immediate harsh messages criticizing the ship for the Cannes debacle, which he attributed—with more hope than expectation—to the emergence of real world tasking.

Just after sunset, Schmidt heaved himself out of the comfortable bridge wing chair and moved down the two ladders to his cabin. He was working through some of the routine paperwork in his In basket and enjoying a bowl of popcorn from the wardroom when his Combat Systems Officer, Lieutenant Commander Moseman, knocked and entered his cabin.

"Hey, CSO. What's up?"

"Captain, we've just gotten a SPECAT message."

Schmidt sat straight up. SPECAT stood for "special category" and could indicate closely held operational orders. Alternatively, it could be a violent ass-chewing from anyone in his chain of command. He hoped it was orders, but guessed it was an ass-chewing.

For once, hope overtook expectation aboard the *Churchill*.

```
FROM: COMSIXTHFLT
TO: USS WINSTON CHURCHILL
INFO: COMGWBATGRU
COMDESRON THREE TWO
USS HARTFORD
SECRET/SPECAT//N03100//
```

1. (S) TAKE POSITION VICINITY 33 6'N 16 4'W NO LATER THAN 0700 ZULU 11 MAY. RENDEZVOUS WITH USS HARTFORD. CONDUCT SURVEILLANCE OPERATIONS AND COORDINATE INTELLIGENCE GATHERING WITH HARTFORD. CHURCHILL DESIGNATED OFFICER IN TACTICAL COMMAND.

2. (S) ANTICIPATE REMAIN ON STATION 30 DAYS. LOGISTICS SUPPORT PLAN WILL BE FORTHCOMING. INDICATE COMMANDER'S ESTIMATE, SURVEILLANCE PLAN, AND LOGISTIC STATE IN DAILY SPECAT SUPPLEMENT TO DAILY OPSTAT.

3. (S) FOR HARTFORD: MAINTAIN PREDESIGNATED SURVEILLANCE PATTERN. REPORT AS PREVIOUSLY ORDERED. BT

"Wow. Brad, read this." Schmidt passed the message to Moseman. The CSO exhaled softly.

"I wonder what this is all about, Captain? My guess is *Hartford* is doing some kind of close-in intelligence gathering, and we're the shotgun. Or maybe a decoy of some kind."

"Yeah, maybe that's our punishment for the Cannes Six incident. We get to play goalie for Gadhafi's Silkworm missile launches." Schmidt smiled tightly. "Well, whatever it is we'd better ratchet up our readiness. Bring up a copy of the Combat Systems Doctrine and the Daily Tactical Orders. We need to adjust the system lineup. I want to put about a dozen standard missiles in a 'ready to fire' mode. And let's upload two live fish in each of the torpedo tubes topside. Have OPS give me a call. And tell the OOD to call the XO and pass the word for an all-officers meeting for half an hour from now in the wardroom."

ON THE *Hartford*, Chet Hollomaker finished reading the same SPECAT message. He also had a detailed intelligence collection message in front of him. He called his XO and Operations Officer into his tiny cabin.

"Mike, we're going all the way into the beach again. Full shifts down in the tank. The same collection protocol. Everything goes up on the bird and direct to home plate. And this time they want it all sent flash."

"Flash?" The Operations Officer gaped at his CO. Flash was the highest precedence for message traffic. This would put it at the head of the queue of all other communications traveling through the worldwide system. The use of flash was very rare except in cases of direct attack or the very highest levels of DEFCON.

Hollomaker ran his hands through his thinning blond hair. "Yeah, OPS. Flash. When you care enough to send the very best. This is prime time, gentlemen. I can't quite put all the pieces together, but my sense is something very, very big is going down. I'm going to the tank."

In the boat's tiny intelligence collection suite, nicknamed "the tank," several cryptologists were listening to military broadcasts, telephone relay intercepts, police shortwave signals, and a variety of other prime intelligence sources. One of the specialists, an Arab linguist, looked very focused on what was coming across the signal set in front of him. Suddenly he leaned back and shook his head.

"Stopped right before he said anything good. He's really cagey. That's the one we're calling 'the engineer,' Captain. He's the prime intelligence source. He keeps talking about something big involving the Tarhouna chemical facility but he always stops before getting to the good stuff."

Hollomaker nodded. "Keep at him. We'll get what they need. And you know the drill—lots of times they just need some little piece of the big puzzle from us. Just keep sending it back to NSA, flash." He wished he felt as confident as he sounded.

As he walked from the tank forward to the boat's control area, Hollomaker vaguely heard a crew member in the torpedo room singing along with his boom box. The lyrics said something about sending lawyers, guns, and money. Thinking back on the communications that *Hartford* had intercepted, Hollomaker added to the lyrics. And gas masks, he thought to himself, lots of gas masks.

ON THE *Churchill*, sailing southeast into the bright Mediterranean sun, Bill Schmidt was calming down his XO, as usual.

"Tom, take it easy. I don't care if the Helmsman was wearing Oakley sunglasses on watch."

"Captain, it undermines the entire concept of uniform regulations, and I just can't run a tight ship if . . ."

"XO, it'll be fine. And by the way, I'm going to start a new thing on the ship—civilian clothes on Fridays. What do you think?"

Ellsworth shuddered. "Captain, you just can't . . ."

"Just kidding, XO. But let the crew wear their sunglasses. I suspect the Navy will survive."

As Ellsworth walked away, Schmidt considered his exec's prickly personality. What really surprised him was Ellsworth's total focus on the minutia around the ship, even as everyone else was honing the ship's combat system for possible action. Actually, the biggest surprise was that he could accurately identify a pair of Oakley sunglasses. He's the last guy on the planet earth under the age of seventy-one still wearing those flip-down sun shades over his regular glasses. Probably inherited them from his dad.

Schmidt finished putting the finishing touches on his combat systems daily tactical orders. He had placed fifteen of his surface-to-air Standard missiles in a ready-to-fire status, and had broken out the two firing keys from a safe in his cabin. They now hung around the neck of the Tactical Action Officer in the Combat Information Center, ready to bring the sophisticated AEGIS combat system to full air warfare readiness. He had also ordered two of the advanced capability MK 46 torpedoes loaded into his topside tubes, and was likewise prepared to launch Harpoon surface-to-surface missiles and electronic decoy rounds as well. Keys and release authority for each had been formally provided to the watch officer in the ship's Combat Information Center.

Word of all these preparations had a galvanizing effect on the crew. People were tense, watchful, and excited.

With the technical assistance of Attila the Hahn, Schmidt and Moseman had worked out both the weapons status upgrades and a new watch bill throughout the night. As *Churchill* swung gently into station at the designated latitude and longitude, Schmidt knew his ship was ready. He found himself thinking of the baseball movie from the late 1980s, *Bull Durham*. Like the Kevin Costner character, he felt like an old veteran guiding a ship full of bright young stars into the big leagues, into the spotlight of the show. Bill Schmidt was smart enough to realize that the show was a place where many people watch and judge every move, weighing and evaluating. He hoped his ship was ready.

Schmidt stepped onto the starboard bridge wing, looking south across the sparkling surface of the Mediterranean Sea, toward the distant and unseen coast of Libya. We'd better get this one right.

16

Thank God I don't have to give Charlie a ride downtown again today, Jim thought. For the past three days he had given his nextdoor neighbor a lift while his car was in the shop. Jim slowly backed down the driveway of his suburban Virginia home, stopping once to move a bicycle out of the way.

Jim and his wife had bought a large brick colonial home in Mount Vernon just before his boss the senator was about to become President. Prior to that, the Schmidts had lived in a cramped townhouse on Capitol Hill. Quaint and convenient, it had also been in the middle of a high-crime zone. With the two boys nearing school age, Jim and his wife felt they needed to move out of the city and into a neighborhood where Kevlar was not the prescribed attire for playing in the front yard. On Capitol Hill, their neighbors were mostly single, young Congressional staffers. In the suburbs, they were surrounded by families like themselves, like Charlie and his wife and three kids. Generally, it was nice to be able to socialize with Charlie. But there were times, like when he was driving to work, that Jim preferred to be alone. It was not that Charlie was such a bad companion. Not at all. But when Jim had other people in the car with him in the morning he felt obliged to tune in National Public Radio's "Morning Edition." It just seemed like the thing well-connected Washingtonians were expected to do. But truth be told, Jim felt the program was elitist, pretentious, and all too often boring. Alone in his car, Jim could channel surf among several oldies stations and periodically listen to Imus. The scatological humor on the program often stung the administration, but Jim found it a much better barometer of what real people were interested in—certainly much more telling than the highbrow stuff on NPR. Besides, Imus was funny.

Jim was making good time traveling up the George Washington Parkway, a leafy pastoral drive along the Potomac River. He started out listening to oldies. On the radio, Little Peggy March's rendition of "I Will Follow Him" ended and the station went into a commercial. Jim switched to Imus to see who they were skewering today.

Imus was in the middle of humping all manner of stuff in one of his interminable commercials. ". . . So call Fred at 1-800-272-1957 and order your 'Delbert McClinton model' harmonica. Then you'll have a harp jus' like the one ol' Delbert used to teach John Lennon how to play."

"Harmonica?" one of Imus's sidekicks exclaimed. "Boy, you'll sell anything won't you? What's next, Autobody Express bagpipes?"

"Yeah, the Secretary of State Windbag model."

Jim groaned and quickly turned off the radio. He drove on in silence to the White House.

After reading his news summary, Jim flipped through the *New York Times* and the *Wall Street Journal*. There weren't any dominant stories out there, which made it a dangerous time to be a press secretary. At times like this the press was really unpredictable. When they had an ongoing crisis or a single major story it was pretty easy to guess what questions might come up in the daily briefing. But now it was silly season. Any kind of off-the-wall story could take on a life of its own. Trivia looks important when nothing of substance is around.

It was hard for Jim to keep his staff focused at times like this. Without the adrenaline rush of an apparent crisis they would sometimes get lazy. But if his staff was distracted, so was he. It was hard to concentrate on his daily press briefing when the second meeting of the crisis working group loomed later, in the afternoon.

The daily press briefing started out uneventfully. Jim opened with a presidential proclamation of a state of emergency as a result of the spring floods in the Mississippi Valley. It was a routine announcement, unless you happened to live along the banks of the Mississippi. After a few additional personnel announcements—the naming of a new federal judge and the makeup of a delegation to an inauguration in Peru—Jim opened the floor to questions.

There were precious few, and for a moment Jim thought that Alice Kenworthy would quickly say "thank you" and grant him an early release. Alice turned around in her front-row seat to look for raised hands before uttering her benediction. At the last moment she saw a hand raised in the back of the room.

Oh no, Jim thought. He saw that the hand was connected to the scrawny arm of Nick Klosterbach, the White House correspondent for the *New Age News*, a publication of the Church of Transcendental Quality. The only thing predictable about questions from Nick were that they weren't of this world.

"Yes, Nick?"

"I have a two-part question. First, what is the White House's reaction to the fact that U.S. Navy personnel have done great harm to American diplomatic efforts as a result of their drunken rampages throughout Europe?"

Jim looked at the front row of reporters. "Another softball question from Nick." When the laughter subsided, he continued. "I suppose your follow-up question will be the tough one." Without waiting for a reaction, Jim gave a reply. "Actually, while I object to the premise of your question, I believe the conduct of military personnel overseas would be best addressed by the Pentagon. I suggest you ask your question there."

"Well, it won't be as easy for you to duck my follow up," Klosterbach replied. "What is the White House's response to allegations floating around town that the captain of the rogue warship *Winston Churchill* is unqualified for his position and received this assignment only because he is related to the President's spokesman?"

"Ooohh," the other members of the press murmured.

Jim took a deep breath and then responded. "This White House is quite busy maintaining a sound economy, protecting Medicare, cutting unemployment, and maintaining world peace. We don't have the time or the inclination to involve ourselves in personnel assignments for Navy commanders. I personally have no doubt about the qualifications of the individual you maligned, but if you want details on his credentials, once again, I suggest you contact the Pentagon."

"Thank you!" Alice Kenworthy said, in a voice even louder than usual. For the first time in his life, Jim felt like kissing her.

Jim quickly went back to his office, closed the door, and listened to oldies. He couldn't find his Neil Diamond tape. Where was "He Ain't Heavy, He's My Brother" when a man needed it? He knew that Bill's qualifications were strong, but it still hurt to be skewered by some sixties leftover about his brother's crew. That's the least of our worries today, he thought. Gotta stay focused on Tarhouna.

In the week that had passed since the first meeting, he hoped that the intelligence community had been able to make some progress checking out the validity of the threat and narrowing in on the location of any weapons stashed in the U.S., if in fact they existed. Jim noticed that he was starting to think and speak like a national security policy wonk. They always called the spy agencies "the intelligence community." It made them sound so, well, family friendly.

WALLY BURNETTE quickly called the meeting to order. Although there were no placards assigning seats, Jim noticed that everyone sat in the same spot that he or she had at the last meeting. Burnette asked the DCI to summarize what progress her organization had made in checking out the threat. It didn't take long.

"Basically, we ah running inta brick walls," Fiona Nelson drawled. "Gadhafi has done a good job of keepin' a lid on progress at Tarhouna. He continues to maintain that Tarhouna is part of his 'Great Man-made Rivah' project. We have been unable ta penetrate the plant and ah having difficulty in comin' up with a list of workers they-ah, something we hoped ta do ta allow us ta locate Mustafa." It was clear to Jim that the DCI was not her usual feisty self. Her disappointment at having no progress to report was clear.

The report from the Director of NSA was equally bleak. "We've tweaked every antenna, satellite, and listening post we have. Our Arabic linguists are working double shifts. But so far, no joy," General Firman admitted.

"How about possible means of delivery, Fiona?" Burnette asked.

"Do you mean against Israel or the U.S.?"

"To start with, let's talk about Israel."

"Let me take a crack at that one," offered General Sundin, the Chairman of the JCS. "We've looked at that and have decided that the Libyan Air Force would be incapable of delivering the ordnance. They don't have any missiles with the range, and as far as fighter aircraft goes, even if they could convince a pilot to make it a one-way suicide mission, they wouldn't have much of a chance of getting through Israel's air defenses." For a moment Jim found himself hoping that this might lead the group to conclude that Gadhafi was simply bluffing. He was wrong.

"So how could they do it?" Burnette asked.

"My best guess is that they would use a terrorist willing to sacrifice himself and make the delivery using a commercial airliner," Sundin said, obviously uncomfortable with being forced to make a prediction.

"We've come ta the same conclusion," Director Nelson added. Her head bobbed up and down slowly. "Ah've got mah people inventoryin' ev'ry commercial aircraft in Libya that would have the range ta reach Tel Aviv. We are also compilin' a list of fundamentalist wackos who know how ta fly."

"Since we remain without a representative from the State Department, let me ask a diplomatic question," the Secretary of Defense injected. "Shouldn't we, at some point, notify our Israeli allies about our suspicions?" Reflexively, Jim looked at the empty chairs at the end of the table.

"I've been struggling with that myself," Burnette said. "But you know the Israelis. If they think they are the target of an imminent attack, they will conduct a preemptive strike of their own. And it'll be conducted with all the subtlety and restraint of Dennis Rodman."

"Can ya blame them?" Director Nelson asked.

"No, but what that does is toss all the cards up in the air. And if Gadhafi survives the Israeli response, and maybe even if he doesn't, we face the possibility of chemical weapons being detonated somewhere within the United States. I'd really like to hold off tipping our hand until we absolutely must."

"Concur fully," General Firman said. "From the NSA point of view, as soon as the Israelis start hammering our Libyan friends, any chance of us intercepting information about the location of the CW in the States goes out the window." Jim knew that there was always a debate between operators and signals intelligence people. It seemed as if the "SIGINT" guys never wanted the military to take action based on the information they obtained, so that they could get more information in the future. The warfighters always wanted to act now, and let future intelligence collection take care of itself.

Jim wasn't comfortable enough yet at these meetings to offer too many opinions, but he thought he would risk a question. "What happens if Israel gets hit by a chemical attack and they later find out that we knew it was coming and didn't warn them?" he asked.

Burnette sighed. "If that should happen, I don't believe even a great spinmeister like you would be able to concoct a reply that would satisfy them."

The Chairman of the Joint Chiefs rubbed his chin. "If that happens, it will be a tough call as to who we have to fear the most . . . the Libyans or the Israelis."

17

Jim dropped his reading glasses on his desk and slowly rubbed his eyes. As much as he tried to force himself to read the advance copy of the free trade report he could not focus on it. I've got to make some sense of this today or I'll never be able to explain it in my briefing tomorrow, he thought.

In the background The Beach Boys were singing "Sloop John B." He shook his head as the chorus exclaimed "This is the worst trip I've ever been on." I'll bet Bill could relate to this song after that *Washington Post* article.

His musings were interrupted by a knock at his office door. It opened quickly, and Natalie bustled in. "Are you ready for the tong? They're all here."

Jim was scheduled to conduct a background briefing for a group of reporters from small and midsized newspapers. The big ones, like the *Washington Post* and *New York Times*, never had any trouble getting in to see senior administration officials for the inside dope. But the little guys had less success, so small groups of them banded together in self-described "tongs" seeking something like equivalent treatment.

Jim wanted to treat all reporters equally, but as a practical matter the TV networks and a handful of big papers were the 800–pound gorillas. Even though the combined circulation of the *Sacramento Bee, St. Louis Post Dispatch, Chicago Sun-Times, Newark Star Ledger, Dallas Morning News,* and *Minneapolis Star Tribune,* all represented in this tong, exceeded that of the *New York Times,* it was impossible to view them as being as important, or as dangerous, as a single *Times* reporter.

"Yeah, send them in. But after about twenty minutes, buzz me on the intercom and tell me my presence is required in the Oval Office, okay?"

The Beach Boys were singing "God Only Knows" as Jim reached back and turned off his stereo. That might be a good theme song for this group, he thought.

The tong ambled in, led by Stanley Kovaleski, the recognized leader of this group due to his longevity and tenacity. Stan was wearing his standard outfit. Checked sports coat, striped shirt, and plaid double-knit trousers. Considerable evidence of lunch was displayed on his tie. Jim admired the fact that Kovaleski was not a slave to fashion. Too many of the younger newsroom denizens had taken to looking like yuppie stockbrokers.

Kovaleski fumbled with his tape recorder, which was held together with masking tape. It was clear that the machine had been dropped on several occasions. As he struggled to turn the recorder on, he knocked a stack a magazines off a coffee table in front of him. Jim smiled as he noticed the felt tip pen that was inserted point down, without a cap, in Kovaleski's shirt pocket.

"Lady and gentlemen, welcome," Schmidt said, hoping that he could successfully fake sincerity. The "lady" was the only female member of the tong, Iris Van Pelt, the White House correspondent for the *Newark Star Ledger.*

From her accent it was clear that Iris was a genuine New Jerseyan. Jim once asked her the name of her hometown. "Exit Sixteen," was her reply.

The reporters placed tape recorders on Jim's desk and punched the start buttons. Though they had all been through this kabuki dance many times before, Jim felt safer by reminding everyone of the ground rules.

"Same rules as always. This is on background, attributable to a senior administration official. No kicking, biting, or punching in the clinches. Stan has the first question."

"Have you sent or received any SOS's from your baby brother lately?" Kovaleski didn't waste any time with social niceties.

"No, I think he probably has his hands full and my duties here have prevented me from being a very good pen pal."

Kovaleski looked at the reporter to his left. They would rotate asking questions until time ran out. "What was the reaction to the 'Schmidt happens' story around the White House?"

"Several senior officials ran down to see the Navy recruiter," Jim deadpanned. "Seems they are convinced of the veracity of that old slogan, Sailors Have More Fun."

Iris was next in the rotation. "You can make light of it if you want, but it sounds like a bunch of cowboys are running around Europe taking a sledgehammer to the delicate framework of international relations."

Jeez, these folks won't give up. "I think the Atlantic Alliance will survive a few pixilated sailors. And I would note that the *Post* story was written by Sue O'Dell. I'm sure you all read her stuff. Frankly, I am in awe at her ability to write about a leaky faucet and make it sound like the Johnstown flood."

"Sure, blame the messenger," one of the reporters muttered.

"And you are willing to assure us that there was no political pressure used to get your brother this assignment, right?"

"Absolutely!" Jim reactively blurted out the response, perhaps a bit too forcefully.

He found himself checking his watch to see if the twenty minutes had passed and if Natalie would be coming to his rescue soon. To his disappointment less than five minutes had elapsed.

Maybe I'd better go on the offensive, Jim thought. "Say, you know tomorrow the free trade report is going to come out and there are some pretty fascinating conclusions. They'd shoot me if the news leaked early, but if you guys will accept it on 'deep background' I can give you some of the highlights."

Not pausing to find out if there was any interest in free trade, Jim pressed ahead and recited every detail he could remember from the report he had just struggled to read. A measure of his skill as a quick study and spinmeister was that he managed to consume the next fifteen minutes in a trade discussion. He scrambled to give examples of potential exports that happened to come from the cities represented by the members of the tong.

Bzzzz. Jim hit the speaker button on his phone with relief. "Yes?"

"General Burnette is here to see you," Natalie said. Dammit, she got that wrong. She was supposed to tell him that he had to go to someone else's office, not that they were here to see him.

"I'm just finishing up with the Kovaleski group. Please tell the general that I will go over to his office in just a minute."

Taking the hint, and having had their fill of free trade, the reporters all picked up their tape recorders from Schmidt's desk and closed their notebooks.

"You better go," Iris said. "It could be a crisis. Maybe the crew of the *Winston Churchill* just stormed the Bastille." The reporters wandered out chuckling.

Getting up from his seat, Jim walked out of his office. He intended to chew out Natalie for the mix-up in signals.

"Nat, you were supposed to say that I was wanted—Oh, hi Wally." The National Security Advisor stood next to Natalie's desk munching on some stale candy left over from the Easter egg roll.

Natalie rolled her eyes. "As I said. The General *is* here to see you."

"Well, why didn't you say so?" Jim ducked back into his office before Natalie could throw anything at him. Well-aged jelly beans could be quite painful. Wally Burnette quickly followed him and closed the door.

"How was the group feeding?" he asked.

"I feel like I've been nibbled to death by ducks."

"What were they interested in?"

"Mostly the cowboys of the *Winston Churchill*, but after a while I managed to get them to bite on the free trade story."

Burnette turned slowly. "What did you say?"

"I gave them a few nuggets on free trade and gave them a day's jump on the big boys. They'll need it to make sense of this report. We'll be lucky if we can get the big guys to write about it at all," Schmidt answered.

"No, I didn't mean that. What was that you said about cowboys?"

"Oh, they were going on and on about what a bunch of loose cannons we have on the *Winston Churchill* and how they were Rending the Fabric of Statecraft," Jim said.

Burnette paused for a moment and scratched his rapidly balding head. "Something you said a moment ago struck a nerve with me. I came over to brainstorm with you about how we can get out of this mess we're in in Libya, and I think you may have given me an idea. Do you remember the *Vincennes* incident?"

"Sure," Jim said. "The Navy ship that accidentally shot down the Iranian airliner a few years ago. Ugly. I think we're still paying compensation."

"Yep. They mistook an Iranian Airbus for an attacking F-14 and blew it out of the sky. There was a lot of criticism at the time because the ship involved, the *Vincennes*, had a reputation of being out of control. The investigations revealed that other ships in the region referred to the *Vincennes* as the 'Robocruiser' and a number of people, perhaps unfairly, called the skipper and his crew 'cowboys.' "

Jim's eyes grew wide. "So are you suggesting that my brother is about to be court-martialed?"

"Oh no, not at all. As soon as that story came out I called the CNO and Bush Custis told me that your brother has a great reputation as a naval officer. He might have inherited all of the fun-loving genes in your family, but other than being your brother, he reportedly is a solid citizen. No, what I was thinking about was the dilemma that we talked about in the Sit Room yesterday. What do we do if Gadhafi is about to launch his attack on Israel and we still haven't identified the location of the chemical weapons in the U.S.? How can we knock down the aircraft without letting Gadhafi know that we are onto his plan?"

"I see your point," Jim said. "We need to bring down the aircraft but can't let on that we're listening in on the party line. At least until we get the word on the location of the chemical weapons."

"Well, I was thinking. If the Libyans launch an aircraft with the intention of hitting Tel Aviv, what if it were 'accidentally' shot down by those cowboys on the *Winston Churchill?* Since the *Washington Post* has already labeled your brother and his crew as 'unguided missiles,' the world—and most importantly Gadhafi—might believe that the *Winston Churchill* could inadvertently shoot down a plane."

18

Most White House officials were blissfully unaware of the threat as they carried out the day-to-day work of running the executive branch of the world's only remaining superpower.

Each year since 1975, the democratically elected leaders of the world's largest industrial economies met to discuss how to fight inflation, bring down trade barriers, and promote prosperity.

Each spring or summer, the countries, once collectively known as the Group of Seven, held what had been known as the "G-7 Summit." Recent meetings had some added spice since the Russians had been allowed to join, making it the G-8.

At the moment, many White House staffers were consumed with preparations to make the President's upcoming trip to Rome for the G-8 Summit a success.

Most of his predecessors found these economic summits mind-numbingly dull, but Jim Schmidt enjoyed them. Multilateral trade negotiations, international investment policy, and farm price supports were the President's strengths, so the G-8 Summit gave the President a chance to shine on the international stage, and helped counter claims that he was a foreign policy lightweight. The President will look good as long as I can keep the Secretary of State under control, Jim thought. Secretary Harden had a penchant for trying to hog the spotlight at events like this. Hell, he'd tap dance naked if he thought it would get him two minutes on the nightly news.

As the summit approached, Jim's staff conducted a number of background briefings for the press prior to the departure for Rome. These sessions were designed to get the media marginally familiar with the issues that would be discussed and to lay the groundwork for the reporters to understand the achievements that the administration knew would come out of the summit. Jim had more than an educated guess about what those achievements would be: high-level representatives from each nation had been working on the summit's final communiqué months before the meeting began. These representatives were known as the Sherpas, in deference to the Himalayan guides, for their role in leading their nation's efforts in the march toward the summit.

Why bother having a meeting if it is already decided how it will come out, those unfamiliar with the ways of Washington might well ask. Without the pressure of having to come up with some significant accomplishments for their bosses to announce at a meeting, the Sherpas would never be able to agree about anything. The fact that the G-8 members knew how the game was going to come out before it was played was no secret to the press, but the White House correspondents went along with the ruse, in part because it enabled them to make predictions which would later prove to be true.

In addition to the general briefings for White House reporters, Jim's staff arranged background sessions at the U.S. Information Agency's press center in the National Press Building. The foreign press took these G-8 meetings much more seriously than their American counterparts did. Another part of the buildup to the summit involved private background briefings for the tongs of second-tier media people, and for specific regional groups that had a particular interest in some agenda item at the summit.

National Security Advisor Wally Burnette did his part to build interest in the event as well. He customarily held a weekly seance with White House reporters from the major news magazines in which he would provide, on "deep background," the color, context, and timelines that the weeklies thrived on. The news magazines were particularly interested in the timelines, which they called "tick tock." During this week's news magazine backgrounder, Wally gave a detailed description of the President's efforts to prepare for the summit. "We have developed five major briefing books for the President on the major issues that we expect to come up at the summit," he said. "He takes one of them with him to the residence each evening and pores over it in bed after dinner."

"What time does he begin working on them and what does the First Lady think about sharing her bed with policy papers on the International Monetary Fund?" the reporter from *Newsweek* asked.

"I don't know the answer to either question, but I can tell you that he called me at home to discuss trade barriers at eleven-thirty last night," Burnette replied. The reporters all busily scribbled this into their notebooks and looked down to ensure that their tape recorders were running properly.

Some might wonder about the fascination over such minutiae. But by including this type of "tick tock" in their stories, the news magazines gave their readers the impression that they were getting the real inside story. After all, if a reporter knew precisely what the President was doing in bed, he must have the details right on policy plans as well.

After another fifteen minutes of questions about the mechanics of how decisions were made, not the substance of what was being decided, the backgrounder was over.

Burnette said good-bye to his guests and walked across the West Wing lobby and down the narrow hallway which led to Jim Schmidt's office. It was his practice to give the Press Secretary a brief readout on any of his contacts with the press. That way if the reporters came back to the Press Secretary with questions about things they'd learned from Burnette, Jim would know the source and the context of the original information.

"I really had a hard time getting them interested in the economic summit," Burnette announced. "It wasn't until I threw some sex in there that I got their attention."

"Sex and the G-8?" Jim asked, clearly impressed. "How'd you manage that?"

"I told them that the President gets aroused by taking his briefing books on farm price supports to bed with him."

Jim laughed. "Fortunately, for a policy wonk from Wyoming, that is not considered an unnatural act."

It was good to share a chuckle over the G-8 plans, but it was clear to Jim that Burnette was still agonizing over the Libyan situation. "Have you come up with any leads on foreign policy problem number one?" Jim asked.

Burnette shook his head slowly. "We're really flying blind on this one, Jim. For all we know, Colonel Gadhafi might be waving bye-bye to a martyr right now who is enroute to an unpleasant landing in Israel."

Jim stared out of his office window. After a moment's reflection he added, "Yeah, and another one of his cohorts could be preparing to set off some of those nasty chemical weapons in downtown Detroit, or somewhere."

"We have got to stop him," Burnette said grimly.

"Are you seriously considering the accidental shootdown ploy?" Jim asked. "I mean, would Gadhafi be dumb enough to believe that?"

"Under most circumstances, no. But thanks to our friends at the *Washington Post* . . ." Burnette paused for a split second. "God, I never thought I'd hear myself say that. But anyway, thanks to that article in the *Post*, we might have a chance. Look, the whole world believes that your brother is a wild man and that his crew are a bunch of idiots. It wouldn't be too much of a stretch to get people to believe that they could make some colossal mistake."

Jim smiled tightly. "It is always a pleasure for the Schmidt family to be of service to our country."

"The tough part would be to keep people in our own government from spilling the beans prematurely. So, if we were to pull off something like this, we could clue in only the absolute minimum number of people. How is your brother at acting? He would have to be pretty damn convincing. And he would have to take a lot of heat from his superiors who might not be privy to the particulars of the operation."

"When we were kids we were always getting into trouble. I talked him into doing some crazy things. More often than not, we'd get caught." In his mind, Jim visualized the time he convinced Bill, then eight years old, to dump a five-pound box of high-sudsing detergent into the Binghamton Mall fountain. Jim winced when he recalled the time the two of them Krazy Glued all the desks shut at Calvin Coolidge Elementary School. "He was pretty good at acting as though he was innocent. But I don't think he's had much experience pretending to be guilty."

"Well, he may get a chance to practice. But since we can't give him an order through the chain of command, you might have to talk him into doing this crazy thing."

Suddenly, Jim had a hollow feeling in the pit of his stomach that he hadn't felt in three decades, not since he had set his little brother on a course to conduct some low-grade vandalism. This time he might have to ask Bill to put his whole career at risk. And he might have to ask him to take someone's life. In fact, he might have to ask him to initiate an act of war.

"Wally," Jim asked querulously, "are you sure this is a good idea?"

"Hell no, I'm not sure. It may be the dumbest thing ever invented in the White House. And that is some stiff competition."

Jim looked at a picture on his desk from the last Schmidt family reunion. At the back of the group photo stood Bill, with a mischievous grin on his face. "Well, should we run your scenario by the Crisis Working Group to see what they think?"

Burnette paused for a moment. "No, at this point, the whole thing is too speculative. I think there is one other person we should discuss it with. Let's go see the President."

IT WAS POURING rain at Andrews Air Force Base on the day the President was to leave for the Rome G-8 Summit. The foul weather was cooperating with Jim's plans.

Air Force One sat on the tarmac, primed and ready for the trip.

A discrete three hundred yards behind it sat the chartered 747 that was to carry most of the White House press corps. Except for a small, rotating pool of twelve reporters and technicians who flew on the presidential aircraft, the majority of the media traveled on the charter plane. Truth be told, most preferred the commercial flight. The food was better, the drinks flowed more freely, and the cabin crew had long ago given up on giving admonitions about being buckled in for takeoffs or landings, or giving warnings about not using electronic devices.

The press charter was wild and raucous. For several hours editors could not reach their reporters, and their onboard competitors were similarly unable to file any stories. No one was beeped and no one was getting beaten. Members of the fourth estate, guardians of the public trust, would often surf down the plane's aisle on overturned serving trays as the aircraft lifted off. The flight could even be profitable; for five dollars, the passengers could enter the "Seato" raffle. On a 747 the reward for having your seat number pulled out of a sack could be substantial.

But before takeoff, there was one last bit of work to perform. On long trips such as this, the charter would remain on the ground so that the media could record any presidential predeparture remarks and videotape his plane's takeoff. The latter was known as the death watch.

Assuming that Air Force One did not crash on takeoff, reporters and cameramen would scramble aboard the charter and take off in pursuit of the President. Somewhere over the Atlantic, the press plane would overtake the presidential jet so that the media could land first and record Air Force One's landing and any comments the leader of the free world cared to make upon deplaning.

As rain pelted down on the bystanders, the President's helicopter, Marine One, landed nearby after its ten-minute flight from the South Lawn of the White House. The President disembarked to salutes from the helicopter's two Marine crewmen. Two Air Force enlisted men took over escort duties, each carrying a large umbrella to keep the commander in chief dry. They walked briskly over to the press area, known as "the pit," and President Walsh made his way to the awaiting microphones.

Jim exited from the rear steps of Marine One thirty seconds after the President and walked unescorted to the press area. There were no airmen holding umbrellas over his head. Normally, Jim took pains to stand out of camera range. Today he stood close enough to the President to be in clear view of the media as he struggled to hear the President's departing remarks above the din of the pouring rain. After five minutes of routine remarks, the President turned and charged up the front steps of Air Force One. Jim and the dozen members of the press corps travel pool scrambled up the back steps. The giant Air Force 747 was rolling before they could dry off and find their seats.

HALFWAY across the Atlantic, Jim walked back to the compartment where the press were confined. He commiserated with them about having stood outside in the rain to hear the President's uninspiring departure comments. He complained that he had yet to warm up from the soaking and took out his handkerchief and loudly blew his nose. As he set off toward the senior staff cabin he muttered something about having a chill and seeking out one of the military physicians who always traveled with the President.

BRAD MOSEMAN couldn't remember the ship ever getting this many SPECAT messages before. He attached the latest to a clipboard, flipped the metal cover down on top of it, and headed off to the commanding officer's cabin. "We've got another SPECAT, Cap'n," he said.

"Jeez Brad, kind of makes you feel important, doesn't it?" Bill Schmidt flipped the cover back on the clipboard and read the latest message.

```
FROM: COMSIXTHFLT
TO: USS WINSTON CHURCHILL
INFO: COMDESRON THREE TWO
COMGWBATGRU
SECRET/SPECAT//N03100//
```

1. (S) DEPART CURRENT POSITION IMMEDIATELY
   AND CLOSE POSITION VICINITY 41 48'N 13
   36'E AT BEST SPEED.
2. (S) MAINTAIN EMCON THROUGHOUT TRANSIT.
3. (S) WHEN ON STATION, DISPATCH SHIP'S HELO
   TO GUARDIA CIVIL HELIPORT 41 48'N 12 36'E
   FOR PICKUP OF ONE DISTINGUISHED VISITOR
   (CODE SIX).
4. (S) HELO SHOULD FERRY DV TO CHURCHILL FOR
   APPROX ONE HOUR VISIT AND THEN RETURN HIM
   TO GUARDIA CIVIL.
5. (S) AFTER VISIT, AND RECOVERY OF HELO,
   RETURN AT BEST SPEED VICINITY OF GULF OF
   SIDRA TO CONTINUE SURVEILLANCE OPS UNTIL
   FURTHER NOTICE. BT.

Hmm, I wonder what the hell this is all about? Bill thought. Curious that they don't name the DV? "Code Six." A four-star flag or general officer or four-star civilian equivalent. If this were COM-SIXTHFLT coming to chew us out over the Cannes incident, they wouldn't be so mysterious.

JIM HELD a presummit press briefing on the evening of the President's arrival in Rome. The White House advance team had established a press filing center in a ballroom of the Excelsior Hotel in Rome. The senior White House staff and most of the traveling press had rooms at the hotel. The president, for security reasons, was staying at the U.S. Embassy nearby.

Hundreds of reporters sat along the rows of narrow tables in the cavernous press center. Who are all these people? Jim thought. The ranks of the White House correspondents swelled on occasions such as this. When a presidential trip included three or four days in a spot like Rome, reporters who only occasionally covered the White House fought to convince their editors that it was crucial for them to be on hand.

Jim sniffled throughout his briefing and mopped his brow on several occasions. The session was intended to review the logistics of the next several days and to restate the President's goals for the summit. Jim hoped that the same turgid phrases he used in Washington would sound more convincing with a Rome dateline.

When the briefing ended, Jim mingled among the correspondents. He solicitously asked the members of the Air Force One pool if they had come down with any illnesses after enduring the Andrews deluge. Thankfully, they said, none had. Late that evening the Press Office staff put out word that Jim was "severely under the weather" and had asked one of his deputies to handle his duties for a day or so until he could recover.

Early the next morning, long before most of the traveling press had arisen, Jim descended in a service elevator to the hotel's garage with the aid of the Secret Service and was whisked into a large black Chevy Suburban van with opaque black windows. The Service called these vehicles war wagons. They usually carried a half-dozen heavily armed agents in presidential motorcades. Air Force transport aircraft flew scores of specialized vehicles in advance to every presidential visit site.

The large van lumbered through the ancient Roman streets, dwarfing the small cars and mopeds favored by the natives. Jim sat alone in back of the vehicle and watched through the tinted windows with amusement and occasional horror as the driver struggled to avoid pedestrians and early morning traffic. I hope this is less eventful than our arrival motorcade was, Jim thought.

When Air Force One arrived in Rome, the President, his official party, the Secret Service, and the press were all escorted into the Eternal City in a seventy-mile-per-hour procession led by *cara-binieri* on motorcycles. The Italian national policemen, splendid looking in their thigh-high leather boots, managed to steer their motorcycles with their legs while waving away oncoming traffic with both hands. It was a magnificent sight until the motorcade had to alter its route unexpectedly because of the presence of a broken-down truck carrying giant bottles of *vino locale*. The lead motorcycle didn't get the word, and sailed off in the wrong direction. When this *carabiniere* noticed that he was no longer leading the parade, he tried to make a sudden stop, lost control, and slid under the wine truck. Remarkably unscathed, he slid off his bike on the other side, sprang to his feet, and saluted as the remainder of the motorcade passed him by.

Minus the President and the *carabinieri*, today's ride turned out to be much less eventful. Before long, Jim found himself at a heliport. As instructed, he remained in the van until the Navy helicopter landed. The aircraft's door slid open and a crew chief stood alongside it with a flotation jacket and helmet for the mysterious passenger. Gotta remember not to call this helicopter a "chopper", Jim thought. His brother Bill had lectured him before that the Army and Air Force called them choppers. In the Navy that was a major faux pas; they were "helos."

Jim jumped out of the van and quickly walked over to the crewman. "Hi, I'm your passenger." The crewman helped Jim put on a dirty white life vest and an earphone/helmet combination, garments known in the fleet as a float coat and cranial.

Jumping aboard the Sikorsky SH-60B helicopter, Jim noted that it was a far cry from the ones he was used to in the presidential fleet. For one thing, it was a lot noisier, and much of the cables, wiring, and piping was exposed on the interior of the aircraft. Strictly utilitarian, Jim thought. Nothing wrong here that a lot of fake wood paneling, some leather seats, and a ton of soundproofing couldn't fix.

The Seahawk helicopter quickly lifted off. Flying low across the landscape, it was soon flying over the Adriatic Sea. Forty-five minutes later Jim looked down and saw the *Churchill* on the horizon.

On the bridge, the Officer of the Deck turned the ship into the wind and had the bosun' call flight quarters on the ship's PA system. "Flight quarters, flight quarters, all hands, man your flight quarters stations."

"If I were a betting man, and of course I am not, I would wager that this is CINCUSNAVEUR, coming out to chastise us about that Cannes incident," Lieutenant Commander Ellsworth said, sounding at once frightened and hopeful.

Bill pulled his ballcap down over his eyes and tried not to show any emotion. "Relax, XO. We were told to pick up a single passenger. When's the last time you saw a four-star Admiral travel without an entourage? But since you are so excited about this, why don't you go back aft and greet our mystery guest and bring him or her to my cabin." Might as well give the XO a thrill.

Before the Captain's words were out of his mouth, the XO was sprinting aft, simultaneously checking his uniform to make sure the military creases in his shirt lined up with the belt loops in his trousers. He didn't have to check to see if his shirttail was tucked in. It was connected to his socks by a sort of jury-rigged garter belt.

Fortunately, the early morning fog that was typical for the region had lifted. The *Churchill*'s helo settled down on the ship's deck with a thud. Crewmen quickly placed chocks in front of and behind the aircraft's wheels and secured the helicopter to the deck with tie-down chains.

Thank God they can land this thing on the boat, umm . . . ship, Jim thought. For a while I thought they were going to have to lower me onto the deck using that horse collar-looking device.

Wearing his cranial, goggles, and float coat, Jim would have been unidentifiable to his mother. Ellsworth hadn't a clue who the visitor might be, but since the passenger was listed as a "Code Six," the XO figured a salute would be in order.

"Welcome aboard *Winston Churchill*, sir!" Ellsworth shouted above the noise of the helicopter.

"Great to be here," Jim shouted in return. "Where's Bill?"

"Bill? Oh, the Captain is in his cabin awaiting you, sir . . . Mr. . . . err . . ."

"I'm sorry, we haven't been formally introduced. I'm Bill's brother, Jim."

The XO led the visitor through a hatch to the interior of the ship. The wind blew the hatch shut behind them with a clang. Oh brother, Ellsworth thought. You mean we left our duty station off of Libya to come screaming up here simply to give the Captain's brother a joy ride? I wonder how many strings were pulled to make this happen.

The XO led the way to the commanding officer's cabin and knocked sharply on the door. "Come in," Bill shouted.

"Captain, I believe you know our guest," the XO said icily. As

Ellsworth stepped aside, Jim Schmidt brushed past him. Ellsworth had never seen his CO look shocked before. Today was a day to remember.

"You said to drop in some time if I was ever in the neighborhood," Jim said. He stuck out his hand and then warmly embraced his astonished younger brother. Bill Schmidt was momentarily speechless.

"Well, next time give me a little warning so I can clean up my room," Bill finally said.

"Don't worry, I won't tell Mom if it's a mess."

Side-by-side it was clear that the two men were brothers. Jim, slightly taller and thicker of the two, had the look of someone who had heard a million stories. Nothing would surprise him. Bill, on the other hand, couldn't conceal the impish gleam in his eyes. He had the look of someone who had told a million stories. "Jeez, bro, it created something of a pucker factor around here when we heard a 'Code Six' was coming." Bill glanced at the XO.

"What's a 'Code Six'?" Jim asked.

The XO took it upon himself to reply. "That's a four-star Admiral, General or their civilian equivalent, sir."

"Well, they told me that being an assistant to the President carried some sort of rank but I never did figure out what I am. 'Code Six,' huh? Sounds pretty good."

The XO showed no signs of leaving and so Bill found a way to gently dismiss him. "XO, how about going back and checking on the aircrew and helo? According to our orders, they've got to be ready to give big brother a ride back to the beach in less than an hour. Mom would never forgive me if they ran out of gas and had to ditch."

"Yes, sir. I'll make sure the craft is airworthy," Ellsworth replied.

What a dipshit, both brothers thought simultaneously.

Bill kept slapping his brother's arm and punching him on the shoulder. It was as if he was trying to convince himself that the visit was for real.

"So, what do you think of my ship?" Bill asked.

"It looks a lot bigger now than it did when I first spotted it out the window of the helo," Jim replied.

Bill nodded with pride. "Yeah, it is surprisingly big."

"And I'll tell you another thing that surprised me. I couldn't help but notice as I was walking to your cabin that you have quite a few women on the crew. I imagine that can be the cause of some additional headaches for you."

"Ah, its not so bad. I just tell the whole crew that the *Churchill* is a family. So if you mess around with another crew member, it's like dating your sister."

"And that dissuades them?" Jim asked skeptically.

"Yeah, except for the ones from West Virginia."

The two brothers shared a laugh but Jim quickly broke the mood.

"I'd like to yuck it up with you, Bill, but we have some business to transact. Sit down, little brother. I've got a story to tell you that you are *not* going to believe. . . ."

19

It would be important to minimize the number of people aboard *Winston Churchill* who had knowledge of the scheme. Bill Schmidt knew he couldn't pull it off by himself.

I'll need the TAO and the CSC in on it at the minimum, he thought. The Tactical Action Officer and the Combat Systems Coordinator were the watch positions in the Combat Information Center, or "CIC," that controlled weapons launches. During the highest alert conditions of General Quarters, the officers who performed these key functions were Hahn and Moseman.

It helped that Brad Moseman and Attila and Hahn were the two members of his wardroom whom Schmidt trusted the most.

Schmidt invited the two officers to his in-port cabin for further discussion. Aboard *Arleigh Burke* destroyers, like most Navy ships, commanding officers have two homes. One, called the "at-sea cabin," was a small, spartan affair, with little more than a desk and bunk, located a few steps aft of the navigation bridge. This is where the Captain would often stay during intense at-sea periods. From here he was able to reach the bridge in an instant, in his skivvies if necessary, to help avoid a collision or other disaster.

A larger, better-appointed cabin was mainly used during in-port periods and for hosting dignitaries.

The reactions of Hahn and Moseman to Schmidt's private briefing were entirely predictable. Hahn, who thought with his heart, would follow his captain anywhere, without question. Moseman, no less loyal to Schmidt, was more analytical and had lots of questions.

"With all due respect, sir, how do we know that your brother isn't . . . well. . . ."

"Crazy?" Schmidt interrupted.

"Well, I might have used another phrase, but that about sums it up."

"Brad, you've got to trust me on this. I've known Jim all my life." Schmidt paused for a second, thinking about how foolish that comment sounded.

Hahn laughed. "Yeah, I'll bet he was like a brother to you."

Schmidt smiled. "Something like that. I know him and I can tell that he still has all his marbles, and he is very, very worried. Besides, if there weren't something going on in Libya, I don't think we'd be sitting off of Gadhafi's coast right now. Instead we'd be up in Gaeta doing a rug dance with COMSIXTHFLT about why our crew keeps finding colorful ways to win friends and influence people around the Med."

Both officers nodded. "Well, I'd be a lot more comfortable if this tasking came down in an OPORDER through the chain of command," Moseman said.

"Yeah, well there's no way you could keep something like that quiet," Hahn replied. "And even though it is *a little* unusual to get tasking via the President's press secretary, maybe this is the only way to do it. I mean, there probably aren't any Standard Operating Procedures for ordering a Navy ship to shoot down an unarmed civilian airliner, so if you were gonna do it . . ."

"Well, can I count on the two of you to help me pull this off?" Schmidt asked.

"Damn straight!" Hahn answered first.

"Yes, sir," Moseman quietly responded.

"Great. This isn't going to be easy. I am going to plant some seeds by telling the wardroom and chiefs that intelligence indicates that the Libyans may be planning an attack, using a civilian airliner as a Trojan horse. The tough part is going to be convincing the crew that a real commercial aircraft is a MiG, or the equivalent."

"Presumably," Moseman said, "the target aircraft will be squawking IFF codes appropriate for commercial air."

"Yeah, and another thing," Hahn added, "he's liable to be making a steady climb out of Libya, which won't look very threatening to our guys on the consoles."

"Here's another problem that I have been rolling around in my head," Schmidt offered. "Under standard practice, we would have to warn this guy many times as he approached us before we engaged him with missiles. If we hail this guy on any of the international frequencies that he guards, however, he'll know that we are on to him and he is likely to turn back."

"I've got another one for you, boss." Despite the obstacles, Moseman was clearly getting excited about the challenge. "If nobody else in our immediate chain of command is in on this, how can we be sure that we are going to get permission to launch weapons, you know, to go 'birds free?' "

"Well, besides that it looks easy, right?"

Hahn guffawed; Moseman chuckled dryly. "Piece of cake, Cap'n." Hahn replied.

If Moseman and Hahn hadn't known their commanding officer so well, they might have been surprised at how willingly and easily he accepted this unorthodox assignment, one that could place at risk everything he had ever worked for. But both officers knew Schmidt to be one of the least introspective people on the planet. On any decision, he considered the facts, made up his mind, and never looked back. Moseman wished he had that ability. It would have saved him many sleepless nights.

"One other thought," the ever practical Moseman added. "If this aircraft is full of chemical weapons and we blow it out of the sky above us, what does that do for air quality around here?"

MOSEMAN and Hahn had faith in their commanding officer. They would follow him because Schmidt had earned their trust. About

400 miles to the south, a small group of Libyan workers were also following the orders of their superiors, but they did so because their leaders had earned their fear.

Deep within tunnel two of the Tarhouna complex, a five-ton Mercedes truck was backing up to an underground loading dock. High-powered halogen lights in the ceiling far above gave off an eerie yellow glow. A slow, rhythmic beeping sound reverberated within the tunnel shaft as the big truck slowly eased backward into position.

The driver of the truck had never been inside the complex before. A member of the powerful Meghrani tribe, the source of Gadhafi's strength in Libya, he felt honored to be allowed to see such an engineering marvel. The honor turned to shock as plant workers arrived on the loading dock with his cargo. Four technicians wearing what appeared to be space suits walked slowly alongside a large yellow forklift transporting a pallet containing eight large metal canisters.

The driver had no idea what the nature of his cargo might be, but it was clearly very dangerous by the way the handlers were treating it. He immediately noticed that he was the only person in the facility without a protective breathing apparatus.

Gingerly, the technicians loaded the pallet onto the truck and then proceeded to cover it with netting and strap it down.

Most modern chemical weapons were produced in binary form. That is, they were made up of two chemicals which were stored separately. Each was relatively harmless in its natural state; it was only when mixed with the other component that they became lethal. The Tarhouna shipment was a unitary supply. Already premixed, it only needed to be dispersed to carry out its deadly mission.

The leader of the loading crew, a man named Abdullah, climbed into the cab of the Mercedes and placed a pistol to the driver's temple. Tactics like that really weren't necessary, but Abdullah found that you rarely had to repeat yourself when you used such an attention getter.

"My friend, your orders are simple. In a few hours, when it is fully dark, you will drive out of this tunnel. There will be three vehicles in front of you as you leave the compound, and three more will follow." Smiling through his gas mask, Abdullah continued with a mechanical sounding voice. "All you need to do is deliver your cargo to hangar three at the airport and you will be free to go."

Abdullah smiled again, knowing that the driver would never have an opportunity to go free. He had seen too much.

"Do you understand your instructions?" Abdullah asked.

The driver nodded slowly but was speechless.

"Oh, and my friend, please drive carefully."

ABOARD THE *Churchill*, a crowd was gathering in the wardroom, the place where the ship's officers took their meals, and which also served as their lounge. Schmidt had called a meeting of his officers and senior enlisted for what he termed a threat briefing.

"I know you all have been wondering what the heck has been going on operationally and why we have been boring a hole in the ocean off the Libyan coast." As Schmidt looked around, he could tell that several of those present hadn't given a moment's thought to the nature of the mission. One part of the ocean looked pretty much like any other.

"What I am about to tell you is highly classified. Needless to say, there will be no mention of it in any of your communications off the ship. And I don't even want you speculating about it among yourselves." There, that ought to get them buzzing. "Ladies and gentlemen, allied intelligence assets believe that members of the Libyan Armed Forces may be planning to strike U.S. naval assets in the Mediterranean in a surprise attack." The eyes of Schmidt's audience grew considerably wider. Boy, I wish I had their attention like this when I had to lecture them on the need to get personnel evaluations submitted on time, Schmidt thought. "Don't ask me why they might do something stupid like that. Colonel Gadhafi has been out in the sun for quite some time and he wasn't real stable on his good days."

Schmidt continued his briefing. "Intelligence indicates that the Libyans may launch a MiG or a Fitter in a kamikaze attack on a Sixth Fleet ship. The aircraft may be equipped with a bogus commercial IFF and could be squawking like a commercial airliner.

They might even respond to radio queries like a civilian aircraft. We can't allow ourselves to be fooled. From now on, I want everyone to be on their toes. Don't jump to conclusions that things are what they seem to be." Schmidt looked out at his audience and noticed that he still held their rapt attention. The XO was busily taking notes. Schmidt knew that Lieutenant Commander Ellsworth saw this as an opportunity to pad his professional résumé.

"We are going to increase the number of watches in CIC, the bridge, and sonar. Starting immediately, we will be going to port and starboard in Combat as opposed to the usual three sections." Port and starboard meant fifty percent of qualified watchstanders would be on duty at any given time. It was rare to have so many people on watch at any given time. Normally that level of staffing only occurred during general quarters drills and at times of actual crisis.

"Weapons Department, I want you to set a few dozen Standard missiles to armed status and upload the Phalanx with full magazines. Are there any questions?"

"Sir!, sir!" Schmidt didn't have to look around to recognize the squeaky voice of Ensign Marshall Madison.

"Yes, Mister Madison?"

"Does this mean we're going to get medals?" The crowd moaned in unison.

Schmidt thought of an immediate reply and momentarily stifled himself. But just for a moment.

"It might, Marshall. The reason I am having this meeting is to try to avoid getting the medals *posthumously*."

20

Ensign Marshall Madison had only been on board *Winston Churchill* for six months but already he was a legend. Most newly commissioned officers and recently enlisted graduates of boot camp come to the fleet somewhat green, but Madison was chartreuse. In a neighborhood where street smarts were the coin of the realm, Ensign Madison was bankrupt.

For this and many other reasons the crew loved him. He was an endless source of fun. Shortly after reporting aboard someone ascertained that the young Ensign enjoyed bowling. "Well, if you get a special request chit signed, you'll be permitted to use *Winston Churchill*'s onboard bowling facilities," he was told.

Having already succumbed to several other scams, Marshall was on his guard. "How can you bowl on a ship that rocks and rolls around?" he asked. The answer: "Gyro stabilization." It was enough to satisfy him.

"Well, where is it? How come I haven't seen it?"

"Below decks. Haven't you heard of the shaft alley?"

The bad news for Madison was that in truth the "shaft alley" was a tiny, nearly airless, elongated space in the bowels of the ship, so named because the ship's twin propeller shafts passed through it. For the better part of a week, Madison went all over the ship from stem to stern. The Chief Master at Arms signed his chit but told him he needed an okay from the corpsman. The doc initialed off but suggested that the supply officer also had to give his approval. Finally, when every other logical authority had signed his request form, the ensign was sent to see his commanding officer.

Bill Schmidt was sitting in his chair on the bridge looking out on the setting Mediterranean sun. "Excuse me, sir," Ensign Madison said in a soft, squeaky voice. "Would you approve my bowling chit, sir?"

Bill looked down at the young ensign, slightly out of breath from having climbed all the way to the bridge while carrying his bowling bag and ball.

"Marshall, I don't know how to tell you this . . . but the bowling alley is . . . ah, well, it is out of order for the rest of the cruise." Schmidt didn't have the heart to tell Madison the truth.

"Darn. I was so looking forward to a few games."

Bill looked out the bridge window to avoid breaking up. "Don't worry, son, I think the crew will find a few other ways to keep you entertained."

A more innocent, guileless twenty-two-year-old had never entered the fleet. How Marshall Madison got a commission and assignment to an *Arleigh Burke*-class destroyer was a source of constant speculation in the wardroom. The leading theory was that somewhere there was a qualified candidate named Madison Marshall and a computer got the names backward, sending the wrong man to the *Winston Churchill.*

Not all of Ensign Madison's habits endeared him to his shipmates. Marshall was "born again." Some said he was born again and again. In any case, he took it upon himself to save any reprobates he might come across. On *Winston Churchill,* this was a full-time job. Temporarily placing his bowling ball in his locker, Madison had filled the bowling bag with religious tracts. When not on watch, he would wander around the ship and leave literature where he thought it was most needed. Often this meant substituting his sacred screed for the crew's *Playboys* and *Penthouses.* Marshall then placed the offending magazines in plastic bags, along with full cans of cream soda for weight, and surrendered them to the deep.

Marshall's seamanship skills were also lacking. He would hum hymns while standing Junior Officer of the Deck watches on the bridge. His mind would wander from the tasks at hand, so much so that most OODs were reluctant to relinquish any authority to the young man.

The general consensus, however, was that if you were going to allow Madison to conn the ship, you should do so early in the watch. Wardroom scuttlebutt was that he would take a pen and write *port* in his left palm and *starboard* in his right. But before long he would forget about his study guides and rub his hairless chin. By the end of a watch, Madison's face would be ink-stained and any shipboard maneuvers he might direct had a somewhat random nature to them.

Madison's cluelessness made him a perfect participant in Schmidt's shootdown scheme. The only way to bring off a deception like the one proposed was to keep most of the crew in the dark. Sailors make the world's worst conspirators because they talk among themselves too much. If the phrase "loose lips sink ships" were true, the fleet would be awfully small, Schmidt thought.

The first step to creating a plausible screwup of mammoth proportions was to assign Ensign Marshall Madison as Fire Control Officer "Air" in CIC, where he would play a vital part in any air engagement.

21

For the first time, USS *Hartford* neared the surface close to the Libyan shoreline. During the previous few weeks of eavesdropping off the northern coast of Africa, the submarine was able to remain fully submerged.

"Our guys in the tank did the best they could," Chet Hollomaker explained to his XO. "But I guess our formerly talkative friend on the beach has gone zip lip. That's why the folks back in Washington have decided to employ a more direct way of gathering intelligence."

"The honchos back in D.C. must want that info awfully badly to risk this," the XO replied.

"This" was the use of a SEAL reconnaissance team. Two nights before, *Hartford* was ordered off-station near Libya and directed to make a high speed run to the Navy submarine base in La Maddalena, Sardinia. There, under a moonless Mediterranean sky, the submarine took on five members of a SEAL Team and their equipment. As soon as the last of the supplies was stored, *Hartford* was underway again, speeding her way back toward the Libyan coast.

The crew of *Hartford* made room for Lieutenant Sammy Diaz and four enlisted SEALs. Hollomaker noticed that most of the SEALs had swarthy complexions. It struck him that there must be a high demand among special operations folks for people who can pass for Arabs.

Hartford was soon back on station off of Tripoli. During the transit, Diaz and his crew checked out their gear in the sub's dry deck shelter, essentially a bubble on the hull placed aft of the submarine's sail and designed to aid in the clandestine insertion of unconventional warfare personnel. A native of El Centro, California, Diaz had gone to UCLA on a wrestling scholarship. Hollomaker noticed that the slight, wiry officer always walked on the balls of his feet, giving the impression that he was perpetually on the verge of taking an opponent down on a mat. There was an intensity about Diaz that was unmatched in any of the officers regularly assigned to the *Hartford*.

In addition to various small arms, radios, and survival gear, Diaz checked the false identification papers and shabby Egyptian-made clothing that he and his troops would adopt, assuming they made it safely to shore without being seen. The clothing and papers were carefully placed in airtight plastic bags, because the SEALs were going in "wet."

Their mode of insertion was to be a twenty-two-foot-long Mark VIII SEAL Delivery Vehicle. The SDV would be launched, fully flooded, from *Hartford*'s dry deck shelter. One SEAL would serve as the craft's operator, delivering his three comrades to an isolated beach west of Tripoli.

Hollomaker, no neophyte to special operations, was nevertheless amazed when Diaz briefed him on the SEALs' mission.

"Well, sir, my men and I have been instructed to make our way ashore and bury our wet suits and other gear. Petty Officers Shaughnessy and Jefferson will bring the SDV back out here to 'mother,' and just as well . . . they don't look too Arab to me. Meanwhile, the three of us on the beach get in our A-rab outfits and turn ourselves into Libyans. That's why me and the guys haven't shaved for a couple days. Then we make our way to the seaside village of

Sabratha. With luck, we hot-wire a truck or something and head south to Tajura where, according to NSA, 'the engineer' is supposed to live." Hollomaker listened wide-eyed and silent.

"Chief Khaury is the best Arabic speaker among us. So we'll use him to try to pin down the exact location of Mustafa's house or apartment. Then, all we have to do is pay the gentleman a visit and see if he'd like to share a bit more information with us."

"What happens if he won't?" Hollomaker asked.

"Oh, he will. We'll relay whatever we learn back to you . . . and that's why it is vital that your commo guys stay on their toes and always monitor the circuits we gave them."

"I've ordered port and starboard watches in the Communications Department," Hollomaker said. The twelve-hour-on and twelve-hour-off rotation would allow him to double the normal allotment of communicators on duty at any given time to listen for word from Diaz and his troops.

"Good. As soon as we transmit whatever we've got, we hightail it out of there and then signal you to dispatch Shaughnessy and Jefferson to pick us up. If any problems crop up, well, at least you've got the inside skinny for the folks in D.C."

"Rog," Hollomaker responded. "But make sure you try real hard to ensure that no 'problems crop up.' The paperwork is a real pain in the butt when a submarine comes back to port with fewer passengers than she left with."

Two nights after leaving La Maddalena with the SEALs, *Hartford* was ready to give her passengers a silent send-off near the Libyan coastline.

Hollomaker was more than a bit uneasy. His concern was exacerbated because his least efficient officer of the deck happened to be on watch. Lieutenant Larry Caffey was technically competent enough, but he was always chattering away. The crew said he "was stuck in the transmit mode."

"Officer of the Deck, any surface contacts?" Hollomaker asked.

"Like I said, Captain, this neighborhood is emptier than a MENSA meeting at West Point."

Among Caffey's many annoying habits was his tendency to start sentences with the words *Like I said* . . . having never before said anything of the like. He also had a propensity for inventing absurd similes.

The captain did a 360-degree turn with the sub's periscope to assure himself of the accuracy of the OOD's observation. It was indeed quiet and dark. Hollomaker ordered the submarine to go dead in the water and he gave the SEALs the green light for launching the SDV.

The run in to the beach went like clockwork. Once ashore, Diaz and his crew quickly buried much of their wet gear and donned their Arab attire. They made their way inland to the small town of Tajura. Once a desolate way station for Bedouin traders, Tajura had lately seen somewhat of a boom as a result of construction on Gadhafi's "Great Man-made River Project." The project, called by Gadhafi the eighth wonder of the world, was viewed by most outsiders as the greatest of all the colonel's follies. It was a $25-billion scheme to bring two million cubic meters of water a day to Tripoli from aquifers in southern Libya. The water would have to cross a thousand miles of desert, making the project spectacularly expensive and implausible.

In fact, the project served several purposes. It gave the Libyan masses the sense that a great enterprise was taking place in their midst. It provided the hope of fresh water in a land where ninety-five percent of the country was without it. And it provided cover for other projects, most notably the Tarhouna chemical weapons facility.

The world's most ambitious public works project meant that there were plenty of vehicles around. In the predawn hours, Diaz's troops made short work of stealing a battered Mercedes truck. The SEALs climbed aboard and headed off toward Tajura. They quickly wished that they had stolen a truck with air-conditioning as the early morning temperature reached the mid-eighties.

By the time they arrived, the sun had risen and the local populace had begun to head off for work. Diaz and his group laid low until midday, when they found their way to the people's "souk" or marketplace, in Tajura. Armed with some ten dinar notes, it took Chief Khaury only three tries to find someone who could direct him to his "cousin Mustafa's" house. Mustafa lived in a modest dwelling surrounded by a white stucco wall on the southeast edge of the town.

Quickly ascertaining that no one was home, the SEALs took only moments to break in. They settled down to wait for the owner to return. "Jeez, get a load of this place. This guy is definitely a bachelor," Chief Khaury said. The home's modest furnishings could barely be seen under a layer of debris. A half-eaten meal of chicken tagine, now covered by flies, lay on a table in what passed for the kitchen. Hidden in a cupboard were several half-empty whiskey bottles, confirming NSA's analysis that Mustafa would have a drop from time to time.

"For an engineer, he is not very orderly," Diaz noted. About a month's worth of newspapers were strewn on the floor. Over near a cushion were a stack of pornographic magazines, apparently of Egyptian origin. The SEALs amused themselves with these while they waited for Mustafa to return.

Just after nightfall, the sound of a car engine being switched off could be heard outside the compound. A key jiggled in the lock and a man in his mid-thirties staggered in.

As the door closed behind him, a hand reached out from behind and clamped across his mouth. A knife was thrust against his throat. "Mustafa, my friend, you have been working late," Chief Khaury said in Arabic in a voice that was anything but friendly.

The engineer's eyes were wide with fright. He wouldn't have been able to say much even without a large hand stretched across his mouth.

"I'm going to remove my hand from your mouth," Khaury continued, "but if you shout out I might get nervous and the hand holding this blade against your throat might slip. Do you understand that?"

Mustafa nodded very slowly.

Khaury's hand dropped from Mustafa's mouth and the engineer mustered the courage to talk. "I . . . I . . . I am not a rich man . . . but whatever I have that you want . . . take it, but please leave me alone. I will not tell the authorities . . . just do not harm me."

"What do you take us for, common thieves? Why, I ought to kill you for that." Khaury found himself enjoying this.

"No, no! I am sorry if I have offended you. What . . . what do you want?"

"Do you speak English?"

Mustafa's confused expression showed he thought that this was an odd question. "Well, yes, it was necessary to learn English when I was earning my degree."

"Good. That will make this a lot easier," came from another voice. Lieutenant Diaz and the other member of his team showed themselves.

Khaury dragged Mustafa over to one of the cushions and pushed him down on the floor, all the while maintaining the light touch of the knife to his throat.

"We're here to find out everything you know about the Tarhouna project," Diaz began.

"It is part of the Great Man-made River Project," Mustafa replied. He made a guttural noise as Diaz kneed him in the groin. "Yeah, and I'm Hosni Mubarak," Diaz said. "Look, we know what it is and we don't have time to play games. It's a chemical weapons production facility and you work there as an engineer."

"I know very little of what goes on there. I am a simple man." *Oompf.* A second knee to the groin.

"Yeah, and you're also a slow learner, Mustafa."

"If anyone speaks about what goes on at Tarhouna the authorities will have them killed!" Mustafa was looking truly frightened.

"Guess you should have thought about that before you discussed it with your brother Ibrahim," Diaz replied.

"Ibrahim? He reported me? It's a lie!" *Oompf.* Another shot to the groin.

"Naw, your brother wouldn't do that. Let's just say that your party line got crossed and we overheard a few things you were sayin'."

Nodding to Chief Khaury, Diaz said, "You got that little recording handy?" With that Khaury brought out a microcassette recorder and hit the Play button. What Mustafa heard next was unmistakably his own voice: "I can't believe he is going to do it. He is planning on dropping a planeload of our 'special product' on the Zionists. Right on the Knesset."

"You're Israelis!" *Oompf.* Yet another blow.

"Damn, Mustafa, I don't believe I've ever seen anyone as dumb as you. You better shut up for a while, I'm getting tired out with all this kicking."

"Why are you doing this to me?"

"Hey, we'd like to read you your Miranda rights and enter into a nice discussion, but frankly, man, we just don't have time. And besides, a Libyan who is about to help gas a lot of innocent people doesn't have many rights."

Mustafa looked confused. The words *Miranda rights* meant nothing to him. "Wha . . . what do you want?"

"Look, man, here's the deal. You tell us everything we want to know, and do everything we tell you, or we give a copy of this little tape to Colonel Gadhafi and friends. When they get done dicing and slicing you and the rest of your family, you'll be camel food."

"I, I understand."

"Good! Maybe you aren't so stupid."

Chief Khaury put a blank tape in the microcassette player and pushed Record. "Okay, man, now here is what we want to know. . . ."

By the end of a five-hour grilling, Diaz was convinced of several things. First, Mustafa didn't know the precise timing of an attack on Israel. Several more well-placed groin kicks revealed that the attack would come soon and that indeed an Air Libya commercial airliner would be used.

Most importantly, Mustafa provided a detailed description of the construction of the Tarhouna plant. Many of the facts he provided jibed with intelligence reports that Diaz had previously heard. The facility consisted of two tunnels approximately 400 feet in length, protected by 100 feet of sandstone and reinforced concrete. Just inside the front entrance to each tunnel, the passageway diverged around huge rock walls that could withstand any nonnuclear blast, Mustafa estimated. Diaz had to draw back his knee only once or twice to get Mustafa to reveal everything he knew about how the facility was constructed and how it was operated.

While the interrogation was going on, another member of Diaz's team, Petty Officer Pete Valdez, was hard at work. The communicator for the squad, Valdez rigged a transmitter to Mustafa's phone line.

Once Mustafa had been milked of every scrap of information he had on Tarhouna, Diaz gave him his assignment. "Mustafa, my friend, you may get to live after all. You'd like that, wouldn't you?"

Mustafa nodded.

"But the only way you are going to live is if you do exactly as I tell you. Do you understand?"

Another nod, this one faster.

"I want you to find out exactly when the aircraft attacking Israel is going to take off. I want details . . . time, where it will be launched from, the course it will fly, tail number. Everything. Is that understood?"

Mustafa seemed to be on the verge of saying something but then just nodded again.

"It might take you a couple days to find this out . . . but I want to know that you are still working on it. So I want you to call your brother Ibrahim every day. If you haven't found out what I want, just say the words *I am working very hard, my brother.* When you do get the information, I want you to work it into a conversation. Tell Ibrahim that you are thinking of taking a vacation and going to Malta. Give him the date, time, and other details of your flight . . . but those details will be for the attack on Israel. Get it?"

"Yes, I understand." Mustafa's demeanor brightened a little.

"That's the easy part, Mustafa. Your most important mission is to find out where your 'special product' is stashed in the United States, and give us the exact—and I mean exact—location. Now, I know what you are thinking," Diaz continued. "You are thinking that all you have to do is tell your brother every day that you are working hard. Well you can do that, but if that flight takes off and you haven't warned us, or if the 'special product' in the U.S. is released and you haven't given us the location, I will send a copy of that tape I played for you to Brother Gadhafi. And he will make sure that you and your entire family die. You understand?"

Mustafa nodded, and the SEAL team began packing up for their trip back to the beach and an SDV ride back home to "mother."

22

After submitting her story on the misadventures of the crew of the *Winston Churchill*, Sue O'Dell lingered in southern France telling her editors that she was doing background research for some future unspecified articles. There is something nice about having your boss six time zones away, Sue thought. Most contact with her editors came through E-mail and voice mail messages, rather than the constant second-guessing and "helpful suggestions" that her colleagues in the newsroom in Washington had to endure.

A beautiful young American woman with an expense account had no trouble attracting potential escorts along the Riviera. But the matter-of-fact boldness that Sue demonstrated in her professional life did not carry through to her private life. Put off by the local lotharios who were magnetically drawn to her bright smile, Sue would often retreat to her hotel and order meals from room service. The bellhops delivering her meals wondered why this lovely blonde woman was dining alone.

Sue enjoyed Europe, but after a while the isolation, the feeling of being disconnected from her homeland began to bother her. Every six months or so, Sue would convince herself that it was time to make a visit to the United States to catch up on the latest office gossip and to make sure that the paper's leadership could put a face to her byline. The concept of having a Style section reporter based in Europe was a new one, and she didn't want her editors to think that she had lost touch and gone native.

But each time she returned to the United States she felt more like a foreigner. She wondered if she would ever feel truly at home anywhere anymore.

Sue's editors used these biannual visits to discuss the stories she had produced over the past several months. They've stored up all that kibitzing and I guess they can't resist, she rationalized. Paul Harper, her editor, was penurious with his praise, and so she was more than a little surprised at his enthusiasm for her recent story on the *Winston Churchill.*

Sitting in Harper's glassed-in office and looking out on the newsroom, Sue basked in her boss's praise. "You really nailed those sailors running amok in the Mediterranean. Great story. Had everything. Sex, lies, and government waste."

"Thanks, I enjoyed it myself. But if you liked it so much, why was it edited so drastically? The story I submitted was considerably longer than the one that got into the paper."

Harper fiddled with some executive toys on his desk which were supposed to reduce stress. For Harper's visitors they only increased it.

"Sorry, Sue. Couldn't be helped. Turns out your story was set to run in the paper on the same day that Lorena Bobbitt announced she was running for Congress. A story on the cutting edge of politics was bound to swamp your gob story." Harper was addicted to terrible puns and would often employ words like *gob*, an archaic reference to sailors.

"Yeah, well, I still feel cheated."

"Hey, I've got an idea!" Harper shouted. He flung his arms wide, knocking a stack of papers to the floor.

Sue hated it when her editors got excited about ideas.

"Why don't you do a follow-up. And since you're here and there is a White House angle to your story, why don't you go see what the skipper's big brother thought of your piece."

For once, she thought, that's not such a bad idea. "Sure. Maybe I can work in some of that fine prose from my first piece that you and Lorena sliced out."

The next day, Sue contacted Jerry Beach, the *Post*'s White House correspondent, to gently tell him about her project. Reporters who cover the White House get very annoyed if they think someone else is poaching on their territory. After a little sweet talking, Sue convinced Beach that she had no long-term designs on his sources or his seat in the press room and that she would soon not only be out of his hair, but out of the country.

Beach contacted one of the young heiresses who worked in the press office to have Sue cleared in to the White House for a one-time visit. You don't have to be an heiress to get a job here, he thought, but it is a lot easier if Daddy made some major contributions to the President's election campaign.

Sue figured scheduling a one-on-one interview with Jim Schmidt would be difficult, particularly because of the edge to her *Winston Churchill* story. So she decided just to show up for the daily press briefing and see if she could get a few minutes with Schmidt afterward, before he had a chance to think up an excuse to get away. Sue arrived just in time to hear one of Schmidt's patented rock 'n' roll briefing introductions. She heard faint music coming out of the briefing room speakers followed by a disembodied voice. "Ladies and gentlemen of the press, the briefing is about to begin. Please take your guidance from the King." The music grew louder and Sue recognized the strains of Elvis Presley's "Don't Be Cruel."

I wonder if someone tipped him off that I'm here, she thought.

The briefing was an easy one for Schmidt; he had a few nuggets to offer. He took a few veiled shots at the Senate Minority Leader for apparently reneging on capital gains tax relief. Nothing really controversial but enough raw meat to keep the animals fed.

Sue stood along the side of the briefing room. Her *Post* colleague would certainly not relinquish his seat to her, and she felt uneasy about sitting in any of the vacant chairs. It would be embarrassing if the rightful occupant showed up in midbriefing and she got evicted. She admired Schmidt's easy banter with the media and his obvious familiarity with the issues. And she noticed some family resemblance with his younger brother. She wouldn't have picked him out of a lineup as Bill's brother, but there was something there. Come to think of it, if either of them were apt to end up in a lineup, it would probably be Bill.

The briefing ended with a whimper rather than a bang; the questions petered out. Finally Alice Kenworthy took pity on Schmidt and said thank you.

Since the briefing was entirely amiable, Schmidt hung around the podium for a few minutes joking with a few of the regulars and providing some additional amplification on his remarks.

As the crowd dwindled, Jerry Beach took Sue in tow and led her to the front of the room.

"Jim, I wonder if you would have a few minutes to meet with one of my colleagues." He nodded toward Sue.

Schmidt had noticed the attractive stranger during the briefing and wondered who she was. He flashed a big smile. "Sure!"

"Jim, I'd like you to meet Sue O'Dell."

Jim already had his hand extended and hoped the shock that ran through his body was not too noticeable. "*The* Sue O'Dell?"

"Yep. Still willing to give me a few minutes?"

"Ah, sure, sure. Might as well give you a chance to try to sink a second Schmidt." Jim did his best to appear unflustered, but his best was none too good.

"Well, I certainly didn't try to sink the other one, just reported the facts." Easy girl, you are sounding pretty defensive, she thought.

"Yeah, I know. The *fact* that my brother's crew modeled themselves on the Vandals is pretty well known. Come on up to the office."

Schmidt led Sue and Jerry out of the briefing room and up the ramp toward the press secretary's office. Jerry stopped in the lower press office to chat with another reporter. Sue nodded with appreciation. It was clear he was letting her have a private moment with Schmidt. Either that or he didn't want to be associated with her.

Jim led Sue into his office and offered her coffee, which she declined with a wave. "I overdosed before coming over today." She looked around the office and admired the furniture, photos, and memorabilia. In one corner was a bust of Thomas Jefferson, which had sported a USS *Winston Churchill* ball cap since her story had come out.

Sue sat on the couch along the wall. Jim found himself sitting in the side chair alongside as opposed to behind his desk. He didn't want to appear too imposing.

"I wanted to get your reaction to my piece on your brother's ship." Might as well take a frontal approach, she thought.

"The only official White House reaction is to refer you to the Pentagon." Jim hoped he didn't sound too snippy. He looked out his office window toward the driveway and wished he were there, or anywhere else.

"Look, I am not after an on-the-record response. We can do this on background, deep background, whatever you want."

"Sue, even on background as a White House official I would be uncomfortable talking about your story. It's not the kind of story the White House would normally touch. No reason to alter that stance just because the captain's name is Schmidt."

Sue smiled, looked down at her empty notebook, and reached out and touched Jim's arm. "How about off the record?"

"It's against my better judgment, but on that basis, I'll tell you that, well, your story is obviously well written. You've got quite a flair for sticking a knife in someone. But where was the balance?"

Sue's smile dimmed. "What do you mean?"

"It is fair game to mention the several ways the crew got themselves in trouble. But why couldn't you at least have included something about the good things they have done. Missions accomplished, orphanages painted, stuff like that."

"Orphanages? What orphanages?"

"There's always orphanages. Bill tells me that every Navy ship paints orphanages. Some orphanages get painted two, three times a month."

Sue found herself smiling, and noticing more and more of a resemblance between the two brothers.

"And you could have mentioned that the ship won the Battenberg Cup."

"What's that?"

"I have no idea. But I heard they won it and, as I understand it, it is a good thing that doesn't involve drinking, abduction, or seduction."

"Sounds pretty boring," Sue opined.

"I recognize, Sue, that there is a reason nobody ever wrote a sea chanty called 'What Do You Do with a Sober Sailor,' but it seems to me you could have found something nice to say."

Looking a little stunned, Sue said, "Boy, I really struck a nerve, didn't I?"

"I'm sure you didn't intend to write a one-sided piece. And I imagine that life aboard a U.S. Navy ship is more foreign to you than the rest of the stuff you cover in Europe."

"Well, I don't know . . ."

"I'll bet that none of your friends in high school or college went into the military, right?"

"Well, yeah, but . . ."

"And I'll bet you've met more people whose names start with Buffy than with Lieutenant or Petty Officer, right?"

"Well, actually, ah . . ."

"And taking a wild guess, I'll wager that your mom and dad's only involvement in the military in the sixties was to demonstrate against the Vietnam War. How am I doing?"

Sue was starting to get more than a little bit pissed. She would have told the SOB off if he wasn't right. "For a guy who wanted to let the Pentagon respond to the story, you are doing pretty well."

"Look, I don't mean to be picking on you. But sometimes people don't recognize how hard folks like Bill's crew have it. Did you know their average age is about twenty? When you and your Buffy friends were that age, I'll bet you got a little rambunctious, pulled a few pranks and the like, eh?"

Sue sighed. "Yeah, those were the days."

Jim had worked himself into quite a head of steam by now. "I'll tell you the thing that most impresses me about Bill's sailors. They are so damn loyal to one another and their skipper. Can you imagine your coworkers banding together to get your boss a date? It wouldn't happen around here, the Home for the Chronically Self-serving." Jim paused. "Hey, I'm sorry for venting on you. But a guy has to stick up for his little brother. Particularly when you can do so off the record."

"Not a problem. I've developed a pretty thick skin. Besides, you make a few good points."

"You probably regret asking my reaction to the story. Anything else I can do for you?"

"Yeah, I was wondering . . . has Bill always been single? I mean, is the Navy his whole life?"

"Lifelong bachelor. Got sort of serious a couple of times. But about the time he'd be pressed for a commitment, he'd get orders to another part of the world. We've accused him of arranging that. Probably true. Why do you ask?"

"Just wondering."

23

Jim felt it only fair that for once he got to lecture a reporter about how journalism should be conducted. After all, every day members of the media gave *him* a tutorial on how government should work. His sense of satisfaction was short lived, however. As he walked up to the lectern for the next day's press briefing he found himself scanning the room to see if Sue O'Dell had come back for a return engagement. No sign of her. He hoped he hadn't hurt her feelings the day before.

Jim's concern was more than humanitarian. Reporters, like animals, were most dangerous when wounded. He knew that the best thing that could happen to brother Bill and the *Winston Churchill* would be for Sue to forget all about them. Despite the fact that he had a room full of White House regulars to deal with, Jim found himself still thinking about yesterday's attractive visitor. He could see why Bill got himself in trouble when she interviewed him. There was something about her that made a person want to keep talking. Bill was a lucky guy, Jim thought. As a bachelor, there was nothing to prevent him from trying to practice hands-on media relations with an alluring reporter like Sue.

Jim was snapped out of his reverie by the grating tones of the *Newark Star Ledger*'s Iris Van Pelt. "Any time, Jim. What's the musical theme for today, 'The Sound of Silence'?"

"Sorry. I just wanted to soak in the warmth and love that permeates this room. Let me say that I have no opening statements and humbly offer to respond to your inquiries, gentle people of the press."

The briefing was typical of its kind. The stenographers who transcribed the session would have no further need for words like *gentle*, *warmth*, or *love*. The excitement of the day revolved around published reports of a book that was about to come out by a recently resigned member of the President's cabinet. Philip Falcona, the former Secretary of Housing and Urban Development had left no mark on the administration. Falcona had a twelve percent name recognition rating, average for most cabinet members, but somewhat weak in this case since it was obtained in a poll of people within his own department. Nobody cared a whit about this guy when he was in office, Jim thought to himself. Now he gets out and writes a book and all of a sudden he is a prophet.

Nick Klosterbach, reporter for the *New Age News*, was particularly dogged in his questioning. "What is your reaction to the secretary's assertion that this administration is without vision and direction?"

"I haven't read his book, Nick, and so I shouldn't comment on allegations that may or may not be in it."

"Well, I've read it and that's what he says. Are you without vision and direction or not?"

"I don't recall the former secretary making that suggestion during any cabinet meetings. Come to think of it, I can't recall him making *any* suggestions . . ." The press corps hooted and scribbled rapidly in their pads. The broadcasters had the sound bite they needed.

The briefing deteriorated from there and it was another thirty minutes before Jim could elicit a thank-you from Alice Kenworthy and make his escape.

Beating a hasty retreat to his office, Jim quickly shut the door and popped a cassette in the tape player. The first song was Three

Dog Night's "Mama Told Me Not to Come." After a few minutes, Natalie entered the office, interrupting Jim's meditation. She filled his In box and dropped off a sheet of paper listing a couple dozen reporters and editors, each of whom wanted just a few minutes of Jim's time, preferably right away.

"Don't forget your regular poker game this afternoon," Natalie said cheerfully. Since the purpose of Jim's increasingly frequent visits to the Situation Room was hush hush, Jim's staff had begun humorously speculating that he and General Burnette were sneaking away to play cards.

"Right. A couple more big wins and I'll be able to quit this rat race and retire."

"What would you do without all this?" Natalie asked.

"Well, one thing I wouldn't do is write a book."

FOR ONCE the members of the Crisis Working Group gathered with a sense that progress was being made. Wally Burnette called the group to order and asked General Sundin to summarize the information that the SEALs had managed to cajole out of Mustafa.

"They had a very productive visit. We've managed to learn an awful lot about Tarhouna, and we have Mustafa digging around to get us more information. The SEALs have turned his telephone into a virtual broadcast superstation. Our folks listening in off shore can now zero in on Radio Free Mustafa without bothering with all the other noise in the region."

There were nods of appreciation around the table. I don't think anyone here knows what kind of courage it takes for a small group of men to conduct a covert operation like that, Sundin thought. Three American servicemen wandering around alone in Gadhafi's Libya would have a life expectancy of nanoseconds if they had been caught.

"We've given a copy of the interrogation of Mustafa to the CIA and asked them to help make sense of the information we got out of this 'engineer.' Perhaps this would be a good point for Fiona to tell us what her analysts learned from the material."

Director Nelson looked down at some notes and cleared her

throat. "It was certainly a job well done to find Mustafa and, ah, enlist his cooperation in foilin' Gadhafi. We evaluate Mustafa's comments as truthful. The SEALs clearly got his attention and he undoubtedly believes that they will kill him if he fails ta cooperate."

"Good thinking on his part," General Sundin interjected.

Jim shuddered. We can't do that without good cause, he thought. Can we?

"The bad news is that he appeahs truthful when he says he doesn't know much about the details of Gadhafi's plan," Director Nelson continued. "We can hope that he will be able to find out the information we need, particulahly the timin' of the attack on Israel and the location of the chemical weapons in the United States. But Gadhafi is very good at compartmentalizin' sensitive information. So we need to accept the fact that Mustafa may nevah be in a position ta learn what we want to know."

"Well, if there is any way to do so, he should be motivated. It scared me just to read the transcripts of the SEALs interrogation," General Firman offered.

Cleveland Forbes Stevens, the Secretary of Defense, mute until now, spoke up. "We've been studying the transcripts as well. There is one part that we find of particular interest."

"What's that?"

"You will recall that as he described the functioning of Tarhouna, at one point Mustafa talked about the sophisticated venting system within the complex. Because the plant is subterranean, with a vaultlike entrance, they've had to install an elaborate system to keep the air inside breathable. Apparently, they need to flush the system every couple of weeks. They do this by opening hidden vents in the air exchanger and blowing out the contaminated air. According to Mustafa, this is done late at night about once every two weeks."

"And what is the significance of that?" Director Nelson asked.

"Let me tackle that one, sir," General Sundin offered. "Madame Director, that information might give us the hope of being able to knock out Tarhouna with a nonnuclear strike."

General Sundin looked around the table. "I think we should

consider a preemptive strike now that we may have a way to take out the plant with conventional means."

"Let me bring this back to reality," Wally Burnette responded. "We still don't know when the attack on Israel might occur and we haven't a clue where the chemicals in the States might be stashed. This air handling information might be useful in helping us retaliate, but we are still at a loss to prevent a strike. Fiona, do you have anything else for us?"

"Ouah people have captured a numbah of Libyan television broadcasts off the satellites," Director Nelson began.

"Great, but what you need to do is to capture some damn Libyans!" General Sundin interrupted.

Director Nelson demonstrated what was for her unusual patience by ignoring the comment and continuing with her point.

"We have doctors on the staff who have studied the recent video of Gadhafi at public ceremonies. He a-peahs ta have lost a great deal of weight, his complexion is wuhse than usual, and he seems ta have developed a tremah in his right hand."

General Sundin fidgeted in his seat until he couldn't take it anymore. "What the hell is the significance of all this?" he growled.

"We believe that he is undah great stress and may have recently suffahed a small stroke. Whatevah his ailments, his recent ill health may add to his sense of mortality and increase the likelihood that he is tryin' ta do somethin' to cinch his place in the history books."

There was a long silence around the table.

Burnette asked the CIA Director if her staff had refined their estimates on how an attack on Israel might take place.

"Yes. As ya know, due ta the UN sanctions against Libya, their national airline, known as Jamahiriya Libyan A-rab Airlines, has been relegated almost exclusively ta a domestic carriyah. They have been denied landin' rights in most countries because of they-ah refusal ta turn over the Pan Am 103 suspects."

"So a commercial flight in the direction of Israel would stand out?" Secretary Stevens asked.

"Right. They ah pretty much restricted to flyin' between Tripoli, Benghazi, and Tobruk. There is an hourly shuttle between

Tripoli and Benghazi. We have discovered an Airbus 300 that is bein' kept in a hangar at Tripoli International Airport under heavy guard. Ouah estimate is that a likely tactic would be for them ta load the aircraft with CW, have it take off to the west en route to Benghazi, and then somewheah en route drop below radar coverage."

"They couldn't fly all the way to Israel at that low an altitude," General Sundin, the old bomber pilot, remarked. "It would consume more fuel than they could carry."

"Concur," Director Nelson said. "We figah they would plan ta remain at low altitude until they could get ta the Cairo air traffic control region. Then they would pop up, mix in with the heavy traffic along that corridor, and try ta sneak in to somewhere in Israel."

Turning to the National Security Advisor, Director Nelson asked, "Have you thought about what we should do about givin' the Israelis notice of an impendin' attack?"

Burnette's and Jim Schmidt's eyes locked. Until this point the rest of the Crisis Working Group was unaware of the *Churchill* scenario.

"Yes. If it comes to that—and God willing it won't—Jim and I have worked up a little plan that might buy us a little time while allowing us to prevent a successful attack on Israel."

Great, Jim thought, he didn't need to mention me. He is about to tell the Secretary of Defense and Chairman of the Joint Chiefs that I have been going around behind their backs enticing their subordinates to start a war. The least he could have done was to tell them that the President has bought off on this crazy plan.

Burnette briefed the CWG on the *Churchill* concept. After considerable discussion, General Sundin summed up the consensus. "That is the craziest plan I've heard since Iran Contra. The odds against it are about a million to one. Which is about the best chance we've got."

24

"Commanding Officer, your presence is requested in the tank!" Chet Hollomaker heard the call on the submarine's announcing system and guessed correctly that Radio Free Mustafa must be on the air again.

It took just a minute to get to the communications spaces from back aft in engineering. "It's him again, Captain. Boy, that transmitter the SEALs installed on his phone line works like a charm. We don't have to bother ferreting out his signal; it comes through like a fifty-thousand-watt blowtorch."

"All the tapes up and running?"

"Yessir, copying all."

"What's been said so far?" Hollomaker asked one of the Arabists who had recently augmented the crew.

"Well, sir, it seems as if old Ibrahim is a bit confused about why he is hearing from Mustafa on a daily basis."

The sailor pressed his earphones closer to his head and paused. "Mustafa is telling him how tired he is from all this hard work and how he is thinking of going on a vacation. He says he is hoping to leave Tripoli next Friday."

There was a lengthy pause. "What's going on now?" Hollo-maker asked.

"Ibrahim asked him where he is going, and he says 'Malta.' "

That's the code, Hollomaker thought. These crazy SOBs are really going to try it.

"Then Ibrahim asked him what he was going to do there, and he said maybe he'd visit the Maltese Parliament."

"Anything else?"

"Yes sir, Ibrahim was sayin' that he was glad Mustafa was going to get away because Mustafa has sounded so stressed out lately. And then Mustafa—he agreed and said he's under a lotta pressure. And he says he misplaced some stuff recently and he still can't find it."

Hollomaker sighed. "As soon as the conversation is completed, let's transmit the audio and a transcript back to Washington. Flash precedence."

ABOARD THE *Winston Churchill*, Bill Schmidt's plan was falling into place. The in-port cabin was the scene of a meeting between the captain and his two coconspirators, Lieutenant Commander Mose-man and Lieutenant Hahn.

"Okay, let's go over this again. Based on the last SPECAT from the White House we can expect an Airbus 300 launching out of Tripoli. It'll probably be squawking IFF codes for a standard commercial airliner. Most likely, after climbing out it will head east and somewhere between Tripoli and Benghazi it will dive for the deck to evade detection by radar in the Cairo Flight Information Region."

"Right," Lieutenant Commander Moseman said. "My guess is that he will do that very soon after reaching altitude. No sense giving the folks at Cairo center too good a look at him." Moseman took off his eyeglasses and wiped some lint off the lenses.

"So if we position ourselves on a track between Tripoli and Ben-ina International, the airport serving Benghazi, we should be aligned to have a good look at the Airbus."

"Yeah, and the Airbus descending at a rapid rate will give our crew the impression that he is coming after us," Hahn suggested. Attila was clearly enjoying the plotting. The analytical Moseman was not.

"What about the standard warnings?" Schmidt asked. "If we hail him on a guard frequency as we are required to do and let him know that we are on to him, he might just turn around and try again another day."

"Got that one taken care of, boss," Moseman replied. "From my seat at the CSO console I can control just about any part of the ship's combat systems. I have the capability of knocking the entire communications suite off line."

"Can you do it without the crew knowing that you caused it?"

"Piece of cake."

"What about the problem of getting the Battle Group Commander's permission to launch our missiles?"

"Brad's self-jamming can work for us there," Hahn said. "You see, we start warning the Airbus a couple hundred miles out to stay away from us. But since he won't hear us, he won't alter course. Then, once the sweat pumps light off in Combat, the Captain calls the Admiral on the *George Washington* requesting permission to go 'birds free.' But the Admiral isn't going to hear us any better than that Libyan kamikaze. And the standard rules of engagement state that the Captain's first priority is to protect his ship."

"And when I hear nothing in return from the *GW*, I take it upon myself to launch?"

"Well, sir, that is why you get the big bucks."

"Good plan."

"Thanks, sir. Planning to screw up is easier than I thought."

"Well, I've been working a little, too," Schmidt said. "You remember the last time we met, Brad had some questions about the air quality if we vaporize a plane carrying CW? I've been hitting the books on that question and here's what I've come up with."

Moseman and Hahn leaned forward in their seats and listened intently.

"Let's assume that we take out the aircraft with a Standard missile at a range of about ten miles. The Standard will most likely knock off a wing. With luck, when the wing shears off, the aircraft will spiral into the ocean with the fuselage intact. If that happens, no problem."

Schmidt looked at his two assistants and could see that they weren't buying that rosy scenario.

"Okay, so maybe that doesn't happen. Worst case, the aircraft explodes in midair and the CW is dispersed at whatever altitude the plane happens to be at. From the intelligence reports we received prior to deployment, we know that the Libyans are primarily believed to be producing VX at Tarhouna. VX is a persistent nerve agent that typically is in a liquid form before it is dispensed." Looks like I have their attention, Schmidt thought. I believe Moseman may be holding his breath. "Once the shell or rocket carrying VX explodes, the liquid is sprayed into the air. Some of it forms a gas. The rest becomes droplets. The heavier droplets fall to the surface. If it were over land, those droplets could evaporate and form a secondary cloud. But we don't have that problem since this will be at sea."

"Just another advantage of sea duty," Hahn said.

Schmidt ignored Attila and continued on. "The smaller droplets mix with the gas in an aerosol. This becomes the primary cloud which drifts over the target, killing its victims in a matter of minutes. Not a pretty way to go, I understand. The question is: How long is that cloud potent? There are a number of factors, mostly meteorological, that drive that answer. Temperature, wind speed and turbulence, and precipitation all factor in. In our situation, we have some good news and some bad news in that regard."

"Well, boss, that's better than the string of luck the *Winnie* has been having. Up till now it's been all bad."

"Right. The area off the Libyan coast has high temperatures and little rain. That can mean a longer-lasting, more potent cloud. But it also has a prevailing strong wind, which the Libyans call the sirocco. And since we'll be close to shore, there should be considerable inversion as a result of the difference between the temperature on the ground and in the water. That should result in a lot of turbulence which should help break up and dissipate the cloud.

"One of the publications we have in the ship's intelligence library gives some complex formulas for figuring out how long a CW cloud should remain toxic. I've done the calculations. It is a little hard to be precise, since we don't know what altitude the aircraft will be at when we take it out, but all things considered, I figure that we should be pretty safe if we can remain at least five miles outside the impact zone for an hour after we splash the Libyans. Any questions?"

"About those calculations, sir?"

"Yeah, Attila?"

"What grade did you get in math at the Academy?"

"You don't want to know."

25

Jim pored through the stack of tapes behind his desk. It gets harder all the time to find the right one, he thought. He considered "Town Without Pity" by Gene Pitney, and "Midnight Confessions" by the Grass Roots, but finally settled on the Rascals' "How Can I Be Sure." Picking up his office telephone and punching the button that enabled the public address function, he started the cassette and intoned, "Ladies and gentlemen of the press, the briefing is about to begin. Gather around and your every question will be confidently and capably answered." He cranked up the volume as the Rascals' vocals kicked in.

The briefing started routinely enough. Jim tried to interest the press corps in the upcoming events the White House was staging to highlight its agenda. The events were often designed to try to put a human face on some complex policy issue. Others were planned to lay groundwork for some larger program yet to be announced. And still others were intended to inoculate the press corps, to take the initiative in announcing bad news before the administration's adversaries could mount their communications efforts. He read an announcement about a forthcoming Rose Garden ceremony to honor the "volunteer of the year," a Korean-American grandmother who was a school crossing guard and taught karate to inner-city youth in her free time. Not much interest in this one, he thought, looking at the bored faces, maybe she'll bring some of her students to kick butt in this place. Then he revealed that the following Monday the administration would be ready to unveil its annual proposal to revise campaign finance laws. I guess I don't blame them for not getting too excited about it, Jim thought. Especially since we are holding that $25,000-a-plate fund-raiser aboard the *QE II* in New York on Sunday. Finally he made a statement about ongoing consultations regarding the probability of soon declaring Iraq a "most-favored nation," a bit of a misnomer given that out of about 180 countries in the world there were only about two left that didn't have MFN status.

The media expressed almost no interest and wanted to move on to address issues on its agenda. Having completed his list of announcements, Jim opened the floor for questions.

"What is the administration's reaction to the Albert Janoska column in the *New York Times* today?" Alice Kenworthy asked. It was unusual for a reporter to cite a competitor's work in their question. Alice chomped down hard on a pencil as she awaited her answer. She was clearly in need of a nicotine fix.

"The punctuation and spelling were quite good. Other than that, could you be a bit more specific, Alice?"

"Sure. Specifically, what is your reaction to complaints from high-ranking State Department officials that the President seems uninterested in foreign policy matters, as illustrated by the fact that he hasn't met privately with the Secretary of State in several weeks?"

"The President values the Secretary's advice and counsel and has benefited from it in many ways. Just because there hasn't been a one-on-one meeting in recent days doesn't mean that he is not receiving a, ah, steady flow of information from the secretary." There were a few knowing snickers from the press. Better be careful, he cautioned himself, don't want another windbag episode.

"Well, that sounds like a one-way communication flow," Alice replied. "Does the President think that the world is so calm that he can devote all his time to karate-teaching grandmothers, and sea-going contributors, and not bother with the affairs of State?"

Boy, Jim thought, she is really on a roll today. As she spoke, Alice was absentmindedly rummaging around her enormous handbag. She probably feels better just touching her cigarettes, Jim figured.

"Alice, you would be amazed at how much time and effort we are spending on foreign affairs and national security issues. By its very nature, much of this work must be done outside the glare of public scrutiny. I know you wish it were otherwise. But let me assure you that this administration is actively engaged in issues beyond our borders. It is a measure of the respect that the President has for his Secretary of State that he does not have to look over the secretary's shoulder constantly. The secretary has full access to the President and he keeps the White House Fully Informed As He Practices His Statecraft." Jeez, I'm starting to sound like Harden, Jim thought.

When the briefing ended, Jim left the room and strode up a ramp, a remnant of FDR's administration, which led to his office. Natalie intercepted him before he could reach his door.

"They just called a meeting of the poker group in the Sit Room. It started ten minutes ago. Gimme your briefing notes. Here's your notebook. Good luck. I hope you win."

Too bad I can't tell the press corps about this, Jim thought, as he reversed course and headed downstairs toward the Sit Room. It was annoying to have to do something immediately following the brief-ing. Jim always felt the need to decompress after a dive in the murky waters of the press briefing. Normally he would replay in his mind the questions reporters had asked, and often would come up with snappy retorts he wished he had been able to think of during the briefing, or had had the courage to deliver. The press accuses us of ignoring international issues, he thought, but the fact is we are spending so much time on that I don't even have time to take a leak.

Jim automatically entered the three-digit code on the cipher lock to gain entrance to the Sit Room. He was getting to be such a regular he didn't even have to think about the combination. The Poker Group had assembled but the door to the conference room was open. Wally Burnette had held off on starting the Crisis Working Group meeting until Schmidt could join the others. While waiting for him, they had amused themselves by listening in to an audio feed of the briefing that was piped into the Situation Room.

When Jim walked into the conference room, Burnette, again sitting in the President's chair, spun around and gleefully announced: "We caught your act!"

"What?"

"We caught your act."

"We heard you trying to fend off the wolves," Secretary Stevens said. "Fine job of attempting to make it sound like Harden is a player."

General Sundin did a passable imitation of Schmidt. "It is a measure of the regard in which we hold the secretary that we never invite him here." The others chuckled.

"Yeah, he measures out pretty low."

"Okay, okay," Burnette interrupted. "If we can suspend the Harden hammering, let's get going." Jim noticed that these meetings had become increasingly informal. The members had gotten more comfortable with one another and despite the gravity of the threat, or perhaps because of it, the participants had adopted a decidedly casual attitude.

"Let me review where we are," Burnette said. "Mustafa tells us that the Libyans are going to launch their attack on Israel on Friday. We don't have a good fix on what time of day . . . but we estimate that it will be in daylight hours, in an effort on their part to maximize casualties."

There were several nods around the table.

"Overhead imagery shows continued high levels of security around an aircraft hangar in Tripoli." Burnette reached into a folder and pulled out a half-dozen eight-by-ten copies of a satellite photo. He slid copies of the imagery down the length of the table. Each Poker Group participant grabbed one and studied it. The photo showed a large aircraft hangar with two perimeter fences. The photo had labels indicating that the fences were made of barbed wire, although that was not immediately discernible to the unskilled eye. There appeared to be sentry shacks at each corner of the hangar and about two dozen troops scattered around the facility.

"This hangar is one of the ones that the U.S. Air Force helpfully built when we operated out of there. The airfield is what once was Wheelus Air Base," General Sundin advised the group.

"Today is Wednesday, so we have somewhere between thirty-six and forty-eight hours to make a decision and prepare," Burnette stated. Several members of the group looked up at the digital clocks along the side of the conference room. One was dedicated to Libyan time, six hours ahead of Washington at the moment because of daylight savings time.

"We've picked up another call from Mustafa to Ibrahim," General Firman offered. "The engineer didn't have anything else for us regarding the stash in the States."

"How do we know that he isn't just stiffin' us?" Director Nelson asked.

"We don't," Burnette replied. "But he sounds pretty frightened. I have to believe that the information about where the CW is planted is very compartmentalized. Mustafa probably is not in the small group with a need to know," Burnette replied.

He turned to the Director of Central Intelligence for an update. "Fiona, what is the latest on the agency's efforts?"

The CIA Director cleared her throat and looked at some notes. "We continyah ta pursue evrah lead we have. We ah checking on evrah known or suspected Libyan agent." Jim noticed that the Director was not as upbeat and bubbly as usual. She looked very, very tired. Normally, she did not look like someone who had spent thirty-five years in government, but today, honest friends would not dispute the fact.

"We have been watchin' the Libyans' command and control centahrs, intelligence headquartahrs, and the half-dozen locations where Gadhafi is known ta spend his nights," Director Nelson continued. "The idea is ta try ta pick up some indicatah or warnin' that something' unusual is up. So fah, no luck."

Several people at the table sadly looked down at their blank notepads. Only General Sundin was writing—a doodle of a B-2 bomber.

Oblivious to the reactions around her, Director Nelson continued. "Workin' with the FBI, we ah trying ta track down all freight shipments that might have gone ta the Libyan delegation to the UN or ta other Libyan fronts in the U.S. So fah, nothing correlates." The CIA's jurisdiction stopped at the U.S. border, so any pursuit of leads within the United States would have to be handled by the FBI.

"Let me stress that we need to be very careful when dealing with FBI and local law enforcement units," Burnette warned. "If word gets back to the Libyans about what we are looking for . . . well, that might trigger a premature release."

"How extensive is our overhead capability?" Secretary Stevens asked.

Director Nelson replied, knowing that the National Reconnaissance Office, the outfit that controlled the satellites, nominally worked for the Defense Department. "We have repositioned a couple of satellites so that we have almost constant coverage of the Tarhouna area as well as the airfield in Tripoli. We don't have hundred pahcent live coverage . . . there is a few minute delay in retrievin' the imagery . . . but it is pretty quick."

"So if an aircraft left its hangar at Wheelus and took off, it might be a few minutes before we knew?"

" 'Fraid so, Wally."

"Let's review the bidding. Sometime in the next forty-eight hours, an airplane loaded with chemical weapons is likely to take off from Tripoli en route to Israel. I see three options. One, we tell Libya that we know what they are up to and to knock it off. That would preempt the near-term attack on the Knesset, but there's no telling when or where the threat would arise again."

"And, there is the little problem about the CW stashed somewheah in the U.S.," Director Nelson added. "We could be open to blackmail."

"Right. Option two, we attack the hangar and take out the aircraft—"

"Potentially releasing a chemical cloud over downtown Tripoli," Secretary Stevens noted. Since his department was soundly excoriated over its handling of the destruction of Iraqi chemical munitions after the Gulf War, Stevens had become acutely sensitive to the potential unintended health effects of toxic clouds.

He wanted to avoid another Gulf War Illness debacle, whether it was based on fact or emotion.

"Good point," Burnette sighed. "Under this scenario, we probably would also want to attack Tarhouna, although we are not at all confident that we can take the facility out." Burnette had been in uniform when White House leaders ordered a number of botched military missions. He didn't want to preside over another. "Finally, there is option three. The *Churchill* scenario. If the Libyan aircraft with the chemical weapons on board takes off, we have USS *Churchill* bring it down. Then we foster the impression that it might have been a mistake, buying more time to try to locate the CW here. Comments?"

"Are you sure you don't have an option number four?" Schmidt asked.

"No, no I don't, Jim," Burnette said sadly.

Having received no substantive comments, Burnette went around the table and asked each participant which option he or she would recommend to the President. The *Churchill* scenario was the unanimous choice.

Jim sensed that the meeting was about to break up, but the Secretary of Defense raised a complication. "Just in case anyone here is getting complacent," Secretary Stevens said, "I thought I would throw in a new wrinkle."

Wally Burnette sighed. "What wrinkle is that, Cleve?"

"You haven't forgotten the War Powers Act, have you?"

General Sundin bit off a chunk of his unlit cigar and spat it out on the table. "War Powers Act? We're not gonna fool around with that nonsense, are we?"

Burnette jumped in to prevent an incident between the Chairman of the JCS and his boss. "Now Leroy, Cleve has a point." Burnette made eye contact with Secretary Stevens and tried to avoid General Sundin's glare. "What we are proposing here is for a U.S. military unit to conduct a preemptive strike on an airplane belonging to another sovereign nation. That is an act of war." Burnette noticed that the Director of the CIA and the President's press secretary were nodding their heads slowly. The two generals at the table were not.

"The law says that since we can reasonably expect hostilities to occur, the commander in chief is supposed to give Congress advance notification," Burnette continued.

"Advance notification to Congress! Why don't we just have the protocol office send an engraved invitation to Gadhafi asking him pretty please not to set off his chemical weapons until we've held a few hearings?" General Sundin thundered.

"Gentlemen, gentlemen." The DCI tried her hand at peace-making. "As Ah see it, what we are proposin' here is a covert action. That bein' the case, the President could sign a findin' and we would have forty-eight hours aftah the *Churchill* takes action before we have ta tell ouah friends on the Hill what the facts ah."

All eyes turned back to Wally Burnette. "Maybe the forty-eight hours after the *Churchill* takes action will be enough time for us to locate the weapons in the United States," he said.

"And if it is not?" Sundin asked.

"If it is not, if it is not . . . well, we will have to cross that bridge when we come to it," Burnette said. "Look, none of this is perfect. Perfect, hell. It is not even satisfactory. But I still haven't heard any better ideas." Burnette paused and looked around the table slowly. "All right, last chance. Anybody got any solutions, or do I tell the President that we recommend executing the *Churchill* scenario?"

There was silence in the room. "All right, I guess I'd better go see the man."

26

Bill Schmidt sat on the bridge of the *Churchill* in his captain's chair worrying about how many things could go wrong with the plan.

The ship had spent the better part of a week steaming back and forth just outside Gadhafi's self-declared "line of death" along the Gulf of Sidra. Normally, destroyers operate as part of a four- to eight-ship battle group. But for this mission, *Churchill* was on her own. *Churchill's* Combat Information Center monitored the regular commercial air traffic along the coast, which was of a moderate volume. The ship's AEGIS weapons system was capable of simultaneously tracking many more aircraft than normally flew out of Tripoli.

At least the UN ban on international flights into and out of Libya makes this a lot easier, Bill thought. With most countries observing the restriction, we only have to keep an eye on the domestic travel.

CIC had noted a regular flow of aircraft from Tripoli to Benghazi and back. During daylight there was typically one flight an hour in each direction. On the eastbound leg, each aircraft would climb northward out of Tripoli, then head out over the Mediterranean. Upon reaching altitude, they would lazily turn to the east and fly toward Benghazi. Shortly after they turned east, the air traffic controllers at Tripoli center would pass control for these aircraft to their counterparts at Benina airfield.

If this guy follows the standard flight path to Benghazi I'll have no plausible reason for shooting, Bill pondered. Sure hope the analysts back in D.C. are right in guessing this guy will dive for the deck in an attempt to sneak underneath the radar.

Bill had met with Brad Moseman and Attila earlier in the day to check on arrangements. He had also called numerous air defense drills over the past few days which gave the crew a heightened sense of concern about the possibility of hostile inbound aircraft. The Weapons Department had loudly tested the ship's Phalanx Close in Weapons System, the ship's last-ditch defense against incoming missiles. The CIWS, pronounced Sea-Whiz, and affectionately known as "Cheez-Whiz," was essentially a gatling gun that threw into the air a wall of depleted uranium shells at a rate of 2,000 rounds a minute. In theory, an attacking missile would hit the wall and be shredded just before hitting the ship. Moseman advised the Captain that he had quietly tested his software patch which rendered the ship's outgoing communications mute, and it worked like a charm.

One of the yeomen from the ship's office came onto the bridge to deliver a copy of *Stripes*, the daily newspaper sent to ships at sea. This desktop publishing version of the European and Pacific *Stars and Stripes* newspapers kept crew members in touch with events back home and around the world. Bill remembered when he first went to sea, when a ship could go for weeks without an update on the news. The paper was received daily on the same 1.2 meter satellite dish that provided the ship with two channels of stateside television, another big improvement in the quality of life, except on those days when the NBA playoffs came on live at 2:00 A.M.

Stripes carried a front-page story about the White House reaction to claims that the administration was uninvolved in foreign affairs. Brother Jim's stirring defense was prominently mentioned in the account picked up from the Associated Press. Well, Jimbo, if we go ahead with this plan, I guess it will demolish complaints that you guys are afraid to engage on the international scene, Bill mused.

At that moment, Bill was interrupted by the Messenger of the

Watch, the most junior member of the bridge watch team. "Excuse me, Captain. We just received a call from Communications. They say you have an incoming phone call on the STU-Three in the radio shack." The STU-III was a telephone that could encode and decode calls over regular telephone transmissions.

"Thanks, Willie. Tell 'em I'll be right down." Wonder what this is about?

Schmidt briskly climbed down the four decks leading to the Communications Department, known as the "radio shack." Though the technology had long surpassed old-fashioned telegraphy, the name still stuck. As he picked up the handset, he turned briskly to the chief who led the watch team. "How 'bout having the guys give me some space here?"

"Sure thing, sir. Hey guys, back off a bit and give the Captain some space, huh?"

Bill punched the flashing button that said Secure. A window at the top of his handset read "Full Duplex . . . Top Secret . . . WHCA." WHCA, Bill knew, stood for White House Communication Agency. "USS *Winston Churchill*, Captain Schmidt speaking." Bill could hear his words being scrambled. There was a slight delay and then he heard a slightly distorted but familiar voice.

"Hey Bill, this is Jim. Have you been keeping out of trouble?"

"Better than you have, or so I've been reading. Why don't you quit being so mean and invite the Secretary of State over to play?"

"Boy, news travels fast. Yeah, you're right. We'll have to have him over for a few brews. By the way, I understand he's a big fan of yours and the *Churchill*'s."

"Great. Remind me to send him one of the ship's ball caps." Bill paused for a second and reflected with wonder on the fact that a mere Navy commander like himself would have come on the radar screen of the Secretary of State. "I've got a hunch that you didn't call to debate which one of us has been getting better press lately. What's up, Jim?"

"It was always hard to put one past you. Bill, you remember the conversation we had when I dropped by for a visit a while back?"

"I seem to recall it." Bill slumped into a chair next to the STU-III.

"Are you guys ready to take on that little project we discussed?"

Bill noted that his brother was speaking fairly cryptically even though they were on a secure call. Probably wise, he thought. He never really believed that these calls were scrambled. There was probably some GS-3 in the bowels of NSA listening in.

"I remind you, sir, that *Churchill* is always ready."

"Good, because it looks like you are going to need to be tomorrow."

"Tomorrow?"

"'Fraid so, little brother. Our friend is expected to come out of Tripoli some time during daylight hours tomorrow. As we explained in that SPECAT message to you, the profile we anticipate is that he will climb to normal cruising altitude and then dive for the deck. He would then proceed toward Benghazi. Once he got into Egyptian airspace he would pop up and mix in with the heavy flow of commercial traffic flying along the Levant. Your mission is to make sure he doesn't get that far."

"Jim, the ship is ready. I've had to bring two of my key officers in on the plan. Other than that, the rest of the crew remains blissfully unaware. If the Libyan flies the profile you describe, we are ready for him. But I've got to tell you that I am more than a little uncomfortable."

"I know. Hey, I can't tell you how sorry I am that you are in this position, little brother."

"My guys have done a good job. I think we have anticipated everything. You'd appreciate one of the questions they asked me."

"What's that?"

"One of them asked me how I knew that you hadn't gone off the deep end." Bill heard a tinny laugh through his handset.

"Good question. What did you tell them?"

"To trust me."

"The fact that they do says a lot about you."

"Yeah, or them." The two brothers paused. More needed to be said but neither could find the words.

"Maybe this will help put you more at ease, Bill. Let me pass the phone to someone who is standing here with me."

"Captain Schmidt, this is President Walsh. I know that we are placing a terrible burden on you. If there were a better way, we would take it, but I don't know of any. You have my thanks and someday you will have the thanks of others. Good-bye and good luck."

"Thank you, sir. *Churchill* out."

27

"Sometime during daylight hours." You'd think with all the intelligence assets in the free world they could be a little more precise, Bill Schmidt muttered to himself. Sure would have been nice if they'd narrowed it down a bit.

Schmidt held a final coordinating meeting with Brad Moseman and Attila the Hahn in his in-port cabin.

"We can't go on meeting like this, Captain."

"Ah, I bet you say that to all the guys."

Hahn chuckled. "The XO keeps giving me the evil eye when he sees me coming down here for these meetings."

"Yeah," Moseman said. "Me too. And afterward I get grilled on what we are doing in here. Last time he got so persistent that I told him we were planning a surprise birthday party for him."

"I'll bet he believed it," Schmidt said.

"Told me it wasn't until October. I allowed as how you can't begin planning too soon."

"Okay, okay," Schmidt interrupted. He was a little uncomfortable taking part in mocking his second in command, even if the man truly was an ass. "We've been told that the Libyan aircraft is going to take off sometime tomorrow during daylight hours. That gives us a pretty broad window. I don't think we can afford to wait until we see it airborne."

"What do you have in mind?"

"I'm thinking about calling away general quarters around oh-five-hundred. That will get us fully manned before first light. We can tell the crew we have intelligence that the Libyans may be planning a sneak attack. That should get everybody on the edge of their seats. Brad, do you suppose you could rig it up so that I receive a bogus warning order?"

"Boss, give me a few minutes at my keyboard and I can make it look like you've won the Publisher's Clearinghouse Sweepstakes."

"I might take you up on that later. But for now, just dummy up a message from Sixth Fleet placing us in a high state of readiness to prepare for a possible attack."

Hahn scratched his chin. "Sir, what happens if the Libyans don't launch their aircraft until five or six at night? If we keep the crew at their GQ stations all day long they'll be punchy by the time the real thing comes along."

"I've thought about that, Attila, but I don't see any way around it. I need to have the GQ watch team in place, particularly you and Brad at your consoles, or else this guy could slip by us. Can't risk that."

THE SMELL of fresh baked bread was wafting over the ship as the mess specialists worked to prepare breakfast that wasn't scheduled to be served for another two hours. The watch team in the comm office called the Captain's at-sea cabin to tell him about the flash message they had just received. "Sorry to wake you, Captain, but we have a hot one."

"Bring it right up, would ya?"

Moments later a Petty Officer knocked on Schmidt's door. Schmidt answered wearing his khaki pants and a T-shirt. The Petty Officer handed Schmidt a metal-covered clipboard.

Rubbing his eyes in an effort to imply that he had just awoken, Schmidt said "Thanks, Petty Officer Taylor."

He flipped the cover up and read the message.

```
FROM: COMSIXTHFLT
TO: COMGWBATGRU
INFO: COMDESRON THREE TWO
USS WINSTON CHURCHILL
USS HARTFORD
TOP SECRET/SPECAT//NO3100//
```

1. (TS) SENSITIVE INTELLIGENCE INDICATES LIBYAN AIR FORCE MAY BE PLANNING A COVERT ATTACK UPON U.S. FORCES IN THE MEDITER-RANEAN.
2. (TS) METHOD OF ATTACK MAY INVOLVE MILITARY AIRCRAFT SIMULATING COMMERCIAL AIRLINERS IN ORDER TO APPROACH U.S. UNITS. AIRCRAFT MAY BE SQUAWKING COMMAIR IFF.
3. (TS) ALL UNITS SHOULD GO TO MAXIMUM STATE OF READINESS AND REMAIN OFF TACTICAL NETS UNLESS ABSOLUTELY NECESSARY.

                                                    BT

"Thanks, Taylor. Take this back down to comm and shred it." That should guarantee that every person on watch will read this message before it hits the shredder, Schmidt thought.

Schmidt picked up the phone in his cabin and pushed the buzzer which rang on the bridge.

"Officer of the Deck, Lieutenant Smith, sir."

"Morning, Debbie. We just got a message in from COMSIX-THFLT which indicates that the Libyans might be feeling kind of frisky."

"Those guys just don't get it, do they sir?"

"Yeah, too much time in the sun, I guess. In any case, we don't want to get caught with our pants down." Schmidt winced. He was still having trouble getting used to having women on board. "I mean . . . we, ah . . . we need to ratchet up our readiness. Since we are on one end of the Gulf of Sidra and the rest of the battle group is on the other, I think it would be prudent for us to put the crew at the highest state of alert. So, how about sounding the alarm for general quarters?"

"Yes sir. Sir, may I give the XO a wake-up call first? I'm afraid he might have a coronary otherwise."

"Good thinking, Debbie. Tell him I asked you to inform him." Better give the XO five minutes to get out of his jammies, Schmidt thought.

"Aye, aye, Captain."

Precisely five minutes later, after having made her wake-up call, Lieutenant Smith called out, "Boatswain's Mate of the Watch, sound the general alarm." The Petty Officer walked aft to the panel affixed to the bulkhead containing the ship's alarms. There were three to choose from. One for collisions, one for chemical attack, and the third labeled "General Alarm." He threw the third lever to the right. The alarm rang out throughout the ship.

Bong, bong, bong, bong . . . whirrup, whirrup, whirrup.

Squeezing the trigger on the 1MC microphone, the Boatswain's Mate read from a well-rehearsed script. "General quarters, general quarters. All hands, man your battle stations. Go up and forward on the port side, down and aft on the starboard. All hands, man your battle stations. This is not a drill." Since GQ caused sailors to sprint in every direction about the ship, it was necessary to give traffic directions, lest there be a pileup in a narrow passageway or at the bottom of some ladder.

The alarm was sounded again, and the call repeated. "General quarters, general quarters. All hands, man your battle stations!"

The words caused a shiver to run down the spines of even the most seasoned crewmen. Sailors who had not yet risen, some of whom had only just gotten to sleep after coming off the midnight to 0400 watch, fairly levitated out of their bunks.

"Did he say 'This is *not* a drill'?"

"He did, unless we're both hearing things."

"Remember the Cap'n told us when we took up station off Libya that there wouldn't be any GQ drills out here?"

"Yeah, this has gotta be real."

The lights came on in every berthing compartment as sailors

scrambled to get into their uniforms. As soon as they could find their shoes they sprinted toward their assigned stations, buttoning and zipping as they ran.

The sound of pounding feet reverberated throughout the ship. The aluminum ladders boomed as sailors charged up and down them.

As the crew reached their battle stations, watertight hatches were slammed shut and dogged down. Sailors donned their sound-powered telephones and reported the readiness of their section. These phones didn't require electricity to work and were designed to remain functional even if the ship was seriously damaged and all the generators were knocked off line. This condition, the ship's engineers' nightmare, was known as dropping the load.

The tradition of a thousand years, that sea captains fought their ships from the navigation bridge, died with the birth of AEGIS ships. No longer was standing next to the helm the best place to control the ship. Commanding officers of AEGIS ships had their GQ station in the Combat Information Center.

Bill Schmidt walked briskly to CIC and sat in front of the two forty-two-inch-square, large screen displays, known as LSDs. The task of navigating the ship during battle now fell to the Executive Officer. Despite his advance warning, Lieutenant Commander Ellsworth was out of breath when he raced to the bridge. He immediately strapped on his battle helmet.

At the consoles to Schmidt's immediate left were the Tactical Action Officer, Lieutenant Hahn, and the Combat Systems Officer, Lieutenant Commander Moseman.

Over his headset, Schmidt could hear the various stations reporting in.

"Engineering, manned and ready!"

"Damage Control Central, manned and ready!"

"Bridge, manned and ready!"

Finally, "Sir, all sections report manned and ready!"

Schmidt looked down at his watch. Five and a half minutes. Not bad.

From his console Schmidt flipped a switch which piped his voice over the 1MC general announcing system.

"Good morning everybody, this is the Captain. Sorry for the slightly early wake-up call. Here's what's going on. We have gotten a warning that the Libyans may be planning a sneak attack on a U.S. unit in the Med. The intelligence says that they may try to disguise themselves as a commercial airliner and sneak up on their victim. *Winston Churchill* is going to be nobody's victim.

"Now, the intell guys say that an attack may come today. If it does, we are going to be ready. I want everybody on your toes. America expects that each sailor will do their duty."

Okay, Bill reflected, so the "America expects" line was a little hokey. He wondered how many of them recognized that he was borrowing from Lord Nelson.

Bill surveyed the scene in the CIC. All nineteen consoles were manned and the room was buzzing with activity. The two large screen displays showed relatively little action. The outline of Libya and the rest of northern Africa was traced on the screen. To the north, the islands of Malta, Sardinia, and Sicily and the lower tip of Italy could be seen.

Well to the east were symbols depicting the remainder of the *George Washington* battle group. Thank God they are way over by the Libyan/Egyptian border, Bill thought. This is going to be hard enough without the Battle Group Commander looking down my throat.

Schmidt looked appreciatively around "Combat," as CIC is often called. For the most part, his strongest people were assigned to watch stations in CIC. Moseman, Hahn, almost the entire team were experienced hands. The one exception was the newly assigned Antiair Warfare Officer, Ensign Marshall Madison.

Schmidt smiled and thought back to the day the previous week when he amazed his wardroom, and particularly Lieutenant Commander Ellsworth, by assigning the ill-starred Ensign to this critical post.

"Relax, XO," he had said. "It takes two keys to launch a missile and I'll be holding both of 'em."

"I know, Captain, but you can never be sure with Marshall. He might try to swap your keys for biblical tracts."

"Don't worry. He's been doing a lot better recently. He's got this port and starboard stuff down pretty good. Now we just have to teach him to shoot at the bad guys rather than save them."

Schmidt looked over at Marshall, who was squinting at a virtually blank console screen. I'll bet somebody turned down the gain when he wasn't looking, he thought.

"Attila, how about giving Mister Madison a hand with his console, would ya?"

"Sure thing, Captain. Might be having a problem with the O-N-O-F-F switch."

The watch team in CIC settled into a routine. They monitored air traffic in and out of Tripoli. The *Churchill's* SPY 1-D radar picked up aircraft moments after they took off from Tripoli's airport. The AEGIS system immediately would label the aircraft as "unknown, assumed enemy," depicted on the blue LSD as a white dot within a half diamond. Everything flying within 250 miles of the ship was displayed on one of the LSDs.

Crewmen in CIC's "air alley" monitored the aircraft. Their consoles sent out coded signals querying the aircraft's Identification Friend or Foe transponders. The response would appear as digital code on the sailor's screens. There were three types of code: Mode I, Mode II, and Mode III. Modes I and II signified military planes. Mode III normally indicated commercial aircraft.

Schmidt keyed his microphone on the internal communications net to speak to the watch team. "Heads up, shipmates. Remember: We cannot assume that aircraft squawking Mode Three are legitimate civilian aircraft. Watch what they do, not what they say."

As an aircraft climbed out of Tripoli, the LSD screen would show a white line extending from the dot in a diamond symbol. The direction of the line indicated the plane's course, and the length of the line indicated speed. The AEGIS system automatically followed each contact, assigning it a track number. With a touch of a button, console operators could call up the flight's speed, course, distance from the ship, altitude, and IFF mode.

The anxiety in Combat rose in parallel with every aircraft taking off. Slowly the tension decreased as a plane climbed to normal cruising altitude, squawked Mode III, and flew a normal flight path.

By shortly after 10:00 A.M. a pattern had emerged. About ten minutes after each hour an aircraft took off, climbed out over the Mediterranean, and banked slowly to the right as it began its eastward journey toward Benghazi. Forty-five minutes past each hour, another aircraft would enter from the East, fly a wide arc out over the Med, and land at the airport some thirty-five kilometers from downtown Tripoli.

These guys are flying some pretty sloppy patterns, Bill observed silently. It's clear they aren't worried about any fuel shortages around here.

The same pattern was followed at 11:00 A.M. and again just after noon.

The crew's nerves jangled less with each passing uneventful flight. A good thing, Schmidt thought to himself, since the early morning GQ call had prevented many of the CIC watch team from applying their usual allocation of Right Guard.

At midday, members of the Supply Department, assisted by nonrated mess cooks, brought in sandwiches and fruit so that the watch team could remain at their stations.

"Enjoy your lunch, ladies and gentlemen, but do me a favor," Schmidt announced over the internal communications system. "Keep one eye on your consoles, and the other on your sodas. The AEGIS system can withstand missile hits, naval gunfire and the like . . . but dump a Coke down it and we might be in the dark for a month."

Shortly after 2:00 P.M. a sailor keyed his mike on the internal communications system. "Here comes the Benghazi shuttle. Fourteen-ten . . . right on time."

Looking at the LSD, Schmidt noted that the system had assigned the aircraft Track Number 6713.

"TN Sixty-seven-thirteen is squawking Mode Three. Appears to be commercial air. Climbing out of ten thousand feet at three hundred fifty knots."

"Roger."

The white symbol on the blue LSD followed the path taken by most of the previous flights of the day.

"Now climbing to fourteen thousand feet, sir."

"Roger."

Another sailor broke into the net. "Tripoli Center just cleared TN Sixty-seven-thirteen to twenty thousand feet and has passed him off to Benghazi."

"Roger."

"Sir! Sir! . . . ah . . . something funny here."

"What is it?" Schmidt felt a knot form in the pit of his stomach.

"Sir, another track just popped up. Sixty-seven-fourteen . . . virtually superimposed on Sixty-seven-thirteen. Unless AEGIS is going haywire, it looks like there are two birds up there. But they must be flying in tight formation for the system to have initially missed it."

Suddenly the room began to buzz.

"Roger. Take TN 6714 under close control."

Immediately the second flight was depicted on the LSD.

"What is he squawking?"

"Mode Three as well, sir."

The LSD displayed an altitude, course, and speed for 6714 that was virtually identical to that of 6713.

"Air guys, have you detected any communications with Tripoli Center by Sixty-seven-fourteen?"

"That's a negative, Captain. No comms at all."

"Range?"

"Seventy-seven miles, Captain."

"Bearing?"

"Aircraft bears Two-six-seven, sir."

"What's Sixty-seven-thirteen doing now?"

"Sir, he has leveled out at twenty thousand feet. Still doing three hundred fifty knots. Heading due east."

"And TN Sixty-seven-fourteen still has his nose up Sixty-seven-thirteen's butt?"

"Captain, they better not flush the heads on Sixty-seven-thirteen or the other guy is going to get a surprise."

"Ah, starting to get separation now."

"What's he doing?"

"Jesus, Sixty-seven-fourteen must be in some kind of dive! That sumbitch is losing altitude like crazy."

"Call it out."

"He's passing fifteen thousand feet, Captain."

"Now fourteen."

"What's his range?"

"Sixty-nine miles, sir. Speed is up to four hundred knots. Course is still essentially due east. His track would take him down our port side. At his current speed he'd be overhead in a little over ten minutes."

"Roger. I don't like the looks of this guy," Schmidt said. He turned to his right, stared hard at Hahn, and nodded slightly. "Brad, we'll probably need to alert the Battle Group Commander shortly. And stand by to issue this guy some warnings."

"Aye, aye, Captain." Moseman looked down at his console and entered a flurry of swift keystrokes. Moments later he looked up and nodded back at his commanding officer.

"Let's go ahead and pass the details of TN Sixty-seven-fourteen to the Battle Group. They should be following the aircraft's movements via their datalink to our system. But let's give them a verbal."

"Aye, aye, sir. Alpha Bravo, this is *Churchill*, over."

"Alpha Bravo, Alpha Bravo, this is *Churchill*, *Churchill*, over."

"That's funny, Captain, the Battle Group Commander's staff is not coming up on the net."

"Try the *George Washington* itself rather than the embarked staff."

"Aye, aye sir. *George Washington*, this is *Churchill*, over. . . . *GW*, *GW*, this is *Churchill*, over."

"*GW*, this is *Churchill*, nothing heard, out."

"That's odd, Captain. We've had great comms with them throughout this at-sea period."

"Well, maybe they are receiving but are having trouble transmitting. Go ahead and transmit in the blind a report on TN Sixty-seven-fourteen."

Schmidt returned his attention to the incoming unidentified aircraft which by now had closed to fifty-eight nautical miles and had leveled off at 2,000 feet.

"Sir, this guy is flying an awfully strange flight profile. Recommend we ask him what the hell he thinks he's doing."

"Concur, Attila, go ahead on both civil and military distress frequencies."

Hahn directed a crewman to break out a standard, preapproved script.

"Unidentified aircraft on course oh-eight-seven, speed four hundred knots, altitude two thousand feet, this is United States Naval Warship range fifty-five miles from you. You are approaching U.S. Naval Warship in international waters. Request you state your intentions, over."

There was no response. There could be none since Moseman's earlier efforts meant that *Winston Churchill* was jamming its own transmissions. The unsuspecting crewmen continued their radio calls. After a few more unsuccessful attempts to communicate they switched to the next higher level of warning.

"Unidentified aircraft on course oh-eight-seven, speed four hundred, altitude two thousand feet, this is U.S. Naval Warship bearing oh-nine-three from you. Request you change course immediately to zero-six-zero. Over."

"Nothing heard, Captain. Contact continues to close at high speed. Now forty-three miles from the ship. Flying straight and level at two thousand feet."

Schmidt toggled his internal communications set to be able to speak to the sailors at the Electronic Warfare consoles.

"EW, how about it, picking up any emissions from this guy? Any communications, fire control radar, anything?"

"Negative, Captain. He's still squawking Mode Three IFF, but other than that we've gotten nothing out of him."

"Roger. Let's move to the next level of warning and tell this guy he is starting to piss us off."

"Aye, sir. Unidentified aircraft on course oh-eight-seven, speed four hundred, altitude two thousand feet, this is U.S. Naval Warship bearing oh-nine-five from you. Turn right immediately and change course to zero-six-zero. If you maintain course you are standing into danger and are subject to U.S. Navy defense measures. Request you change course to one-three-zero, repeat one-three-zero, over."

"Any luck on raising the flagship?"

"Negative, Captain. We're checking everything in Radio. I don't recall ever losing comms over all circuits like this before."

"Okay, keep trying. Continue to provide updates of our situation. Somebody make sure we are logging all these attempts to communicate, both to the unidentified aircraft and the flagship."

Schmidt punched a button on a speaker box next to his chair and called Lieutenant Commander Ellsworth on the bridge.

"XO."

"XO, this is the Captain. Tom, I am sure you have been following this up there." In fact, Schmidt thought, he's probably developed a laundry problem over it.

"Yes, sir."

"We've got an inbound unidentified aircraft approaching at high speed and at a very low altitude. He seems to be ignoring our calls to turn away. To make it a perfect day, we seem to have lost communications with the flagship and the rest of our adult leadership."

"Sir, I recommend we alter course and head north away from Libya."

"XO, we're fast, but we can't outrun an airplane. Besides, I have no intention of giving the appearance that he has us on the run. We are well in international waters, even beyond the area Gadhafi claims to be below his 'line of death.' "

"Yes, sir, but . . ."

"No buts, XO. If he keeps coming, we will take him with missiles if he gets inside ten nautical miles."

"How about sending a message to the flagship requesting guidance, sir?"

"There is no time for paperwork, XO. It is my responsibility to protect the ship. I will not be the recipient of the first shot."

"Yes, sir, but I feel I should point out that the aircraft is still squawking Mode Three. For all we know it could be a commercial airliner." Sailors on the bridge and in CIC who overheard the conversation exchanged wary glances, some rolling their eyes.

"Flying at four hundred knots and two thousand feet? I don't think so. If he has no evil motives he would certainly alter course. Maintain course and speed, XO."

Schmidt punched off his squawk box.

"Status report?"

"Captain, the bogey is twenty miles out, maintaining course and speed."

"Keep making those warnings, both military and civilian frequencies. I want to know the instant anyone detects him altering course!"

The tension in CIC was palpable. The last remaining remnants of Right Guard were overcome by the strain.

"TAO, light him up. Illuminate inbound track with fire control radar. If he is a military aircraft, this should get his attention."

"Aye, aye, sir."

Attila's hands were flying across his console. "Captain, at his altitude, if this guy gets within the ten nautical mile point we may fall inside the effective range of the Standard missiles."

Schmidt nodded. "Call out the range by the mile!"

All eyes were staring at the white dot in a half-diamond symbol as it drew ever closer to the ship.

"Fifteen miles, sir." Every ten seconds another mile closer. "Fourteen, sir." The seconds seemed like hours. Some crewmen's eyes darted about the darkened room but most were fixed upon their captain.

"Thirteen, sir!" It was as if everyone in Combat had stopped breathing.

"Twelve miles, sir!" Schmidt punched the squawk box button for the bridge. "Standby on the bridge."

"Eleven miles, sir!"

"Last chance, anybody detect a course or altitude change?"

Silence.

"Ten miles, sir!"

Schmidt reached to his left and turned two keys granting firing permission. All eyes shifted to Ensign Madison, the Fire Control Officer.

"Is that a take order?"

"YES, DAMMIT, TAKE!"

Two Standard missiles roared out of the vertical launch tubes on the ship's bow.

The crew held its breath. In keeping with normal operating procedures, Schmidt placed his hand near a button which could have destroyed the missiles in flight. His hand never moved.

"Estimated flight time twenty-two seconds!"

"Roger." In Combat all eyes were fixed on a single dot on the blue LSD. It was the longest twenty-two seconds in Bill Schmidt's life. And then the dot was gone.

The bridge watch team reported a bright flash, low on the horizon.

A cheer went up from the crew. "Knock it off! Knock it off!" The Captain seemed quite agitated.

"Check your logs."

28

"Captain, this is the XO."

"Yeah, Tom?"

"Recommend we head over to the vicinity of the flash to see if there is a pilot in the water or anything."

Good old Tom, Schmidt thought. Now he wants to earn his life-saving badge.

"I don't think so, XO. We don't know what that guy might have been carrying if he was planning on attacking us."

"If, sir? We just shot him down. I sure hope he was planning on attacking."

"Well, just in case, let's set Circle William and turn into the wind, unless doing that would take us toward the site where the aircraft came down. I don't want to head there just yet. Oh, and let's activate the CPS."

Ellsworth reacted instantly. "Boatswains Mate of the Watch," he shouted, "set Circle William." The Boatswains Mate repeated the announcement over the 1MC and crew members throughout the ship dashed for nearby fans and vents. Circle William was a readiness condition in which the ship sealed itself off from the outside atmosphere. The sailors turned off the fans and quickly fastened metal covers over openings to prevent the recirculation of potentially poisoned air.

A few moments later, the XO directed Damage Control Central to start up the CPS or Countermeasures Protective System, a sophisticated filtration system that protected the quality of the air inside the skin of the ship.

The Circle William order told the XO all he needed to know about his captain's concerns. Circle William was used only in cases of chemical, biological, or nuclear attack.

Moments later Schmidt upped the ante. "XO, Captain. Just to be on the safe side, let's activate the topside sprinklers and increase speed to thirty-five knots." One more indication of Schmidt's fears. *Churchill*, like all U.S. Navy ships, was equipped with a sprinkler system designed to hose down exposed portions of the ship in case of chemical or biological attack.

As Ellsworth busied himself with measures to minimize the impact of exposure to poisonous gas, Schmidt prepared to reestablish communications with higher command. "Brad, how about checking on that communications problem with the Battle Group staff? I feel a need to call home to 'mother.' "

Moseman nodded and began making keystrokes on his console that would eliminate the self-jamming he had caused.

Anxiety and ambivalence coexisted among the crew. There was the excitement of having done their jobs in defending the ship from an apparent attack, and yet many shared an uneasiness because of the lack of communications with their chain of command or their enemy. They had shot down an aircraft that they had never seen and never heard.

Ten minutes passed before Moseman reported to his captain that communications had been reestablished with the *George Washington* battle group, 400 miles away at the other end of the Gulf of Sidra.

The admiral embarked in the *GW* was instantly on the line.

"Alpha Bravo, this is *Churchill*, Charlie Oscar, over."

"This is Alpha Bravo actual. Bill, what the hell is going on, over?"

Since we broke our data link with them, they couldn't have followed the action, Schmidt thought. I guess he is just reacting to the fact that we dropped off the net for forty-five minutes. Wait till he hears why.

Schmidt proceeded to give a blow-by-blow account of the afternoon's actions leading up to the shootdown. The Admiral broke in frequently with questions about the precise behavior of the aircraft and the ship's crew.

"Have you spotted any wreckage yet?"

"Negative, sir. As a precaution I stood off for a while . . . went to Circle William . . . took a few other steps. Didn't know what kind of payload the Libyan was carrying and thought I would be prudent."

"Well, that is a concept that hasn't always been associated with your ship, Bill."

Ouch. It was not like the Admiral to bust Schmidt's chops. "Admiral, I think enough time has passed so UNODIR, I plan to reverse course and head back toward the impact zone." UNODIR was one of Schmidt's favorite Navy concepts. The acronym stood for "Unless Otherwise Directed." It meant that you never had to ask for permission—you just announced what you planned to do and essentially dared your seniors to overrule you.

"Roger. Let us know as soon as you find anything. We will get busy notifying Washington that you apparently have been forced to take defensive action."

Schmidt didn't like the tone of that *apparently*. He kept the crew at their battle stations, telling them it was a precaution against any additional attacks.

By the time *Winston Churchill* reached the impact area an hour later, much of the wreckage had sunk, but what little remained on the surface left little doubt about the type of aircraft it once was.

Lieutenant Commander Ellsworth punched the squawk box button. "Combat, bridge."

"Go ahead, bridge." The XO's voice was very faint.

"Captain, you'd better come up here, right away, please."

"On my way, Tom."

Seconds later the Boatswain's Mate of the Watch called out the traditional notice. "The Captain's on the bridge." Schmidt's presence was duly recorded in the ship's log.

Five hundred yards off the ship's bow floated a huge chuck of what was once a wing.

"Doesn't look like a MiG, does it?" Schmidt said quietly.

"No sir, no it doesn't," was Ellsworth's barely audible reply.

The ship was going as slowly as it could while still being able to maneuver as it entered a field of floating wreckage.

Schmidt grabbed a pair of binoculars and scanned the debris. He was relieved to see no bodies floating amidst the wreckage and hoped that was an indication that the airliner carried no passengers. The pilot and copilot must have been trapped in the cockpit and went to the bottom with the plane.

A lookout posted on the bow took a boat hook and caught a cushion that was drifting by. Using his sound-powered phone he notified the bridge about his find.

"There's some writing on it in Arabic and then below that it says something in English about Libyan Arab Airlines."

Ellsworth walked briskly to the rear of the bridge, reached for a trash can, and threw up.

Two HOURS later, after gathering more pieces of wreckage and reporting the find to the flagship, Schmidt called a meeting of the crew. All hands except those standing essential watches gathered on the aft portion of the ship near the shelter that served as a helicopter hangar.

"By now you know that the aircraft we shot down earlier today appears to have been an airliner. I say 'appears' because all we know is that the wreckage we found is consistent with that. I want you to know that the crew of *Winston Churchill* performed magnificently today. The ship was approached by an aircraft traveling at high speeds and exhibiting a very unusual flight pattern. We warned the aircraft on numerous occasions to stand clear. In my judgment, the aircraft displayed what the rules of engagement call 'hostile intent.' "

The crew, at first silent, slowly nodded their heads and started to murmur.

"Presented with this threat, the crew of this ship did their jobs precisely as America expected them to do. If—and I emphasize if—there were any screwups, they were mine and mine alone."

One crewman shouted out, "No! You're the best, Captain."

"Thanks . . . but we'll leave it up to others to judge me. The important thing is for each of you to believe in yourselves. The days ahead are going to be difficult ones. You will be under intense scrutiny. We need to preserve all the logs, all the computer tapes, all the records. The investigators will want to see what we did. When they understand, when they fully understand, we'll come out all right."

Some of the crew murmured among themselves. The name of Ensign Madison was on the mind of many sailors. The guy was a Jonah. He might have been responsible for this, some said.

Looking into the eyes of his crew, Schmidt could tell that they were scared. "I want you to stand together. Help one another. Believe in one another and in USS *Winston Churchill*. In the end, I guarantee, I guarantee that your faith will be rewarded. That is all."

The XO was unconvinced. He had asked Lieutenant Debbie Smith to meet him in the ship's office for an "unofficial chat." Smith had been on the bridge with the XO during the shootdown.

After closing the door, Ellsworth pounded a desk. "I can't believe he shot down an unarmed civilian airliner!"

"XO, with all due respect, it wasn't 'he' that shot it down . . . it was 'we.' And I think there was sufficient cause." Smith said the words with more certitude than she felt.

"I just want you to remember that I told the Captain we should move out of the track of the inbound aircraft and he rejected my suggestion. If he had listened to me this would not have happened."

"XO, the Captain told us to stick together. I don't think second-guessing the action was what he had in mind."

"I should have known. You are among the members of the wardroom who are under his spell. You're always rationalizing the things he does that get this ship in trouble. Well, this is one screwup that he is not going to be able to talk his way out of. Even his high-powered brother isn't going to get him out of this mess."

"Sir . . ." Lieutenant Smith started to say something and stopped.

"What is it?"

"Ah, never mind."

"No, I want to hear what you were going to say."

"Well, if you insist. I was going to ask you how you could be so disloyal to your commanding officer."

"Disloyal! Disloyal! Do you know what he has done to me?" A gob of spittle slipped out of Ellsworth's mouth.

"You?" Smith was truly puzzled now.

"The selection board considering me for commander meets next month. It should be beyond question that I would be selected. But now, now . . . the board is going to see that I am the XO of this Godforsaken ship. My last fitness reports were signed by this bozo Schmidt. What are they going to think about me? What?"

"Oh, so that's it. When you started whining about the shoot down, I thought for a moment you might have been concerned about the passengers on that airplane."

29

Beepers went off all around Washington. The first reports were pretty sketchy. An unidentified aircraft from Libya had been shot down by a U.S. Navy destroyer after failing to turn away when warned.

Since it was late on a spring Friday afternoon in the nation's capital by the time the incident was reported, duty officers in half a dozen agencies—Defense, State, and CIA among them—had to track down their senior leadership in order to provide them with the details.

Secondary reports discussed the aircraft's unusual flight pattern and the number of times it was warned off. The third round of flash precedence messages from the fleet carried the disturbing news that the downed aircraft appeared to be a civilian passenger jet.

The CNO, Admiral Bushrod Custis, wanted to be the one to inform the Secretary of the Navy. The Navy Command Center paged the secretary's aide and received a return call informing them that the secretary was playing in a fund-raising tennis tournament being held by the Senatorial Wives Club. The aide got the CNO on the line and then handed his cellular phone to the secretary.

"Mr. Secretary, I am sorry to take you away from your game. But I thought you would want to know that *Winston Churchill* has gotten herself into a peck of trouble."

"What did it do?" Despite having been Navy Secretary for two years, Fred Fiske still had trouble grasping the concept that a ship named after a man could be called "she."

"Well, sir, let me emphasize that all we have are initial reports, and initial reports are always wrong . . ."

"I know, Bushrod, and so are second, third, fourth, and final reports."

"Well, sometimes. In any case, it appears that the *Churchill* may have shot down an unarmed civilian airliner—a Libyan airliner. No word yet on the number of casualties but it could be that our friend Commander Schmidt, the fellow who got all that notoriety in the *Washington Post* a while back, might have been a little quick on the trigger. I spoke with the Commander of the Sixth Fleet. It seems that there was a communications glitch between the ship and higher command. So this fellow Schmidt took it upon himself to launch."

"Jesus Christ!" Fiske exclaimed. Several of the senatorial wives turned to look at him shouting into his cellular phone alongside the indoor tennis courts.

Sensing his agitation, Custis set to work. "Yessir, I know what you are thinking. You remember that you and I were very concerned about the reports that this guy might be some sort of a cowboy. But we had assurances that he was under control. And with his ties to the White House, well, we didn't want to overreact."

"Yes, of course, we didn't want to overreact."

"And naturally, while deployed, the ship is under the operational control of the U.S. European Command. And it wouldn't be appropriate for us to tell that Army four-star General how to run his shop. Although in retrospect, I wish he had been more vigilant."

"Yes, a little vigilance would have helped."

"Mr. Secretary, right now I would recommend that we let the DoD and the Joint Staff handle public comment on the incident. I'll have my staff provide some 'off-the-record' context for the major media and we'll just see how this thing plays out."

"Right, well thank you for the briefing. Keep me advised." With that, Fiske returned to his tennis match and promptly double-faulted.

The State Department Operations Center reached its secretary at his office, where he was preparing to host a black-tie dinner for the Ambassadors to the Organization of American States in the Benjamin Franklin Room of the department's Foggy Bottom headquarters. Harden's aides briefed him on what was known about the incident.

"Outrageous! See, I Told You So! This Man Is a Menace. Even More So Than His Brother!" The Secretary thundered on in his usual overwrought style. He asked if there had been any contact from the Libyans. Not yet—since the U.S. had no diplomatic relations, contact would be made through intermediaries. Switzerland handled U.S. interests in Libya. Morocco represented Libya in the U.S.

"Get Me a Copy of All the Relevant Reports!"

After reading the initial reports and calming down a bit, Harden had his assistant place a call to Al Janoska of the *New York Times*. No comments for attribution—Harden just wanted to make sure that the newspaper of record had the right perspective on the story that was about to break.

The senior leadership at the CIA and National Security Agency were not taken by surprise by the downing of the aircraft. Director Nelson and General Firman heightened the state of alert of their staffs and immediately began to monitor Libya's reaction to the event.

"I want everything we've got focused on the Libyan leadership," Firman directed. "We need to know what they are saying about this incident . . . and how, if at all, they are going to respond."

From the White House Situation Room, National Security Advisor Burnette called each of the members of the Crisis Working Group. He asked them to redouble their efforts to locate the chemical weapons stash in the U.S. "If we don't find the stash in the next forty-eight hours, we will have to let Congress in on the secret," he reminded them. The whole plan would fall apart if the U.S. were unable to convince the Libyans that the aircraft downing was a genuine mistake.

The first public announcement about the incident came from the Pentagon. Just after the evening network news programs aired, the top Pentagon spokesman issued a "Blue Topper," so named because they were once printed on stationery with a large blue header. Even though press releases were now often issued via the Internet or by some other electronic means, they were still called Blue Toppers.

Reference: No. 196-00
(703) 697-5131 (media)
(703) 697-3189 (copies)
(703) 697-5737 (public/industry)
IMMEDIATE RELEASE
Washington—May 16

A U.S. Navy guided missile destroyer, the USS *Winston Churchill*, shot down an unidentified aircraft that it believed was displaying hostile intent in the Mediterranean this afternoon.

The incident occurred in international waters and airspace approximately 200 miles northeast of Tripoli at approximately 2:27 P.M. local time today.

The *Winston Churchill* was conducting independent operations at sea at the time of the incident. No other United States units were involved.

Initial reports indicate that an unidentified aircraft approached the ship at high speed and at a low altitude. Numerous attempts to get the aircraft to identify itself and to change course were apparently not received or were ignored.

Believing that it was under attack, USS *Winston Churchill* launched two Standard surface-to-air missiles destroying the aircraft.

An inspection of the wreckage revealed that the aircraft apparently was a passenger jet belonging to Jamahiriya Libyan Arab Airlines. No survivors were found at the scene.

The Secretary of Defense has ordered an immediate investigation into the incident.

It is premature to speculate on the cause of the incident. Nevertheless, if innocent lives were lost, the United States government deeply regrets it.

USS *Winston Churchill* is homeported in Norfolk, Virginia, and is commanded by Commander William C. Schmidt, 38, of Binghamton, New York.

-30-

Note for Pentagon correspondents: A press briefing will be held at 10:00 A.M. on Saturday, May 17th in the Pentagon briefing room. General Leroy Sundin, Chairman of the Joint Chiefs of Staff, will conduct the briefing.

The reaction around Washington was swift and judgmental. In a city where jumping to conclusions could be an Olympic sport, it did not take long for conventional wisdom to determine that the *Winston Churchill* was guilty.

In newsrooms around the city, researchers were asked to retrieve copies of the story that had recently run in the *Washington Post*. Defense correspondents dug out their old files on the incident involving USS *Vincennes* and the downing of an Iranian airliner in 1988. The parallels were compelling.

CNN was the first to air a report on the shoot down. The network flashed a Breaking News on the screen and interrupted "Crossfire" with an account based on the Blue Topper. An unmanned robot camera in the network's cubical along the Pentagon's Correspondent's Corridor captured the CNN defense reporter's rendition of the bare bones release. The anchor in Atlanta repeatedly grilled the correspondent for more details and refused to give up until long after it was apparent that there were no more facts available.

Paul Harper, the Style section editor for the *Washington Post*, was in his office wrapping up the next day's assignments when the CNN report aired. The TV in his office was on but the sound was turned down. When he saw the Breaking News title, Harper fumbled for his remote control.

It took him a few seconds to increase the volume, but he did so in time to hear the story repeated several times. "Hey, is Sue O'Dell on her way back to Europe yet?" he shouted into the news room. "Wherever she is, get her!"

Since most of the support staff had gone home for the day, it took several phone calls to determine that Sue was still in Washington. Harper remembered that he had suggested that she do a follow-up story on the *Winston Churchill* and wondered why he had never seen any copy from her.

"I hope to hell she has some more details about that boat and its captain. Facts about the *Churchill* are going to be awfully valuable over the next few days."

Moments later Sue was on the line. "What's up, Paul? I was just finishing packing. I'm flying back to Europe tomorrow."

"Have you heard about your friends on the *Churchill?*"

"No! What did they do this time, moon the Queen?"

"They wish. Looks like they shot down an airliner full of innocent Libyans," Harper said.

"Oh, no!"

"Oh, yes! And you, missy, are the world's leading expert on the ship and its skipper. How are you coming on your follow-up story?"

Sue was slightly dazed. She didn't respond immediately.

"Well, do you have something for me or not?"

"Frankly, Paul, I haven't come up with much. The ship has a good reputation in the fleet and although the crew tends to be a bit colorful they are reportedly pretty good at what they do. They even won the Battenburg Cup."

"What the hell is the Battenburg Cup?"

Sue had no idea and regretted mentioning it as soon as the words left her mouth. "It just means they are among the best . . . ah . . . oh, I don't have time to explain it to you."

"So, can you bang out a sidebar for me for tomorrow's editions?"

"Well, I suppose . . . but you know, I think it would be better if I headed out to Dulles right now. If I hurry I can still get a flight to Rome tonight. Undoubtedly, there is going to be a big investigation and I want to be there for it."

Harper sighed. His visions of an in-depth story for tomorrow's edition about the men behind the news dissolved. By the next day, everyone would have had time to generate a feature article on the ship in the news.

"You sure you don't have five hundred words in you about the antics of these cowboys?"

"Paul, let's not convict them before all the facts are in."

"Jeez, that doesn't sound like the Sue O'Dell I know. Okay, go ahead and get back to Europe. Check in the minute you arrive. This is not going to be a one-day story, so I hope you had a nice rest while you were in the States."

30

Several hours after the Pentagon issued its Blue Topper, the Libyans responded. Their reply, when it finally came, was predictable.

Why, in the name of Allah, did the Americans continue to torment the peace-loving people of the Libyan Arab Jamahiriya? The Jamahiriya was Gadhafi's concept of a state of the masses, self-governed by the populace through local councils. In fact, the country was ruled by the iron hand of Gadhafi, who nonetheless continued to feign no official role in the government. The press release put out in the name of the Revolutionary Leader went on to condemn the treachery of the United States in knowingly destroying a civilian aircraft which, according to Gadhafi, had carried 190 souls.

Gadhafi decried the butchery and bullying of the United States and finished with a call for the United Nations to impose a ban on all commercial flights into and out of the U.S. until those responsible for the heinous act were brought to justice in a Libyan people's tribunal.

NSA intercepted and translated the Libyan press statement and

General Firman immediately called the White House to read it to Burnette. "Nice touch that last bit," Burnette told Firman.

"Yes, in light of the fact that Libya is still under UN sanction for refusing to give up the two agents suspected in the Pan Am 103 bombing, I'd say it was a clever twist on their part."

"Gadhafi goes on for quite a few pages. Do you want me to read more, Wally?"

"Not necessary, Lew, thanks. We just got the full text from MSNBC."

"Well, so much for our vaunted intelligence network."

"I am more interested in anything that you are picking up that is a bit more sensitive than press releases. Got anything there, Lew?"

"Analysis shows that shortly after the plane was shot down there was a spike in the amount of communications between Gadhafi's headquarters and the command center for the Istikhbara al Askariya, the Libyan intelligence service."

"What was that all about?"

"We don't have it completely analyzed yet, but our best guess is that there was one hellacious debate going on about whether we knew what they were up to or not. After CNN did its report on the Pentagon press release expressing regret there was another spike in communications. It was only then that they put together their own statement taking us to task."

"Well, what do you think? Did they buy it? Do they really believe that we accidentally shot down their airplane which happened to be loaded with chemical weapons?"

"They seem skeptical, Wally. But right now, thanks to CNN and the advance work done by the *Washington Post*, they are giving us the benefit of the doubt. Seems they are ready to believe we are just inept."

"I hope they continue to believe that for a while. Any luck getting information on where the weapons here are stashed?"

"Nothing yet. But maybe the shoot down will spur somebody to talk about it, somebody whose phone calls we listen to."

The headlines in the next day's newspapers around the world made it clear that it wasn't only the Libyans who were ready to believe the U.S. was inept.

The *New York Times* headline read: "U.S. Ship Brings Tragedy to Mediterranean."

The *Washington Post*'s story was titled: "Error-Prone Ship Sparks Catastrophe," and it had the subheading "White House Spokesman's Brother At Helm."

The *Washington Times* led with "Defects in AEGIS System? Setback for Missile Defense."

The *New York Daily News* had a full-page photo of the *Winston Churchill* on its cover with the simple headline: "Oops!"

Jim Schmidt had all the papers spread out across his spacious desk in his West Wing office. The press were clamoring for a statement from the White House, but other than a two-sentence release expressing regret at any innocent loss of life, Schmidt steadfastly referred all questions to the Pentagon.

Schmidt picked up the handset on his secure phone and called the office of the Chairman of the JCS. General Sundin came on the line and Schmidt discussed with him how to handle the press conference scheduled for later that morning.

"General, as I see it, your task is easy. You have to convince the press that the U.S. government, as embodied by my little brother, are a bunch of screwups. Never has a senior military official gone into battle with an easier objective."

"Jim, if you think this is going to be so easy, why don't you do the briefing yourself?" Sundin laughed.

"Much as I'd like to, I'm afraid I'll have to recuse myself due to my family ties. On a more serious note, let me recommend that you try not to say anything in your briefing that you know is untrue. I don't want your credibility ruined when this crisis is over."

"How do you recommend I avoid lying?"

"Easy. Just be vague. For any tough questions just say that the whole matter is under investigation and that it is premature to speculate. Keep saying that we regret the loss of any innocent life and that, while it may take some time for the facts to emerge, we are confident that in the end we will be able to get to the bottom of this."

"Easy for you to say."

"Just keep up your mantra. Our finest minds are investigating at this very moment. We regret the loss of innocent life. Premature to speculate."

"Yeah, I imagine the press will do all the speculating we need."

AT PRECISELY 10:00 A.M. General Sundin strode into room 2E781, the Pentagon's press briefing room. The room number indicated that it was on the second floor, on the outside or "E" ring, and located off the seventh corridor. The E-ring hallway between the seventh and eighth corridors, known as the Correspondent's Corridor, was the place where Pentagon reporters were allowed to set up small offices. The Pentagon press corps only had to walk a few feet to reach the briefing room.

General Sundin marched up to the lectern. He projected a commanding image but felt quite naked since his staff had convinced him to go out without one of his trademark cigars. Behind him hung an oval sign that read *The Pentagon*. By design, it mimicked the sign that adorned the White House briefing room—a clear case of signage envy.

The room was packed. Thirty television cameras were crammed onto a riser at the back of the room. Two large "mult boxes" nearby provided places where the media could plug in and receive a direct audio feed. This eliminated the unsightly mass of microphones often seen lashed to less sophisticated lecterns. An overflow crowd of correspondents packed the rest of the room, eager for any fresh details on the shoot down. The heat from the reporters' bodies and the television lights quickly overcame the high-powered air-conditioning system which normally kept the briefing room at a temperature consistent with that of a meat locker.

An easel had been set up to one side of the General. The information to be displayed was covered so as not to distract until the appropriate point in his opening statement.

The Chairman began with a brief recitation of the facts. He stressed that the information he was providing was based on initial reports and that undoubtedly additional information, perhaps even some that might be contradictory, would later emerge.

The General went to the easel and uncovered a map of the southern Mediterranean. The chart had a silhouette to illustrate the position of the *Winston Churchill* and a dotted line to show the flight path of the ill-starred aircraft. After running through the unusual flight path of the aircraft, the warnings sent, responses not received, and other details, General Sundin paused and asked if there were any questions.

Hands shot up around the room. The General realized that asking if there were any questions was the first silly question of the day.

"General, this ship was a source of trouble throughout its deployment. Are you at all concerned that you have a rogue ship out there and that this was an accident looking for a place to happen?"

"As I said in my opening statement, a very thorough investigation is underway. It would be inappropriate for me to speculate on what the outcome of that investigation might be. Clearly, no one believed that this was, as you say, an accident looking for a place to happen. There may have been tragic results, but beyond that. . . ."

More hands shot up. Voices shouted to be heard above the others.

"Sir, who ordered the ship to fire? The Battle Group Commander? Sixth Fleet? Who, sir?"

"Well, as it turns out, the ship was having communications difficulty at the time of the incident." The crowd of reporters buzzed. Many looked down, checking that their tape recorders were rolling. Others scribbled furiously in their notepads.

"The ship was unable to talk to higher command. *Churchill*'s commanding officer has said that he believed the aircraft was displaying hostile intent and under peacetime rules of engagement, believing that his ship was in imminent danger, he took defensive action."

"General, is it your belief that the error was human? Was it the result of a faulty AEGIS system, or perhaps both?"

The heat in the room was beginning to get to the tall, four-star General. He instinctively mopped his brow. As his hand reached his forehead, scores of motor drives fired and the still photographers captured an image that Sundin's aides later described as the "Oy vey!" shot.

"Ah, as I said earlier. The whole matter is under investigation. I wouldn't want to jump to any conclusions. The AEGIS system has been reliable in the past and . . . and so have the crew of this particular ship. So let's just wait until the investigation. . . ."

"General, how can you say they are reliable when there have been stories in the *Washington Post* detailing how they have caroused their way across Europe?"

"Well, I, look . . . it does no good to speculate about these things without specific knowledge. I came out here today because I knew there would be tremendous demand for information. I also knew that I would not be in a position to provide you with many of the answers you want. So let me simply repeat what I have been saying: We regret the loss of any innocent life . . . a thorough investigation is underway . . . and it would be inappropriate for me to speculate beyond that."

With that, Sundin executed a left face and strode out of the briefing room.

Four television correspondents immediately stood up and faced the back of the room where they could look into their network's camera and provide instant analysis and dialogue with anchors back in the studios. Newspaper correspondents went out of their way to amble through the shots.

31

On a submarine you can't get very far away from people who annoy you and there was something about Larry Caffey that really annoyed Chet Hollomaker.

Caffey had never heard that submarine duty was supposed to be the "silent service," Hollomaker mused. The young lieutenant could be counted on to have a comment for every occurrence, and to announce an opinion at every opportunity. Behind his back, the crew called him "Chatty Caffey." But as Captain, Hollomaker could hardly avoid him, particularly when he was the Conning Officer.

Caffey spotted Hollomaker fifteen feet away.

"Yo ho, Captain. Pleased to report the best submarine in the world's finest, semi-undefeated, partially nuclear Navy is trim, full of vim, and ready to swim, sir!"

"Pleased to hear it."

Hollomaker theorized that if he kept his responses to Caffey to a minimum, he might not inspire additional verbal riffs. The theory didn't work.

"Like I said, Captain, we're slicing through this Libyan goo like a Swiss Army knife through a Boy Scout's finger."

I can't take any more of this, Hollomaker thought. "Jeez, Larry, you say whatever pops into your head, don't you?"

"No sense having all those fine thoughts clogging up your head, Captain. Why, I literally have millions of pertinent phrases beating up on each other trying to get out."

And another thing that bugs me about this guy, Hollomaker reflected, is that he always says *literally* when he means *figuratively*. At least he thought that's what he meant. "Yeah, well, I'm glad you don't waste any energy stifling yourself. But how about coming up for a breath every once in a while. Remember, we have to make our own air on this boat."

"Captain, are you implying that I talk too much? Because if that were true, sir, I would be very, very upset. No, sir, there is no way, shape, or form that I would want to be known as loose-lipped. Not at all. Every word is measured, weighed, calculated, caressed."

"Well, I . . ."

"There is not a single day that goes by that I don't ask myself, Larry, I say, how have you contributed to social discourse on dis-boat."

"Dis-boat?"

"And I truly believe that freedom of speech is our most important liberty and while I may be a bit freer than the average bear, I've gotta say . . ."

Hollomaker despaired at getting a word in and simply shook his head. The other members of the watch team smothered laughs. Maybe I need that SEAL team to work this guy over, Hollomaker thought. Maybe they're as good at getting people to shut up as they are at making them talk.

He could take only so much of Caffey and his limit was at hand, so Hollomaker found an excuse to be somewhere, anywhere, else. "I'm going to check in with the SIGINT guys. They've been under a lot of pressure to feed more data back to NSA. Better see how they are doing."

"Right you are, Captain. Always good to check up on those guys and make sure they aren't listening to heavy metal on those headphones. Bad for the ears, literally blows your brains out. . . ."

Hollomaker could hear Caffey yammering on in full automatic mode as he walked away.

The relative silence of the narrow, closet-size compartment devoted to communications intercepts was a blessed relief.

"Hey guys, how's the fishing?"

"Oh, hi, Captain. So, so."

That's what Hollomaker liked. A man of few words.

"Any unusual trends?"

"We picked up a spike in traffic on the Monarch circuits after the *Churchill* splashed the Libyan." Monarch referred to communications channels devoted to supporting a foreign government's leadership.

"And there was a second spike right after CNN reported the shoot down."

"Any sense of what they were saying?" Hollomaker asked.

"Most of that stuff is pretty well encrypted. We are sending the data back to NSA to be deciphered. We can judge the quantity of transmissions here but not the content."

"I see. Any news from Radio Free Mustafa?"

"Not yet, sir, but it is getting to be about time for his daily call to his brother. We'll let you know when he phones home."

Hollomaker headed back to his stateroom and wished there was a way of getting there without passing by the Mouth of the Med, Lieutenant Caffey. Alas, the only route to his small cabin took him by Caffey's perch.

Just as Hollomaker was about to be hosed down by a verbal broadside from Lieutenant Caffey, there was an interruption by a buzz on one of the internal communications circuits. The SIGINT guys urgently requested the Captain's presence. Must be getting some action from the beach, Hollomaker thought. Saved by the buzzer. He quickly made his way forward. He arrived to see the chief petty officer in charge of the watch team reviewing some notes.

"Captain, Mustafa came on line again. Called his brother. At first he had some explaining to do because the brother had expected Mustafa to have gone on vacation."

"Yeah? How'd he get out of that one?"

"Mustafa says that he had to cancel because something came up at work." Hollomaker's interest was piqued.

"At this point, Ibrahim breaks in and says you need some time off my brother, you've been working too hard. You been sounding stressed-out lately."

"Yeah, if only he knew," Hollomaker said.

"So here comes the interesting part. He says, 'I've been having these strange dreams lately. In my dreams I have lost something very important . . . but I cannot find where it is.' And then he said it two more times: 'I cannot find where it is.' "

"That's not what I wanted to hear, Chief."

"Yessir, but at the very end of the conversation, Mustafa says, 'In my dream I cannot find where it is . . . all I know is that this important stuff is in some tanks.' "

"Tanks? Like Army tanks?" Hollomaker asked incredulously.

"No, sir. He said 'khazzanat,' the Arabic word for tanks, as in canisters or containers. If he meant armored tanks the word would have been 'dababat.' "

"Very interesting, Chief. You know the procedure on a Mustafa call. Get the transcript and full audio off to Washington. Make it flash."

32

The aircraft wreckage had barely reached the bottom of the Mediterranean before the bureaucratic response began. A long series of messages arrived instructing the *Winston Churchill* about what to do and especially what not to do. First, they were directed to secure all the ship's logs, tapes, and records. The crew was instructed not to speculate among themselves about the incident, a directive with no chance of being followed. Since the ship was instructed to cut off contact with the outside world, the crew's Internet access and use of ship-to-shore telephones was immediately suspended.

Cutting off the phones was especially tough on morale. Using satellite technology, ships had only recently given the crew a simple mechanism for phoning home while at sea. "POTS," the Plain Old Telephone System, was a major boost to the quality of life.

The commander of the Sixth Fleet appointed a three-man Board of Inquiry to investigate the shoot down. The team was to be led by Rear Admiral Norbert Arnold, the senior surface warfare officer in the European theater.

Uh oh, Bill Schmidt thought. He's the last guy on active duty in the Navy with a crew cut. He had his sense of humor surgically removed. They say his nickname is "Norbert." This investigation is going to be a barrel of laughs.

Winston Churchill was ordered to proceed at best speed to Naples. Normally, when in Naples, the ship moored alongside a pier. This time she was ordered to anchor about a half-mile from Fleet Landing. Probably don't want to make it too easy for Libyans, reporters, or other kinds of terrorists to get to us, Schmidt reflected.

The XO had regained none of his color after the shoot down incident. Crew members noticed that he was spending more time than usual in his cabin. When out, he was often seen mumbling to himself. He also maintained his distance from his commanding officer, something to which Schmidt did not object.

Schmidt, too, was unusually detached and remained largely by himself except for occasional meetings with Moseman and Hahn.

A messenger knocked loudly on the door to the Captain's in-port cabin.

"Whadya got, Taylor?"

"Another SPECAT from Sixth Fleet, Captain. They've sure been burning up the wires lately."

Schmidt signed for the message and handed an empty clipboard and pen back to the sailor.

"Always nice to know that the higher-ups are thinking about us, Taylor." Yeah, he thought, shoot down one civilian airliner and they never let you hear the end of it.

The latest message informed Schmidt that prior to the ship's arrival in Naples, two officers were to be flown out to the ship to assist him, one a JAG from the Navy Legal Services Office in Naples and the other a PAO from the naval station. Schmidt groaned to himself. One guy to tell him not to say anything, and another to tell him how to say it, he thought. Great.

Schmidt's cynicism subsided when the two officers arrived. The lawyer, a commander by the name of Wiley Copeland, advised him of his rights to be represented by any defense attorney within the Navy Department and asked if there were any that he particularly wanted.

"Although this ship has had a colorful deployment, I haven't had to become acquainted with too many Navy lawyers. Got any you'd recommend? Who's the best?"

"Well, in my humble opinion sir, I am," Copeland replied.

"You sure you're not an aviator?"

"Nah, that's for wimps."

"Okay, you're hired."

The PAO, Lieutenant Commander Abe Epstein, also won Schmidt's respect. Epstein gave Schmidt a quick tutorial on the intense media interest that he was about to face and discussed techniques on how to answer the questions he wanted to answer and deflect the ones he didn't.

"Don't ever answer a speculative question. If it begins with 'what if' . . . don't bite. But never, ever, ever say 'No comment.' That will be taken as a sure sign of guilt. Say something like, 'I am not in a position to answer that question right now,' or 'Let me take that question and get back to you.' "

"Maybe I should have talked to you, Abe, before I met with that reporter from the *Washington Post*."

"As a matter of fact, I thought the same thing when I read her story in the Early Bird. Sue's quite a handful. She's made mincemeat out of a lot of media-savvy folks."

"Always nice to be in good company."

Long before *Winston Churchill* dropped anchor, media helicopters and fixed-wing aircraft had been buzzing overhead trying to get fresh video of the ship for the evening news. Several enterprising reporters hired pilot boats to approach the destroyer as she entered Naples harbor and shouted questions to sailors visible on the weatherdecks. Since they also had been briefed by the newly embarked PAO, none responded, neither verbally nor with the hand gestures that came to mind.

Thirty minutes after reaching the anchorage, *Winston Churchill* was approached by a boat carrying Admiral Arnold, the senior member of the Board of Inquiry. Arnold had borrowed the barge belonging to the commander of Fleet Air Mediterranean, a two-star officer based in Naples.

As the barge neared, Schmidt noticed that Arnold himself was at the helm. Executing a sharp turn on the approach, the barge made a perfect landing at *Churchill*'s accommodation ladder. Turning to the boat's coxswain, Arnold could be heard shouting "Now *that's* how you shoot an approach, sailor." Schmidt waited at the top of the ladder, clear that the Admiral coming aboard was someone with firmly held opinions.

Bong, bong . . . bong, bong . . . bong, bong . . . "Rear Admiral, United States Navy, arriving," the ship's announcing system blared. Arnold bounded up the ladder, saluted the American flag, known as the national ensign, flying from the ship's stern, and then saluted the Officer of the Deck. As his foot hit *Churchill*'s main deck, a final *bong* was sounded.

"Admiral Arnold, welcome aboard, sir. I'm Bill Schmidt, the commanding officer."

"Let's go to the in-port cabin. Just you and me," the Admiral said.

Hmmm. Not much for small talk.

"Yes sir, right this way, please."

Once in the cabin, Arnold got to the point. "Look, there is a lot of pressure to find out what happened and why. I expect you to fully cooperate. You've got a week to prepare your defense. Meanwhile, I want access to your files, logs, tapes, and the like. My investigators are coming out in about an hour. They will want to talk to you, your XO, TAO, CSO, and other key people from CIC. You can have your lawyer present if you want. I'd recommend it. Any questions?"

"Sir, we'll be happy to work with you of course . . ."

"Good, but you don't have a choice."

"Er, right. But anyway, I was wondering if starting the hearings within a week was rushing things a bit much. Seems to me you'll want to analyze the computer tapes from CIC and that can't be done in theater. They'll need to be shipped back to the Naval Surface Weapons Center in Dahlgren to be completely read." Schmidt hoped to buy more time in the hope that the location of the chemicals hidden in the U.S. would be uncovered and he would be able to testify truthfully about his actions. His hopes were dashed.

"Nonsense. Already thought of that. I have a plane standing by. Once you give me the tapes—as you are going to do in a few minutes—I will have them flown back to Virginia later this afternoon. The people in Dahlgren are standing by to receive them and promise a quick turnaround. Any other questions?"

The Admiral's no-nonsense attitude did not inspire much hope within Schmidt for what he was about to ask. "Sir, my crew has been under a lot of pressure. It would be nice if we could grant them some liberty."

"Not now. I need all hands on board twenty-four hours a day to be available for my investigators. Maybe after we have taken all the statements we might grant some limited shore leave."

Schmidt was struck by the Admiral's use of the term "shore leave," a phrase that had been out of general use for some forty years. Where has this guy been? he wondered. "I understand, sir."

Without a further word, the Admiral stood up and strode toward the quarterdeck and his awaiting barge.

Seconds after the Admiral had been *bong*ed off the ship, the XO appeared at the Captain's side.

"How did it go, sir?" Ellsworth asked with a querulous voice.

"Great, Tom. I have been assured that there will be no executions until after a fair trail."

Ellsworth failed to see the humor. "Sir, I believe I should obtain separate legal counsel in this case."

Schmidt looked quizzically at the XO. "Why, Tom? You were on the bridge. You didn't do anything wrong. If anyone gets hanged over this it'll be me. Moseman and Hahn and the folks in CIC might be at some risk, but you . . ."

"I agree I did nothing wrong . . ."

Sure you do, Schmidt thought.

". . . but would feel better if my interests were protected."

"Okay, why don't you go see Commander Copeland. I'm sure he can fix you up with another attorney. If there is anything we've got a lot of in this Navy, it's lawyers."

True to the Admiral's word, a boatload of his investigators arrived an hour later. Clearly, each had been previously given a specific assignment. They spread throughout the ship and immediately set about conducting interviews and gathering documents and evidence.

The investigators were polite but relentless. Over the next several days they examined the incident from almost every possible angle. Some investigators asked members of the CIC watch team what they did, what they saw, and what they thought. Others examined the ship's radar and weapons systems for signs of flaws. Another group of investigators closely inspected the ship's records for evidence of the training and qualifications of the crew.

After the investigators left the ship following a second day of inquiry, Schmidt called his coconspirators, Moseman and Hahn, to his in-port cabin. "It is clear to me that Admiral Arnold and friends are not read in on the plan. From what I can see they are taking this thing deadly seriously. How about you guys? What is your take on how the investigation is going?"

"These investigators are thorough, sir. They've asked every possible question six ways from Sunday," Moseman said.

"Every question but one," Hahn observed.

"What's that, Attila?"

"If we did it on purpose."

ON THE THIRD day the Admiral returned to *Churchill* and asked for a private meeting with Schmidt.

"As you know, we are still in the fact-finding phase, and won't begin the formal inquiry until next week."

"Yessir."

"But my investigators have come across something unusual that I want to talk to you about."

"What's that, Admiral?"

"Quite a few of your crew whom we interviewed mentioned intelligence warnings about possible attacks from the Libyans. We checked with the Fleet intell office and they say they don't know about any such warning. Can you explain that?"

"Admiral, I . . . I . . . I think I'd better take a pass on that question until I can consult with my lawyer." Schmidt hated the way his response sounded. If I were the Admiral, he thought, I would take that as an admission of guilt. But Schmidt could think of no other way to deflect the question.

The Admiral stared long and hard at Schmidt. There was a long silence. "Very well." Then the Admiral executed a right face, and marched out of cabin.

A shaken Bill Schmidt went to his secure phone to seek advice from the only person who could help him, his brother Jim.

After telling Jim about the line of questioning and the pressure he and the crew were under, Bill asked for permission to "read in" Admiral Arnold on what really transpired. "I'm telling you, Jim, this guy makes Al Gore look animated. His eyes bore in on you and you just want to plead guilty to every crime ever committed. Why can't I brief him on what really happened? He'd never leak it. Hell, you couldn't get the time of day out of him with a rubber hose."

Jim Schmidt felt awful for having put his younger brother in this kind of a dilemma. "Bill, as soon as they announced the Arnold investigation, I went to Wally Burnette and asked if we could tell the Admiral that you were acting under the President's orders."

"And?" Bill knew what the answer would be.

"And, he said no. Sorry. But our only hope of fooling the Libyans is to make this inquiry absolutely authentic. If Arnold appears less than his usual dogged self in going after you, it might blow the whole scenario."

Bill Schmidt rubbed his eyes and sank down in his seat. In a low voice he pleaded, "Well, can I at least tell the true story to my lawyer?"

It was the lowest that Jim Schmidt had ever heard his brother sound. "Sorry, bro'. But hang in there. This will all work out. We just need to buy some more time."

"Okay," Bill sighed. "But tell those guys to hurry up. I don't want my next call to you to be a request for a presidential pardon. *Churchill* out."

33

The poker group met again in the Sit Room to review the situation. Unmentioned but widely felt was a sinking feeling that a slippery slope had just turned into a gorge.

"I've gotta tell you I am awful uncomfortable not clueing in some of the other senior folks at the Pentagon," the Chairman of the Joint Chiefs offered. "The CNO and Secretary of the Navy aren't much interested in Admiral Arnold's investigation. They are ready to have young Commander Schmidt keelhauled today, 'for the good of the service,' you understand." The tension in the room was palpable. Even though the shoot down scenario had gone as planned, no one felt very good about the situation.

"Well, they have to get in line behind the Secretary of State," Wally Burnette added. "I understand he is calling every reporter he knows and on 'shallow background' telling them that Jim and Bill are actually twins who shared a womb and seventy-five IQ points between them."

The Secretary of Defense spoke up. "Shallow background? That's a new one on me."

"Yeah, that's where the Secretary of State pretends he is telling you something in confidence, but you and he know that you are going to reveal the information and your source to everyone you meet."

Burnette tried to get the meeting back on track. "Okay, let's go over where we stand. The first part of the plan went off as well as could be expected. The western world seems to be totally convinced that Commander Schmidt and friends screwed up big time and shot down some innocent civilians."

General Firman, head of the National Security Agency, added the perception as seen in Tripoli. "From our intercepts we can tell that the Libyans are confused. There seems to be a debate going on at the highest levels over whether we are inept and lucky or clever and devious. 'Inept and lucky' seem to be winning at the moment."

The National Security Advisor turned to the Director of Central Intelligence. "Fiona, what the hell is going on with the CIA? You haven't made a bit of progress in locating the CW in the United States. Or am I wrong?"

Director Nelson shifted uncomfortably in her chair. "Well, ah think we have made progress in pinnin' down places where the weapons aren't, but admittedly that leaves a lot of sites unchecked."

There was an uncomfortable silence. "What do you make of the latest call from Mustafa?" Secretary Stevens finally asked.

"It's not much hep. Mustafa seems ta be genuinely tryin' ta locate the stash. Tellin' us that it is in tanks isn't much hep."

The participants struggled to find some way to resolve the stalemate. General Sundin was always in favor of action. "What about another clandestine effort? Snatch someone who knows where the stuff is and 'encourage' them to talk?" Sundin asked.

"Leroy, we don't know who ta grab. Strong arm the wrong person and we run the risk of premature use of the weapons."

"What is the good of having all these spies you have on your payroll if you can't ever use them?" Sundin responded, adopting a refrain often heard around Washington. Ironically, it was a theme often used against the military as well. Civilian bureaucrats were usually more willing to commit troops to battle than were the admirals and generals.

"You sound like the fatheads at mah Senate confirmation hearing." Director Nelson reflected on several members of her oversight committee who could not understand why the CIA didn't have a mole inside the palace, bedroom, and mind of every tin pot dictator on the planet.

"All right, no hitting below the belt, Fiona." Burnette tried to restore order. "Lew, anything else you are picking up from the Libyans that might give us a lead on the stash? They have got to be saying something useful." All eyes turned to General Firman who had been trying to maintain a low profile in order to avoid the food fight at the other end of the table.

"No. But I can tell you that it appears that they have decided to score some publicity points over the shoot down." A slight smile creased Firman's normally taciturn visage. "Gadhafi has decided to crank up his PR machine and ask why the big bad bully Uncle Sam is picking on him again."

"Yeah, well that was to be expected," General Sundin snorted.

"This time he is pulling out all the stops. We picked up a call last night in which one of the colonel's top aides was trying to find the phone number for CNN. Apparently Gadhafi wants to go on 'Larry King Live.' "

Secretary Stevens turned to the National Security Advisor and asked a question that was on everyone's mind but which no one wanted to think about. "Wally, about forty-eight hours have passed since the shoot down. What is President Walsh going to do about congressional notification? Remember, whether we call this a covert action or a standard military engagement, the clock is running and he is going to have to tell Congress or break the law."

"That's a helluva note!" General Sundin thundered. "Lives, maybe thousands of lives, are at stake and we have to spill our guts to the World's Greatest Sievelike Body. Stupid, I tell ya, just stupid. I wouldn't trust those empty suits as far as I could throw 'em."

The color was rising in Secretary Stevens's face. "I would remind you, General, that until a few years ago, I was one of those 'empty suits' and so, I might add, was the Commander in Chief!"

Sundin was taken slightly aback. "Sorry, Cleve. I didn't mean you guys. But Jeez Louise, I can't say I trust everybody up on the Hill the way I trust you guys."

Burnette cleared his throat. "The President has come up with a plan on congressional notification. This afternoon he is getting on the phone and calling the Big Eight plus the Intelligence Oversight Chairmen and ranking members." The Big Eight referred to the Speaker of the House, the House Minority Leader, the Majority and Minority Leaders in the Senate, and the Chairman and ranking minority members of the Senate Armed Services Committee and House National Security Committee.

"Jesus H. Christ! He's not going to tell all those folks, is he? And not on the phone, for crying out loud," General Sundin pleaded.

Wally Burnette looked sternly at Sundin. "Well, yes and no." Sundin was clearly confused.

"The President is going to invite all those gents up to Camp David tonight. He is going to tell them that they are going to have a domestic budget summit and fly-fishing contest. Once he gets them up in the mountains he'll brief them on the *Churchill* scenario. He is going to pull the plug on all outgoing communications from the camp, just in case any of these folks can't resist sharing the news with someone else. It turns out that the Navy, who run the camp, even have the capability to jam outgoing cellular phone calls from the location. These Senators and Congressmen are going to be having communications withdrawal pains."

Ever the practical one, Jim Schmidt raised a logical question. "He can't keep them up there forever. What happens if we don't discover the weapons stash in a day or two?"

"We've got a plan for that, too," Burnette smiled. "We have drawn up a list of every pork barrel project scheduled for the States or districts of these members of Congress. The President is going to promise them that if the true story leaks, he will kill every one of those projects in each one of their districts. Since we never are able to identify the sources of leaks, the President is going to tell them that if the *Churchill* story leaks, he plans to punish all of them, in order to be sure to hurt the guilty party."

There was laughter around the table. "Brilliant!" Director Nelson shouted. "Each membah will pressure the others not ta leak. The stakes will be too high."

As if they weren't already high enough, Jim thought.

• • •

GADHAFI and his troops had no intention of limiting their public relations offensive to a single outlet. It was midday when Paul Harper got a call in his office at the *Washington Post*.

"Style. Harper."

A heavily accented voice responded. The quality of the phone line was bad—clearly, the call was not local. "Meester Harper, I am representative of the Popular Socialist Libyan Arab Jamahiriya. I try to reach Mees Sue O'Dell. Can you connect her with me?"

"Sue is back in Europe. Who'd you say you were again?"

"I call on behalf of Libyan peoples to offer Mees O'Dell opportunity to meeting weeth Revolutionary Leader, Colonel Moammar al-Gadhafi. Mees O'Dell could be interested, yes?"

"Yes, absolutely yes!"

Less than twenty-four hours later, Sue found herself en route to Tripoli. There was no easy way to get from Italy to Libya. There were no direct flights, thanks to the UN ban. The two best options were to fly to an airport on the island of Djerba in neighboring Tunisia and then endure a five-hour drive through the desert or take the course Sue chose, which was to fly to Malta and take a ferry to Tripoli.

Originally, Sue had planned to be in Naples to cover the Board of Inquiry into the shoot down. When the opportunity for a one-on-one interview with Gadhafi arose, however, her editors told her to drop everything and head for Libya.

It was clear to Sue why she had received this invitation. Obviously, they read the *Washington Post* in Libya, she thought. Gadhafi and friends must have liked the story she did on the *Winston Churchill*. That is a heck of a note, she mused, when a story you do is sharply criticized by the White House Press Secretary and applauded by the dictatorial leader of one of the world's most disreputable countries.

When the ferry landed, Sue was met by a man who identified himself as Jamal and said he represented the General People's Congress. She was led, without stopping, past the immigration and passport control and placed in the backseat of a shiny white Mercedes.

The car took Sue to the Marhaba Hotel in downtown Tripoli. Jamal took her directly to her room. There was no need to check in.

"Please stay here. You may freshen up from your journey and prepare for your interview. We shall return when it is time for you to meet with the Revolutionary Leader."

"When will that be?" she asked.

There was no answer. Jamal simply turned away, closing the door as he departed.

Sue looked around the room. Utilitarian, not plush, and her hosts had kindly left some reading material to help her prepare for her interview. Displayed on a desk at the foot of the bed was a copy of Gadhafi's thin *Green Book*, his manifesto of a few decades ago in which he had outlined his philosophy of a third way between capitalism and communism. Also at hand was a fact sheet on the Great Man-made River Project and a chronological list of incidents in which the western world, principally the United States, had been nasty to the Libyan Arab Jamahiriya. To round out the press kit was a sheaf of papers containing quotes lauding the "Revolutionary Leader." With a few exceptions, such as Louis Farrakhan, the authors of the quotes were unknown to Sue. Three of the quotes compared Gadhafi to the prophet Muhammed and two to Muhammed Ali. Nothing like an unbiased opinion, she thought. He's compared favorably to everybody but Ali MacGraw.

While she waited, Sue scanned the official biography of the revolutionary leader that had been provided by her hosts. She read of his Bedouin upbringing during which he reportedly learned to love nature. It was out in the desert where the idea for the Third Universal Theory came to the young Moammar.

Sue flipped through the *Green Book* and tried to get a sense of the man who wrote it. She didn't get far. She'd always found it impossible to take any writer seriously who used the word *dialectic*, and Gadhafi, or his ghost writer, was no exception.

By mid-afternoon Sue looked out her hotel room window and noticed the heavy traffic going by. A guidebook she brought with her explained that normal business hours in Libya were from 7:00 A.M. to 2:00 P.M. Some shops opened again from 4:30 to 8:30 P.M. Not much different than Spain, but a lot less fun, she mused.

Despite the lack of diversions, Sue was pleased to be there. Reporters at her level were not routinely invited to conduct one-on-one interviews with heads of state, particularly those who were so newsworthy. Some of the columnists at the *Post* who specialized in foreign policy might be accustomed to being summoned to see world leaders, but it was a new experience for Sue and one which she fully intended to enjoy.

By late afternoon Sue was getting hungry. She didn't want to leave her room and miss a call summoning her to see Gadhafi. A call to the front desk revealed that the concept of room service had not reached this part of the world. She lamented that she'd declined the little bag of peanuts on her flight to Malta. She supposed that the chances that there would be a minibar hidden somewhere in the room was slim in this Islamic paradise. Sue rarely drank hard liquor, but the enforced absence of it made her long for a gin and tonic.

It was well after 10:00 P.M. when a knock on her door broke up a dream about a sizzling steak with a bourbon marinade. Her escort, Jamal, had returned. "Are you enjoying your stay?" he asked.

"Yes, marvelous."

"Come with me, please."

"Where are we going? Are you taking me to dinner?

"I am taking you to see the Revolutionary Leader."

Sue grabbed her notebook and tape recorder as she dashed out the door.

Her guide led Sue swiftly through the hotel lobby and gestured to the rear door of another Mercedes, this one black. Jamal got into the front passenger seat. As soon as the doors slammed the driver pulled away.

Sue noticed that there were curtains on all the rear windows. Between the front and back seats was an opaque glass partition and curtains around the side and back windows.

Sue had read that vehicles like this one were common in the more fundamentalist Islamic states, so that women could be driven around without seeing or being seen by members of the opposite sex. But Libya, she knew, treated women differently. Gadhafi had made a big point about feminine emancipation. Thank goodness for that, she thought. Sue wouldn't have been able to stand it if this were one of the fundamentalist countries that required women to cover themselves head to toe. There were some lines she would not cross, no matter how great the story.

They didn't want her to know where Gadhafi lived, she reasoned. She supposed it beat having them throw her in the trunk, or put a bag over her head.

The Mercedes zigged and zagged through the congested Tripoli streets. The driver used the horn as often as the brakes and made countless turns. Finally Sue felt the car make a sharp left-hand turn and noticed that it seemed to be driving up a ramp. The sound of the Mercedes's engine was noticeably different, and then it died. She heard doors of cars in front and in back of her slam and guessed that her vehicle must have been in the middle of a motorcade.

Suddenly the right rear door opened. Jamal leaned in and gestured for Sue to get out. Looking rearward she could see that the motorcade had entered a covered archway that penetrated a stone building. In front was a ramp that appeared to lead to an open center court.

"Walk this way, please."

Sue followed Jamal and noticed that every few feet along the way armed guards eyed her closely. As she proceeded, Sue could see for the first time that she was in an uncovered central courtyard in the middle of a rectangular building. On one side of the enclosure was an antiaircraft gun. On the far side was a large Bedouin tent. Sue was led to the tent, which turned out to have a series of smaller tents within it. Standing just outside the entrance were two more heavily armed guards, pretty young women.

"Let me hold your notepad and recorder for a moment," Jamal offered.

"Oh, that's not . . ." Sue suddenly realized she was about to be searched. She placed the notepad in one of Jamal's hands and the tape recorder in the other, then she took her handbag and hung it over his right shoulder. Turning back to the armed women, she held out her arms as instructed and was given a very thorough patting down. She felt the wall of cold air just before she heard the whine of an air conditioner. Sue then retrieved her things and was led into the main tent, which was empty save for the center, containing nothing but large pillows scattered about the floor. The area was lit by large candles, which flickered dramatically.

Someone approached Sue carrying a large metal urn and asked if she would like a drink.

"Yes, very much so."

She was handed a small brass cup, big enough for only a thumbful of liquid. Skillfully manipulating the urn, the server aimed a short stream of dark liquid into the tiny receptacle. Jamal accepted the same offering and downed it with a quick tilt of his head.

Sue tried to copy the move and struggled mightily to avoid spitting out the fluid.

"Do you like our coffee?"

So that's what it was. Sue was relieved. For a moment she thought it might have been camel piss.

"It's quite different."

Jamal gestured for Sue to sit on one of the cushions, and followed suit. "Would you like something to eat before you meet with Brother Gadhafi?"

"Yes, that would be quite nice," Sue replied without thinking.

Jamal looked around and nodded. A young man arrived with a platter, in the center of which was shredded meat, lamb, Sue guessed, on a bed of lettuce. Ringing the platter were what appeared to be grapes. Circling the entire tray was a squadron of flies. Sue blanched. Some of them were big enough to be house pets.

There were no plates or utensils. Sue looked at Jamal, who nodded eagerly, so she reached towards the middle of the platter and grabbed a small handful of meat. Holding her breath, she quickly swallowed it. Jamal smiled and followed suit. That wasn't so bad. Sue smiled and grabbed a bigger clump of meat and downed it again. Jamal returned the smile and did the same. Emboldened, Sue grabbed one of the grapelike objects and popped it in her mouth as Jamal began to speak.

"Most westerners are put off by the sheep eyes. I am glad to see you enjoy this delicacy."

She would later claim that it was a triumph of her tough journalistic mind that she swallowed the eye whole; in fact, it went down accidentally, in mid-gasp.

Fortunately, Jamal was distracted by a minion who came up and whispered in his ear. As Sue struggled to gain her composure he stood and said reverentially, "The Revolutionary Leader is here."

She turned and saw two more armed guards, this time men, enter the tent. They looked around the area and then stepped aside. A second later, in strode Colonel Moammar Gadhafi himself.

He was wearing a flight suit, leather jacket, and sunglasses. This despite the fact that it was over ninety degrees outside and had been dark for two hours. Gadhafi had apparently decided to adopt the attire of a Libyan Airlines pilot. From her research, Sue knew that Gadhafi's choice of garb was entirely unpredictable. In quick succession he could appear dressed as a general, admiral, surgeon, or banker. This guy was a one-man version of The Village People, she thought.

Gadhafi paused for a moment at the entrance to the tent and appeared to look skyward. My God, he's posing, she thought.

The Revolutionary Leader sauntered over to where Sue was standing. When Jamal introduced her, he daintily held out his cupped hand, with the palm facing downward. Sue reached out but only managed a fingershake. Gadhafi's eyes lingered on her, looking her over appreciatively and unself-consciously. "Thank you for responding so quickly to my invitation," he said with a smile. "It is kind of you to come to hear the story of my people, people who have suffered greatly at the hands of your country." Gadhafi spoke in a low, sing-song voice, as if he were making a speech. It was the voice of someone who once knew English well but now rarely used it.

"I believe that you, like most Americans, do not wish us harm. If you only know the truth, you will speak it," Gadhafi continued. "You see, I have read your work and admire it." Quite an endorsement, Sue thought.

He gestured for Sue to sit on one of the cushions.

Sue pulled out her tape recorder. "Do you mind if I record

our interview, sir? It would help me ensure that I quote you accurately."

"Not at all. I see the press as being messengers between me and the world. You may record my words because I have many things to say."

To prove it, he started out by explaining the concept of the Jamahiriya, his state of the masses, governed by the populace through local councils. Then, without pausing for questions, perhaps sensing that Sue had none, he launched into a lecture about the role of women and the media in society. Sue had paged through enough of the *Green Book* at her hotel to know that he was expanding upon information from his Libyan best-seller.

An hour had passed and Gadhafi was driving home for the third time the importance of treating women equally, despite the fact that they became enfeebled on a monthly basis. Sue looked down at her tape recorder and silently cursed herself for bringing only one spare cassette. She wondered if he would notice if she reused the tape that she'd been using for the past hour? He hadn't yet said a thing worth reporting.

As she was starting up the second tape, Gadhafi abruptly changed subjects. "And why, you may ask, is a country as forward thinking as this one, so constantly abused by great powers such as the United States? I will tell you . . ." He proceeded with a rambling half hour recitation of perceived unprovoked transgressions by the United States.

Finally, Sue managed to get in a question. "That is all very interesting, sir, but I don't quite get why you think that the West is picking on your nation. What is the West's motivation?"

"This I will tell you, Sue O'Dell. The West, and particularly the American government know that I stand for the Third Way. Not for communism, not for capitalism, but for the people. America knows I am champion of the people. People such as our Palestinian brothers who must . . . I say must . . . have returned to them the homeland on the West Bank that was taken away by the Zionists. I will fight for this!"

At the end of his response, Gadhafi stood up and shouted:

"Why, why did the American Navy find it necessary to kill so many Libyan babies and their mothers? Why did they shoot at unarmed innocents? Why?"

"Sir, was the airplane full of women and children? I have never heard an accurate accounting of the death toll."

Gadhafi stiffened slightly. "Tragic, tragic," he muttered.

Sue decided to try another approach. "Sir, I was wondering, would it be possible for me to meet with the families of some of the victims? It would be helpful for me so that I might be able to describe the full impact of the tragedy."

Gadhafi pursed his lips and squinted at Sue. There was silence for what seemed to be a full minute. Finally he replied, "No. I will not permit the families to have their grief exploited. American journalists always must ask the families of victims how they feel about their loss. I will tell you. They feel as though their hearts have been ripped from their bodies. They feel as though a powerful giant has smashed their most prized possession. No, I will not subject these women and children to further heartbreak." So much for that angle, Sue thought.

The aggressive air-conditioning in the tent meant that Gadhafi had no need to remove his leather flight jacket. Sue, less well prepared, shivered on her cushion as she tried another question.

"Sir, do you hate Americans?"

"Hate? I do not hate. Do you know that I am a student of your history? Yes, it is true. Once your country, too, was a champion of the people. Once your Navy and Marines had a glorious history fighting for the liberation of enslaved peoples. Yes, I have studied this. Belleau Wood, Chateau Thierry, Pearl Harbor, Java Sea, Wake, Coral Sea, Midway, Savo Islands. And now? Now they add to this list the slaughter of innocent women and children. I do not hate. But for this they must be punished."

Gadhafi rambled on for another half hour and then abruptly rose and declared the interview over.

Sue shut off her tape recorder, collected her notes, and quickly followed Jamal to the waiting Mercedes.

"Jamal, there aren't any McDonald's drive-ins on our way back to the hotel, are there?"

He stared stonily back at her. "Was it good for you?"

"What? The sheep's eye?"

"No, the interview."

"Oh. I've never had one quite like it before."

34

"This is getting old," Brad Moseman said to no one in particular at dinner in the wardroom.

Attila nodded silently, preoccupied with a plate full of surf and turf. The ship's cooks were going out of their way to try to take the crew's minds off the fact that they were unable to go ashore.

"Yeah, I don't know how many times I can answer the same question." Debbie Smith was particularly annoyed since as a bridge watch stander during the incident she had little to tell Admiral Arnold's team about what happened that day. Being grilled repeatedly on the same question offended her sense of dignity. Didn't they believe her the first time?

"What did they ask you, Debbie?"

Attila offered a guess. "I'll bet it was, 'Hey, good-looking, how about a date.' "

The XO grimaced from the head of the table. Ever since the shoot down, the Captain had taken to having his meals in his cabin. "Not much chance of them asking that question, Mister Hahn. That would be a conflict of interest for the investigators."

"Ah, XO, that was a joke."

"I'll tell you what the joke is," Debbie Smith interjected. "It is the fact that they are holding this crew hostage while they drag this on and on."

"Right," Hahn said. "It is kinda cruel on the crew. They can see the lights of Naples, when the wind is right they can smell it, but they can't go ashore. Hey XO, why don't you ask Admiral Arnold to cut this ship a break and let the crew go on liberty before the formal hearing begins?"

"Yeah, weren't you telling us that when Arnold was a junior officer he served under your dad?" Lieutenant Smith asked.

The XO sat more erect in his chair. "Well, yes, I understand he does consider Father his role model."

"Isn't that a conflict of interest?" Debbie Smith asked. There were snickers around the wardroom table.

"I don't think the investigation is so horrible," Ensign Madison offered, always a few beats behind in any conversation.

"Why is that, Marshall?"

"Well, you get to meet a lot of important people. And another thing, it gave me a chance to leave some of my Bible tracts with them."

"You didn't swap them for their porno did you?" Hahn quickly asked. "I mean, if you did, no wonder they're so ornery."

"No, I didn't swap anything. But you know those big, square briefcases they carry around with them?"

The members of the wardroom looked around at one another, afraid of what would come next.

"Marshall, they call them litigation bags. They use them to keep their files and evidence in order," Brad Moseman explained.

"Yeah, well, when the investigators took a lunch break today they left their briefcases in the ship's office. So I just opened them up and put in some Bible study material in the files."

The XO looked as if he was going to have a coronary. "Did you put that stuff in every briefcase?"

"Oh no, sir, just the Admiral's."

•   •   •

THE XO reported immediately to Bill Schmidt that Marshall had been tampering with the evidence. Schmidt laughed until he cried.

"Well, that should convince the Admiral that we are all straight arrows around here."

"Captain, don't you think he might think that we were trying to get a peek at the documents he has been collecting?" Ellsworth asked.

"Nah. I doubt that even Admiral Arnold will think we're dumb enough to do that. I'll just call him and say that one of our officers' evangelistic instincts sometimes exceed his common sense. I need to talk to the Admiral anyway."

"What about, sir, if I may ask?"

"I'm going to make another pitch for the crew to get some liberty. They are starting to go stir crazy."

The XO pursed his lips. Bill could tell Ellsworth was getting up the gumption to say something dumb.

"I don't believe it's wise to let the crew go ashore, Captain. If there is another liberty incident while this investigation is ongoing . . . well, any chance we have for a fair hearing will go out the window. I know Admiral Arnold. He does not have much of a sense of humor."

Coming from Thomas Oliver Ellsworth III, that was quite an indictment, Bill thought. "No, the crew has been under too much pressure, XO. We need to see that they have an opportunity to get away from this ship for a few hours. You, too. You need some attitude adjustment. In fact, I am going to direct Attila to take you out on the town and show you some of the cultural attractions."

"Well, I, I, I . . . don't really think that . . . "

"Nope. No getting out of it. If I can convince the Admiral to let me grant some liberty, I want you on the first boat. We'll switch off. You go on liberty tonight and I'll stay aboard. Tomorrow I'll hit the beach and you can mind the store."

As it turned out, the Admiral was fairly understanding. Since his investigators were coming to the end of their work and the formal tribunal was about to begin, he granted Schmidt's request to allow a portion of the crew to go ashore. He was even understanding about

Ensign Madison's contributions to the investigation files. "Made good reading. I was wondering where that stuff came from."

The next morning Schmidt announced to the crew that two-thirds of them would be allowed to go ashore that afternoon. The rest would have an opportunity the next day. Morale brightened considerably throughout the ship, except for the XO, who was unhappy about being ordered to associate with a rough-hewn LDO like Lieutenant Hahn.

"Tom, this is nonnegotiable. I want you to hit the beach with Attila and don't come back until your attitude has been fully adjusted."

"Aye, aye, sir. But you know, I would much rather stay on board and rehearse my testimony."

Schmidt fought to avoid rolling his eyes. "This ain't the Lincoln Center, Tom. All you do is tell the investigators what you remember. In the meantime, I want you to go out with Attila and kill a few brain cells."

After the XO left Schmidt's cabin, the Captain called in Lieutenant Hahn and gave him his mission.

Hahn had a toothpick drooping from his mouth and a sad look on his face. "Cap'n, have I done somethin' to piss you off?"

"No, Attila, why?"

"Well if I haven't, why are you making me go on liberty with the XO? His idea of a wild time is straightening up the books at the base library."

Bill put both hands on Hahn's shoulders and gave him an understanding smile. Getting people to undertake tasks they find unappealing is a big part of leadership, Bill reflected. "Attila, the XO is wound tighter than a two-dollar watch. I need someone . . . I need you . . . to get his mind off the shoot down and himself. I swear, if Admiral Arnold's board asks him one tough question, he's liable to go postal on us."

"I don't think he would shoot anyone, Captain. But he might bore a few to death."

Schmidt smiled. "So, you're going to help him lighten up, right?"

"Okay, boss, I'll do it. But I want you to know that while I will shoot down civilian airliners with you, after tonight I'm drawing the line when it comes to baby-sitting bozos."

Ellsworth was late in meeting Hahn at the ship's brow. When the XO finally showed up he explained that he had lost track of time while inspecting the ship's laundry.

"How are the button crunchers holding up, XO?"

"Caught them skimping on the starch again. I was quite peeved. They act like they're paying for the stuff."

"Gee, I hate to drag you away from a major bust like that XO, but the boss has ordered me to show you a good time in Naples or not come back. God, I love a challenge."

The two officers boarded the first liberty launch. Hahn was wearing a blue chambray shirt and khaki trousers. Ellsworth wore plaid polyester pants, a striped long-sleeve shirt, and a liberal dose of some English Leather cologne, purchased in the early 1980s.

On the ride into port, the *Churchill*'s boat ran parallel for a while with a ferry that was returning from a day trip to the nearby isle of Capri. The tourists onboard seemed to be enjoying themselves immensely, waving and shouting at each passing craft. An elderly crewman aboard the ferry walked among the passengers with a large plastic trash bag, carefully collecting the beer and soda cans, sandwich wrappers, and empty cigarette packs. Ellsworth was about to remark on the care the ferry took in preserving cleanliness when he observed the crewman tie a knot in the plastic bag and fling it into the sea. The liberty boat's coxswain had to maneuver sharply to avoid the still-floating trash. The XO and Attila rode on in silence until the boat deposited them on the pier near where the rest of the Navy's ships were moored.

Hahn proceeded to lead the XO on a lengthy hike through the streets of Naples.

"Are you sure you know where you are going? It looks like we have passed many suitable places already."

"Relax, XO. I'm going to take you to the finest pizza restaurant in all of Naples."

"Pizza? I was looking forward to something somewhat . . . well, classier."

"Classy? The joints in this town don't get any classier than the one I am taking you to."

The two officers walked along the narrow, winding, ancient streets. Ellsworth noticed that all of the business establishments and most of the churches had big metal fences across their doors and windows.

"That's to cut down on the robbery," Attila observed.

"Who would rob a church?"

Before Hahn could respond, both officers heard a loud *beep, beep* behind them. They dove into a doorway barely eluding a Vespa that was bearing down on them.

"What kind of idiot would drive his motorbike down a sidewalk?" Ellsworth asked incredulously as he checked his clothing for smudges or wrinkles.

"Probably the same kind of guy who would rob a church," Hahn replied. "There are tons of 'em around here." The XO wasn't sure if Hahn meant Vespas, robbers, or churches.

Ellsworth was about to give up when Hahn finally led him into Antonio's, a local eating establishment known by generations of sailors and locals for its pasta and pizza. It was dark inside and it took a while for their eyes to adjust. They were shown to a table in the back of the restaurant. Attila ordered a bottle of Chianti and some bread while they perused the menu.

"I'm not normally much of a drinker, but when in Rome . . ." Ellsworth lifted his glass in a toast to his companion.

"Really? That surprises me. I would have thought that since you come from a long line of sea-going men, alcohol tolerance would be in your genes."

"Well yes, like Dad, I was once known for my hollow leg. But in recent years, I just haven't seen the point in imbibing." Ellsworth raised his glass and tossed back a healthy slug of wine.

The waiter assigned to their table seemed indifferent to the two officers. Gestures to lure him over to take their orders were ignored.

"Good thing we got this bread and wine when we arrived. We might starve waiting for Giuseppe here."

When the waiter finally came over and took their orders, the bottle of Chianti was practically empty.

"Bring us another one of these, pal, wouldja?" Hahn asked.

Ellsworth started to say something, then stopped.

The bottle arrived in moments, but not the food. The waiter explained that the kitchen was running behind because the restaurant was unusually crowded.

Closely surveying the trattoria for the first time, Ellsworth noticed a table full of sailors from *Winston Churchill*'s Deck Department. He pointed them out to Hahn. "I thought you told me this place had some class. Since when do Boatswains Mates patronize sush stablishments?"

Attila noted that the XO's speech was beginning to slur. "That's how you identify a class joint, XO. Boatswain Mates know the best eating spots in every port. If you go into any restaurant around the Med and don't see some deck ape . . . turn around, it ain't no good."

Hahn was not yet slurring his speech but his grammar had returned to its natural state and he began to use slang like *deck ape* to refer to Deck Department sailors.

"Well, I doan know." Ellsworth turned again to look at his shipmates and, for the first time, made eye contact with them.

"Hey look, it's the XO and Mister Hahn. Never thought I'd see the two of them out steaming together," one of the sailors told his group.

Moments later the waiter showed up at Ellsworth and Hahn's table. The officers were disappointed to see that their dinners had still not arrived. Instead the waiter presented a third bottle of wine.

"Compliments of the . . . gentlemen . . . at the table across the room."

"Nah, we can't ashshept any thin' like that . . ." Ellsworth said raising both hands.

"We've gotta, Tom." Hahn used the XO's first name for the first time. "We can't insult them. That would be bad form. It would be against protocol."

"Well, can't be agains' protocol, I guess."

The two officers sped up their work on bottle number two so

they could begin to make a dent in number three. By the time their dinners came, both were well and truly sloshed.

Most of the evening they had managed to avoid discussion about their work and the cloud hanging over their ship. But no matter what subject Hahn brought up—motor racing, computers, baseball, family—Ellsworth seemed disinterested and surly. Finally, Hahn could take no more.

"Wass amatter with you, XO? How come you is always in such a piss-poor mood, huh?"

Ellsworth looked around the room and leaned well forward. His chin almost touched the table. "How can I not be mad after what he did to me?" he hissed.

"He who?"

"He the captain he."

"Whad he do to you?"

"This whole shoot down thing. Doan he know that I am about to be up for promoshun for commander? What's this gonna do to my chances?"

Through his alcohol-induced haze Hahn sighed. "Ah, you must have a strong record. They'll probably promote you anyway. Besides, this investiga-shun is gonna go on forever. The board is only 'sposed to consider what is in your record. None of this has been documented yet."

Sitting straight up, Ellsworth pounded the table with both fists. "No, no, no. My faffer was on plenty of boards. He tole me that everyone has a strong record. Everyone is a water walker. On paper everone iss purfeck. The board looks for little things to give them an excuse *not* to vote for somebody. This Libyan thing will give 'em more 'n enuf reason."

Hahn placed his head in his hands, partially as a result of the wine and partially as a result of the whine. It was Attila's turn to lean far forward. In a voice intended to be a whisper he said, "Look, you dumb sumbitch. The Captain, he dint do nothin' wrong. He did jus' what they wanted him to. Someday everybody'll know."

Ellsworth squinted at his dinner companion in a vain attempt to understand the last remark. The XO opened his mouth several times as if to speak, but then slowly closed it.

"Wha, whadya talkin' about?"

For a second time Hahn placed his head in his hands. After a long pause, he lifted his eyes toward Ellsworth. "Lookit. Do ya rememmer when the Cap'n's brother came aboard off Italy. Whaddya think that was all about? A soshal call?"

The XO tried without luck to make some sense of what Hahn was saying. "Well, I figgered it was jus' the Cap'n breakin' rules as always."

"Nah, hiss brother come out to tell him that we needed to shoot down a Libyan airliner and make it look like an assident."

Ellsworth's eyes widened and his jaw dropped. He considered Hahn's story for a few moments. "Why would we wanna do that?"

Hahn was beginning to get frustrated. "'Cause it was full of chemical weapons!" he practically shouted. Catching himself, Attila lowered his voice to a whisper. "Why do you think the Cap'n set Circle William right after we shot the plane down?"

From the look on Ellsworth's face it was clear that he was beginning to believe Hahn.

"Yeah, well, but we shot them down, so how come we doan just announce what we did now. We'd be heroes, not under investigashun."

By this point, Hahn's conscience was bothering him. The Captain told him to not come back until the XO's morale improved. But he never should have tried to lift Ellsworth's spirits by letting him in on the secret. Attila made a fist and pounded himself on the forehead.

"Well, how do you 'splain that?" the XO continued to press.

"Look. I shunta tole you what I did. XO, do me a favor. Jus forgetaboutit." For the first time that evening a broad smile came across Ellsworth's face. He told Hahn to call him Tom and he ordered another bottle of wine before picking up the check. The two stumbled back to the *Churchill* like two old shipmates.

35

Ellsworth woke up with the worst hangover of his life, which wasn't hard, because despite what he had told Hahn the night before, it was his first. Still, he managed a weak smile as he shaved. There may be some hope for my career yet, he mused. They can't pass over the XO of a ship that successfully carried out secret missions for the good of the country.

After concocting a reason to check on something ashore, Ellsworth had the ship's boat take him to the beach. Once there, he caught a taxi to the Navy Exchange, a shopping complex at the Naval Support Activity, which was what the Navy called its base in Naples. Between a minimart and a video rental shop was a building that contained a bank of telephones to meet the needs of visiting ships' crews.

Using the calling card his mother gave him before the deployment, Ellsworth reached information and asked for the number for the *Washington Post*. It took a couple of transfers to reach the Style section editor.

"Style, Harper."

"Yes, I urgently need to contact Ms. Sue O'Dell. Can you tell me where to find her?"

Harper noticed that the phone connection was weak. He looked at the caller ID function on his telephone and saw that the number was unavailable.

"She is on assignment in Italy. Who is calling, please?"

"I know she is on assignment and I don't want to give my name. But I have some vital information about the downing of the Libyan aircraft. Do you think she wants it, or should I simply call the *New York Times?*"

"Easy fella, you really know how to hurt a guy, don't you? Look, I just can't give out the number where Sue O'Dell is. Why don't you give me a number where she can get back to you?"

"No can do. I need to talk to her now."

Harper noticed that the caller's voice was somewhat muffled and wondered if this clown was using a handkerchief over the mouthpiece. Still, there was something about the call that made him think it might be worth pursuing.

"Okay, tell you what. Let me try to reach her on the other line. No telling where she is right now. But if I can find her I can conference the calls together and put you on the line, okay?"

"Yes, but be quick about it."

Harper knew that Sue was operating out of the oddly named Hotel Jolly in Naples. He swiftly dialed the number and was relieved when she answered the room phone on the first ring.

"Sue O'Dell."

"What are you doing in your room? You should be out covering this story!"

"Paul, is that you? I . . ."

"Never mind. I have some guy calling for you. Won't give his name. Says he has some hot information on the Libyan thing. Probably a crackpot, but ya never know. I'm going to connect his call to you, just in case. Are you ready?

"Let me get a pad and pen. Okay, go ahead."

After punching a few buttons the lines were connected.

"Hey buddy, can you hear me?"

"Yes, yes I can."

"Sue, how about you?"

"Loud and clear."

"You've been hanging with those Navy guys too much, Sue."

"Okay, Bud, you're talking to Sue, whadya got?"

"I am calling to tell you that the downing of the Libyan aircraft was no accident."

"What do you mean?"

"I mean that w . . . they shot it down on purpose."

"Who am I talking to please?"

"I can't tell you. It isn't safe."

Uh, oh, Sue thought, another one of these conspiracy nuts. Wonder if this is Pierre Salinger on the line.

"Okay, why would the ship intentionally shoot down a passenger jet?"

"Because it was carrying chemical weapons."

"All right, if I accept that, why wouldn't the U.S. government announce what the ship had done? If the plane was carrying chemical weapons, as you say, why not admit shooting it down and take credit for it?"

There was a long pause. This guy is a nut, Sue thought. He doesn't even have a plausible story.

"I can't tell you exactly why it is such a big secret. I don't know. But I can tell you who ordered the shoot down."

Here it comes, she thought. Elvis, I'll bet. "And who is that, sir?"

"Jim Schmidt, the President's spokesman. He flew out to the *Winston Churchill* when the President was in Rome for that summit meeting. Schmidt flew out all alone and told his brother about the plan. Next thing you know . . . *boom* . . . we, err, they shoot down this Libyan."

"Do you have any proof about this, sir?" There was a long pause. "Sir?"

"Ah, well, you're the reporter. Go check it out. But I'm telling you that it's true. You need to write something about this real soon."

"We aren't going to print anything until we can confirm it. Don't you have anything else to offer as confirmation?"

"Isn't that enough?"

There was exasperation in Sue's voice. "It's not very damn

much. If you get any additional proof, leave a message for me at the Hotel Jolly in Naples."

The caller snorted. "Look, blondie, just do your job, okay?" And then he hung up.

"You still on the line, Paul?"

"Yeah."

"What do you think?"

"He's a nut case."

"Yeah, probably." She paused. "Hey Paul, how did he know I was blonde?"

"I dunno. You kind of sound like one on the phone."

After cursing Harper, Sue agreed that they both would do some rudimentary checks on the anonymous caller's story. Harper was back on the line with her about an hour later.

"Hey Sue, you aren't going to believe this. I checked with our White House correspondents. They said that Jim Schmidt disappeared for about twenty-four hours during the Rome Summit. Said he had the flu. It was May seventh."

"Yeah, well listen to this. I called a friend who works at Fumicino Airport in Rome and asked about unusual military traffic during the Rome summit. Naturally there were lots of transport aircraft coming in from the States with presidential support. But when he was going over his log he found another entry. A helicopter from USS *Winston Churchill* flew in, departed, and returned about three hours later."

"Hmmm. Very interesting."

"Yeah, and Paul?"

"Yes."

"The log showed that this happened on May seventh."

The caller was right, Sue knew. It was time for her to do her job. She needed to confront Bill Schmidt and ask him point blank about this bizarre claim. But how could she get to him? The Navy had seen to it that the *Winston Churchill* was anchored in Naples harbor. Security boats circled the destroyer at all hours of the day and night. The gambit she used when they first met in Cannes, hiring a boat to take her out to the ship, would not work this time.

Sitting down at the desk in her room, Sue pulled out some Hotel Jolly stationery and penned a note to Bill Schmidt. That was the easy part.

She left her hotel and took a cab to the waterfront. Once there, she wandered back and forth, keeping her eyes peeled for sailors. Whenever she saw a group of them, she would quickly walk over and silently inspect their uniforms.

I'll be lucky if I don't get arrested or assaulted doing this, she thought.

The Navy helpfully required that a name badge be sewn on the shoulders of their white uniforms, identifying the command to which a sailor was assigned, and Navy men and women wearing their blue dungaree working uniforms wore baseball caps with their command's name and crest embroidered above the bill.

Sue first sidled up to a sailor who turned out to be from USS *George Washington*. Then another from USS *Barry*. Three more from the *George Washington* followed. With over 5,000 people aboard, there would be lots around.

She ran up to another sailor and eyed the tab on his shoulder. Damn, she thought, another guy from the *Barry*.

The sailor gave her the once over in return. "Hey babe, what's happening?"

"Ah, sorry, I mistook you for someone else."

"Well listen, if you don't find him, give me a call, will ya?"

Don't hold your breath, Romeo. She was beginning to despair of finding someone who could help her when she saw a short, stocky sailor in his blue dungarees uniform walking toward the pier with his head down.

"What the hell, might as well check him out." Sue ran to catch up with him and checked his hat. "USS *Winston Churchill*." Bingo! Sue looked at the sailor's shirt. Stenciled above the breast pocket was MADERIAS, J. M.

"Excuse me, ah, Mr. Maderias. Could I talk to you for a moment?"

Maderias stopped and looked up at the pretty blonde woman. He smiled. "Any time."

"I'm trying to get a message to my friend, Bill Schmidt. Do you know him?"

Maderias guffawed. "Know him? He's just the best damn destroyer driver in the fleet. Yeah, I know him."

"Well, I need to get a message to him, but the Navy seems to be keeping the ship out of touch. Can you help me?"

Maderias thought back to his failed attempts to arrange a date for his captain. "You say you are a friend of his?"

"Yes. And I wrote this note. I would be ever so grateful if you could help me get it to Bill." Sue reached in her handbag and pulled out the note. When she had signed and sealed it she put a drop of perfume on the envelope. It seemed kind of silly at the time, but as she handed it to Maderias, she could see that tactic made an impression on the sailor.

"Yes, ma'am. I'm heading out to *Winnie* now. I'd be happy to see that—Bill—gets it." Reaching out to take the note Maderias gave the envelope a quick sniff. "Does your note tell him how to contact you?"

"It sure does. Thanks so very much." Sue reached out and gave Maderias a hug, and flashed him a big smile.

Maderias headed off to where the ship's boat was tied up, thinking that if the Captain didn't follow up on this one he was crazy for sure.

Arriving aboard the ship, Maderias headed directly for the Captain's in-port cabin and knocked loudly on the door.

"Enter! Oh hey, Boats. What's up?" Schmidt knew that Maderias was not on watch, so it was a little unusual for him to be knocking on his captain's door. God, I hope he hasn't gotten himself into any more trouble, he thought.

But then Schmidt noticed that Maderias had an ear-to-ear grin, a just-won-the-lottery look on his face.

"Captain, remember when me and the guys tried to fix you up with a date in Cannes?"

"I've been trying to forget. Why?"

"Well, I am about to make things up to you. Seems like a date just found you. Pretty little thing, too. If I might say so, sir."

"What are you talking about, Boats?"

Maderias reached behind his back and pulled the note out of the waistband of his pants. He hadn't wanted to wrinkle it. Handing the note over to his captain, Maderias gave an impish smile and departed.

Bill opened the envelope and pulled out the note. Am I crazy, he asked himself, or is this thing perfumed? He began to read:

Dear Bill,

I desperately hope that this note reaches you. It seems that although you are here in Naples, the powers that be are keeping you out of sight. There doesn't seem to be any way to contact you directly—I'd much prefer to ask you face-to-face. But since I can't, I have had to resort to this written communication.

I'll get right to the point. I need your help. Someone has contacted me with a wild story. They say that you intentionally shot down that Libyan airliner. This source told me that you were on secret orders from the White House to knock down the plane because it was carrying chemical weapons.

It sounds crazy to me but my editors are pressing me to write the story. What gives it credibility is that the tipster said that your brother delivered the shoot down orders himself when the President was in Rome. As it turns out, Jim did disappear for a day or so and there are records of your helicopter making a couple of trips to the Rome airport on the same day. And there is more.

So you see, Bill, someone who believes in grand conspiracies might put some credence in this tale. My editors won't let up on me. Only you can help me.

I hope you weren't too distressed by the first story I did on the *Winston Churchill*. When I was in Washington last week, I met with your brother, Jim. He convinced me that I may not have been very fair with you. I want an opportunity to do right by you this time.

Won't you please help me? I don't want to rush into print with half the facts. Please help.

The letter included her room number and phone number at the Hotel Jolly and was simply signed, "Sue."

36

Bill read the letter over four times. He knew that the right thing to do was to call his brother Jim, but for some reason he resisted.

It sure sounds like she regrets screwing us the last time, Bill thought. I think I really did get through to her before. It was probably those left-wing editors in Washington who turned her story into a hatchet job.

Schmidt found himself thinking about their last meeting. He wanted another chance to win her over. I should call Jim, he thought, but he'll probably just try to talk me out of seeing Sue. We really need to find out more about what she knows. Damn! Who is behind this leak?

He sighed, picked up his STU-III, and dialed his brother's now-familiar number. After reaching the White House and making the connection secure, Bill broke the news to Jim that someone had shared the nation's biggest secret with the *Washington Post*. Jim also tried to fathom who might have leaked the story. "Frankly, I'm not surprised that it leaked, but I expected it to come out of Washington."

"How do you know that it wasn't from someone inside the Beltway?" Bill asked. He was feeling a bit defensive.

"Just a guess, little brother. But if you were in Washington and wanted to leak this story, you wouldn't call a reporter in Italy to do it. No need to invest in an international call if you are here. Everyone in D.C. knows the *Post*'s phone number."

"I guess you're right. What do we do now?"

There was a pause, so long that Bill felt as if he had lost his connection. "I could have the President call Donnie Graham at the *Post*, I suppose. He could give him all the details and then appeal to his sense of humanity to sit on the story."

"Do you think they would agree not to print it?" Bill asked.

"They might. They have acted responsibly before. Once or twice."

Bill's laughter sounded eerie over the scrambled phone line.

"But what concerns me," Jim continued, "is that whoever is peddling this story might try to leak it elsewhere if the *Post* doesn't bite. I really wish we had a better idea who Sue's source was."

"Well, why don't I go to see her and ask?" Bill offered.

"It doesn't work that way, little brother," Jim laughed. "She is a professional and would never tell you. Still, you might be able to pick up some information which might give us a clue about who we are up against."

"Yeah, you know, in her letter to me she makes the allegation and then says 'and there is more.' I think I better go find out what the 'more' means."

"Well, okay, but remember, *you* are going to get information out of *her*, not the other way around."

"Gotcha, bro. Trust me. She'll get only name, rank, and serial number from me."

Jim snorted. "Yeah, right. You forget, little brother. I've seen her."

BILL SCHMIDT called the Command Duty Officer to tell him that he would be going ashore a little early and to leave instructions concerning the ship's routine while at the anchorage. He changed into civilian clothes, breaking out his civilian sports coat for the first time during the deployment. Schmidt eschewed his standard lace-up shiny shoes for an expensive pair of loafers he had purchased at the BX just before leaving the States.

After splashing on some aftershave, he bounded down to the quarterdeck and had the ship's boat take him ashore. During the ride in to the pier, he found himself brooding again on how word of the shoot down scheme could have gotten out. He had to believe it was a leak in Washington, despite what Jim had said.

Once ashore, Bill grabbed a cab and ordered the driver to take him to the Hotel Jolly. The driver seemed to wind through every street in Naples before pulling up to the hotel, only a mile or two from the pier. Schmidt knew he was being conned but had neither the time nor the inclination to argue. He thrust a ten-thousand lira note into the cabbie's hands, jumped out of the taxi, and ran up the hotel steps.

He pulled the letter from his back pocket to recheck the room number—314. Taking the stairs to the third floor, he found the room and knocked on the door.

A familiar voice came from within. "Hello, room service? Please leave the tray outside my door. I just got out of the shower."

Hmmm, Bill thought. Is this a sailor's dream or what? He said nothing and knocked again.

"Just leave it, I said!"

Bill waited a moment and then knocked for a third time.

The door opened a crack. The security chain was still on.

"I said leave it . . . oh! It's you! I was expecting room service. I, I thought you would call."

"Just part of our media outreach program. I like to respond to press queries in person."

"Please, come in." Sue removed the security chain and opened the door.

Bill walked tentatively into the room. Sue was wearing a thick white terry cloth robe and had a towel wrapped around her head.

Sue had the hotel radio tuned to the Armed Forces Network. Schmidt recognized the song, a 1972 hit by the Cornelius Brothers & Sister Rose, "Too Late to Turn Back Now."

"Forgive me. I, I wasn't expecting company," Sue stammered.

"Not a problem. My last girlfriend had an outfit just like that."

He was surprised to see Sue blush. He hadn't imagined that a reporter for the *Washington Post* was capable of such a display.

Sue motioned him over to a chair near the window. Bill was impressed with the room. "Wow, looks like the *Post* sprang for a suite."

"Yeah, well, they owe me one. You should have seen the dive I had to stay in last week in Tripoli."

"Tripoli? Like the one in Libya? What were you doing there?"

"That's a story for another time. But now I have some questions for you."

Sue laid out the entire story of the anonymous caller and his tip about the shoot down, repeatedly emphasizing the amount of pressure her editors were putting on her to produce a story. Her eyes locked onto Bill's.

"Who do you think your caller was?" he asked.

"I haven't a clue. But if I did, I couldn't tell you. It wouldn't be, well, ethical," she said. "But you shouldn't be asking me questions. I need to ask them of you. You won't believe the way my editors are hounding me to write this story." As she spoke, Sue reached out and touched Bill's arm. "But I learned my lesson the last time. There is always more to the story than meets the eye. I don't want to write anything that will be unfair to you and your crew." She gave Bill a warm smile.

"Then don't write anything," he said sternly. Bill's comments were immediately followed by a knock at the door. This time is was room service with a small pizza and good bottle of local wine. They shared both.

When the waiter left, Sue replied. "It's not as simple as just not writing. I've got to know the truth. Did your brother fly out to the ship? Did he give you some secret orders? And did you intentionally shoot down that plane?"

Bill took another sip of wine as he contemplated his response. "I don't think I should comment on any of that." He reminded himself of his promise to Jim: name, rank, and serial number only.

Reaching out again, Sue touched him and gave a sad smile. "Don't you see? My editors would be happy to go with that. We could write the allegations and say that you refused to deny them. Come on, Bill, please. I want to understand."

How did I get myself into this mess? Bill asked himself. "What kind of business are you in? Are you comfortable writing allegations about stuff you don't understand and letting the chips fall where they may?"

Sue looked at him and shook her head slowly. "Believe it or not, I often wonder what kind of business I *am* in. I'm uncomfortable about things we do all the time. But you have to understand. I can only be as good as the information I have. Someone, I don't know who, has dropped this bombshell in my lap. You refuse to help me in any way. What in God's name am I supposed to do?"

Bill sighed and tried to think of a way out. "What if I told you the truth . . . off the record. If I convince you, you don't write anything. If I don't . . . well, you do what you must, but you only go as far as to write that Navy officials refused to deny your story?"

Sue, who was sitting at the edge of a small sofa, leaned forward and grabbed both of Bill's hands. "I am not supposed to enter into that kind of agreement without the approval of my bosses."

Bill was momentarily taken aback. He assumed that reporters entered into the kind of pact he proposed all the time. "Well, I am not supposed to tell you anything without the approval of *my* bosses. And I can pretty much assure you that they would not approve." Sue looked him in the eye and nodded slowly. "But I am willing to go out on a limb and tell you what you want to know, off the record, and take a chance that I can convince you that it is important to keep that information under wraps for now. Are you willing to take a chance with me?"

Sue took a deep breath and replied. "It's a deal. And Bill?"

"Yeah?"

"You *can* trust me. Honest."

Schmidt began to talk, and the holes in Sue's story were soon filled in.

Sue's eyes grew wide. Bill wondered whether she was amazed by the plan or simply thinking about the size of her scoop. There was a brief silence.

"Here is what I don't get, Bill. Why was it necessary then, or now for that matter, to make it look like an accident? Why not take out the aircraft and let the world know what you did? No rational person would have a problem with that kind of preemptive action."

Schmidt took a deep breath and thought about how to continue. Sue reached out once again and touched his hand. This time he grasped hers and looked directly in her eyes, seeking strength and reassurance for what he was about to tell her.

"The reason it had to be a secret is because we didn't want the Libyans to know that we were on to them." Bill paused and slowly exhaled. "We didn't want to reveal that we knew they had smuggled a bunch of chemical weapons into the United States."

Sue's eyes widened. "The United States? Where?"

"That's the point. We don't know where. I guess the CIA, FBI, FEMA—whoever—are desperately trying to find the stuff. But if you write your story, Gadhafi will know that the jig is up and he might . . . he just might set the stuff off. Could you live with yourself if he did that?"

Bill watched her eyes for a sign. Now it was Sue's turn to tighten her grip for strength. Slowly she shook her head, no. A soft "Jesus H. Christ" was the only comment she could muster.

"Sue, I have trouble believing that even the Libyans are crazy enough to set off some chemical weapons in a populated area. But how can we take the chance?"

"I don't."

"You don't what?"

"I don't have a problem seeing the Libyans doing it. Remember I mentioned my recent visit to Tripoli?"

"Yeah?"

"Well, I met with Gadhafi." Sue proceeded to tell Bill all about her visit with the Revolutionary Leader. The story cascaded from her lips. She had been dying to tell someone all the details of her bizarre encounter. "It was surreal," she said. "I swear the man appeared to be wearing makeup. And he kept talking about his place in history." Bill smiled at Sue's description of the air-conditioned tent, and chuckled on hearing about the sheep's eye treat.

It occurred to Bill that Sue's visit to Gadhafi would be of great interest to the spooks. He was savvy enough to know that no self-respecting reporter would provide a report to the intelligence community, but if she kept talking to him, perhaps she would mention something he could relay to the analysts that might prove useful.

"It must have been fascinating!" he said. "Did Gadhafi say anything interesting, or was he mostly posturing?"

Sue appeared delighted to be able to relive the visit. "Bill, you wouldn't believe the rambling dissertation he gave me. His comments were elliptical, illogical . . . hell, they were all over the lot."

"Were there any hints about doing anything to the United States?"

"I don't think so," she said slowly. "In fact, he said he was once an admirer of the U.S. military, and a student of our history. I've got my tape recording of the interview here. Do you want to listen to it? If you have nothing better to do for the next few hours."

"Would I?" Bill said. "I'd love to hear how he sounded. You know, Gadhafi's actions have influenced how the U.S. Navy has operated in the Mediterranean since before I was a plebe. As a result, he has always been demonized. I'd love to stay with you—and hear how you handled him."

Sue was delighted to have the company. She ordered another pizza and bottle of wine from room service, started the tape, and excused herself to go get dressed.

By the time she returned wearing jeans and a sweater and with freshly blow-dried hair, Bill had reached the part of the tape where Gadhafi was reciting from the *Green Book*. Shortly thereafter, the room service order arrived and Bill temporarily stopped the tape.

After pouring the two of them more wine, Schmidt started up the tape again. Bill kept telling himself that he had to try to remember as much of the interview as possible so that he could provide a briefing to the Fleet Intelligence officers.

As they were draining the bottle, he reached the point in the recording where Gadhafi was expounding on his interest in U.S. military history.

The audio quality was grainy but audible. Schmidt heard Gadhafi say: "Once your Navy and Marines had a glorious history fighting for the liberation of enslaved peoples. Yes, I have studied this.

Belleau Wood, Chateau Thierry, Pearl Harbor, Java Sea, Wake, Coral Sea, Midway, Savo Islands. And now? Now they add to this list the slaughter of innocent women and children . . ."

A puzzled look crossed Bill's face. He reached out and stopped the tape, then rewound it a bit.

"Is something wrong?" Sue asked.

"I just want to hear that part again."

"Belleau Wood, Chateau Thierry, Pearl Harbor, Java Sea, Wake, Coral Sea, Midway, Savo Islands. And now? Now they add to this list the slaughter of innocent women and children . . ."

"There's something about that list."

"What?"

Bill played the tape again. And again.

He closed his eyes and struggled to remember. No luck. Then he closed his eyes and let his mind drift. There was something so very familiar about "Belleau Wood, Chateau Thierry, Pearl Harbor, Java Sea, Wake, Coral Sea, Midway, Savo Islands."

After listening to the remainder of the interview, Bill and Sue returned to discussing why the explanation for the actions of USS *Churchill* needed to remain secret. "Let me ask your assessment," he said. "Did Gadhafi strike you as the kind of person who could order a chemical weapons attack on innocent civilians?"

Sue paused. "I don't know if I am qualified to answer that. I mean, what kind of person would do that? It is hard to believe that anyone could order something like that, and yet . . ." Her words trailed off.

"The intelligence reports tell us that he has ordered the use of chemical weapons before," Bill said. "He did so in Chad, for instance. So I guess a better question would be, do you think he is mad enough at the United States to conduct an attack on us there? Or could he simply be . . . mad?"

Bill noticed for the first time that Sue's hands were trembling. She nervously picked at her cuticles. "I, I, I just can't say. He might. He might. I can't be sure."

This time Bill reached out and steadied her trembling hands. "If you can't say for sure that he isn't planning that kind of operation, I don't see how a reasonable person would be willing to write a story about what my ship did and run the risk of triggering a chemical attack in the U.S." Sue nodded slowly in agreement.

Bill looked at his watch. "Sue, one last question. Was there anything, anything at all in your interview, that might give you a sense of where Gadhafi might choose to attack—assuming that was his plan?"

"No. I don't remember anything that would provide that kind of hint. But you heard the tape. What do you think?"

Bill stared out Sue's hotel room window into the Neapolitan darkness. "No. No, I have no idea."

He reluctantly decided that he had to return to his ship. The liberty boats stopped running at midnight. Given the scrutiny that *Winston Churchill* was under, now was not the time to spend a night away from the ship, no matter how alluring the prospect might be.

"Sue, I'd like to stay with you. To hear more about your trip to Libya, I mean," he quickly stammered. "But I gave the crew Cinderella liberty: they turn into pumpkins if they aren't back by midnight. I can't very well have a different rule for myself."

Sue gave him a look of genuine disappointment. "But we have to think this through. You can't go until we've solved it."

"There are a bunch of people who are a whole lot smarter than me working on it," Schmidt said sadly. "If they haven't figured it out yet, I don't suppose I'm likely to tonight."

Sue sighed. "What am I going to do?"

"Do? Nothing I hope. I mean, I trust you, Sue. I've shared with you the biggest secret I've ever known. But please, promise me that you won't tell your editors or anyone else. If word of this gets out, it could be catastrophic."

"Bill, I have to tell my editors. If they learn that I've withheld something this important from them, they'd kill me."

"Yeah? Well, what if you tell them and they run the story, or tip off Gadhafi by checking it out? There will be a lot more people killed than just one gorgeous reporter."

"Gorgeous?"

"Ah, sorry. The Navy keeps sending me to these remedial sensitivity training courses, but they don't seem to work."

"No apology necessary. I like a slow learner."

Schmidt quickly changed the subject and suggested that Sue hold off doing anything for another couple of days. "Give us that long to sort things out. I promise you can have exclusive access to me, for an interview I mean, once I am free to talk."

Sue reached out and grabbed Bill's hands. "Well . . . okay. But call me. . . . No, visit me tomorrow, all right?"

"Deal." Bill pulled her toward him to give her a hug and a chaste kiss on the cheek. Coward, he thought to himself. She felt so soft, so warm. He could have done a lot better than that.

On the boat ride back to the ship, as Bill tried to analyze what he'd heard on the Gadhafi tape, he found it strangely hard to focus on the subject at hand.

37

Jim retreated to his office to recover from another brutal press briefing. The press corps seemed to delight even more than usual in toying with him that day.

Alice Kenworthy had set the tone. "Would it be fair to say that the administration's Middle East policy is adrift?" she asked.

"No, that would be totally erroneous," Jim confidently replied.

"Well, that's what the Secretary of State was overheard saying at a dinner party last evening. It seems he thinks that his counsel is not being followed by the President and senior White House advisors." The other members of the press corps laughed and held their pens at the ready, sensing that Jim was facing another opportunity to make news.

"I wasn't eavesdropping on Secretary Harden last night. But I would guess that if he said anything like that, his comments were probably taken out of context. You'll have to ask him what he said and what he meant. As for the administration, we are pursuing a sound and reasoned approach regarding the Middle East. The President values and often implements the advice of our friends at Foggy Bottom."

Several reporters sighed with disappointment, hoping for another "windbag" moment.

Sensing danger in this line of discussion, Jim looked to the back of the briefing room and called on Amy Wainright, a reporter who represented a financial newsletter. She could always be counted on to change the subject.

"Do you know the OMB position on the CBO scoring of the Omnibus Reconciliation Bill?"

"No, but if you hum a few bars, I'll fake it."

The remainder of the press corps groaned. But the ploy worked: Jim could sense the room's interest in the Secretary of State's after-dinner remarks wane.

Back in his office a half hour later, Jim shook his head and marveled that he had escaped relatively unscathed. It was hard keeping focused when you knew there was a bat shit Bedouin who might be planning to gas a large American city.

HE WAS leaning back in his chair and listening to a tape of the Four Tops singing "Shake Me, Wake Me When It's Over" when Natalie knocked on the door and bustled in.

"Here is your call sheet. A lot of folks following up on that Secretary Harden story. And it's about time for the poker group meeting."

Shoulders slumping, Jim looked at the list. "I'll bet the old windbag said exactly what Alice quoted. Give him a few glasses of wine with dinner and you get a couple of hours of *whine* with dessert."

He trundled downstairs to the Sit Room to meet with the now-familiar group. As always, General Burnette kicked off the meeting.

"Look, lady and gents, the President is getting pretty unhappy with the lot of us. He wants to know why we can't find those chemical weapons and what we are going to do about Tarhouna."

Everyone present looked down at their notepads; no one made eye contact with the national security advisor.

"We can't keep this charade up forever. Sooner or later this is going to leak or worse yet, Gadhafi is going to figure out that we are on to him and decide he might as well set off his weapons and go out with a bang. Now, has anybody got anything for me to take back to the President that won't get my tail feathers singed . . . again?"

After a long silence, Director Nelson went first, much to the relief of the others at the table. "We ah drawin' blanks evahwhere. One guess is that the group involved is so small that it is not leavin' any wake. If they ah self-contained and don't talk out of school, they ah goin' ta be verra hard ta find. I wish I could tell you that we had some solid leads . . ."

"I wish so, too," Burnette interjected. "Leroy, what have you got?"

The Chairman of the Joint Chiefs of Staff straightened some papers before him and cleared his throat. "Each of the services have what are called 'Chemical/Biological Medical Strike Teams' which are trained to treat toxically exposed patients. We have put all of those teams on alert."

"Great," Burnette said with a voice dripping in sarcasm. "That'll be a great comfort to the people of Chicago after they have been gassed. Or Denver, or St. Louis."

"Well, the Marines have a 'Chemical/Biological Incident Response Force.' They are affectionately known as the Bugs and Gas Guys. I guess that's because it is hard to pronounce their acronym—CBIRF. They are trained to detect, monitor, and decontaminate chemical and biological weapons. We have these guys on full alert as well. They are based at Camp Lejeune, but for the time being are attached to the Presidential Protective Detail of the Secret Service."

Several heads snapped toward General Sundin. Jim Schmidt was the first to speak. "Do you mean to imply that we have some reason to believe that Gadhafi's threat is directed against the President?"

"Nothing specific. But going back a number of years there has been speculation that the White House would make a good target."

Burnette nodded his head grimly. "In addition to the military forces that Leroy has, we have the folks at FEMA on alert, and the Energy Department's NEST team are on their toes . . ."

"Aren't they supposed to combat nuclear accidents and incidents?" the head of the National Security Agency asked.

"Yes, but some of their skills carry over into the chemical and biological areas as well," Burnette replied. "And we have the FBI engaged since they are the lead agency for antiterrorism within the United States. The biggest problem with them is that they want to take over the whole investigation. I've had to remind the Director that this is a sensitive national security issue that requires more subtlety than they demonstrated at Waco and Ruby Ridge. Although the Bureau swears that they got over those bad habits years ago. Now, does *anybody* have any good news?" he pleaded.

Secretary of Defense Stevens tentatively lifted his hand. "We may be on to something regarding Tarhouna."

"What have you got, Cleve?"

"Remember Mustafa telling our SEALs about how they flush the air system at the plant every few weeks through large vents? Using our infrared satellites, we now have observed them doing it. Because of the dramatic change in temperature on the desert floor when the vents are open, the pictures are quite striking. The vents appear to be computer controlled. I've got our top computer geeks working on it."

"Who is working on what, exactly?"

"The propeller heads who are trying to ensure that our own computers aren't subject to some kind of electronic Pearl Harbor some day."

It was clear that Secretary Stevens had lost most of the group sitting around the table.

"Here's the bottom line: I think our hackers can get control of their computer system and order all the vents and doors to open at the same time. If we can do that and put some bombs on target at the same instant, Tarhouna will be a Great Man-made Hole in the Ground."

38

Bill awoke with a hollow feeling in the pit of his stomach. Had he done the right thing by revealing the truth about the Libyans? And there was a nagging unease about the Gadhafi interview. Most of all, there was a hunger to be with Sue again. He vowed that next time he would not be so timid if he had a chance to kiss her. He hadn't felt that awkward since junior high.

During the morning, the ship conducted training for the crew. There were damage control drills, CPR training, and practice sessions for upcoming Scholastic Aptitude tests that *Churchill*'s educational services office was planning to administer. Bill wanted to keep the crew occupied as much as possible to keep their minds off the upcoming Board of Inquiry.

At mid-morning, Bill received word from Admiral Arnold that the investigators had completed their work and would be ready in the next day or so to begin the formal hearings. Bill sent word back that it might take him another few days to prepare his defense, news that surprised many crew members, since the Captain didn't seem to be spending much time with his lawyer.

•   •   •

A FEW MINUTES before noon, at nearly 6:00 A.M. East Coast time, the XO appeared in the Communications Department office demanding to know if the Early Bird news clippings had been received yet by satellite. The communicators expressed surprise, since Ellsworth had never before shown an interest in the publication.

"Somebody must have told him the Early Bird carries the polo scores," one crewman suggested. When the twenty-page publication was received and printed, Ellsworth grabbed the first copy and madly pored over its contents. Upon reaching the last page a frustrated look came over his face.

"Looking for something in particular, XO?"

"Err, ah, no. Always good to keep up with current events."

ALL DAY long Bill wanted to call Sue but held back. He didn't want to seem too anxious, and besides, what would he say? But she said to call. No, visit. So he supposed he really shouldn't leave her in limbo. He tortured himself further: what if he called and said the wrong thing and she decided she had to brief her editors about the shoot down? Or, what if he didn't call and she got pissed off at him and decided to spill the beans. What if he called and she thought he was only interested in her? What if he didn't call and she thought he wasn't?

The internal argument raged until early afternoon, when Bill did what he wanted to do all day: he called.

Sue answered on the first ring. "Hello?"

"I think you are supposed to say *pronto* in this country."

"What do you know about *pronto*? I've been waiting for you to call all day."

Damn, he knew he should have called sooner. "Sorry. I really wanted to, but I needed to tend to some things around here."

"Any word on whether all those smart folks you were talking about have figured out where the weapons are?"

"Looks like they might be about as smart as me."

"Well, smartie, did you ever figure out what was bothering you about that interview?"

"No, I agonized about it a lot but it still hasn't come to me. Do you have the tape recorder handy? Because if you do, could you play that one part for me one more time?"

After taking a minute to cue the tape up to the correct point, Sue held the recorder up to the phone. "Here goes."

Gadhafi's slightly muffled voice came through. "Once your Navy and Marines had a glorious history fighting for the liberation of enslaved peoples. Yes, I have studied this. Belleau Wood, Chateau Thierry, Pearl Harbor, Java Sea, Wake, Coral Sea, Midway, Savo Islands. And now? Now they add to this list the slaughter of innocent women and children."

And then it came to him. His mind went back to his days at Annapolis. As a member of the brigade of Midshipmen he was required to attend all home football games at the Academy's War Memorial Stadium. There, on the facade of the upper deck, were listed the great battles of Navy and Marine Corps history. Belleau Wood, Chateau Thierry, Pearl Harbor, Java Sea, Wake, Coral Sea, Midway, Savo Islands. "Sue, I've got it! That list, it's displayed in Annapolis. At the football stadium."

"That's nice, Bill . . . but, so what?"

"Don't you get it?" Bill said excitedly. "Those battles are displayed in the stadium at Annapolis in precisely that order. Gadhafi might be a student of U.S. Naval history—I doubt it, but let's say he is. Even then, there is no way he would come up with that list of battles in exactly the same order that they are displayed around the stadium. Obviously, he has been studying pictures of the stadium. And I think I can guess why!"

"You don't think that that . . ." Sue didn't finish her sentence.

"I sure do. That has to be it!"

"What are you going to do?" Sue asked.

"Ah, tell somebody. Quick. Look, gotta go. I'll be back to you as soon as I can. Don't go anywhere. And Sue?"

"Yes?"

"Don't let your journalistic instincts overwhelm your good judgment. Please, please don't call anyone. Remember, go along with me and the second it is safe, I guarantee you I will be all yours. Bye." Bill hung up without waiting for an answer. Quickly opening his office safe, he pulled out a big plastic key that looked like a child's toy. The key was needed to activate the STU-III secure phone in his in-port cabin. A second later he realized that in his excitement he could not remember the corresponding secure phone number for his brother's office.

A dusty directory that had been sitting under the STU-III for a couple years listed the number for the White House Communications Agency switchboard.

After three rings someone answered. "WOCKA?" Wocka was the phonetic pronunciation of W-H-C-A.

"This is an emergency. I need the secure phone number for Jim Schmidt, the President's spokesman." It took several minutes to find the number.

Jim's secretary, Natalie, heard the phone ringing behind the spokesman's desk and was sure it was another wrong number. Calls rarely came in on the special phone and when they did they were usually misdirected.

"Mr. Schmidt's office. Natalie speaking."

"Natalie, this is Bill Schmidt, Jim's brother . . ."

"Oh, hi! How are you? We've all been very concerned about you. I hope you are keeping your chin up."

"Yeah, right, chin up. Look, Nat, I've gotta speak to Jim. Is he there? Put him on, will you?"

"No, he's on a day trip with the President. Do you want me to have him call you when he gets back? You are in Italy, right? It might be early evening your time before he returns."

"Where is he?"

"The President is making another one of those college commencement speeches. A lot of work goes into them and hardly anything ever gets reported."

"Can Jim be reached on the road? Can you have him call me right away?"

"I'll try to have him get back to you. It's funny you should call today."

I really don't have time for this small talk, Bill thought. "Why?"

"Yeah, well, remember I said the President is out making a college graduation speech?"

"Yeah?"

"Well, what with you being in the Navy and all, that's why it is a coincidence. It's not really a college graduation he is doing. He is speaking at the graduation at the Naval Academy."

"What?"

"Oh yeah, you went there, didn't you? Then you probably know the President speaks at one of the service academies each year. It is just Annapolis's turn. It is a beautiful day for it, although I understand it gets hot in that football stadium."

"Natalie, I need to speak with Jim now. This instant. I can't explain why, but there is not a second to spare."

39

A puzzled Natalie placed Bill on hold and pushed a button to reach one of the White House military operators. "Signal," the young man answered. The White House has two separate phone systems. One, manned by civilians, provides the basic infrastructure for calls from the executive mansion. The other, operated by the military's White House Communications Agency, provides complete telephone service for the President and his staff wherever they travel.

"Hi, Signal. This is Natalie in Mr. Schmidt's office. I need to speak with my boss right away. Can you buzz the press filing center for me?"

Each time the President traveled, the White House press corps went along, even if the commander in chief was only going out to dinner at a local Chinese restaurant. If he planned to spend more than an hour or so at any location, a makeshift press center was constructed for the media's convenience. Called "the filing center," these facilities were often located in hotel ballrooms, high school gymnasiums, or, on this day, in a tent just outside the Navy-Marine Corps War Memorial Stadium.

Row upon row of narrow tables, just wide enough to support a laptop computer, were laden with telephones installed solely for the day's event. Light refreshments were available at the back of the filing center for those reporters who could not leave their posts due to deadline pressure or sheer inertia. The audio, and on many occasions closed circuit video, of the President's remarks was piped into the center, and many correspondents chose to cover the speech from the filing center instead of walking a few yards to see the event in person. Like the baby boomers most of them were, the press corps didn't consider an event to be real unless they could see it on TV.

At the front of the filing center behind a partition was a work area for the Press Office staff. One of the young staff assistants answered the constant ringing of the White House phone, known as a "drop."

"Press Office."

"Angie, this is Natalie. I need to speak to Jim right away. Is he in the filing center?"

"No, Nat. Haven't seen him in quite a while." Putting her hand partially over the mouthpiece, Angie shouted to her colleagues. "Anybody seen Jim?"

"What?"

"Hey Natalie, somebody said they thought he was going over to the Senior Staff Holding Room. Apparently the President made some last-minute changes to his remarks and Jim's discussing the inserts with General Burnette."

"Thanks." Hanging up quickly Natalie pushed the phone button that directly connected to Signal.

"Hi, it's me again. Can you ring the drop in the Senior Staff Holding Room for me, please? And hurry. It's important."

Natalie realized that she didn't know why it was important, but she would have to take Bill Schmidt's word for it. Meanwhile, Bill agonized on the other line, able to hear only Natalie's side of the calls.

"Senior staff, Hart."

"Jack, this is Natalie. Is my boss hanging around there?"

"Sure is, Natalie. He says he meets a nicer class of people in here than he does in the press tent."

"Put him on, will you? It's kind of urgent." About twenty seconds passed.

"Jim Schmidt."

"Jim, I have your brother Bill calling in on the STU-Three. He says he needs to talk to you urgently. I can try to transfer his call to you on this line, although you won't be able to talk secure."

"Go ahead, Nat. I'll see what is on his mind."

Natalie pushed a few buttons and said a silent prayer. "Well, here goes."

"Jim, Jim. This is Bill. You've got to get everyone out of there. It's Annapolis!"

"Oh, so that explains all those folks in the sailor suits. Yeah, I know it's Annapolis, little brother. You haven't been overindulging on liberty again, have you?"

"No, you idiot! The chemical weapons are stashed in Annapolis! I don't have time to tell you how I have figured it out . . . but trust me. Gadhafi has been studying the place. It has to be Annapolis!"

With his voice rising several octaves, Jim Schmidt squeezed the telephone handset. "Bill, I need a little more to go on. Tell me how you know."

"Have you been in the stadium yet?"

"No, I'm in a little area near the locker room under the stands. It looks like the trainer's room. I haven't been on the field yet."

"Jim, Gadhafi gave an interview to Sue a few days ago and he described the Navy's and Marine Corps' great battles of the past."

"Sue? Sue O'Dell?"

"Right. And he rattled off the battles in this precise order: Belleau Wood, Chateau Thierry, Pearl Harbor, Java Sea, Wake, Coral Sea, Midway, Savo Islands."

"You've lost me, Bill."

"Go outside onto the field and look around the rim of the upper deck at the stadium. Along the facade are displayed the greatest battles ever fought by sailors and Marines. The list goes, Belleau Wood, Chateau Thierry, Pearl Harbor, Java Sea, Wake, Coral Sea, Midway, Savo Islands."

"Jesus H. . . . ." Jim dropped the phone and sprinted toward the field.

Several members of the senior staff looked amused as Schmidt scrambled toward the stadium.

"Did the coach call and tell you to suit up, Jim? Don't forget your helmet and protective cup."

Jim sprinted onto the field and looked up at the facade of the stadium. Belleau Wood, Chateau Thierry, Pearl Harbor . . . "Holy shit."

Nearly one thousand Midshipmen, soon to be Ensigns and Second Lieutenants, were marching into the stadium and taking their places on seats on the field. In the stands, tens of thousands of proud parents, relatives, and friends watched the spectacle. Several thousand of the underclassmen observed the proceedings from the upper deck.

A stiff breeze blew across the crowded stadium. The sky was cloudless, making the day perfect for the anticipated flyby of the Navy's Blue Angels, scheduled to kick off the day's ceremonies.

On the south side, at the closed end of the horseshoe-shaped stadium, stretched a stage with a dozen wooden captain's chairs that awaited the imminent arrival of the commander in chief and other top brass.

Facing the stage were fifty rows of chairs for the graduates. Beyond the graduating Midshipmen, on a platform built of pipe and plywood, were the camera crews from the national press, and one or two hearty reporters who planned to cover the event "live" rather than from the cooler press filing room.

The Secret Service had erected some tents behind the stage to shield the President's entrance to the stadium area.

The noise was deafening. Jim noticed that he was standing next to a huge speaker that was blasting the Naval Academy band's rendition of "Pomp and Circumstance" to the farthest reaches of the upper deck.

Parents, girlfriends, and boyfriends were shouting to the graduates to try to get them to wave to the cameras.

Amidst the confusion, Jim's eyes darted wildly, seeking the diminutive form of Wally Burnette, the National Security Advisor.

The graduation and commissioning ceremony was late in starting due to huge traffic jams on Routes 50 and 301 leading to the stadium and a massive backup entering the facility as everyone was forced to go through metal detecting magnetometers manned by uniformed division members of the Secret Service.

Jim dashed toward the area where he knew the President would be waiting for the music of "Ruffles and Flourishes," his cue to go on.

Although Jim's face was well known and he was wearing his senior staff lapel pin identifying him to law enforcement officials as someone who was allowed to be near the President, the sight of an obviously agitated man sprinting toward the President caused a half-dozen agents to reach for their weapons.

It was only when Jim saw a female agent drop the flap on her briefcase to reveal an Uzi submachine gun that he recognized he might be in some danger from the good guys.

Slowing to a brisk walk he held up both hands. "It's just me. Don't shoot the messenger." He could tell from the reaction that the agents had heard that one before. "I've got to find General Burnette right away. Has anyone seen him?"

Two agents moved between Schmidt and the President. A third pointed to an area in the far side of the tent where a large woman in a flowery sun hat was talking animatedly. Moving in that direction, Jim could see that the woman, the wife of the Academy Commandant, had the General cornered and was busy lecturing him.

"Excuse me, ma'am." Jim tried to get past the woman but she stepped sideways, effectively blocking his path.

Burnette leaned to the right and tried to look around her.

"Wally, Wally. We've got to get the President out of here. I think this is the place!"

Before Burnette could answer, the Admiral's wife interrupted. "The President is not going anywhere, young man, until he has shaken one thousand hands and returned one thousand salutes!"

Burnette used the diversion to make a run around the woman's port side.

"What do you mean, this is the place?"

"I don't have time to explain it now. But my brother . . . my brother says that Gadhafi gave an interview in which he displayed intimate knowledge of this stadium and he expressed his annoyance at the President and the Navy!"

The Admiral's wife interrupted again. "I don't know who your brother is, young man, but he has no business being annoyed with the President or the United States Navy!"

Burnette managed to break free and ran over to the Secret Service agent leading the presidential protective detail. He whispered a few words in the man's ear. Pausing for just a second, the agent held his left sleeve up to his mouth and spoke into it. In seconds two other agents bracketed the President, grabbed his upper arms, lifted, and hustled him out of the tent. A stunned President protested as he was dragged through a tunnel and tossed into his waiting armored limo. The jaws of bystanders in the tent dropped in unison.

A buzz arose among the VIPs waiting in the holding area. The Admiral's wife marched over to her husband to report how rude the somewhat familiar-looking young man and General Burnette had been to her. "What do you expect from an Army man?" he asked.

Burnette dragged Schmidt over to the side of the tent. "Look, if we try to evacuate this place there will be panic and gridlock. And if you are right about the weapons being planted here, as soon as we ask everyone to quickly file out, the Libyans will set them off. We need to alert the Chemical Response Force without tipping our hand." Jim said nothing but was clearly uneasy about leaving 20,000 people sitting in a stadium that might be laden with chemical weapons.

"We've got to buy some time!"

"All right, I'll tell the band to keep on playing. I wonder if they know anything by the Beach Boys."

The Secretary of the Navy, the Chief of Naval Operations, and other dignitaries who were scheduled to be potted palms on the platform for the graduation came over to Burnette to ask what was going on.

"Ah, something has come up that the President has to attend to. Hopefully it won't take too long. Looks like a beautiful day for a commissioning, doesn't it? Why don't you all go out and mingle with the moms and dads for a while. It'll be great PR, and they'll be thrilled to meet you."

Frederic Fiske, the Secretary of the Navy, thought that was a brilliant suggestion and darted out to shake hands along the first rows of the stadium's lower deck. It was an exercise he enjoyed immensely. He never realized that none of the people whose hands he shook had the slightest idea who he was.

Meanwhile, Burnette alerted the chemical weapons team, who had personnel throughout the stadium, all in civilian clothes. The head of the Secret Service's presidential protective detail briefly questioned the plausibility of the warning.

"Them weapons can't be in here, General! We've magged everyone coming in . . . we've had bomb dogs sniffing for explosives for the past two days. We've got control of the airspace, and Stinger teams standing by to shoot down anything attempting to overfly us. If those chemical weapons are here, where the hell are they?"

"Damned if I know. The only clue we have is that they may be in the stadium . . . and an old clue, one that our man in Libya provided, that the weapons are in the 'tanks' . . ."

"Tanks, sir? Begging the General's pardon, sir, but these anchor clankers don't have too many tanks around here."

Meanwhile the Response Force members were poring over the stadium, looking under the stands, in the locker rooms, checking out buses and vehicles in the nearby parking lot. Many carried Chemical Agent Monitors, small hand-held devices that detected vapors of chemical agents by sensing molecular ions of specific mobilities. Using timing and microprocessor techniques, the five-and-a-half-pound CAMs could detect and discriminate between vapors of nerve and blister agents.

Jim was a nervous wreck, literally not knowing if his next breath would be his last. He also began briskly walking around the stadium looking for a likely place to stash some weapons of mass destruction, quickly realizing that he had no idea what they might look like. The sun was now high in the Maryland sky and the temperature on the floor of the stadium had risen to the low nineties. Patches of sweat shone on Jim's forehead.

Jim decided to check the area under the stands. He jumped over a low railing in front of the lower tier of seats near a sign memorializing the Vietnam riverine operation known by the code name "Market Time." He jogged up a ramp that led to an area below the upper deck. As he worked his way past the crowd, he felt a stiff breeze blow in from the nearby Chesapeake Bay, through the opening, and down toward the field. It felt good. Upon entering the cool, shady area below the upper deck of the stadium, Jim noticed a concession stand. He wished he had time to grab a quick soda to quench his thirst. Surprisingly, the concessionaire was not doing any business. An OUT OF ORDER sign hung on the stand's soda dispensers. Despite the breeze from the Bay, a large industrial-size fan behind the counter was blowing out toward the concourse. The two swarthy men in the stand didn't seem to be trying to fix the soda dispenser.

Those guys are never going to own their own 7-Eleven with a work ethic like *that*, Jim thought. And then he immediately felt guilty for having such a politically incorrect thought. Those guys could be making a mint here today if they had their machine working. He wondered what was wrong with their tank.

Then he froze in his tracks, and he looked hard at the two men, who returned his stare. Taking a deep breath, he tried to look nonchalant and walked down the ramp and back onto the field.

As soon as he got out of sight of the concession stand, he began running. Sprinting onto the field he ran into some of the same Secret Service agents as before. This time they were somewhat less jumpy since the President was no longer on the scene.

"Where's General Burnette? Find him! Now!"

The agents started to tell Schmidt that they didn't take orders from a mere press spokesman, but there was something about his tone that caused them to make an exception. The lead agent bent down and spoke into his sleeve. His two nearest colleagues each stopped and held a hand over their ear pieces.

Moments later an agent dragged Burnette onto the field and pointed out where Schmidt was standing. The General was accompanied by a man in civilian clothes but with an obvious military haircut.

"What have you got, Jim?"

"Up there, in the concession stand. There are two Arab-looking guys standing at a dysfunctional concession stand!"

"You've got that in every stadium in America, Jim."

Schmidt grabbed the General's arm and started leading him up the ramp.

"No, don't you see? They have an 'OUT OF ORDER' sign hanging on a bunch of *tanks* connected to the soda machine. And the stand is only twenty yards upwind from where the President is supposed to be sitting right now!"

The man with the military haircut pulled a walkie-talkie out of his inside jacket pocket and barked some orders into it. Seconds later a group of fifteen similarly attired, very muscular men with short haircuts assembled on the edge of the field at the base of the ramp.

After a quick consultation they divided up and, using different routes, headed underneath the stands.

Three minutes later, two of the men stopped ten feet from the concession stand and began a loud argument over whether Navy should have tried to go for a two-point conversion in the final seconds of the last Army-Navy game.

"Ah, you're an idiot. They weren't able to run the ball all afternoon. What makes you think they would have been able to get past the Army line for the extra points?"

"Look, dummy, they were able to get by them to score the damn touchdown, weren't they? What good did it do to kick the extra point? Tying Army is like winning a date with Ellen DeGeneres. It ain't worth the trouble."

All eyes on the concourse, including those of the concessionaires, were on the two argumentative young men as they walked off to the right.

Suddenly, from the left, four other men leapt over the counter and slammed the two concessionaires up against the wall. In an instant, weapons were drawn and the men were wrestled to the ground.

As he was carried backward by the pouncing undercover Special Forces soldiers, one of the concessionaires managed to thrust out his right hand and reach for the knob atop the canisters with the OUT OF ORDER sign. Before he could attain his goal, his attackers placed their knees on his forearms and bent his arms back until there was a loud snap. The screaming was only slightly muffled by the shouts of more Special Forces troops leaping over the counter.

40

The traveling White House press corps was within a hundred yards of the biggest story in years; unfortunately, their attention was focused on the refreshments in the press filing center, and they missed the Libyan takedown entirely.

As the Secret Service swept the stadium and determined that there was only one stash of weapons on the grounds, Burnette and Jim placed a priority call to the Chairman of the Joint Chiefs.

"Leroy . . . we found it! The stash. It was here in Annapolis. We got to it before they could do anything! They were going to gas the President and thousands of people at the academy graduation." Schmidt noticed that they were both speaking several octaves higher than usual. "The bust went down like clockwork. We need to act now to take out Tarhouna. We've got to put them out of business before they can export another shipment of their special product."

The Chairman could be heard shouting for his operations deputy to be summoned immediately.

"Wally, are the press aware of the bust?"

"Amazingly, I don't think so."

"Good. I recommend that the President continue on as if nothing has happened. It will take us some time to implement the strike package. Try to buy us all the time you can."

The President, who had been whisked across town and upwind, was quickly driven back to the stadium. Burnette briefed him on what had transpired and got his okay to press ahead with planning an attack on the Libyan facility.

The press and the parents buzzed amongst themselves about what had caused the delay. The Midshipmen, who had waited four years for this day, fidgeted anxiously in their seats. Reporters in the filing center wanted to ask Jim Schmidt about the delay but the spokesman was nowhere to be found. Finally, the President mounted the stage and the ceremony began about an hour and a half late.

The speech that had been prepared for the President was to have been the third in a series of commencement remarks in which he laid out his vision for the economy and gave a paean to volunteerism. The press, in keeping with standard practice, had been given copies of the prepared text of his remarks several hours earlier, and many had already written their stories long before the President had begun his speech.

The President was ten or twelve paragraphs into his remarks when he abandoned the prepared text. It took another minute or two for someone in the press filing center to notice the change. A general scurrying took place as reporters reached for their text and tried to follow where the President was going with his remarks.

"Dammit, I'm going to have to listen to this thing now."

"You? I've already written my story and pitched it to my editor. The President better get back to his text or I'll be mighty pissed!"

But the President did not return to the script. Instead, he delivered a heartfelt and impromptu speech about the meaning of service and sacrifice. He ended by telling the graduates that their commissions meant that, in the near future, they might be called on to do the unpopular thing on behalf of their country. "Anyone can serve," he said, "when service is honored and appreciated. But you, like others who have gone before you, may have to accept unwarranted criticism and scorn. Like the best of those in whose footsteps you now walk, I know that you have the strength and the courage to pursue the ultimate good."

By the time the President had finished his remarks and presented commissions to the 900 or so graduates, the Joint Staff back at the Pentagon had completed their warning order for an attack on Tarhouna.

On board the *Winston Churchill*, the Executive Officer had been stewing all day about why the *Washington Post* had failed to do a story based on his hot tip. *That awful woman is taking her sweet time trying to confirm the story. Since when did the Washington Post develop journalistic ethics,* he thought.

Ellsworth never imagined it would be so difficult to leak top-secret information. Well, if it was confirmation she required, he would have to provide it. The XO changed into civilian clothes, double-knit trousers and a Banlon shirt from the seventies. He neatly folded his uniform and carried it with him in a gym bag. Ellsworth never liked to be without a uniform nearby. Then he ordered up the ship's boat and had it take him to the pier. Once on the beach, Ellsworth hailed a cab and asked to be taken to the Navy Exchange. The crowds had dwindled in the midweek early evening hours.

After struggling with a fist full of 500 lira coins and a brace of Italian telephone operators, Ellsworth finally was put through to the Hotel Jolly. Once again, he deployed a handkerchief to cover the phone's mouthpiece and in his best imitation French accent, asked to be connected to Miss Sue O'Dell's room.

The phone was answered on the first ring.

"*Pronto!*"

"Mademoiselle O'Dell?"

"Ah, yes." There was disappointment in Sue's voice.

"Mademoiselle, Ah em callink choo to teeping choo eff. Choo see, zee Americain Navee hess ben chuting dowen Lee-bee-yen aeroplains weeth intenshun. Be-cass dee Lee-bee-yens hass ben plenning chemi-cal a-tax. Dees sheep *Chur-shill* ees really quite e-roic. Choo must, how choo say? Choo must repore dees story rye away. Good-bye."

The phone went silent as the caller hung up, but not before Sue decided that she was talking to the same individual who gave her the original tip. That was the worst fake French accent she'd ever heard. Someone was awfully desperate for her to report the story. She wondered, why?

Meanwhile, Bill Schmidt waited aboard the ship, at anchor in Naples harbor. Alone in his cabin, he anxiously watched the satellite television feed of CNN for any report from Annapolis. He knew that if he was wrong, and they disrupted the entire academy graduation for nothing because of his hysterical tip, they'd have his head. If there was a bust or, God forbid, a successful attack, Schmidt knew he would hear about it on CNN long before official channels reported the incident. But there was nothing. Bill endured a two-hour-long "Talk Back Live" program where callers and in-studio guests gave their views on the social significance of cosmetic surgery.

Finally, at the turn of the hour, CNN broke in with a news update. The fourth story was a brief item about the President's speech which featured the familiar video of newly commissioned officers throwing their hats in the air at the end of the ceremony.

Schmidt's emotions yo-yoed between "Thank God nothing happened," and "Oh shit! Nothing happened." *What little credibility I had left is shot.* His discomfort was interrupted by a sharp knock on his cabin door.

"Yes?"

"Captain, this is Brad Moseman. I've got a hot one for you!"

Schmidt lumbered out of his chair like an old man. Shoulders slumped, he shuffled over to open the door.

"Now what, Brad?" he said softly.

Moseman was holding a silver-colored metal clipboard with a cover to protect the message from prying eyes. "We just got this flash message directing us to get underway within thirty minutes and to make the best possible speed toward a particular posit . . . which happens to be just outside Libyan claimed waters. Looks like we might be out of the dog house, at least for the moment."

Schmidt paused to reflect on the meaning of the message and quickly decided he had no idea what it meant. But, as was his wont, he decided it was good news. His posture immediately improved at the prospect of getting down to the business of going to sea. "How many people do we have ashore?"

"The crew was pretty worn out after several nights of liberty. I'd estimate that no more than a third of them are on the beach. I've already issued an emergency recall. We'll get as many back on board as possible, but we've got enough people on board to fight the ship right now."

"Great. I want to get underway in precisely thirty minutes. Anyone who can't make it back . . . well, we'll have to do without 'em. Any key people unaccounted for?"

Moseman paused for a moment. "No. Not unless you count the XO, sir." They exchanged meaningful looks.

"Tell you what, Brad. Let's get underway in twenty-five minutes instead."

TOM ELLSWORTH was feeling pretty good about himself and his efforts to deceive Sue O'Dell. He was sure that his fake French accent would make her think she had the second source she needed and convince her of the necessity of immediately writing the story of the *Winston Churchill* and her heroic crew. He felt a surge of optimism that lasted the entire taxi ride back to fleet landing, right up until the moment he observed his ship sailing over the horizon.

Ellsworth stood speechless on the pier. No sound came from his throat, but his lips slowly formed the words, *He . . . can't . . . do . . . this . . . to . . . me.*

He could, and he did. On the bridge of the *Winston Churchill,* Bill Schmidt ordered the sea and anchor detail to expedite the ship's departure from its anchorage. *Arleigh Burke* destroyers, like no other Navy vessels, are uniquely well suited to respond to such a command. With the power generated from the ship's four GE-2500 gas turbine engines, the same type of engines used to power DC-10 aircraft, Schmidt could bring his ship up to full speed from a standing start in sixty seconds. He waited until the ship had cleared the harbor, and ordered flank speed.

Exhilarated from having been released from the bonds of their anchorage, the crew of *Winston Churchill* cheered as their captain set a direct course for "the line of death," an artificial boundary that Gadhafi had drawn across the international waters of the Gulf of Sidra. Schmidt ordered the ship to maintain flank speed, something rarely done in these days of caution and economy.

As the ship sped toward Libya, the details of a battle plan, known as an OP order, were being transmitted from the Pentagon to the European Command Headquarters near Stuttgart, Germany.

All OP orders call for careful timing, but this one called for unheard-of precision. The key was with a small group of computer programmers at the Defense Technical Information Center, known as "Dee-Tick," at Fort Belvoir, Virginia. For two weeks, a handful of experts had been trying to hack into a computer system five thousand miles away in Tarhouna.

The tricky part was to avoid revealing their efforts to the Libyans. They were able to access the computer system with ease, but it was impossible to tell whether they could control the system without tipping their hand.

General Leroy Sundin and the Joint Staff decided that real-time intelligence was essential if the plan were to work. Putting men on the ground was deemed unacceptably risky and highly likely to fail. Normal surveillance satellites were not timely enough and were subject to technical failure or weather complications.

"Once the DTIC gets control over the vents and hatches—if they get control—we will have only a few minutes before the Libyans are able to override the computers and close the barn doors," Sundin observed in a meeting in the JCS conference room known as "the Tank."

"If we can't get the vents open, we're just going to have to have the entire U.S. Air Force conduct bombing practice on the place and hope we get lucky," Defense Secretary Stevens offered.

There were actually two plans. The first, the wildly optimistic one, called for the DTIC tekkies to grab control of the Tarhouna computer system just as a Sea Ferret reconnaissance missile was flying overhead. The missile, launched from the submarine USS *Hartford*, would relay live infrared video back to the battle group commander aboard the *George Washington*. In turn, the video would be relayed to command centers in Stuttgart and Washington.

If the Sea Ferret's cameras confirmed that the vents were open, Strike Fighter F/A-18s from the *George Washington*, which would be circling just outside Libyan-claimed airspace, would dash in and drop precision-guided munitions into the gaping orifices. The initial attack would be followed by Tomahawk cruise missiles launched from the fleet.

If the hackers failed in their mission, the F/A-18s would stand down until Air Force F-117s and B-2 bombers could arrive in theater.

That arrival would take an extra day since several European allies had refused to grant overflight rights again. Therefore, the U.S.-based aircraft would have to take a very circuitous route to the target. As a result, once in Europe, Air Force regulations called for the aircraft to land and for the pilots to achieve the requisite amount of crew rest before pressing the attack. A similar overflight refusal in 1986 forced Air Force bombers to circumnavigate France before pressing an attack. Some observers felt that the added flight time may have contributed to the loss of one F-111 bomber.

The OP order was sent from the Pentagon to the European Command in Stuttgart. Simultaneously, it went to the Navy's European Headquarters in London and to the Sixth Fleet command ship in Italy. At each level, planners added their own after-action reporting requirements and fleshed out the tasking.

Bill Schmidt could scarcely believe his eyes when the plan reached *Winston Churchill*. The Sea Ferret was a new weapons system, never before tried in actual combat. It was so new that few Navy ships had been equipped with it yet.

Poor old Chet Hollomaker, Schmidt thought. Eighteen years in the Navy. Finally gets to fire a missile in anger, and all it has for a warhead is a TV camera.

On board the *Churchill*, Weapons Department crewmen were feeding new targeting data into the guidance sets of the ship's cruise missiles. The data was received via satellite from targeting decision centers ashore.

This time if we shoot, Schmidt thought, it will be with the blessing of the entire chain of command.

41

The silence was killing Sue. Eight hours had passed since Bill came up with what he thought was the answer to Gadhafi's riddle. And it had been eight hours since he begged her not to notify her editors. The tug on her emotions was immense as she sat by her phone waiting for Schmidt to call. Finally, when she could stand it no longer, Sue called her office.

"Style, Harper."

"Paul, this is Sue. What's going on?" She hoped that her question sounded innocent enough.

"Not much, Sue. Just another episode in the life of a great metropolitan daily. Have you found out anything that would back up the story of our conspiracy theorist?"

Sue pretended that she had not heard the question.

"Paul, I was wondering. Have you heard of anything unusual happening at the Naval Academy commencement today? The President was supposed to have been there."

"Aw, we've got a story about it for tomorrow's paper. Let me call it up on my screen." Obviously, nothing of great significance could have happened.

"Here it is. Looks like your standard graduation speech. The only thing unusual is that the President apparently showed up an hour late. A lot of grousing from the families of the grads and apparently from the wife of the Academy's Commandant. Why do you ask?"

"Oh, nothing. Never mind. Look, I've got to go. Talk to you later. 'Bye."

Sue hung up the phone and winced at the thought that Bill Schmidt must be suffering from terminal embarrassment for having raised a false alarm at Annapolis. No wonder he hasn't called me, she thought. Poor thing, his male pride must be wounded.

Since there was no way for her to call out to the ship, Sue decided to write Bill a note and once again go down to the waterfront in search of a sailor to play postman.

She sat down and drafted a warm and supportive note, urging Schmidt to keep his chin up and not feel too embarrassed for crying wolf. This time she put two drops of perfume on the letter, telling herself she was only ensuring that the letter got through.

It was 11:00 P.M. by the time she finished her note. She rushed to the hotel lobby to catch a taxi, figuring that with Cinderella liberty in effect for the ship, liberty boats would stop running around midnight.

The cab driver asked, in broken English, if Sue was sure about going down to the waterfront at this hour of night. "Ees no so safe, Signorina."

Sue assured him that she would be all right, but asked if the taxi would stand by and wait for her. "I won't be long. I just need to drop something off."

Minutes later the taxi pulled up to the pier. Sue jumped out and began looking for a candidate to be a courier. Since this was after working hours, most sailors in the area were wearing civilian clothes, so there was no way to identify their ship.

She started approaching people who looked like sailors and asked the same question. "Excuse me. You wouldn't be from the *Winston Churchill*, would you?"

The first five said no, and sometimes colorfully so. On the sixth attempt she struck pay dirt.

"Yes, ma'am. I surely am." The sailor sounded somehow forlorn. He sat looking out at the harbor, taking slow sips out of a big bottle of beer.

"I wonder if I could trouble you to take this letter to my good friend, Bill Schmidt?" Sue smiled hopefully.

"Wish I could, ma'am. But that ain't exactly possible."

"Look, it would mean a lot to me. Suppose I were to offer you fifty dollars for your trouble."

"I guess you haven't heard, ma'am," the sailor sadly as he pointed out into the black night. "If you look out thataway, that was where the *Winnie* used to be. Seems she got underway in a big hurry this afternoon and left me and a bunch of the rest of the crew on the beach."

"They left?"

"Yes, ma'am. Just up and left. The Navy gave us rooms in the barracks and said we could join up with the ship later. But no one will tell us where she went. I've never missed ship's movement before, and I am not feeling too good about it. *Winnie* is my home. That's where I belong."

Sue patted the disconsolate sailor on the arm and started to walk back to the waiting taxi. Then she paused and walked back to the sailor. She pulled out $50 and handed it to the bewildered man.

"Here, take this. Round up your other stranded shipmates and buy them a drink on me, would you?"

Visibly brightening, the sailor gingerly took the money. "Gee, thanks. I know they will all appreciate it. Well, except maybe the XO. But the rest of 'em are in need of a drink. Thanks!"

Sue ran back to her cab and asked the driver to rush back to the Hotel Jolly. Once there, she agonized, once again, about whether she should tell her editors what she knew, and what she suspected. In the end, the cautions she received from Bill won out.

How could she live with herself if she screwed up a chance to prevent a terrorist attack on the United States, just for a story?

Suzy, you are never going to make it in this business if you keep thinking like that, she admonished herself.

•   •   •

THE SUN was rising over Libya as U.S. forces gathered to conduct a strike. At the same time, close to midnight in Washington, a debate raged in the White House Situation Room as to whether to wait until nightfall to launch or to strike immediately before the Libyans detected the armada off their shores.

"Look," CIA Director Nelson said, "the Libyans now know that the attack at the Naval Academy didn't work. Evrah second we wait gives them moah time ta figah out what happened and prepayuh a defense."

General Firman, the head of the National Security Agency, shook his head. "We noticed a huge spike in the amount of traffic between Gadhafi and the senior leadership about the time of the graduation ceremony. From those communications which we can monitor, it appears that there is great confusion over what happened. But they don't seem to know. We believe that they didn't have a backup crew watching the guys at the concession stand."

"Probably pretty hard to get folks to volunteer to stand around in the middle of a gas attack," Jim Schmidt offered.

Wally Burnette nodded his agreement. "Not exactly prime duty, I would say. Leroy, how do you rate the advantages and downsides of launching now?"

The Chairman of the JCS looked down at briefing notes prepared by his staff and cleared his throat. "We can launch in daylight, but we run the risk of our reconnaissance bird being shot down and not knowing if the vents are open. We also run a much greater risk of losing aircraft on the attack run. And finally, there is some likelihood that a successful attack will release some chemical agents in the air around Tarhouna. A daylight attack would probably result in higher collateral damage."

"You mean we might kill more of the guys who have been making chemical weapons," Secretary of Defense Stevens said.

"Well, yes sir."

"I didn't notice them being too concerned when they planned on a midday attack on Annapolis!"

"It seems to me that the major concern has to be, will a daylight attack put more of our people at risk, and will it significantly diminish the mission's chances of knocking out Tarhouna for good," Wally Burnette summarized.

In the end, the group elected to present both options to the President with the news that half of them preferred the daylight option while the others preferred night.

Wally Burnette called and woke the President, who invited the entire group to come over to the Family Quarters on the second floor of the White House residence. With the President in his bathrobe, Burnette laid out both options and said a good case could be made for either.

"It's advice like that that makes it so rewarding to be President," the commander in chief noted dryly. "No matter what I do, half the group will write in their memoirs that they advised me to do otherwise."

"Not if you pick the right option," Burnette observed wryly.

"Okay, let's wait until dark."

ABOARD THE *Hartford*, preparations for launching the Sea Ferret were about complete.

Much to Chet Hollomaker's discomfort, Lieutenant Larry Caffey was once again officer of the deck.

"Oh Captain, my captain! Mighty pleased to report that we've got that snooping bird stuffed into its tube and ready to blanket Libya like the *National Enquirer* covers Liz Taylor's weddings."

Whatever the hell, that means, Hollomaker thought. "Ah, thanks, Larry."

"Don't mention it. Well, I guess you already did, but no further mention is required. When do we shoot?"

Hollomaker sighed. "Our orders are to launch at precisely twenty-two fifteen Zulu time. It'll be plenty dark by then. The bird is programmed to overfly the least-populated areas enroute to Tarhouna. It'll be going in at about fifty feet and will pop up on the perimeter of the facility and then orbit the place. Hopefully, it will send back a solid signal to the flagship showing them what they want to see."

Aboard USS *George Washington,* Captain Mike "Spider" Webb sat in the Strike Ops office, making final plans for an Alpha Strike, a consolidated attack by the majority of the air wing.

Webb was commander of the carrier's air wing, and was known as the "CAG." The acronym dated back to the time, more than four decades before, when the air wing was called an air group. Old ways die hard in the Navy. Spider Webb and his planners had labored for six hours to assemble a document known as the Air Tasking Order, which would orchestrate the attack.

S-3B tankers from the VS-32 Maulers would launch first to be ready to refuel their colleagues as soon as necessary. F/A-18 Super Hornet attack jets from three different squadrons, the Sidewinders, Street Cars, and T-Bolts, would follow. Then would come EA-6B Prowlers from VAQ 137, known as the Rooks, to jam and supress enemy radar, and finally F-14 Tomcat fighters from the VF-102 Diamondbacks, which would defend the entire force from any Libyan aerial response.

Once the plan was finalized, each squadron gathered the aviators in their respective ready rooms to handle some ominous administrative details. An intelligence officer briefed them on escape and evasion plans. If their aircraft were shot down and they had to eject over land, the crew had specific instructions on locations they should try to reach to await rescue. Each officer was given a document called a "blood chit." Made of indestructible fibrous paper, the document carried a statement in Arabic promising the reader that if they helped a downed airman escape capture, the U.S. government would guarantee them a payment of $1,500.

Next the aviators were asked to go over data in a file that would be used by rescue personnel to verify the identity of the airmen. Name, rank, and Social Security number would not be enough to dispatch a "SAR" search and rescue helo to pick them up. Downed flyers calling in support on emergency radios would be quizzed on things like the name of their first dog or the color of their wife's car to verify their identity.

On normal missions the aircrew flew without personal weapons. This would not be a normal mission. The ship's Master at Arms issued .38 caliber pistols to the flight crews. Some of the more experienced pilots had their own, more powerful Ruger pistols which had been locked away for occasions such as this.

Finally, the aircrew were given their personnel files and asked to verify the name, address, and phone number of their next of kin.

When the administrative details were taken care of, the aircrews were allowed to take a final meal in the ship's wardroom, return to their bunkrooms to try to rest, or, hardest of all, find a quiet spot on board the giant carrier to reflect on what lay ahead of them.

As the sun began to set, each squadron held another AOM, all officer meeting, in which the precise details of the impending attack were laid out. Closed-circuit television monitors flickered on and delivered a threat briefing from the CVIC, the carrier's intelligence center, which discussed the massive amount of antiaircraft guns and surface-to-air missiles arrayed around the Tarhouna facility.

Over the 1MC announcing system came the shrill whistle of a Bo'sun's pipe demanding the attention of all hands. *George Washington*'s captain praised the hard work of all on board and then passed the microphone to the Admiral who reminded everyone that this was what they trained for and voiced his confidence that they would all carry out their responsibilities with courage and skill. Finally, the voice of the ship's senior chaplain was heard seeking God's protection for those who were about to go in harm's way.

The Captain waited a few minutes to give everyone a chance to reflect on the chaplain's word, then he had the Boatswain Mate of the Watch call flight quarters on the 1MC. "Flight quarters, flight quarters, all hands, man your flight quarters stations."

The flight deck crew, in their cranial helmets, goggles, and multicolored jerseys, were expecting the announcement. The carrier was quickly ready to conduct flight operations.

Nearly sixty aircraft launched from the four-acre flight deck and ascended to altitude. They began flying in a long, lazy racetrack pattern, awaiting orders to proceed.

At precisely 2215 Zulu, the submerged *Hartford* launched the Sea Ferret which skimmed the surface at 500 miles per hour en route to Tarhouna.

Aboard the *George Washington*, in the Admiral's command center known as Flag Plot, watchstanders anxiously waited to receive the Sea Ferret's signal. It would show nothing identifiable while over water. Only when it went "feet dry," over land, would it be possible to tell if the signal was transmitting properly.

Five thousand miles away, in suburban Virginia, the technicians at DTIC were told to hack away. The preparation done days earlier to probe but not try to control the system paid off. Fingers flew over their keyboards as they attempted to break into the Tarhouna computer system. Entry into the overall system's architecture proved relatively simple.

"Boy, these guys are pretty lax about their system security," the lead hacker noted.

"Thank goodness for that," the civilian in charge of the work center offered.

"Damn!"

"What's wrong?"

"Ran into a password protect feature on the computer that runs the environmental controls . . . air handler and stuff like that."

Worried looks were exchanged around the room. "Let's run that password generator program and see what we get."

All eyes fixed on the screen. It flashed fifty times a second as various passwords were attempted.

Five, ten, fifteen minutes passed and then suddenly the screen changed.

"We're in!"

Fingers shaking, the programmer typed a few quick strokes and examined the result. A screen popped up with a list of devices. Unfortunately, the list was in Arabic.

"Translator!" Fortunately, the planners had foreseen this possibility and arranged for linguists to be standing by.

"Read me this list!"

"Water pump one, water pump two, three, four . . . so on. Lighting bank one, two, three, . . . you get the idea."

"Yeah, anything about air vents?" he shouted as he scrolled down the list.

"Let's see . . . air conditioners, air handlers . . . yes! Air vents one, two, three, it goes down to twelve."

"And what is the column to the right of these devices?"

"They all say 'secured.' "

Taking the mouse next to his keyboard, the technician dragged it down over the twelve air vent entries and hit the enter key. Suddenly a different word appeared after each air vent entry.

"What does it say now?"

"It says 'open.' "

ABOARD THE *George Washington*, whoops and cheers went up in Flag Plot when the first pictures came in from the Sea Ferret. As programmed, the missile slowed down as it approached its target. Gaining altitude, the missile began circling the Tarhouna complex. The infrared camera sent back a photo negative-type video picture to the carrier offshore.

"That's as clear as day!" the Admiral exclaimed. Some action on the ground could be observed. Small trucks and Jeep-like vehicles were darting around. As the sailors watched, the vehicles went to a series of hatches embedded in the desert floor. Each hatch appeared to be open.

The Admiral signaled the Alpha Strike leader to proceed with the attack, and sixty aircraft broke from the circling formation and headed directly for Tarhouna.

Back at Fort Belvoir, the hackers had one more task to complete. As soon as they were notified that the air vents were open, the technicians took charge of the computer system one last time.

Going back to the equipment list, the operators asked the linguists to point out the Arabic words for electric generators. It took only moments to find them, highlight them, and with a keystroke of finality, turn them off.

The screen in Virginia went blank as the computer in Libya and all other electrical equipment at Tarhouna lost power. The vents were now locked in an open position, and the plant was plunged into darkness.

In the few minutes it took for emergency generators to kick in to provide minimal power for the facility, the *George Washington* airwing raced toward its target.

The EA-6 Prowlers, escorted by Tomcats, led the way. As Libyan air defense radars picked up the approaching aircraft, the Prowlers turned on their powerful jammers. The land-based air defense radar screens turned to snow. At first the operators thought their systems had suffered mechanical breakdowns. When radio calls among the dispersed sites determined that the loss of signal was widespread, the senior radar operator on duty alerted the interceptors of the Libyan Air Force. As he did so, the EA-6s maneuvered themselves within range to launch their HARM, High Speed Anti-Radiation Missiles, which were intended to knock out the defenses.

Confusion reigned on the ground. Plant maintenance and security people scurried about the facility cursing the faulty workmanship they presumed caused such a power failure and breakdown to occur.

Before they could figure out the cause of the problem, the first of the Super Hornets streaked in over the horizon and toward the compound. Two aircraft had been assigned to each opening in the plant's air vents. One after another, the pilots "pickled off" their precision-guided munitions, which slammed into the air ducts.

Huge bursts of flame shot out from each target. The concussions from hit after hit roiled through the plant.

The sleeping Libyan Air Force finally awakened. A handful of Soviet-built SU-17 Fitter aircraft took to the skies. Unaccustomed to night flight, let alone night fighting, most of the pilots were easy targets for the F-14s. But one of the Fitters was flown by a pilot who clearly had been trained by skilled airmen. He juked, climbed, dove, and managed to elude the pursuing Tomcats.

In the Flag Plot aboard the *George Washington*, watchstanders could listen in to the radio calls of the GW air wing. "Mace Two-oh-one, bandit on your tail!"

"Mace, breaking right," came the calm reply. The Libyan broke with him.

A buzzer went off in the F-14's cockpit indicating that the aircraft had been locked on with a fire control radar. The Tomcat dove for the deck and broke left a split second before an air-to-air missile streaked past his right wing tip and slammed into the ground. Listeners in the Command Centers could hear the pilot's labored breathing dramatically increase with each new maneuver.

Mace 201's wing man pulled six Gs as he looped around behind the Fitter. As he leveled out he illuminated the Libyan with his fire control radar and launched an AIM 9X Sidewinder missile which flew up the aircraft's tail and exploded in a huge orange ball of flame.

The heavens above Tarhouna were lit as if it were daytime. Antiaircraft guns peppered the sky as surface-to-air missiles streaked toward the attacking jets.

Decision makers on board the *George Washington* as well as in Washington watched the whole scene unfold thanks to infrared video broadcast by the still-circling Sea Ferret.

"Unbelievable!" was the only statement Jim Schmidt could muster as he watched the attack from the comfortable confines of the White House Situation Room.

Soon, their weapons expended, the aircraft reached "bingo" status when their fuel supplies were diminished and they were forced to head north to return to the *George Washington*.

"What do you think, Leroy?" Wally Burnette asked the Chairman of the JCS over a telephone link to the Pentagon.

"It looks like a very successful mission. But I can't say with certainty that we have knocked the plant out for good. I'd recommend we pump a few Tomahawks into the place for good measure. If that doesn't work, we can hit it again in daylight with the B-2s and F-117s."

Burnette quickly consulted with the President and gave General Sundin the go-ahead.

The authorization was flashed to the fleet and within moments the order was received on the two Tomahawk-capable platforms off Libya. USS *Hartford* and USS *Winston Churchill* each made preparations to launch a salvo of missiles.

"Officer of the Deck, prepare to launch Tomahawk from VLS tubes one, two, three, and four," Chet Hollomaker ordered aboard the *Hartford*.

"Aye, aye, sir. Ready to stuff these suckers up Gadhafi's butt like a . . ."

"Knock it off, Larry. Just pipe down for once."

"Yes sir, pipe down. Got ya covered, sir. . . . Why, I—"

"Officer of the Deck, fire one."

"Fire one, aye, sir."

Aboard the *Winston Churchill* things were slightly less chaotic. Bill Schmidt, from his chair in CIC, checked with the weapons officer and was assured that all was in readiness.

Schmidt tried to reassure a clearly nervous watch team in the Combat Information Center. "Ladies and gentlemen, we are about to launch some missiles. We are doing so with the complete authority of our entire chain of command. With these missiles, just like the Standard missiles we launched a while back, we are protecting the security of our nation. Batteries released!"

Eight TLAM-C land-attack Tomahawk missiles with conventional warheads streaked toward Tarhouna. Joined by the four launched from the vertical launch tubes of the *Hartford*, they shared two targets, the main doorways leading to the tunnels of Tarhouna.

The sense of anticipation in *Churchill*'s Combat Information Center was intense. All eyes focused on the large screen displays. All eyes except those of Ensign Madison, who was feeling vindicated . . . and playful. Marshall walked over to Lieutenant Hahn's console. When Attila wasn't looking, Madison reached over and turned down the gain on the TAO's scope.

As Attila's attention returned to his console, he was momentarily startled by the darkness. "What the hell?"

"Let me help you with that, Lieutenant," Madison offered. He reached over and turned up the gain. "Maybe you were having a problem with the O-N-O-F-F switch, sir." The CIC watchstanders erupted in laughter.

Schmidt stifled a smile. "Okay, okay, let's knock it off. Marshall, quit picking on Attila."

Ashore in Tarhouna, the situation was anything but a laughing matter. Fires set by bombs from the attacking aircraft continued to rage inside the chemical weapons plant. Smoke billowed from each of the vents that had been struck.

In the command center aboard the *George Washington*, crewmen calculated that the Sea Ferret would soon run out of fuel and the picture of Tarhouna would be lost, and with it the ability to provide instant bomb damage assessment.

In the National Military Command Center in the Pentagon and the White House Situation Room, officials watched and counted down the time until the cruise missiles were due to strike.

Thirty seconds before the first missile was scheduled to arrive, the military leadership watched in amazement as Tarhouna's main tunnel doors slowly opened.

"They must have gotten some power back!" a watch officer observed.

"Looks like the fire and smoke inside the facility is too much for them," another added.

A handful of plant workers could be seen running from the facility. At that moment the first of the Tomahawks reached the target and flew directly through one of the open tunnel doors.

A split second later, the next TLAM flew into the adjacent tunnel opening. Each was followed by a massive blast. As the billowing smoke subsided, another missile flew into the same opening; and another, and another, until all twelve had struck home.

The Sea Ferret showed the plant erupting: the entire mountain seemed to implode. Then the reconnaissance missile ran out of fuel; the ground rapidly filled the screen. Then, all went black.

42

The atmosphere of calm professionalism that prevailed in the Pentagon command center and the Combat Information Centers of USS *George Washington* and USS *Winston Churchill* was in stark contrast to the chaotic atmosphere of the *Washington Post*'s newsroom.

"We're going to kick the *New York Times*'s ass so badly on this story that those bloody *Times*men will be too embarrassed to show their faces in the Harvard Club for months!" editor Branford Clay shouted at no one in particular.

Clay called a meeting of his top editors to discuss the *Post*'s strategy for covering the day's extraordinary events involving Libya.

"We're going to ride this story all the way to the finish line!" Clay exulted. "I don't know how Sue O'Dell is getting all the great stuff she's sending in, but I tell ya, this thing smells like a Pulitzer to me."

The editors looked out of Clay's glass-enclosed office at the newsroom, which was buzzing with activity. Their aging editor's enthusiasm was infectious.

"Here's what we're going to do," Clay barked. "First we are going to run a six-column headline, right across the whole freaking front page. In the upper right we'll run a two-column subhead with a lead-all story summarizing the whole shebang under Sue O'Dell's byline."

The National editor interrupted with an objection. "Brad, Sue's done some nice work on this story but the meat of it will have to come from my guys at the White House, Pentagon, and State Department. I think Sue's material should run as a sidebar to the main show."

Before Clay had a chance to respond, another objection was raised by the Metro editor. "To me the big story is the attempted gas attack at the Naval Academy. My Annapolis bureau chief is pounding the pavement on that one, right now."

The National editor rolled his eyes. "This isn't the kind of story you lift from the police blotter, you twit!" Several of the Metro editor's colleagues had to physically restrain him. "This is a story that requires sources at the highest levels of government, not the lowest!"

"Sit down and shut up!" Clay shouted above the din. "Maybe you guys weren't listening to me. Sue O'Dell is getting the byline on the lead story. If we use National and Metro stuff in her piece we'll give your reporters a tagline at the end of her story. You know, 'also contributing to this story were . . . yadda, yadda, yadda.'

"Tell the art department I want a graphic showing the weapons plant in flames with all kinds of arrows streaking toward it from the sea." Clay was barking out orders faster than anyone could take them down. "See if we can get the Pentagon to release some satellite imagery of the burning plant. And, oh yeah, somebody get their hands on a candid shot of the skipper of that *Winston Churchill* boat. Get Jerry Beach to go up to Jim Schmidt's office and steal a family photo if that's the only way to get one.

"National, I want your Pentagon guys to give me everything they can get on these ships and the planes and missiles that took out the Libyans." The National editor was scribbling notes to himself at breakneck speed.

"Foreign desk, I want you to get reaction from damn near every capital in the world. I mean, what do they think about this in Tel Aviv? Cairo? New goddamn Delhi? Got it?" Clay did not pause to wait for an answer. He had built up quite a head of steam. "Tomorrow morning, the only question I want left in our readers' minds is 'How in the hell am I going to be able to lift this huge son-of-a-bitch of a paper?' "

The *Washington Post*
U.S. Ships and Planes Destroy Libyan
Chemical Warfare Plant
Plot Against Life of President Foiled
Page A-1
by Sue O'Dell

Naples, Italy—The United States conducted a massive attack on a chemical weapons facility in Tarhouna, Libya, last night. The assault was conducted in retaliation for what was a narrowly averted Libyan effort to use chemical weapons against Israel and the United States.

The *Washington Post* has learned, exclusively, that a Libyan attempt to use chemical weapons on Tel Aviv was thwarted by USS *Winston Churchill*. The destroyer, under the leadership of Commander Bill Schmidt, brother of presidential spokesman Jim Schmidt, shot down a Libyan airliner laden with chemical weapons two weeks ago.

Commander Schmidt permitted suspicion to be cast upon himself and his crew in order to allow investigators time to discover the location of additional Libyan chemical weapons believed to be hidden somewhere in the United States.

A tangled trail of clues painstakingly put together by a network of analysts, experts, and operatives stretching from Fort Meade, Maryland, to Langley, Virginia, and within Libya itself finally led to the discovery of the hidden weapons. Commander Schmidt was the individual who eventually put all the pieces of the puzzle together and determined that the weapons were secreted at the football stadium used by the U.S. Naval Academy in Annapolis, Maryland.

The weapons were discovered and rendered harmless just moments before the President was scheduled to speak at commencement exercises being held at the stadium.

Once the weapons were neutralized, U.S. officials ordered a retaliatory attack on the chemical weapons plant at Tarhouna.

Although damage assessments are preliminary, officials involved with the attack, who spoke to the *Post* under the condition that they remain anonymous, said the chemical plant appears to have been destroyed. . . .

Sue's byline was on four of the six stories on the paper's front page. She even received credit for stories she hadn't written. Clay wanted to hype the central role she played in the affair. He could see the series of stories resulting not only in a Pulitzer Prize but also in the establishment of a major star amongst the paper's pantheon of reporters. Despite Clay's promotional efforts, there were a few important stories on the subject which didn't carry Sue's name.

The *Washington Post*
Worldwide Praise for Raid
But Harden Resigns
Page A-1
by Jerry Beach

Washington, D.C.—Reaction from international capitals to last night's raid on Tarhouna was swift and positive. Praise rained in from allied capitals as details of the attack emerged.

One sour note for the administration was a report, first carried in early editions of the *New York Times*, that Secretary of State Blair D. Harden III reportedly plans to resign his post due to anger and frustration at having been left out of all planning for the attack.

White House spokesman Jim Schmidt, who was contacted at home last night for comment, said no resignation letter had been received from Harden and that if the reports were true, the President would view the news "with some regret."

Navy Secretary Frederic C. Fiske issued a press release last night lauding the crew of USS *Winston Churchill* for their role in thwarting the attack on Israel and in the strike on Libya.

"I regret that it was necessary to allow some members of the public to jump to the conclusion that *Winston Churchill* was at fault in the Libyan shoot down and to question the capability of the crew and the ship."

Secretary Fiske's statement concluded with the comment that "those of us in the know always had confidence in Commander Schmidt and his fine crew. This action once again proves that the AEGIS destroyer is the Cadillac of all Navy ships."

Despite his statement of support, senior administration officials, who spoke on the condition of anonymity, said Fiske might soon be returning to the private sector. Before coming to government, Fiske had been a car dealer.

43

Once again a swarm of press helicopters and fixed-wing aircraft covered USS *Winston Churchill*'s arrival as it entered Naples harbor.

This time it's not so bad, Schmidt thought. Crewmen poured onto the deck and waved their ballcaps at the cameramen overhead. The ship's signalmen asked for and received permission to fly the holiday Ensign, an American flag that was twice as large as the one generally flown. Once again the fleet commander had ordered *Winston Churchill* to anchor out. This time, however, the decision was made to protect the ship from admirers rather than to fend off hostile attack.

Standing on the pier amidst a throng of well wishers was Sue O'Dell. She found herself standing next to a familiar-looking Navy Lieutenant Commander, the only person on the pier not smiling.

"Isn't this great?" she asked.

"Yeah great," the officer responded in a monotone. "Really heroic."

Sue detected more than a little resentment in the voice. And there was something else about it.

"I'm Sue O'Dell of the *Washington Post*. I'd like to quote you in my story. You are . . ."

Her companion turned and silently walked away, but not before she noticed his name tag: ELLSWORTH.

Sue had come prepared with a note for the ship's Captain and went in search of someone who could deliver it to the *Winston Churchill*. She soon found a sailor who said he was Coxswain for the Admiral's barge and would be among the first to go out to the ship.

A warm smile and a twenty-dollar bill was all the persuasion he needed to agree to deliver her letter. Less than thirty minutes later, Bill was reading the note in his cabin.

> Dearest Bill,
>
> Congratulations on your tremendous victory. You have my undying thanks for that ship-to-shore telephone call giving me the details and the go-ahead to write my story. I hope you approve of the job I've done.
>
> I also hope you haven't forgotten that when you left so suddenly, you promised you would come back and be all mine.
>
> I intend to hold you to that promise, Commander. There are so many questions I'd still like to ask. For instance, what the hell is the Battenburg Cup?
>
> Love, Sue
>
> P. S. Since there is so much to talk about . . . could we dispense with this Cinderella liberty nonsense?

44

As he drove to work, Jim Schmidt gave a moment's thought to tuning in to National Public Radio. Nah, who cares what those windbags have to say! Hah, *windbags.* There's a word he never thought he'd enjoy using again.

Jim punched the button for one of his favorite oldies stations and sang along with the 1956 hit "The Great Pretender," by the Platters. Using his cellular phone and an assumed name, Jim called the station with a request. He asked to hear "Secret Agent Man," and sang along loudly and badly as they played the Johnny Rivers recording.

As he crossed the Fourteenth Street Bridge, the oldies station went to a commercial, so Jim switched to AM and tuned in to Imus in the Morning.

"I've gotta admit," he heard the "I Man" say, "I used to think the President was just some fat pant load who didn't know anything about how to conduct foreign affairs. But after this Libya deal . . . well, I, I, I, I gotta say this . . . he's a fat pant load who *does* know something about how to deal with a terrorist nation."

I guess that's as good an endorsement as you can hope to get, Jim thought.

As his Volvo pulled up to the southwest gate of the White House, Jim noticed that the guards were being especially careful as they checked incoming cars, but unless he was mistaken, they seemed to show extra deference when it was his turn for inspection.

Quickly cleared in, Jim parked in his usual space and walked to the West Wing basement entrance of the White House with a spring in his step. The Uniformed Division guard looked around. Finding no one else in sight, he stood up and shook Jim's hand.

The spokesman passed by the White House mess. There was neither need nor time for extra sustenance today. He bounded up the stairs and turned left toward his office. There, blocking the entrance, as she did so often, was Alice Kenworthy.

"So, how do you justify keeping all this information from the American public?" she asked, a twinkle in her eye. "Intentionally shooting down airplanes, foiling terrorist attacks, nearly getting the President gassed . . . not to mention the White House press corps. And you don't tell us anything? How can that be?"

"Well, Alice, I guess you could say that Schmidt happens."